The Decameron of Giovanni Boccaccio- part II

Giovanni Boccaccio

Translated by John Payne

Esprios.com

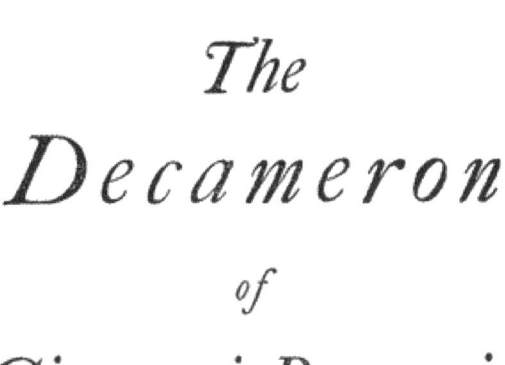

The Decameron

of

Giovanni Boccaccio

*Translated by
John Payne*

WALTER J. BLACK, INC.
171 Madison Avenue
NEW YORK, N. Y.

Contents

DAY THE SIXTH

THE FIRST STORY. A gentleman engageth to Madam Oretta to carry her a-horseback with a story, but, telling it disorderly, is prayed by her to set her down again

THE SECOND STORY. Cisti the baker with a word of his fashion maketh Messer Geri Spina sensible of an indiscreet request of his

THE THIRD STORY. Madam Nonna de' Pulci, with a ready retort to a not altogether seemly pleasantry, imposeth silence on the Bishop of Florence

THE FOURTH STORY. Chichibio, cook to Currado Gianfigliazzi, with a ready word spoken to save himself, turneth his master's anger into laughter and escapeth the punishment threatened him by the latter

THE FIFTH STORY. Messer Forese da Rabatta and Master Giotto the painter coming from Mugello, each jestingly rallieth the other on his scurvy favour

THE SIXTH STORY. Michele Scalza proveth to certain young men that the cadgers of Florence are the best gentlemen of the world or the Maremma and winneth a supper

THE SEVENTH STORY. Madam Filippa, being found by her husband with a lover of hers and brought to justice, delivereth herself with a prompt and pleasant answer and causeth modify the statute

THE EIGHTH STORY. Fresco exhorteth his niece not to mirror herself in the glass if, as she saith, it irketh her to see disagreeable folk 308

THE NINTH STORY. Guido Cavalcanti with a pithy speech courteously flouteth certain Florentine gentlemen who had taken him by surprise

THE TENTH STORY. Fra Cipolla promiseth certain country folk to show them one of the angel Gabriel's feathers and finding coals in place thereof, avoucheth these latter to be of those which roasted St. Lawrence

DAY THE SEVENTH

THE FIRST STORY. Gianni Lotteringhi heareth knock at his door by night and awakeneth his wife, who giveth him to believe that it is a phantom; whereupon they go to exorcise it with a certain orison and the knocking ceaseth

THE SECOND STORY. Peronella hideth a lover of hers in a vat, upon her husband's unlooked for return, and hearing from the latter that he hath sold the vat, avoucheth herself to have sold it to one who is presently therewithin, to see if it be sound; whereupon the gallant, jumping out of the vat, causeth the husband scrape it out for him and after carry it home to his house

THE THIRD STORY. Fra Rinaldo lieth with his gossip and being found of her husband closeted with her in her chamber, they give him to believe that he was in act to conjure worms from his godson

THE FOURTH STORY. Tofano one night shutteth his wife out of doors, who, availing not to re-enter by dint of entreaties, feigneth to cast herself into a well and casteth therein a great stone. Tofano cometh forth of the house and runneth thither, whereupon she slippeth in and locking him out, bawleth reproaches at him from the window

THE FIFTH STORY. A jealous husband, in the guise of a priest, confesseth his wife, who giveth him to believe that she loveth a priest, who cometh to her every night; and whilst the husband secretly keepeth watch at the door for the latter, the lady bringeth in a lover of hers by the roof and lieth with him

THE SIXTH STORY. Madam Isabella, being in company with Leonetto her lover, is visited by one Messer Lambertuccio, of whom she is beloved; her husband returning, [unexpected,] she sendeth Lambertuccio forth of the house, whinger in hand, and the husband after escorteth Leonetto home

THE SEVENTH STORY. Lodovico discovereth to Madam Beatrice the love he beareth her, whereupon she sendeth Egano her husband into the garden, in her own favour, and lieth meanwhile with Lodovico, who, presently arising, goeth and cudgelleth Egano in the garden

THE EIGHTH STORY. A man waxeth jealous of his wife, who bindeth a piece of packthread to her great toe anights, so she may have notice of her lover's coming. One night her husband becometh aware of this device and what while he pursueth the lover, the lady putteth another woman to bed in her room. This latter the husband beateth and cutteth off her hair, then fetcheth his wife's brothers, who, finding his story [seemingly] untrue, give him hard words

THE NINTH STORY. Lydia, wife of Nicostratus, loveth Pyrrhus, who, so he may believe it, requireth of her three things, all which she doth. Moreover, she solaceth herself with him in the presence of Nicostratus and maketh the latter believe that that which he hath seen is not real

THE TENTH STORY. Two Siennese love a lady, who is gossip to one of them; the latter dieth and returning to his companion, according to premise made him, relateth to him how folk fare in the other world

DAY THE EIGHTH

THE FIRST STORY. Gulfardo borroweth of Guasparruolo certain monies, for which he hath agreed with his wife that he shall lie with her, and accordingly giveth them to her; then, in her presence, he telleth Guasparruolo that he gave them to her, and she confesseth it to be true

THE SECOND STORY. The parish priest of Varlungo lieth with Mistress Belcolore and leaveth her a cloak of his in pledge; then, borrowing a mortar of her, he sendeth it back to her, demanding in return the cloak left by way of token, which the good woman grudgingly giveth him back

THE THIRD STORY. Calandrino, Bruno and Buffalmacco go coasting along the Mugnone in search of the heliotrope and Calandrino thinketh to have found it. Accordingly he returneth home, laden with stones, and his wife chideth him; whereupon, flying out into a rage, he beateth her and recounteth to his companions that which they know better than he

THE FOURTH STORY. The rector of Fiesole loveth a widow lady, but is not loved by her and thinking to lie with her, lieth with a serving-wench of hers, whilst the lady's brothers cause the bishop find him in this case

THE FIFTH STORY. Three young men pull the breeches off a Marchegan judge in Florence, what while he is on the bench, administering justice

THE SIXTH STORY. Bruno and Buffalmacco, having stolen a pig from Calandrino, make him try the ordeal with ginger boluses and sack and give him (instead of the ginger) two dogballs compounded with aloes, whereby it appeareth that he himself hath had the pig and they make him pay blackmail, and he would not have them tell his wife

THE SEVENTH STORY. A scholar loveth a widow lady, who, being enamoured of another, causeth him spend one winter's night in the snow awaiting her, and he after contriveth, by his sleight, to have her abide naked, all one mid-July day, on the summit of a tower, exposed to flies and gads and sun

THE EIGHTH STORY. Two men consorting together, one lieth with the wife of his comrade, who, becoming aware thereof, doth with her on such wise that the other is shut up in a chest, upon which he lieth with his wife, he being inside the while

THE NINTH STORY. Master Simone the physician, having been induced by Bruno and Buffalmacco to repair to a certain place by night, there to be made a member of a company, that goeth a-roving, is cast by Buffalmacco into a trench full of ordure and there left 406

THE TENTH STORY. A certain woman of Sicily artfully despoileth a merchant of that which he had brought to Palermo; but he, making believe to have returned thither with much greater plenty of merchandise than before, borroweth money of her and leaveth her water and tow in payment

DAY THE NINTH

THE FIRST STORY. Madam Francesca, being courted of one Rinuccio Palermini and one Alessandro Chiarmontesi and loving neither the one nor the other, adroitly riddeth herself of both by causing one enter for dead into a sepulchre and the other bring him forth thereof for dead, on such wise that they cannot avail to accomplish the condition imposed

THE SECOND STORY. An abbess, arising in haste and in the dark to find one of her nuns, who had been denounced to her, in bed with her lover and, thinking to cover her head with her coif, donneth instead thereof the breeches of a priest who is abed with her; the which the accused nun observing and making her aware thereof, she is acquitted and hath leisure to be with her lover

THE THIRD STORY. Master Simone, at the instance of Bruno and Buffalmacco and Nello, maketh Calandrino believe that he is with child; wherefore he giveth them capons and money for medicines and recovereth without bringing forth

THE FOURTH STORY. Cecco Fortarrigo gameth away at Buonconvento all his good and the monies of Cecco Angiolieri [his master;] moreover, running after the latter, in his shirt, and avouching that he hath robbed him, he causeth him be taken of the countryfolk; then, donning Angiolieri's clothes and mounting his palfrey, he maketh off and leaveth the other in his shirt

THE FIFTH STORY. Calandrino falleth in love with a wench and Bruno writeth him a talisman, wherewith when he toucheth her, she goeth with him; and his wife finding them together, there betideth him grievous trouble and annoy

THE SIXTH STORY. Two young gentlemen lodge the night with an innkeeper, whereof one goeth to lie with the host's daughter, whilst his wife unwittingly coucheth with the other; after which he who lay with the girl getteth him to bed with her father and telleth him all, thinking to bespeak his comrade. Therewithal they come to words, but the wife, perceiving her mistake, entereth her daughter's bed and thence with certain words appeaseth everything

THE SEVENTH STORY. Talano di Molese dreameth that a wolf mangleth all his wife's neck and face and biddeth her beware thereof; but she payeth no heed to his warning and it befalleth her even as he had dreamed

THE EIGHTH STORY. Biondello cheateth Ciacco of a dinner, whereof the other craftily avengeth himself, procuring him to be shamefully beaten

THE NINTH STORY. Two young men seek counsel of Solomon, one how he may be loved and the other how he may amend his froward wife, and in answer he biddeth the one love and the other get him to Goosebridge

THE TENTH STORY. Dom Gianni, at the instance of his gossip Pietro, performeth a conjuration for the purpose of causing the latter's wife to become a mare; but, whenas he cometh to put on the tail, Pietro marreth the whole conjuration, saying that he will not have a tail

DAY THE TENTH

THE FIRST STORY. A knight in the king's service of Spain thinking himself ill guerdoned, the king by very certain proof showeth him that this is not his fault, but that of his own perverse fortune, and after largesseth him magnificently 462

THE SECOND STORY. Ghino di Tacco taketh the Abbot of Cluny and having cured him of the stomach-complaint, letteth him go; whereupon the Abbot, returning to the court of Rome, reconcileth him with Pope Boniface and maketh him a Prior of the Hospitallers

THE THIRD STORY. Mithridanes, envying Nathan his hospitality and generosity and going to kill him, falleth in with himself, without knowing him, and is by him instructed of the course he shall take to accomplish his purpose; by means whereof he findeth him, as he himself had ordered it, in a coppice and recognizing him, is ashamed and becometh his friend

THE FOURTH STORY. Messer Gentile de' Carisendi, coming from Modona, taketh forth of the sepulchre a lady whom he loveth and who hath been buried for dead. The lady, restored to life, beareth a male child and Messer Gentile restoreth her and her son to Niccoluccio Caccianimico, her husband

THE FIFTH STORY. Madam Dianora requireth of Messer Ansaldo a garden as fair in January as in May, and he by binding himself [to pay a great sum of money] to a nigromancer, giveth it to her. Her husband granteth her leave to do Messer Ansaldo's pleasure, but he, hearing of the former's generosity, absolveth her of her promise, whereupon the nigromancer, in his turn, acquitteth Messer Ansaldo of his bond, without willing aught of his

THE SIXTH STORY. King Charles the Old, the Victorious, falleth enamoured of a young girl, but after, ashamed of his fond thought, honourably marrieth both her and her sister

THE SEVENTH STORY. King Pedro of Arragon, coming to know the fervent love borne him by Lisa, comforteth the lovesick maid and presently marrieth her to a noble young gentleman; then, kissing her on the brow, he ever after avoucheth himself her knight

THE EIGHTH STORY. Sophronia, thinking to marry Gisippus, becometh the wife of Titus Quintius Fulvus and with him betaketh herself to Rome, whither Gisippus cometh in poor case and conceiving himself slighted of Titus, declareth, so he may die, to have slain a man. Titus, recognizing him, to save him, avoucheth himself to have done the deed, and the true murderer, seeing this, discovereth himself; whereupon they are all three liberated by Octavianus and Titus, giving Gisippus his sister to wife, hath all his good in common with him

THE NINTH STORY. Saladin, in the disguise of a merchant, is honourably entertained by Messer Torello d'Istria, who, presently undertaking the [third] crusade, appointeth his wife a term for her marrying again. He is taken [by the Saracens] and cometh, by his skill in training hawks, under the notice of the Soldan, who knoweth him again and discovering himself to him, entreateth him with the utmost honour. Then, Torello falling sick for languishment, he is by magical art transported in one night [from Alexandria] to Pavia, where, being recognized by his wife at the bride-feast held for her marrying again, he returneth with her to his own house

THE TENTH STORY. The Marquess of Saluzzo, constrained by the prayers of his vassals to marry, but determined to do it after his own fashion, taketh to wife the daughter of a peasant and hath of her two children, whom he maketh believe to her to put to death; after which, feigning to be grown weary of her and to have taken another wife, he letteth bring his own daughter home to his house, as she were his new bride, and turneth his wife away in her shift; but, finding her patient under everything, he fetcheth her home again, dearer than ever, and showing her her children grown great, honoureth and letteth honour her as marchioness

CONCLUSION OF THE AUTHOR

Here Beginneth the Book Called Decameron and Surnamed Prince Galahalt Wherein Are Contained an Hundred Stories in Ten Days Told by Seven Ladies and Three Young Men

The Decameron of Giovanni Boccaccio - Part II

Day the Sixth

HERE BEGINNETH THE SIXTH DAY OF THE DECAMERON WHEREIN UNDER THE GOVERNANCE OF ELISA IS DISCOURSED OF WHOSO BEING ASSAILED WITH SOME JIBING SPEECH HATH VINDICATED HIMSELF OR HATH WITH SOME READY REPLY OR ADVISEMENT ESCAPED LOSS, PERIL OR SHAME

THE moon, being now in the middest heaven, had lost its radiance and every part of our world was bright with the new coming light, when, the queen arising and letting call her company, they all with slow step fared forth and rambled over the dewy grass to a little distance from the fair hill, holding various discourse of one thing and another and debating of the more or less goodliness of the stories told, what while they renewed their laughter at the various adventures related therein, till such time as the sun mounting high and beginning to wax hot, it seemed well to them all to turn homeward. Wherefore, reversing their steps, they returned to the palace and there, by the queen's commandment, the tables being already laid and everything strewn with sweet-scented herbs and fair flowers, they addressed themselves to eat, ere the heat should grow greater. This being joyously accomplished, ere they did otherwhat, they sang divers goodly and pleasant canzonets, after which some went to sleep, whilst some sat down to play at chess and other some at tables and Dioneo fell to singing, in concert with Lauretta, of Troilus and Cressida. Then, the hour come for their reassembling after the wonted fashion,[294] they all, being summoned on the part of the queen, seated themselves, as of their usance, about the fountain; but, as she was about to call for the first story, there befell a thing that had not yet befallen there, to wit, that a great clamour was heard by her and by all, made by the wenches and serving-men in the kitchen.

The seneschal, being called and questioned who it was that cried thus and what might be the occasion of the turmoil, answered that the clamour was between Licisca and Tindaro, but that he knew not the cause thereof, being but then come thither to make them bide quiet, whenas he had been summoned on her part. The queen bade him incontinent fetch thither the two offenders and they being come, enquired what was the cause of their clamour; whereto Tindaro offering to reply, Licisca, who was well in years and somewhat overmasterful, being heated with the outcry she had made, turned to him with an angry air and said, "Mark this brute of a man who dareth to speak before me, whereas I am! Let me speak." Then, turning again to the queen, "Madam," quoth she, "this fellow would teach me, forsooth, to know Sicofante's wife and neither more nor less than as if I had not been familiar with her, would fain give me to believe that, the first night her husband lay with her, Squire Maul[295] made his entry into Black Hill[296] by force and with effusion of blood; and I say that it is not true; nay, he entered there in peace and to the great contentment of those within. Marry, this fellow is simple enough to believe wenches to be such ninnies that they stand to lose their time, abiding the commodity of their fathers and brothers, who six times out of seven tarry three or four years more than they should to marry them. Well would they fare, forsooth, were they to wait so long! By Christ His faith (and I should know what I say, when I swear thus) I have not a single gossip who went a maid to her husband; and as for the wives, I know full well how many and what tricks they play their husbands; and this blockhead would teach me to know women, as if I had been born yesterday."

What while Licisca spoke, the ladies kept up such a laughing that you might have drawn all their teeth; and the queen imposed silence upon her a good half dozen times, but to no purpose; she stinted not till she had said her say. When she had at last made an end of her talk, the queen turned to Dioneo and said, laughing, "Dioneo, this is a matter for thy jurisdiction; wherefore, when we shall have made an end of our stories, thou shalt proceed to give final judgment thereon." Whereto he answered promptly, "Madam, the judgment is already given, without hearing more of the matter; and I say that Licisca is in the right and opine that it is even as she saith and that Tindaro is an ass." Licisca, hearing this, fell a-laughing and turning to Tindaro, said, "I told thee so; begone and God go with thee; thinkest thou thou knowest better than I, thou whose eyes are not yet dry?[297] Gramercy, I have not lived here below for nothing, no, not I!" And had not the queen with an angry air imposed silence on her and sent her and Tindaro away, bidding her make no more words or clamour, an she would not be flogged, they had had nought to do all that day but attend to her. When they were gone, the queen called on Filomena to make a beginning with the day's stories and she blithely began thus:

THE FIRST STORY

A GENTLEMAN ENGAGETH TO MADAM ORETTA TO CARRY HER A-HORSEBACK WITH A STORY, BUT, TELLING IT DISORDERLY, IS PRAYED BY HER TO SET HER DOWN AGAIN

"YOUNG ladies, like as stars, in the clear nights, are the ornaments of the heavens and the flowers and the leaf-clad shrubs, in the Spring, of the green fields and the hillsides, even so are praiseworthy manners and goodly discourse adorned by sprightly sallies, the which, for that they are brief, beseem women yet better than men, inasmuch as much speaking is more forbidden to the former than to the latter. Yet, true it is, whatever the cause, whether it be the meanness of our[298] understanding or some particular grudge borne by heaven to our times, that there be nowadays few or no women left who know how to say a witty word in due season or who, an it be said to them, know how to apprehend it as it behoveth; the which is a general reproach to our whole sex. However, for that enough hath been said aforetime on the subject by Pampinea,[299] I purpose to say no more thereof; but, to give you to understand how much goodliness there is in witty sayings, when spoken in due season, it pleaseth me to recount to you the courteous fashion in which a lady imposed silence upon a gentleman.

As many of you ladies may either know by sight or have heard tell, there was not long since in our city a noble and well-bred and well-spoken gentlewoman, whose worth merited not that her name be left unsaid. She was called, then, Madam Oretta and was the wife of Messer Geri Spina. She chanced to be, as we are, in the country, going from place to place, by way of diversion, with a company of ladies and gentlemen, whom she had that day entertained to dinner at her house, and the way being belike somewhat long from the place whence they set out to that whither they were all purposed to go afoot, one of the gentlemen said to her, 'Madam Oretta, an you will, I will carry you a-horseback great part of the way we have to go with one of the finest stories in the world.' 'Nay, sir,' answered the lady, 'I pray you instantly thereof; indeed, it will be most agreeable to me.' Master cavalier, who maybe fared no better, sword at side than tale on tongue, hearing this, began a story of his, which of itself was in truth very goodly; but he, now thrice or four or even half a dozen times repeating one same word, anon turning back and whiles saying, 'I said not aright,' and often erring in the names and putting one for another, marred it cruelly, more by token that he delivered himself exceedingly ill, having regard to the quality of the persons and the nature of the incidents of his tale. By reason whereof, Madam Oretta, hearkening to him, was many a time taken with a sweat and failing of the heart, as she were sick and near her end, and at last, being unable to brook the thing any more and seeing the gentleman engaged in an imbroglio from which he was not like to extricate himself, she said to him pleasantly, 'Sir, this horse of yours hath too hard a trot; wherefore I pray you be pleased to set me down.' The gentleman, who, as it chanced, understood a hint better than he told a story, took the jest in good part and turning it off with a laugh, fell to discoursing of other matters and left unfinished the story that he had begun and conducted so ill."

THE SECOND STORY

CISTI THE BAKER WITH A WORD OF HIS FASHION MAKETH MESSER GERI SPINA SENSIBLE OF AN INDISCREET REQUEST OF HIS

MADAM Oretta's saying was greatly commended of all, ladies and men, and the queen bidding Pampinea follow on, she began thus: "Fair ladies, I know not of mine own motion to resolve me which is the more at fault, whether nature in fitting to a noble soul a mean body or fortune in imposing a mean condition upon a body endowed with a noble soul, as in one our townsman Cisti and in many another we may have seen it happen; which Cisti being gifted with a very lofty spirit, fortune made him a baker. And for this, certes, I should curse both nature and fortune like, did I not know the one to be most discreet and the other to have a thousand eyes, albeit fools picture her blind; and I imagine, therefore, that, being exceeding well-advised, they do that which is oftentimes done of human beings, who, uncertain of future events, bury their most precious things, against their occasions, in the meanest places of their houses, as being the least suspect, and thence bring them forth in their greatest needs, the mean place having the while kept them more surely than would the goodly chamber. And so, meseemeth, do the governors of the world hide oftentimes their most precious things under the shadow of crafts and conditions reputed most mean, to the end that, bringing them forth therefrom in time of need, their lustre may show the brighter. Which how Cisti the baker made manifest, though in but a trifling matter, restoring to Messer Geri Spina (whom the story but now told of Madam Oretta, who was his wife, hath recalled to my memory) the eyes of the understanding, it pleaseth me to show you in a very short story.

I must tell you, then, that Pope Boniface, with whom Messer Geri Spina was in very great favour, having despatched to Florence certain of his gentlemen on an embassy concerning sundry important matters of his, they lighted down at the house of Messer Geri and he treating the pope's affairs in company with them, it chanced, whatever might have been the occasion thereof, that he and they passed well nigh every morning afoot before Santa Maria Ughi, where Cisti the baker had his bakehouse and plied his craft in person. Now, albeit fortune had appointed Cisti a humble enough condition, she had so far at the least been kind to him therein that he was grown very rich and without ever choosing to abandon it for any other, lived very splendidly, having, amongst his other good things, the best wines, white and red, that were to be found in Florence or in the neighbouring country. Seeing Messer Geri and the pope's ambassadors pass every morning before his door and the heat being great, he bethought himself that it were a great courtesy to give them to drink of his good white wine; but, having regard to his own condition and that of Messer Geri, he deemed it not a seemly thing to presume to invite them, but determined to bear himself on such wise as should lead Messer Geri to invite himself.

Accordingly, having still on his body a very white doublet and an apron fresh from the wash, which bespoke him rather a miller than a baker, he let set before his door, every morning, towards the time when he looked for Messer Geri and the ambassadors to pass, a new tinned pail of fair water and a small pitcher of new Bolognese ware, full of his good white wine, together with two beakers, which seemed of silver, so bright they were, and seated himself there, against they should pass, when, after clearing his throat once or twice, he fell to drinking of that his wine with such a relish that he had made a dead man's mouth water for it. Messer Geri, having seen him do thus one and two mornings, said on the third, 'How now, Cisti? Is it good?' Whereupon he started to his feet and said, 'Ay is it, Sir; but how good I cannot give you to understand, except you taste thereof.' Messer Geri, in whom either the nature of the weather or belike the relish with which he saw Cisti drink had begotten a thirst, turned to the ambassadors and said, smiling, 'Gentlemen, we shall do well to taste this honest man's wine; belike it is such that we shall not repent thereof.' Accordingly, he made with them towards Cisti, who let bring a goodly settle out of his bakehouse and praying them sit, said to their serving-men, who pressed forward to rinse the beakers, 'Stand back, friends, and leave this office to me, for that I know no less well how to skink than to wield the baking-peel; and look you not to taste a drop thereof.' So saying, he with his own hands washed out four new and goodly beakers and letting bring a little pitcher of his good wine, busied himself with giving Messer Geri and his companions to drink, to whom the wine seemed the best they had drunken that great while; wherefore they commended it greatly, and well nigh every morning, whilst the ambassadors abode there, Messer Geri went thither to drink in company with them.

After awhile, their business being despatched and they about to depart, Messer Geri made them a magnificent banquet, whereto he bade a number of the most worshipful citizens and amongst the rest, Cisti, who would, however, on no condition go thither; whereupon

Messer Geri bade one of his serving-men go fetch a flask of the baker's wine and give each guest a half beaker thereof with the first course. The servant, despiteful most like for that he had never availed to drink of the wine, took a great flagon, which when Cisti saw, 'My son,' said he, 'Messer Geri sent thee not to me.' The man avouched again and again that he had, but, getting none other answer, returned to Messer Geri and reported it to him. Quoth he, 'Go back to him and tell him that I do indeed send thee to him; and if he still make thee the same answer, ask him to whom I send thee, [an it be not to him.]' Accordingly, the servant went back to the baker and said to him, 'Cisti, for certain Messer Geri sendeth me to thee and none other.' 'For certain, my son,' answered the baker, 'he doth it not.' 'Then,' said the man, 'to whom doth he send me?' 'To the Arno,' replied Cisti; which answer when the servant reported to Messer Geri, the eyes of his understanding were of a sudden opened and he said to the man, 'Let me see what flask thou carriedst thither.'

When he saw the great flagon aforesaid, he said, 'Cisti saith sooth,' and giving the man a sharp reproof, made him take a sortable flask, which when Cisti saw, 'Now,' quoth he, 'I know full well that he sendeth thee to me,' and cheerfully filled it unto him. Then, that same day, he let fill a little cask with the like wine and causing carry it softly to Messer Geri's house, went presently thither and finding him there, said to him, 'Sir. I would not have you think that the great flagon of this morning frightened me; nay, but, meseeming that which I have of these past days shown you with my little pitchers had escaped your mind, to wit, that this is no household wine,[300] I wished to recall it to you. But, now, for that I purpose no longer to be your steward thereof, I have sent it all to you; henceforward do with it as it pleaseth you.' Messer Geri set great store by Cisti's present and rendering him such thanks as he deemed sortable, ever after held him for a man of great worth and for friend."

THE THIRD STORY

MADAM NONNA DE' PULCI, WITH A READY RETORT TO A NOT ALTOGETHER SEEMLY PLEASANTRY, IMPOSETH SILENCE ON THE BISHOP OF FLORENCE

PAMPINEA having made an end of her story and both Cisti's reply and his liberality having been much commended of all, it pleased the queen that the next story should be told be Lauretta, who blithely began as follows, "Jocund ladies, first Pampinea and now Filomena have spoken truly enough touching our little worth and the excellence of pithy sayings, whereto that there may be no need now to return, I would fain remind you, over and above that which hath been said on the subject, that the nature of smart sayings is such that they should bite upon the hearer, not as the dog, but as the sheep biteth; for that, an a trait bit like a dog, it were not a trait, but an affront. The right mean in this was excellently well hit both by Madam Oretta's speech and Cisti's reply. It is true that, if a smart thing be said by way of retort, and the answerer biteth like a dog, having been bitten on like wise, meseemeth he is not to be blamed as he would have been, had this not been the case; wherefore it behoveth us look how and with whom, no less than when and where, we bandy jests; to which considerations, a prelate of ours, taking too little heed, received at least as sharp a bite as he thought to give, as I shall show you in a little story.

Messer Antonio d'Orso, a learned and worthy prelate, being Bishop of Florence, there came thither a Catalan gentleman, called Messer Dego della Ratta, marshal for King Robert, who, being a man of a very fine person and a great amorist, took a liking to one among other Florentine ladies, a very fair lady and granddaughter to a brother of the said bishop, and hearing that her husband, albeit a man of good family, was very sordid and miserly, agreed with him to give him five hundred gold florins, so he would suffer him lie a night with his wife. Accordingly, he let gild so many silver poplins,[301] a coin which was then current, and having lain with the lady, though against her will, gave them to the husband. The thing after coming to be known everywhere, the sordid wretch of a husband reaped both loss and scorn, but the bishop, like a discreet man as he was, affected to know nothing of the matter. Wherefore, he and the marshal consorting much together, it chanced, as they rode side by side with each other, one St. John's Day, viewing the ladies on either side of the way where the mantle is run for,[302] the prelate espied a young lady,—of whom this present pestilence hath bereft us and whom all you ladies must have known, Madam Nonna de' Pulci by name, cousin to Messer Alessio Rinucci, a fresh and fair young woman, both well-spoken and high-spirited, then not long before married in Porta San Piero,—and pointed her out to the marshal; then, being near her, he laid his hand on the latter's shoulder and said to her, 'Nonna, how deemest thou of this gallant? Thinkest thou thou couldst make a conquest of him?' It seemed to the lady that those words somewhat trenched upon her honour and were like to sully it in the eyes of those (and there were many there) who heard them; wherefore, not thinking to purge away the soil, but to return blow for blow, she promptly answered, 'Maybe, sir, he would not make a conquest of me; but, in any case, I should want good money.' The marshal and the bishop, hearing this, felt themselves alike touched to the quick by her speech, the one as the author of the cheat put upon the bishop's brother's granddaughter and the other as having suffered the affront in the person of his kinswoman, and made off, shamefast and silent, without looking at one another or saying aught more to her that day. Thus, then, the young lady having been bitten, it was not forbidden her to bite her biter with a retort."

THE FOURTH STORY

CHICHIBIO, COOK TO CURRADO GIANFIGLIAZZI, WITH A READY WORD SPOKEN TO SAVE HIMSELF, TURNETH HIS MASTER'S ANGER INTO LAUGHTER AND ESCAPETH THE PUNISHMENT THREATENED HIM BY THE LATTER

LAURETTA being silent and Nonna having been mightily commended of all, the queen charged Neifile to follow on, and she said, "Although, lovesome ladies, a ready wit doth often furnish folk with words both prompt and useful and goodly, according to the circumstances, yet fortune whiles cometh to the help of the fearful and putteth of a sudden into their mouths such answers as might never of malice aforethought be found of the speaker, as I purpose to show you by my story.

Currado Gianfigliazzi, as each of you ladies may have both heard and seen, hath still been a noble citizen of our city, liberal and magnificent, and leading a knightly life, hath ever, letting be for the present his weightier doings, taken delight in hawks and hounds. Having one day with a falcon of his brought down a crane and finding it young and fat, he sent it to a good cook he had, a Venetian hight Chichibio, bidding him roast it for supper and dress it well. Chichibio, who looked the new-caught gull he was, trussed the crane and setting it to the fire, proceeded to cook it diligently. When it was all but done and gave out a very savoury smell, it chanced that a wench of the neighbourhood, Brunetta by name, of whom Chichibio was sore enamoured, entered the kitchen and smelling the crane and seeing it, instantly besought him to give her a thigh thereof. He answered her, singing, and said, 'Thou shalt not have it from me, Mistress Brunetta, thou shalt not have it from me.' Whereat she, being vexed, said to him, 'By God His faith, an thou give it me not, thou shalt never have of me aught that shall pleasure thee.' In brief, many were the words between them and at last, Chichibio, not to anger his mistress, cut off one of the thighs of the crane and gave it her.

The bird being after set before Messer Currado and certain stranger guests of his, lacking a thigh, and the former marvelling thereat, he let call Chichibio and asked him what was come of the other thigh; whereto the liar of a Venetian answered without hesitation, 'Sir, cranes have but one thigh and one leg.' 'What a devil?' cried Currado in a rage. 'They have but one thigh and one leg? Have I never seen a crane before?' 'Sir,' replied Chichibio, 'it is as I tell you, and whenas it pleaseth you, I will cause you see it in the quick.' Currado, out of regard for the strangers he had with him, chose not to make more words of the matter, but said, 'Since thou sayst thou wilt cause me see it in the quick, a thing I never yet saw or heard tell of, I desire to see it to-morrow morning, in which case I shall be content; but I swear to thee, by Christ His body, that, an it be otherwise, I will have thee served on such wise that thou shalt still have cause to remember my name to thy sorrow so long as thou livest.' There was an end of the talk for that night; but, next morning, as soon as it was day, Currado, whose anger was nothing abated for sleep, arose, still full of wrath, and bade bring the horses; then, mounting Chichibio upon a rouncey, he carried him off towards a watercourse, on whose banks cranes were still to be seen at break of day, saying, 'We shall soon see who lied yestereve, thou or I.'

Chichibio, seeing that his master's wrath yet endured and that needs must be made good his lie and knowing not how he should avail thereunto, rode after Currado in the greatest fright that might be, and fain would he have fled, so but he might. But, seeing no way of escape, he looked now before him and now behind and now on either side and took all he saw for cranes standing on two feet. Presently, coming near to the river, he chanced to catch sight, before any other, of a round dozen of cranes on the bank, all perched on one leg, as they use to do, when they sleep; whereupon he straightway showed them to Currado, saying, 'Now, sir, if you look at those that stand yonder, you may very well see that I told you the truth yesternight, to wit, that cranes have but one thigh and one leg.' Currado, seeing them, answered, 'Wait and I will show thee that they have two,' and going somewhat nearer to them, he cried out, 'Ho! Ho!' At this the cranes, putting down the other leg, all, after some steps, took to flight; whereupon Currado said to him, 'How sayst thou now, malapert knave that thou art? Deemest thou they have two legs?' Chichibio, all confounded and knowing not whether he stood on his head or his heels,[303] answered, 'Ay, sir; but you did not cry, "Ho! Ho!" to yesternight's crane; had you cried thus, it would have put out the other thigh and the other leg, even as did those yonder.' This reply so tickled Currado that all his wrath was changed into mirth and laughter and he said, 'Chichibio, thou art in the right; indeed, I should have done it.' Thus, then, with his prompt and comical answer did Chichibio avert ill luck and made his peace with his master."

THE FIFTH STORY

MESSER FORESE DA RABATTA AND MASTER GIOTTO THE PAINTER COMING FROM MUGELLO, EACH JESTINGLY RALLIETH THE OTHER ON HIS SCURVY FAVOUR

NEIFILE being silent and the ladies having taken much pleasure in Chichibio's reply, Pamfilo, by the queen's desire, spoke thus: "Dearest ladies, it chanceth often that, like as fortune whiles hideth very great treasures of worth and virtue under mean conditions, as hath been a little before shown by Pampinea, even so, under the sorriest of human forms are marvellous wits found to have been lodged by nature; and this very plainly appeared in two townsmen of ours, of whom I purpose briefly to entertain you. For that the one, who was called Messer Forese da Rabatta, though little of person and misshapen, with a flat camoys face, that had been an eyesore on the shoulders of the foulest cadger in Florence, was yet of such excellence in the interpretation of the laws, that he was of many men of worth reputed a very treasury of civil right; whilst the other, whose name was Giotto, had so excellent a genius that there was nothing of all which Nature, mother and mover of all things, presenteth unto us by the ceaseless revolution of the heavens, but he with pencil and pen and brush depicted it and that so closely that not like, nay, but rather the thing itself it seemed, insomuch that men's visual sense is found to have been oftentimes deceived in things of his fashion, taking that for real which was but depictured. Wherefore, he having brought back to the light this art, which had for many an age lain buried under the errors of certain folk who painted more to divert the eyes of the ignorant than to please the understanding of the judicious, he may deservedly be styled one of the chief glories of Florence, the more so that he bore the honours he had gained with the utmost humility and although, while he lived, chief over all else in his art, he still refused to be called master, which title, though rejected by him, shone so much the more gloriously in him as it was with greater eagerness greedily usurped by those who knew less than he, or by his disciples. Yet, great as was his skill, he was not therefore anywise goodlier of person or better favoured than Messer Forese. But, to come to my story:

I must tell you that Messer Forese and Giotto had each his country house at Mugello and the former, having gone to visit his estates, at that season of the summer when the Courts hold holiday, and returning thence on a sorry cart-horse, chanced to fall in with the aforesaid Giotto, who had been on the same errand and was then on his way back to Florence nowise better equipped than himself in horse and accoutrements. Accordingly, they joined company and fared on softly, like old men as they were. Presently, it chanced, as we often see it happen in summer time, that a sudden shower overtook them, from which, as quickliest they might, they took shelter in the house of a husbandman, a friend and acquaintance of both of them. After awhile, the rain showing no sign of giving over and they wishing to reach Florence by daylight, they borrowed of their host two old homespun cloaks and two hats, rusty with age, for that there were no better to be had, and set out again upon their way.

When they had gone awhile and were all drenched and bemired with the splashing that their hackneys kept up with their hoofs—things which use not to add worship to any one's looks,—the weather began to clear a little and the two wayfarers, who had long fared on in silence, fell to conversing together. Messer Forese, as he rode, hearkening to Giotto, who was a very fine talker, fell to considering his companion from head to foot and seeing him everywise so ill accoutred and in such scurvy case, burst out laughing and without taking any thought to his own plight, said to him, 'How sayst thou, Giotto? An there encountered us here a stranger who had never seen thee, thinkest thou he would believe thee to be, as thou art, the finest painter in the world?' 'Ay, sir,' answered Giotto forthright, 'methinketh he might e'en believe it whenas, looking upon you, he should believe that you knew your A B C.' Messer Forese, hearing this, was sensible of his error and saw himself paid with money such as the wares he had sold."[304]

The Decameron of Giovanni Boccaccio - Part II

THE SIXTH STORY

MICHELE SCALZA PROVETH TO CERTAIN YOUNG MEN THAT THE CADGERS OF FLORENCE ARE THE BEST GENTLEMEN OF THE WORLD OR THE MAREMMA AND WINNETH A SUPPER

THE ladies yet laughed at Giotto's prompt retort, when the queen charged Fiammetta follow on and she proceeded to speak thus: "Young ladies, the mention by Pamfilo of the cadgers of Florence, whom peradventure you know not as doth he, hath brought to my mind a story, wherein, without deviating from our appointed theme, it is demonstrated how great is their nobility; and it pleaseth me, therefore, to relate it.

It is no great while since there was in our city a young man called Michele Scalza, who was the merriest and most agreeable man in the world and he had still the rarest stories in hand, wherefore the young Florentines were exceeding glad to have his company whenas they made a party of pleasure amongst themselves. It chanced one day, he being with certain folk at Monte Ughi, that the question was started among them of who were the best and oldest gentlemen of Florence. Some said the Uberti, others the Lamberti, and one this family and another that, according as it occurred to his mind; which Scalza hearing, he fell a-laughing and said, 'Go to, addlepates that you are! You know not what you say. The best gentlemen and the oldest, not only of Florence, but of all the world or the Maremma,[305] are the Cadgers,[306] a matter upon which all the phisopholers and every one who knoweth them, as I do, are of accord; and lest you should understand it of others, I speak of the Cadgers your neighbors of Santa Maria Maggiore.'

When the young men, who looked for him to say otherwhat, heard this, they all made mock of him and said, 'Thou gullest us, as if we knew not the Cadgers, even as thou dost.' 'By the Evangels,' replied Scalza, 'I gull you not; nay, I speak the truth, and if there be any here who will lay a supper thereon, to be given to the winner and half a dozen companions of his choosing, I will willingly hold the wager; and I will do yet more for you, for I will abide by the judgment of whomsoever you will.' Quoth one of them, called Neri Mannini, 'I am ready to try to win the supper in question'; whereupon, having agreed together to take Piero di Fiorentino, in whose house they were, to judge, they betook themselves to him, followed by all the rest, who looked to see Scalza lose and to make merry over his discomfiture, and recounted to him all that had passed. Piero, who was a discreet young man, having first heard Neri's argument, turned to Scalza and said to him, 'And thou, how canst thou prove this that thou affirmest?' 'How, sayest thou?' answered Scalza. 'Nay, I will prove it by such reasoning that not only thou, but he who denieth it, shall acknowledge that I speak sooth. You know that, the ancienter men are, the nobler they are; and so was it said but now among these. Now the Cadgers are more ancient than any one else, so that they are nobler; and showing you how they are the most ancient, I shall undoubtedly have won the wager. You must know, then, that the Cadgers were made by God the Lord in the days when He first began to learn to draw; but the rest of mankind were made after He knew how to draw. And to assure yourselves that in this I say sooth, do but consider the Cadgers in comparison with other folk; whereas you see all the rest of mankind with faces well composed and duly proportioned, you may see the Cadgers, this with a visnomy very long and strait and with a face out of all measure broad; one hath too long and another too short a nose and a third hath a chin jutting out and turned upward and huge jawbones that show as they were those of an ass, whilst some there be who have one eye bigger than the other and other some who have one set lower than the other, like the faces that children used to make, whenas they first begin to learn to draw. Wherefore, as I have already said, it is abundantly apparent that God the Lord made them, what time He was learning to draw; so that they are more ancient and consequently nobler than the rest of mankind.' At this, both Piero, who was the judge, and Neri, who had wagered the supper, and all the rest, hearing Scalza's comical argument and remembering themselves,[307] fell all a-laughing and affirmed that he was in the right and had won the supper, for that the Cadgers were assuredly the noblest and most ancient gentlemen that were to be found not in Florence alone, but in the world or the Maremma. Wherefore it was very justly said of Pamfilo, seeking to show the foulness of Messer Forese's visnomy, that it would have showed notably ugly on one of the Cadgers."

THE SEVENTH STORY

MADAM FILIPPA, BEING FOUND BY HER HUSBAND WITH A LOVER OF HERS AND BROUGHT TO JUSTICE, DELIVERETH HERSELF WITH A PROMPT AND PLEASANT ANSWER AND CAUSETH MODIFY THE STATUTE

FIAMMETTA was now silent and all laughed yet at the novel argument used by Scalza for the ennoblement over all of the Cadgers, when the queen enjoined Filostrato to tell and he accordingly began to say, "It is everywise a fine thing, noble ladies, to know how to speak well, but I hold it yet goodlier to know how to do it whereas necessity requireth it, even as a gentlewoman, of whom I purpose to entertain you, knew well how to do on such wise that not only did she afford her hearers matter for mirth and laughter, but did herself loose from the toils of an ignominious death, as you shall presently hear.

There was, then, aforetime, in the city of Prato, a statute in truth no less blameworthy than cruel, which, without making any distinction, ordained that any woman found by her husband in adultery with any her lover should be burnt, even as she who should be discovered to have sold her favours for money. What while this statute was in force, it befell that a noble and beautiful lady, by name Madam Filippa, who was of a singularly amorous complexion, was one night found by Rinaldo de' Pugliesi her husband, in her own chamber in the arms of Lazzerino de' Guazzagliotri, a noble and handsome youth of that city, whom she loved even as herself. Rinaldo, seeing this, was sore enraged and scarce contained himself from falling upon them and slaying them; and but that he feared for himself, an he should ensue the promptings of his anger, he had certainly done it. However, he forbore from this, but could not refrain from seeking of the law of Prato that which it was not permitted him to accomplish with his own hand, to wit, the death of his wife. Having, therefore, very sufficient evidence to prove the lady's default, no sooner was the day come than, without taking other counsel, he lodged an accusation against her and caused summon her before the provost.

Madam Filippa, being great of heart, as women commonly are who are verily in love, resolved, although counselled to the contrary by many of her friends and kinsfolk, to appear, choosing rather, confessing the truth, to die with an undaunted spirit, than, meanly fleeing, to live an outlaw in exile and confess herself unworthy of such a lover as he in whose arms she had been the foregoing night. Wherefore, presenting herself before the provost, attended by a great company of men and ladies and exhorted of all to deny the charge, she demanded, with a firm voice and an assured air, what he would with her. The magistrate, looking upon her and seeing her very fair and commendable of carriage and according as her words testified, of a lofty spirit, began to have compassion of her, fearing lest she should confess somewhat wherefore it should behoove him, for his own honour's sake, condemn her to die. However, having no choice but to question her of that which was laid to her charge, he said to her, 'Madam, as you see, here is Rinaldo your husband, who complaineth of you, avouching himself to have found you in adultery with another man and demanding that I should punish you therefor by putting you to death, according to the tenor of a statute which here obtaineth; but this I cannot do, except you confess it; wherefore look well what you answer and tell me if that be true whereof your husband impeacheth you.'

The lady, no wise dismayed, replied very cheerfully, 'Sir, true it is that Rinaldo is my husband and that he found me last night in the arms of Lazzarino, wherein, for the great and perfect love I bear him, I have many a time been; nor am I anywise minded to deny this. But, as I am assured you know, laws should be common to all and made with the consent of those whom they concern; and this is not the case with this statute, which is binding only upon us unhappy women, who might far better than men avail to satisfy many; more by token that, when it was made, not only did no woman yield consent thereunto, but none of us was even cited to do so; wherefore it may justly be styled naught. However, an you choose, to the prejudice of my body and of your own soul, to be the executor of this unrighteous law, it resteth with you to do so; but, ere you proceed to adjudge aught, I pray you do me one slight favour, to wit, that you question my husband if at all times and as often as it pleased him, without ever saying him nay, I have or not vouchsafed him entire commodity of myself.'

Rinaldo, without waiting to be questioned of the provost, straightway made answer that undoubtedly the lady had, at his every request, accorded him his every pleasure of herself; whereupon, 'Then, my lord provost,' straightway rejoined she, 'if he have still taken of me that which was needful and pleasing to him, what, I ask you, was or am I to do with that which remaineth over and above his requirements? Should I cast it to the dogs? Was it not far better to gratify withal a gentleman who loveth me more than himself, than to leave it waste or spoil?' Now well nigh all the people of Prato had flocked thither to the trial of such a matter and of so fair and famous a lady, and hearing so comical a question, they all, after much laughter, cried out as with one voice that she was in the right of it and that she said well. Moreover, ere they departed thence, at the instance of the provost, they modified the cruel statute and left it to apply to those women only who should for money make default to their husbands. Thereupon Rinaldo, having taken nought but shame by so fond an emprise, departed the court, and the lady returned in triumph to her own house, joyful and free and in a manner raised up out of the fire."

THE EIGHTH STORY

FRESCO EXHORTETH HIS NIECE NOT TO MIRROR HERSELF IN THE GLASS, IF, AS SHE SAITH, IT IRKETH HER TO SEE DISAGREEABLE FOLK

THE story told by Filostrato at first touched the hearts of the listening ladies with some little shamefastness and they gave token thereof by a modest redness that appeared upon their faces; but, after looking one at another, they hearkened thereto, tittering the while and scarce able to abstain from laughing. As soon as he was come to the end thereof, the queen turned to Emilia and bade her follow on, whereupon, sighing no otherwise than as she had been aroused from a dream, she began, "Lovesome lasses, for that long thought hath held me far from here, I shall, to obey our queen content myself with [relating] a story belike much slighter than that which I might have bethought myself to tell, had my mind been present here, recounting to you the silly default of a damsel, corrected by an uncle of hers with a jocular retort, had she been woman enough to have apprehended it.

A certain Fresco da Celatico, then, had a niece familiarly called Ciesca,[308] who, having a comely face and person (though none of those angelical beauties that we have often seen aforetime), set so much store by herself and accounted herself so noble that she had gotten a habit of carping at both men and women and everything she saw, without anywise taking thought to herself, who was so much more fashous, froward and humoursome than any other of her sex that nothing could be done to her liking. Beside all this, she was so prideful that, had she been of the blood royal of France, it had been overweening; and when she went abroad, she gave herself so many airs that she did nought but make wry faces, as if there came to her a stench from whomsoever she saw or met. But, letting be many other vexatious and tiresome fashions of hers, it chanced one day that she came back to the house, where Fresco was, and seating herself near him, all full of airs and grimaces, did nothing but puff and blow; whereupon quoth he, 'What meaneth this, Ciesca, that, to-day being a holiday, thou comest home so early?' To which she answered, all like to die away with affectation, 'It is true I have come back soon, for that I believe there were never in this city so many disagreeable and tiresome people, both men and women, as there are to-day; there passeth none about the streets but is hateful to me as ill-chance, and I do not believe there is a woman in the world to whom it is more irksome to see disagreeable folk than it is to me; wherefore I have returned thus early, not to see them.' 'My lass,' rejoined Fresco, to whom his niece's airs and graces were mighty displeasing, 'if disagreeable folk be so distasteful to thee as thou sayest, never mirror thyself in the glass, so thou wouldst live merry.' But she, emptier than a reed, albeit herseemed she was a match for Solomon in wit, apprehended Fresco's true speech no better than a block; nay, she said that she chose to mirror herself in the glass like other women; and so she abode in her folly and therein abideth yet."

THE NINTH STORY

GUIDO CAVALCANTI WITH A PITHY SPEECH COURTEOUSLY FLOUTETH CERTAIN FLORENTINE GENTLEMEN WHO HAD TAKEN HIM BY SURPRISE

THE queen, seeing Emilia delivered of her story and that it rested with none other than herself to tell, saving him who was privileged to speak last, began thus, "Although, sprightly ladies, you have this day taken out of my mouth at the least two stories, whereof I had purposed to relate one, I have yet one left to tell, the end whereof compriseth a saying of such a fashion that none, peradventure, of such pertinence, hath yet been cited to us.

You must know, then, that there were in our city, of times past, many goodly and commendable usances, whereof none is left there nowadays, thanks to the avarice that hath waxed therein with wealth and hath banished them all. Among these there was a custom to the effect that the gentlemen of the various quarters of Florence assembled together in divers places about the town and formed themselves into companies of a certain number, having a care to admit thereinto such only as might aptly bear the expense, whereof to-day the one and to-morrow the other, and so all in turn, hold open house, each his day, for the whole company. At these banquets they often entertained both stranger gentlemen, whenas there came any thither, and those of the city; and on like wise, once at the least in the year, they clad themselves alike and rode in procession through the city on the most notable days and whiles they held passes of arms, especially on the chief holidays or whenas some glad news of victory or the like came to the city.

Amongst these companies was one of Messer Betto Brunelleschi, whereinto the latter and his companions had studied amain to draw Guido, son of Messer Cavalcante de' Cavalcanti, and not without cause; for that, besides being one of the best logicians in the world and an excellent natural philosopher (of which things, indeed, they recked little), he was very sprightly and well-bred and a mighty well-spoken man and knew better than any other to do everything that he would and that pertained unto a gentleman, more by token that he was very rich and knew wonder-well how to entertain whomsoever he deemed deserving of honour. But Messer Betto had never been able to win and to have him, and he and his companions believed that this betided for that Guido, being whiles engaged in abstract speculations, became much distraught from mankind; and for that he inclined somewhat to the opinion of the Epicureans, it was reported among the common folk that these his speculations consisted only in seeking if it might be discovered that God was not.

It chanced one day that Guido set out from Orto San Michele and came by way of the Corso degli Ademari, the which was oftentimes his road, to San Giovanni, round about which there were at that present divers great marble tombs (which are nowadays at Santa Reparata) and many others. As he was between the columns of porphyry there and the tombs in question and the door of the church, which was shut, Messer Betto and his company, coming a-horseback along the Piazza di Santa Reparata, espied him among the tombs and said, 'Let us go plague him.' Accordingly, spurring their horses, they charged all down upon him in sport and coming upon him ere he was aware of them, said to him, 'Guido, thou refusest to be of our company; but, harkye, whenas thou shalt have found that God is not, what wilt thou have accomplished?' Guido, seeing himself hemmed in by them, answered promptly, 'Gentlemen, you may say what you will to me in your own house'; then, laying his hand on one of the great tombs aforesaid and being very nimble of body, he took a spring and alighting on the other side, made off, having thus rid himself of them.

The gentlemen abode looking one upon another and fell a-saying that he was a crack-brain and that this that he had answered them amounted to nought seeing that there where they were they had no more to do than all the other citizens, nor Guido himself less than any of themselves. But Messer Betto turned to them and said, 'It is you who are the crackbrains, if you have not apprehended him. He hath courteously and in a few words given us the sharpest rebuke in the world; for that, an you consider aright, these tombs are the houses of the dead, seeing they are laid and abide therein, and these, saith he, are our house, meaning thus to show us that we and other foolish and unlettered men are, compared with him and other men of learning, worse than dead folk; wherefore, being here, we are in our own house.' Thereupon each understood what Guido had meant to say and was abashed nor ever plagued him more, but held Messer Betto thenceforward a gentleman of a subtle wit and an understanding."

THE TENTH STORY

FRA CIPOLLA PROMISETH CERTAIN COUNTRY FOLK TO SHOW THEM ONE OF THE ANGEL GABRIEL'S FEATHERS AND FINDING COALS IN PLACE THEREOF, AVOUCHETH THESE LATTER TO BE OF THOSE WHICH ROASTED ST. LAWRENCE

EACH of the company being now quit of his[309] story, Dioneo perceived that it rested with him to tell; whereupon, without awaiting more formal commandment, he began on this wise, silence having first been imposed on those who commended Guido's pregnant retort: "Charming ladies, albeit I am privileged to speak of that which most liketh me, I purpose not to-day to depart from the matter whereof you have all very aptly spoken; but, ensuing in your footsteps, I mean to show you how cunningly a friar of the order of St. Anthony, by name Fra Cipolla, contrived with a sudden shift to extricate himself from a snare[310] which had been set for him by two young men; nor should it irk you if, for the complete telling of the story, I enlarge somewhat in speaking, an you consider the sun, which is yet amiddleward in the sky.

Certaldo, as you may have heard, is a burgh of Val d' Elsa situate in our country, which, small though it be, was once inhabited by gentlemen and men of substance; and thither, for that he found good pasture there, one of the friars of the order of St. Anthony was long used to resort once a year, to get in the alms bestowed by simpletons upon him and his brethren. His name was Fra Cipolla and he was gladly seen there, no less belike, for his name's sake[311] than for other reasons, seeing that these parts produce onions that are famous throughout all Tuscany. This Fra Cipolla was little of person, red-haired and merry of countenance, the jolliest rascal in the world, and to boot, for all he was no scholar, he was so fine a talker and so ready of wit that those who knew him not would not only have esteemed him a great rhetorician, but had avouched him to be Tully himself or may be Quintilian; and he was gossip or friend or well-wisher[312] to well nigh every one in the country.

One August among others he betook himself thither according to his wont, and on a Sunday morning, all the goodmen and goodwives of the villages around being come to hear mass at the parish church, he came forward, whenas it seemed to him time, and said, 'Gentlemen and ladies, it is, as you know, your usance to send every year to the poor of our lord Baron St. Anthony of your corn and of your oats, this little and that much, according to his means and his devoutness, to the intent that the blessed St. Anthony may keep watch over your beeves and asses and swine and sheep; and besides this, you use to pay, especially such of you as are inscribed into our company, that small due which is payable once a year. To collect these I have been sent by my superior, to wit, my lord abbot; wherefore, with the blessing of God, you shall, after none, whenas you hear the bells ring, come hither without the church, where I will make preachment to you after the wonted fashion and you shall kiss the cross; moreover, for that I know you all to be great devotees of our lord St. Anthony, I will, as an especial favour show you a very holy and goodly relic, which I myself brought aforetime from the holy lands beyond seas; and that is one of the Angel Gabriel's feathers, which remained in the Virgin Mary's chamber, whenas he came to announce to her in Nazareth.' This said, he broke off and went on with his mass.

Now, when he said this, there were in the church, among many others, two roguish young fellows, hight one Giovanni del Bragioniera and the other Biagio Pizzini, who, after laughing with one another awhile over Fra Cipolla's relic, took counsel together, for all they were great friends and cronies of his, to play him some trick in the matter of the feather in question. Accordingly, having learned that he was to dine that morning with a friend of his in the burgh, they went down into the street as soon as they knew him to be at table, and betook themselves to the inn where he had alighted, purposing that Biagio should hold his servant in parley, whilst Giovanni should search his baggage for the feather aforesaid, whatever it might be, and carry it off, to see what he should say to the people of the matter.

Fra Cipolla had a servant, whom some called Guccio[313] Balena,[314] others Guccio Imbratta[315] and yet others Guccia Porco[316] and who was such a scurvy knave that Lipo Topo[317] never wrought his like, inasmuch as his master used oftentimes to jest of him with his cronies and say, 'My servant hath in him nine defaults, such that, were one of them in Solomon or Aristotle or Seneca, it would suffice to mar all their worth, all their wit and all their sanctity. Consider, then, what a man he must be, who hath all nine of them and in whom there is neither worth nor wit nor sanctity.' Being questioned whiles what were these nine defaults and having put them into doggerel rhyme, he would answer, 'I will tell you. He's a liar, a sloven, a slugabed; disobedient, neglectful, ill bred; o'erweening, foul-spoken, a dunderhead; beside which he hath divers other peccadilloes, whereof it booteth not to speak. But what is most laughable of all his fashions is that, wherever he goeth, he is still for taking a wife and hiring a house; for, having a big black greasy beard, him-seemeth he is so exceeding handsome and agreeable that he conceiteth himself all the women who see him fall in love with him, and if you let him alone, he would run after them all till he lost his girdle.[318] Sooth to say, he is of great assistance to me, for that none can ever seek to speak with me so secretly but he must needs hear his share; and if it chance that I be questioned of aught, he is so fearful lest I should not know how to answer, that he straightway answereth for me both Ay and No, as he judgeth sortable.'

Now Fra Cipolla, in leaving him at the inn, had bidden him look well that none touched his gear, and more particularly his saddle-bags, for that therein were the sacred things. But Guccio, who was fonder of the kitchen than the nightingale of the green boughs, especially if he scented some serving-wench there, and who had seen in that of the inn a gross fat cookmaid, undersized and ill-made, with a pair of paps that showed like two manure-baskets and a face like a cadger's, all sweaty, greasy and smoky, leaving Fra Cipolla's chamber and all his gear to care for themselves, swooped down upon the kitchen, even as the vulture swoopeth upon carrion, and seating himself by the fire, for all it was August, entered into discourse with the wench in question, whose name was Nuta, telling her that he was by rights a gentleman and had more than nine millions of florins, beside that which he had to give others, which was rather more than less, and that he could do and say God only knew what. Moreover, without regard to his bonnet, whereon was grease enough to have seasoned the caldron of Altopascio,[319] and his doublet all torn and pieced and enamelled with filth about the collar and under the armpits, with more spots and patches of divers colours than ever had Turkey or India stuffs, and his shoes all broken and hose unsewn, he told her, as he had been the Sieur de Châtillon,[320] that he meant to clothe her and trick her out anew and deliver her from the wretchedness of abiding with others,[321] and bring her to hope of better fortune, if without any great wealth in possession, and many other things, which, for all he delivered them very earnestly, all turned to wind and came to nought, as did most of his enterprises.

The two young men, accordingly, found Guccio busy about Nuta, whereat they were well pleased, for that it spared them half their pains, and entering Fra Cipolla's chamber, which they found open, the first thing that came under their examination was the saddle-bags wherein was the feather. In these they found, enveloped in a great taffetas wrapper, a little casket and opening this latter, discovered therein a parrot's tail-feather, which they concluded must be that which the friar had promised to show the people of Certaldo. And certes he might lightly cause it to be believed in those days, for that the refinements of Egypt had not yet made their way save into a small part of Tuscany, as they have since done in very great abundance, to the undoing of all Italy; and wherever they may have been some little known, in those parts they were well nigh altogether unknown of the inhabitants; nay the rude honesty of the ancients yet enduring there, not only had they never set eyes on a parrot, but were far from having ever heard tell of such a bird. The young men, then, rejoiced at finding the feather, laid hands on it and not to leave the casket empty, filled it with some coals they saw in a corner of the room and shut it again. Then, putting all things in order as they had found them, they made off in high glee with the feather, without having been seen, and began to await what Fra Cipolli should say, when he found the coals in place thereof.

The simple men and women who were in the church, hearing that they were to see the Angel Gabriel's feather after none, returned home, as soon as mass was over, and neighbor telling it to neighbor and gossip to gossip, no sooner had they all dined than so many men and women flocked to the burgh that it would scarce hold them, all looking eagerly to see the aforesaid feather. Fra Cipolla, having well dined and after slept awhile, arose a little after none and hearing of the great multitude of country folk come to see the feather, sent to bid Guccio Imbratta come thither with the bells and bring his saddle-bags. Guccio, tearing himself with difficulty away from the kitchen and Nuta, betook himself with the things required to the appointed place, whither coming, out of breath, for that the water he had drunken had made his belly swell amain, he repaired, by his master's commandment, to the church door and fell to ringing the bells lustily.

When all the people were assembled there, Fra Cipolla, without observing that aught of his had been meddled with, began his preachment and said many words anent his affairs; after which, thinking to come to the showing of the Angel Gabriel's feather, he first recited the Confiteor with the utmost solemnity and let kindle a pair of flambeaux; then, pulling off his bonnet, he delicately unfolded the taffetas wrapper and brought out the casket. Having first pronounced certain ejaculations in praise and commendation of the Angel Gabriel and of his relic, he opened the casket and seeing it full of coals, suspected not Guccio Balena of having played him this trick, for that he knew him not to be man enough; nor did he curse him for having kept ill watch lest others should do it, but silently cursed himself for having committed to him the care of his gear, knowing him, as he did, to be negligent, disobedient, careless and forgetful.

Nevertheless, without changing colour, he raised his eyes and hands to heaven and said, so as to be heard of all, 'O God, praised be still thy puissance!' Then, shutting the casket and turning to the people, 'Gentlemen and ladies,' quoth he, 'you must know that, whilst I was yet very young, I was dispatched by my superior to those parts where the sun riseth and it was expressly commanded me that I should seek till I found the Privileges of Porcellana, which, though they cost nothing to seal, are much more useful to others than to us. On this errand I set out from Venice and passed through Borgo de' Greci,[322] whence, riding through the kingdom of Algarve and Baldacca,[323] I came to Parione,[324] and from there, not without thirst, I came after awhile into Sardinia. But what booteth it to set out to you in detail all the lands explored by me? Passing the straits of San Giorgio,[325] I came into Truffia[326] and Buffia,[327] countries much inhabited and with great populations, and thence into the land of Menzogna,[328] where I found great plenty of our brethren and of friars of other religious orders, who all went about those parts, shunning unease for the love of God, recking little of others' travail, whenas they saw their own advantage to ensue, and spending none other money than such as was uncoined.[329] Thence I passed into the land of the Abruzzi, where the men and women go in clogs over the mountains, clothing the swine in their own guts;[330] and a little farther I found folk who carried bread on sticks and wine in bags. From this I came to the Mountains of the Bachi, where all the waters run down hill; and in brief, I made my way so far inward that I won at last even to India Pastinaca,[331] where I swear to you, by the habit I wear on my back, that I saw hedge-bills[332] fly, a thing incredible to whoso hath not seen it. But of this Maso del Saggio will confirm me, whom I found there a great merchant, cracking walnuts and selling the shells by retail.

Being unable to find that which I went seeking, for that thence one goeth thither by water, I turned back and arrived in those holy countries, where, in summer-years, cold bread is worth four farthings a loaf and the hot goeth for nothing. There I found the venerable father my lord Blamemenot Anitpleaseyou, the very worshipful Patriarch of Jerusalem, who, for reverence of the habit I have still worn of my lord Baron St. Anthony, would have me see all the holy relics that he had about him and which were so many that, an I sought to recount them all to you, I should not come to an end thereof in several miles. However, not to leave you disconsolate, I will tell you some thereof. First, he showed me the finger of the Holy Ghost, as whole and sound as ever it was, and the forelock of the seraph that appeared to St. Francis and one of the nails of the Cherubim and one of the ribs of the Verbum Caro[333] Get-thee-to-the-windows and some of the vestments of the Holy Catholic Faith and divers rays of the star that appeared to the Three Wise Men in the East and a vial of the sweat of St. Michael, whenas he fought with the devil, and the jawbone of the death of St. Lazarus and others. And for that I made him a free gift of the Steeps[334] of Monte Morello in the vernacular and of some chapters of the Caprezio,[335] which he had long gone seeking, he made me a sharer in his holy relics and gave me one of the teeth of the Holy Rood and somewhat of the sound of the bells of Solomon's Temple in a vial and the feather of the Angel Gabriel, whereof I have already bespoken you, and one of the pattens of St. Gherardo da Villa Magna, which not long since at Florence I gave to Gherardo di Bonsi, who hath a particular devotion for that saint; and he gave me also of the coals wherewith the most blessed martyr St. Lawrence was roasted; all which things I devoutly brought home with me and yet have. True it is that my superior hath never suffered me to show them till such time as he should be certified if they were the very things or not. But now that, by certain miracles performed by them and by letters received from the patriarch, he hath been made certain of this, he hath granted me leave to show them; and I, fearing to trust them to others, still carry them with me.

Now I carry the Angel Gabriel's feather, so it may not be marred, in one casket, and the coals wherewith St. Lawrence was roasted in another, the which are so like one to other, that it hath often happened to me to take one for the other, and so hath it betided me at this present, for that, thinking to bring hither the casket wherein was the feather, I have brought that wherein are the coals. The which I hold not to have been an error; nay, meseemeth certain that it was

God's will and that He Himself placed the casket with the coals in my hands, especially now I mind me that the feast of St. Lawrence is but two days hence; wherefore God, willing that, by showing you the coals wherewith he was roasted, I should rekindle in your hearts the devotion it behoveth you have for him, caused me take, not the feather, as I purposed, but the blessed coals extinguished by the sweat of that most holy body. So, O my blessed children, put off your bonnets and draw near devoutly to behold them; but first I would have you knew that whoso is scored with these coals, in the form of the sign of the cross, may rest assured, for the whole year to come, that fire shall not touch him but he shall feel it.'

Having thus spoken, he opened the casket, chanting the while a canticle in praise of St. Lawrence, and showed the coals, which after the simple multitude had awhile beheld with reverent admiration, they all crowded about Fra Cipolla and making him better offerings than they were used, besought him to touch them withal. Accordingly, taking the coals in hand, he fell to making the biggest crosses for which he could find room upon their white smocks and doublets and upon the veils of the women, avouching that how much soever the coals diminished in making these crosses, they after grew again in the casket, as he had many a time proved. On this wise he crossed all the people of Certaldo, to his no small profit, and thus, by his ready wit and presence of mind, he baffled those who, by taking the feather from him, had thought to baffle him and who, being present at his preachment and hearing the rare shift employed by him and from how far he had taken it and with what words, had so laughed that they thought to have cracked their jaws. Then, after the common folk had departed, they went up to him and with all the mirth in the world discovered to him that which they had done and after restored him his feather, which next year stood him in as good stead as the coals had done that day."

This story afforded unto all the company alike the utmost pleasure and solace, and it was much laughed of all at Fra Cipolla, and particularly of his pilgrimage and the relics seen and brought back by him. The queen, seeing the story and likewise her sovantry at an end, rose to her feet and put off the crown, which she set laughingly on Dioneo's head, saying, "It is time, Dioneo, that thou prove awhile what manner charge it is to have ladies to govern and guide; be thou, then, king and rule on such wise that, in the end, we may have reason to give ourselves joy of thy governance." Dioneo took the crown and answered, laughing, "You may often enough have seen much better kings than I, I mean chess-kings; but, an you obey me as a king should in truth be obeyed, I will cause you enjoy that without which assuredly no entertainment is ever complete in its gladness. But let that talk be; I will rule as best I know."

Then, sending for the seneschal, according to the wonted usance, he orderly enjoined him of that which he should do during the continuance of his seignory and after said, "Noble ladies, it hath in divers manners been devised of human industry[336] and of the various chances [of fortune,] insomuch that, had not Dame Licisca come hither a while agone and found me matter with her prate for our morrow's relations, I misdoubt me I should have been long at pains to find a subject of discourse. As you heard, she avouched that she had not a single gossip who had come to her husband a maid and added that she knew right well how many and what manner tricks married women yet played their husbands. But, letting be the first part, which is a childish matter, methinketh the second should be an agreeable subject for discourse; wherefore I will and ordain it that, since Licisca hath given us occasion therefor, it be discoursed to-morrow OF THE TRICKS WHICH, OR FOR LOVE OR FOR THEIR OWN PRESERVATION, WOMEN HAVE HERETOFORE PLAYED THEIR HUSBANDS, WITH OR WITHOUT THE LATTER'S COGNIZANCE THEREOF."

It seemed to some of the ladies that to discourse of such a matter would ill beseem them and they prayed him, therefore, to change the theme proposed; wherefore answered he, "Ladies, I am no less cognizant than yourselves of that which I have ordained, and that which you would fain allege to me availed not to deter me from ordaining it, considering that the times are such that, provided men and women are careful to eschew unseemly actions, all liberty of discourse is permitted. Know you not that, for the malignity of the season, the judges have forsaken the tribunals, that the laws, as well Divine as human, are silent and full licence is conceded unto every one for the preservation of his life? Wherefore, if your modesty allow itself some little freedom in discourse, not with intent to ensue it with aught of unseemly in deeds, but to afford yourselves and others diversion, I see not with what plausible reason any can blame you in the future. Moreover, your company, from the first day of our assembling until this present, hath been most decorous, nor, for aught that hath been said here, doth it appear to me that its honour hath anywise been sullied. Again, who is there knoweth not your virtue? Which, not to say mirthful discourse, but even fear of death I do not believe could avail to shake. And to tell you the truth, whosoever should hear that you shrank from devising bytimes of these toys would be apt to suspect that you were guilty in the matter and were therefore unwilling to discourse thereof. To say nothing of the fine honour you would do me in that, I having been obedient unto all, you now, having made me your king, seek to lay down the law to me, and not to discourse of the subject which I propose. Put off, then, this misdoubtance, apter to mean minds than to yours, and good luck to you, let each of you bethink herself of some goodly story to tell." When the ladies heard this, they said it should be as he pleased; whereupon he gave them all leave to do their several pleasures until supper-time.

The sun was yet high, for that the discoursement[337] had been brief; wherefor Dioneo having addressed himself to play at tables with the other young men, Elisa called the other ladies apart and said to them, "Since we have been here, I have still wished to carry you to a place very near at hand, whither methinketh none of you hath ever been and which is called the Ladies' Valley, but have never yet found an occasion of bringing you thither unto to-day; wherefore, as the sun is yet high, I doubt not but, an it please you come thither, you will be exceeding well pleased to have been there." They answered that they were ready and calling one of their maids, set out upon their way, without letting the young men know aught thereof; nor had they gone much more than a mile, when they came to the Ladies' Valley. They entered therein by a very strait way, on one side whereof ran a very clear streamlet, and saw it as fair and as delectable, especially at that season whenas the heat was great, as most might be conceived. According to that which one of them after told me, the plain that was in the valley was as round as if it had been traced with the compass, albeit it seemed the work of nature and not of art, and was in circuit a little more than half a mile, encompassed about with six little hills not over-high, on the summit of each of which stood a palace built in guise of a goodly castle. The sides of these hills went sloping gradually downward to the plain on such wise as we see in amphitheatres, the degrees descend in ordered succession from the highest to the lowest, still contracting their circuit; and of these slopes those which looked toward the south were all full of vines and olives and almonds and cherries and figs and many another kind of fruit-bearing trees, without a span thereof being wasted; whilst those which faced the North Star[338] were all covered with thickets of dwarf oaks and ashes and other trees as green and straight as might be. The middle plain, which had no other inlet than that whereby the ladies were come thither, was full of firs and cypresses and laurels and various sorts of pines, as well arrayed and ordered as if the best artist in that kind had planted them; and between these little or no sun, even at its highest, made its way to the ground, which was all one meadow of very fine grass, thick-sown with flowers purpurine and others. Moreover, that which afforded no less delight than otherwhat was a little stream, which ran down from a valley that divided two of the hills aforesaid and falling over cliffs of live rock, made a murmur very delectable to hear, what while it showed from afar, as it broke over the stones, like so much quicksilver jetting out, under pressure of somewhat, into fine spray. As it came down into the little plain, it was there received into a fair channel and ran very swiftly into the middest thereof, where it formed a lakelet, such as the townsfolk made whiles, by way of fishpond, in their gardens, whenas they have a commodity thereof. This lakelet was no deeper than a man's stature, breast high, and its waters being exceeding clear and altogether untroubled with any admixture, it showed its bottom to be of a very fine gravel, the grains whereof whoso had nought else to do might, an he would, have availed to number; nor, looking into the water, was the bottom alone to be seen, nay, but so many fish fleeting hither and thither that, over and above the pleasure thereof, it was a marvel to behold;

nor was it enclosed with other banks than the very soil of the meadow, which was the goodlier thereabout in so much as it received the more of its moisture. The water that abounded over and above the capacity of the lake was received into another channel, whereby, issuing forth of the little valley, it ran off into the lower parts.

Hither then came the young ladies and after they had gazed all about and much commended the place, they took counsel together to bathe, for that the heat was great and that they saw the lakelet before them and were in no fear of being seen. Accordingly, bidding their serving maid abide over against the way whereby one entered there and look if any should come and give them notice thereof, they stripped themselves naked, all seven, and entered the lake, which hid their white bodies no otherwise than as a thin glass would do with a vermeil rose. Then, they being therein and no troubling of the water ensuing thereof, they fell, as best they might, to faring hither and thither in pursuit of the fish, which had uneath where to hide themselves, and seeking to take them with the naked hand. After they had abidden awhile in such joyous pastime and had taken some of the fish, they came forth of the lakelet and clad themselves anew. Then, unable to commend the place more than they had already done and themseeming time to turn homeward, they set out, with soft step, upon their way, discoursing much of the goodliness of the valley.

They reached the palace betimes and there found the young men yet at play where they had left them; to whom quoth Pampinea, laughing. "We have e'en stolen a march on you to-day." "How?" asked Dioneo. "Do you begin to do deeds ere you come to say words?"[339] "Ay, my lord," answered she and related to him at large whence they came and how the place was fashioned and how far distant thence and that which they had done. The king, hearing tell of the goodliness of the place and desirous of seeing it, caused straightway order the supper, which being dispatched to the general satisfaction, the three young men, leaving the ladies, betook themselves with their servants to the valley and having viewed it in every part, for that none of them had ever been there before, extolled it for one of the goodliest things in the world. Then, for that it grew late, after they had bathed and donned their clothes, they returned home, where they found the ladies dancing a round, to the accompaniment of a song sung by Fiammetta.

The dance ended, they entered with them into a discourse of the Ladies' Valley and said much in praise and commendation thereof. Moreover, the king, sending for the seneschal, bade him look that the dinner be made ready there on the following morning and have sundry beds carried thither, in case any should have a mind to lie or sleep there for nooning; after which he let bring lights and wine and confections and the company having somedele refreshed themselves, he commanded that all should address themselves to dancing. Then, Pamfilo having, at his commandment, set up a dance, the king turned to Elisa and said courteously to her, "Fair damsel, thou has to-day done me the honour of the crown and I purpose this evening to do thee that of the song; wherefore look thou sing such an one as most liketh thee." Elisa answered, smiling, that she would well and with dulcet voice began on this wise:

Love, from thy clutches could I but win free,
Hardly, methinks, again
Shall any other hook take hold on me.
I entered in thy wars a youngling maid,
Thinking thy strife was utmost peace and sweet,
And all my weapons on the ground I laid,
As one secure, undoubting of defeat;
But thou, false tyrant, with rapacious heat,
Didst fall on me amain
With all the grapnels of thine armoury.

Then, wound about and fettered with thy chains,
To him, who for my death in evil hour
Was born, thou gav'st me, bounden, full of pains
And bitter tears; and syne within his power
He hath me and his rule's so harsh and dour
No sighs can move the swain
Nor all my wasting plaints to set me free.

My prayers, the wild winds bear them all away;

He hearkeneth unto none and none will hear;
Wherefore each hour my torment waxeth aye;
I cannot die, albeit life irks me drear.
Ah, Lord, have pity on my heavy cheer;
Do that I seek in vain
And give him bounden in thy chains to me.

An this thou wilt not, at the least undo
The bonds erewhen of hope that knitted were;
Alack, O Lord, thereof to thee I sue,
For, an thou do it, yet to waxen fair
Again I trust, as was my use whilere,
And being quit of pain
Myself with white flowers and with red besee.

Elisa ended her song with a very plaintive sigh, and albeit all marvelled at the words thereof, yet was there none who might conceive what it was that caused her sing thus. But the king, who was in a merry mood, calling for Tindaro, bade him bring out his bagpipes, to the sound whereof he let dance many dances; after which, a great part of the night being now past, he bade each go sleep.

HERE ENDETH THE SIXTH DAY
OF THE DECAMERON

Day the Seventh

HERE BEGINNETH THE SEVENTH DAY OF THE DECAMERON WHEREIN UNDER THE GOVERNANCE OF DIONEO IS DISCOURSED OF THE TRICKS WHICH OR FOR LOVE OR FOR THEIR OWN PRESERVATION WOMEN HAVE HERETOFORE PLAYED THEIR HUSBANDS WITH OR WITHOUT THE LATTER'S COGNIZANCE THEREOF

EVERY star was already fled from the parts of the East, save only that which we style Lucifer and which shone yet in the whitening dawn, when the seneschal, arising, betook himself, with a great baggage-train, to the Ladies' Valley, there to order everything, according to commandment had of his lord. The king, whom the noise of the packers and of the beasts had awakened, tarried not long after his departure to rise and being risen, caused arouse all the ladies and likewise the young men; nor had the rays of the sun yet well broken forth, when they all entered upon the road. Never yet had the nightingales and the other birds seemed to them to sing so blithely as they did that morning, what while, accompanied by their carols, they repaired to the Ladies' Valley, where they were received by many more, which seemed to them to make merry for their coming. There, going round about the place and reviewing it all anew, it appeared to them so much fairer than on the foregoing day as the season of the day was more sorted to its goodliness. Then, after they had broken their fast with good wine and confections, not to be behindhand with the birds in the matter of song, they fell a-singing and the valley with them, still echoing those same songs which they did sing, whereto all the birds, as if they would not be outdone, added new and dulcet notes. Presently, the dinner-hour being come and the tables spread hard by the fair lakelet under the thickset laurels and other goodly trees, they seated themselves there, as it pleased the king, and eating, watched the fish swim in vast shoals about the lake, which gave bytimes occasion for talk as well as observation. When they had made an end of dining and the meats and tables were removed, they fell anew to singing more blithely than ever; after which, beds having been spread in various places about the little valley and all enclosed about by the discreet seneschal with curtains and canopies of French serge, whoso would might with the king's permission, go sleep; whilst those who had no mind to sleep might at their will take pleasure of their other wonted pastimes. But, after awhile, all being now arisen and the hour come when they should assemble together for story-telling, carpets were, at the king's commandment, spread upon the grass, not far from the place where they had eaten, and all having seated themselves thereon hard by the lake, the king bade Emilia begin; whereupon she blithely proceeded to speak, smiling, thus:

THE FIRST STORY

GIANNI LOTTERINGHI HEARETH KNOCK AT HIS DOOR BY NIGHT AND AWAKENETH HIS WIFE, WHO GIVETH HIM TO BELIEVE THAT IT IS A PHANTOM; WHEREUPON THEY GO TO EXORCISE IT WITH A CERTAIN ORISON AND THE KNOCKING CEASETH

"My Lord, it had been very agreeable to me, were such your pleasure, that other than I should have given a beginning to so goodly a matter as is that whereof we are to speak; but, since it pleaseth you that I give all the other ladies assurance by my example, I will gladly do it. Moreover, dearest ladies, I will study to tell a thing that may be useful to you in time to come, for that, if you others are as fearful as I, and especially of phantoms, (though what manner of thing they may be God knoweth I know not, nor ever found I any woman who knew it, albeit all are alike adread of them,) you may, by noting well my story, learn a holy and goodly orison of great virtue for the conjuring them away, should they come to you.

There was once in Florence, in the quarter of San Brancazio, a wool-comber called Gianni Lotteringhi, a man more fortunate in his craft than wise in other things, for that, savoring of the simpleton, he was very often made captain of the Laudsingers[340] of Santa Maria Novella and had the governance of their confraternity, and he many a time had other little offices of the same kind, upon which he much valued himself. This betided him for that, being a man of substance, he gave many a good pittance to the clergy, who, getting of him often, this a pair of hose, that a gown and another a scapulary, taught him in return store of goodly orisons and gave him the paternoster in the vulgar tongue, the Song of Saint Alexis, the Lamentations of Saint Bernard, the Canticles of Madam Matilda and the like trumpery, all which he held very dear and kept very diligently for his soul's health. Now he had a very fair and lovesome lady to wife, by name Mistress Tessa, who was the daughter of Mannuccio dalla Cuculia and was exceeding discreet and well advised. She, knowing her husband's simplicity and being enamoured of Federigo di Neri Pegolotti, a brisk and handsome youth, and he of her, took order with a serving-maid of hers that he should come speak with her at a very goodly country house which her husband had at Camerata, where she sojourned all the summer and whither Gianni came whiles to sup and sleep, returning in the morning to his shop and bytimes to his Laudsingers.

Federigo, who desired this beyond measure, taking his opportunity, repaired thither on the day appointed him towards vespers and Gianni not coming thither that evening, supped and lay the night in all ease and delight with the lady, who, being in his arms, taught him that night a good half dozen of her husband's lauds. Then, neither she nor Federigo purposing that this should be the last, as it had been the first time [of their foregathering], they took order together on this wise, so it should not be needful to send the maid for him each time, to wit, that every day, as he came and went to and from a place he had a little farther on, he should keep his eye on a vineyard that adjoined the house, where he would see an ass's skull set up on one of the vine poles, which whenas he saw with the muzzle turned towards Florence, he should without fail and in all assurance betake himself to her that evening after dark; and if he found the door shut he should knock softly thrice and she would open to him; but that, whenas he saw the ass's muzzle turned towards Fiesole, he should not come, for that Gianni would be there; and doing on this wise, they foregathered many a time.

But once, amongst other times, it chanced that, Federigo being one night to sup with Mistress Tessa and she having let cook two fat capons, Gianni, who was not expected there that night, came thither very late, whereat the lady was much chagrined and having supped with her husband on a piece of salt pork, which she had let boil apart, caused the maid wrap the two boiled capons in a white napkin and carry them, together with good store of new-laid eggs and a flask of good wine, into a garden she had, whither she could go, without passing through the house, and where she was wont to sup whiles with her lover, bidding her lay them at the foot of a peach-tree that grew beside a lawn there. But such was her trouble and annoy that she remembered not to bid the maid wait till Federigo should come and tell him that Gianni was there and that he should take the viands from the garden; wherefore, she and Gianni betaking themselves to bed and the maid likewise, it was not long before Federigo came to the door and knocked softly once. The door was so near to the bedchamber that Gianni heard it incontinent, as also did the lady; but she made a show of being asleep, so her husband might have no suspicion of her. After waiting a little, Federigo knocked a second time, whereupon Gianni, marvelling, nudged his wife somewhat and said, 'Tessa, hearest thou what I hear? Meseemeth there is a knocking at our door.'

The lady, who had heard it much better than he, made a show of awaking and said, 'Eh? How sayst thou?' 'I say,' answered Gianni, 'that meseemeth there is a knocking at our door.' 'Knocking!' cried she. 'Alack, Gianni mine, knowst thou not what it is? It is a phantom, that hath these last few nights given me the greatest fright that ever was, insomuch that, whenas I hear it, I put my head under the clothes and dare not bring it out again until it is broad day.' Quoth Gianni, 'Go to, wife; have no fear, if it be so; for I said the Te Lucis and the Intemerata and such and such other pious orisons, before we lay down, and crossed the bed from side to side, in the name of the Father, the Son and the Holy Ghost, so that we have no need to fear, for that, what power soever it have, it cannot avail to harm us.'

The lady, fearing lest Federigo should perchance suspect otherwhat and be angered with her, determined at all hazards to arise and let him know that Gianni was there; wherefore quoth she to her husband, 'That is all very well; thou sayst thy words, thou; but, for my part, I shall never hold myself safe nor secure, except we exorcise it, since thou art here.' 'And how is it to be exorcised?' asked he; and she, 'I know full well how to exorcise it; for, the other day, when I went to the Pardon at Fiesole, a certain anchoress (the very holiest of creatures, Gianni mine, God only can say how holy she is,) seeing me thus fearful, taught me a pious and effectual orison and told me that she had made trial of it several times, ere she became a recluse, and that it had always availed her. God knoweth I should never have dared go alone to make proof of it; but, now that thou art here, I would have us go exorcise the phantom.'

Gianni answered that he would well and accordingly they both arose and went softly to the door, without which Federigo, who now began to misdoubt him of somewhat, was yet in waiting. When they came thither, the lady said to Gianni, 'Do thou spit, whenas I shall bid thee.' And he answered, 'Good.' Then she began the conjuration and said, 'Phantom, phantom that goest by night, with tail upright[341] thou cam'st to us; now get thee gone with tail upright. Begone into the garden to the foot of the great peach tree; there shalt thou find an anointed twice-anointed one[342] and an hundred turds of my sitting hen;[343] set thy mouth to the flagon and get thee gone again and do thou no hurt to my Gianni nor to me.' Then to her husband, 'Spit, Gianni,' quoth she, and he spat. Federigo, who heard all this from without and was now quit of jealousy, had, for all his vexation, so great a mind to laugh that he was like to burst, and when Gianni spat, he said under his breath '[Would it were] thy teeth!'

The lady, having thrice conjured the phantom on this wise, returned to bed with her husband, whilst Federigo, who had not supped, looking to sup with her, and had right well apprehended the words of the conjuration, betook himself to the garden and finding the capons and wine and eggs at the foot of the great peach-tree, carried them off to his house and there supped at his ease; and after, when he next foregathered with the lady, he had a hearty laugh with her anent the conjuration aforesaid. Some say indeed that the lady had actually turned the ass's skull towards Fiesole, but that a husbandman, passing through the vineyard, had given it a blow with a stick and caused it spin round and it had become turned towards Florence, wherefore Federigo, thinking himself summoned, had come thither, and that the lady had made the conjuration on this wise: 'Phantom, phantom, get thee gone in God's name; for it was not I turned the ass's head; but another it was, God put him to shame! and I am here with my Gianni in bed'; whereupon he went away and abode without supper or lodging. But a neighbour of mine, a very ancient lady, telleth me that, according to that which she heard, when a child, both the one and the other were true; but that the latter happened, not to Gianni Lotteringhi, but to one Gianni di Nello, who abode at Porta San Piero and was no less exquisite a ninny than the other. Wherefore, dear my ladies, it abideth at your election to take whether of the two orisons most pleaseth you, except you will have both. They have great virtue in such cases, as you have had proof in the story you have heard; get them, therefore, by heart and they may yet avail you."

THE SECOND STORY

PERONELLA HIDETH A LOVER OF HERS IN A VAT, UPON HER HUSBAND'S UNLOOKED FOR RETURN, AND HEARING FROM THE LATTER THAT HE HATH SOLD THE VAT, AVOUCHETH HERSELF TO HAVE SOLD IT TO ONE WHO IS PRESENTLY THEREWITHIN, TO SEE IF IT BE SOUND; WHEREUPON THE GALLANT, JUMPING OUT OF THE VAT, CAUSETH THE HUSBAND SCRAPE IT OUT FOR HIM AND AFTER CARRY IT HOME TO HIS HOUSE

EMILIA'S story was received with loud laughter and the conjuration commended of all as goodly and excellent; and this come to an end, the king bade Filostrato follow on, who accordingly began, "Dearest ladies, so many are the tricks that men, and particularly husbands, play you, that, if some woman chance whiles to put a cheat upon her husband, you should not only be blithe that this hath happened and take pleasure in coming to know it or hearing it told of any, but should yourselves go telling it everywhere, so men may understand that, if they are knowing, women, on their part, are no less so! the which cannot be other than useful unto you, for that, when one knoweth that another is on the alert, he setteth himself not overlightly to cozen him. Who, then, can doubt but that which we shall say to-day concerning this matter, coming to be known of men, may be exceeding effectual in restraining them from cozening you ladies, whenas they find that you likewise know how to cozen, an you will? I purpose, therefore, to tell you the trick which, on the spur of the moment, a young woman, albeit she was of mean condition, played her husband for her own preservation.

In Naples no great while agone there was a poor man who took to wife a fair and lovesome damsel called Peronella, and albeit he with his craft, which was that of a mason, and she by spinning, earned but a slender pittance, they ordered their life as best they might. It chanced one day that a young gallant of the neighbourhood saw this Peronella and she pleasing him mightily, he fell in love with her and importuned her one way and another till he became familiar with her and they took order with each other on this wise, so they might be together; to wit, seeing that her husband arose every morning betimes to go to work or to find work, they agreed that the young man should be whereas he might see him go out, and that, as soon as he was gone,—the street where she abode, which was called Avorio, being very solitary,—he should come to her house. On this wise they did many times; but one morning, the good man having gone out and Giannello Strignario (for so was the lover named) having entered the house and being with Peronella, it chanced that, after awhile, the husband returned home, whereas it was his wont to be abroad all day, and finding the door locked within, knocked and after fell a-saying in himself, 'O my God, praised be Thou ever! For, though Thou hast made me poor, at least Thou hast comforted me with a good and honest damsel to wife. See how she locked the door within as soon as I was gone out, so none might enter to do her any annoy.'

Peronella, knowing her husband by his way of knocking, said to her lover, 'Alack, Giannello mine, I am a dead woman! For here is my husband, whom God confound, come back and I know not what this meaneth, for never yet came he back hither at this hour; belike he saw thee whenas thou enteredst here. But, for the love of God, however the case may be, get thee into yonder vat, whilst I go open to him, and we shall see what is the meaning of his returning home so early this morning.' Accordingly, Giannello betook himself in all haste into the vat, whilst Peronella, going to the door, opened to her husband and said to him, with an angry air, 'What is to do now, that thou returnest home so soon this morning? Meseemeth thou hast a mind to do nought to-day, that I see thee come back, tools in hand; and if thou do thus, on what are we to live? Whence shall we get bread? Thinkest thou I will suffer thee pawn my gown and my other poor clothes? I, who do nothing but spin day and night, till the flesh is come apart from my nails, so I may at the least have so much oil as will keep our lamp burning! Husband, husband, there is not a neighbour's wife of ours but marvelleth thereat and maketh mock of me for the pains I give myself and all that I endure; and thou, thou returnest home to me, with thy hands a-dangle, whenas thou shouldst be at work.'

So saying, she fell a-weeping and went on to say, 'Alack, woe is me, unhappy woman that I am! In what an ill hour was I born, at what an ill moment did I come hither! I who might have had a young man of such worth and would none of him, so I might come to this fellow here, who taketh no thought to her whom he hath brought home! Other women give themselves a good time with their lovers, for there is none [I know] but hath two and some three, and they enjoy themselves and show their husbands the moon for the sun. But I, wretch that I am! because I am good and occupy myself not with such toys, I suffer ill and ill hap. I know not why I do not take me a lover, as do other women. Understand well, husband mine, that had I a mind to do ill, I could soon enough find the wherewithal, for there be store of brisk young fellows who love me and wish me well and have sent to me, proffering money galore or dresses and jewels, at my choice; but my heart would never suffer me to do it, for that I was no mother's daughter of that ilk; and here thou comest home to me, whenas thou shouldst be at work.'

'Good lack, wife,' answered the husband, 'fret not thyself, for God's sake; thou shouldst be assured that I know what manner of woman thou art, and indeed this morning I have in part had proof thereof. It is true that I went out to go to work; but it seemeth thou knowest not, as I myself knew not, that this is the Feast-day of San Galeone and there is no work doing; that is why I am come back at this hour; but none the less I have provided and found a means how we shall have bread for more than a month, for I have sold yonder man thou seest here with me the vat which, as thou knowest, hath this long while cumbered the house; and he is to give me five lily-florins[344] for it.' Quoth Peronella, 'So much the more cause have I to complain; thou, who art a man and goest about and should be versed in the things of the world, thou hast sold a vat for five florins, whilst I, a poor silly woman who hath scarce ever been without the door, seeing the hindrance it gave us in the house, have sold it for seven to an honest man, who entered it but now, as thou camest back, to see if it were sound!' When the husband heard this, he was more than satisfied and said to him who had come for the vat, 'Good man, begone in peace; for thou hearest that my wife hath sold the vat for seven florins, whereas thou wast to give me but five for it.' 'Good,' replied the other and went his way; whereupon quoth Peronella to her husband, 'Since thou art here, come up and settle with him thyself.' Giannello, who abode with his ears pricked up to hear if it behoved him fear or be on his guard against aught, hearing his mistress's words, straightway scrambled out of the vat and cried out, as if he had heard nothing of the husband's return, 'Where art thou, good wife?' whereupon the goodman, coming up, answered, 'Here am I; what wouldst thou have?' 'Who art thou?' asked Giannello. 'I want the woman with whom I made the bargain for this vat.' Quoth the other, 'You may deal with me in all assurance, for I am her husband.' Then said Giannello, 'The vat appeareth to me sound enough; but meseemeth you have kept dregs or the like therein, for it is all overcrusted with I know not what that is so hard and dry that I cannot remove aught thereof with my nails; wherefore I will not take it, except I first see it clean.' 'Nay,' answered Peronella, 'the bargain shall not fall through for that; my husband will clean it all out.' 'Ay will I,' rejoined the latter, and laying down his tools, put off his coat; then, calling for a light and a scraper, he entered the vat and fell to scraping. Peronella, as if she had a mind to see what he did, thrust her head and one of her arms, shoulder and all, in at the mouth of the vat, which was not overbig, and fell to saying, 'Scrape here' and 'There' and 'There also' and 'See, here is a little left.'

Whilst she was thus engaged in directing her husband and showing him where to scrape, Giannello, who had scarce yet that morning done his full desire, when they were interrupted by the mason's coming, bethought himself to accomplish it as he might; wherefore, boarding her, as she held the mouth of the vat all closed up, on such wise as in the ample plains the unbridled stallions, afire with love, assail the mares of Parthia, he satisfied his juvenile ardour, the which enterprise was brought to perfection well nigh at the same moment as the scraping of the vat; whereupon he dismounted and Peronella withdrawing her head from the mouth of the vat, the husband came forth thereof. Then said she to her gallant, 'Take this light, good man, and look if it be clean to thy mind.' Giannello looked in and said that it was well and that he was satisfied and giving the husband seven florins, caused carry the vat to his own house."

THE THIRD STORY

FRA RINALDO LIETH WITH HIS GOSSIP AND BEING FOUND OF HER HUSBAND CLOSETED WITH HER IN HER CHAMBER, THEY GIVE HIM TO BELIEVE THAT HE WAS IN ACT TO CONJURE WORMS FROM HIS GODSON

FILOSTRATO had not known to speak so obscurely of the mares of Parthia but that the roguish ladies laughed thereat, making believe to laugh at otherwhat. But, when the king saw that his story was ended, he bade Elisa tell, who accordingly, with obedient readiness, began, "Charming ladies, Emilia's conjuration of the phantom hath brought to my memory the story of another conjuration, which latter, though it be not so goodly as hers, nevertheless, for that none other bearing upon our subject occurreth to me at this present, I will proceed to relate.

You must know that there was once in Siena a very agreeable young man and of a worshipful family, by name Rinaldo, who was passionately enamored of a very beautiful lady, a neighbour of his and the wife of a rich man, and flattered himself that, could he but find means to speak with her unsuspected, he might avail to have of her all that he should desire. Seeing none other way and the lady being great with child, he bethought himself to become her gossip and accordingly, clapping up an acquaintance with her husband, he offered him, on such wise as appeared to him most seemly, to be godfather to his child. His offer was accepted and he being now become Madam Agnesa's gossip and having a somewhat more colourable excuse for speaking with her, he took courage and gave her in so many words to know that of his intent which she had indeed long before gathered from his looks; but little did this profit him, although the lady was nothing displeased to have heard him.

Not long after, whatever might have been the reason, it came to pass that Rinaldo turned friar and whether or not he found the pasturage to his liking, he persevered in that way of life; and albeit, in the days of his becoming a monk, he had for awhile laid on one side the love he bore his gossip, together with sundry other vanities of his, yet, in process of time, without quitting the monk's habit, he resumed them[345] and began to delight in making a show and wearing fine stuffs and being dainty and elegant in all his fashions and making canzonets and sonnets and ballads and in singing and all manner other things of the like sort. But what say I of our Fra Rinaldo, of whom we speak? What monks are there that do not thus? Alack, shame that they are of the corrupt world, they blush not to appear fat and ruddy in the face, dainty in their garb and in all that pertaineth unto them, and strut along, not like doves, but like very turkey-cocks, with crest erect and breast puffed out; and what is worse (to say nothing of having their cells full of gallipots crammed with electuaries and unguents, of boxes full of various confections, of phials and flagons of distilled waters and oils, of pitchers brimming with Malmsey and Cyprus and other wines of price, insomuch that they seem to the beholder not friars' cells, but rather apothecaries' or perfumers' shops) they think no shame that folk should know them to be gouty, conceiving that others see not nor know that strict fasting, coarse viands and spare and sober living make men lean and slender and for the most part sound of body, and that if indeed some sicken thereof, at least they sicken not of the gout, whereto it is used to give, for medicine, chastity and everything else that pertaineth to the natural way of living of an honest friar. Yet they persuade themselves that others know not that,—let alone the scant and sober living,—long vigils, praying and discipline should make men pale and mortified and that neither St. Dominic nor St. Francis, far from having four gowns for one, clad themselves in cloth dyed in grain nor in other fine stuffs, but in garments of coarse wool and undyed, to keep out the cold and not to make a show. For which things, as well as for the souls of the simpletons who nourish them, there is need that God provide.

Fra Rinaldo, then, having returned to his former appetites, began to pay frequent visits to his gossip and waxing in assurance, proceeded to solicit her with more than his former instancy to that which he desired of her. The good lady, seeing herself hard pressed and Fra Rinaldo seeming to her belike goodlier than she had thought him aforetime, being one day sore importuned of him, had recourse to that argument which all women use who have a mind to yield that which is asked of them and said, 'How now, Fra Rinaldo? Do monks such things?' 'Madam,' answered he, 'when as I shall have this gown off my back,—and I can put it off mighty easily,—I shall appear to you a man fashioned like other men and not a monk.' The lady pulled a demure face and said, 'Alack, wretched me! You are my gossip; how can I do this? It were sadly ill, and I have heard many a time that it is a very great sin; but, certes, were it not for this, I would do that which you wish.' Quoth Fra Rinaldo, 'You are a simpleton, if you forbear for this; I do not say that it is not a sin, but God pardoneth greater than this to whoso repenteth. But tell me, who is more akin to your child, I who held him at baptism or your husband who begat him?' 'My husband is more akin to him,' answered the lady; whereupon, 'You say sooth,' rejoined the friar. 'And doth not your husband lie with you?' 'Ay doth he,' replied she. 'Then,' said Fra Rinaldo, 'I, who am less akin to your child than is your husband, may lie with you even as doth he.' The lady, who knew no logic and needed little persuasion, either believed or made a show of believing that the friar spoke the truth and answered, 'Who might avail to answer your learned words?' And after, notwithstanding the gossipship, she resigned herself to do his pleasure; nor did they content themselves with one bout, but foregathered many and many a time, having the more commodity thereof under cover of the gossipship, for that there was less suspicion.

But once, amongst other times, it befell that Fra Rinaldo, coming to the lady's house and finding none with her but a little maid of hers, who was very pretty and agreeable, despatched his comrade with the latter to the pigeon-loft, to teach her her Paternoster, and entered with the lady, who had her child in her hand, into her bedchamber, where they locked themselves in and fell to taking their pleasure upon a daybed that was there. As they were thus engaged, it chanced that the husband came home and making for the bedchamber-door, unperceived of any, knocked and called to the lady, who, hearing this, said to the friar, 'I am a dead woman, for here is my husband, and now he will certainly perceive what is the reason of our familiarity.' Now Rinaldo was stripped to his waistcoat, to wit, he had put off his gown and his scapulary, and hearing this, answered, 'You say sooth; were I but dressed, there might be some means; but, if you open to him and he find me thus, there can be no excuse for us.' The lady, seized with a sudden idea, said, 'Harkye, dress yourself and when you are dressed, take your godchild in your arms and hearken well to that which I shall say to him, so your words may after accord with mine, and leave me do.' Then, to the good man, who had not yet left knocking, 'I come to thee,' quoth she and rising, opened the chamber-door and said, with a good countenance, 'Husband mine, I must tell thee that Fra Rinaldo, our gossip, is come hither and it was God sent him to us; for, certes, but for his coming, we should to-day have lost our child.'

The good simple man, hearing this, was like to swoon and said, 'How so?' 'O husband mine,' answered Agnesa, 'there took him but now of a sudden a fainting-fit, that methought he was dead, and I knew not what to do or say; but just then Fra Rinaldo our gossip came in and taking him in his arms, said, "Gossip, these be worms he hath in his body, the which draw near to his heart and would infallibly kill him; but have no fear, for I will conjure them and make them all die; and ere I go hence, you shall see the child whole again as ever you saw him." And for that we had need of thee to repeat certain orisons and that the maid could not find thee, he caused his comrade say them in the highest room of our house, whilst he and I came hither and locked ourselves in, so none should hinder us, for that none other than the child's mother might be present at such an office. Indeed, he hath the child yet in his arms and methinketh he waiteth but for his comrade to have made an end of saying the orisons and it will be done, for that the boy is already altogether restored to himself.' The good simple man, believing all this, was so straitened with concern for his child that it never entered his mind to suspect the cheat put upon him by his wife; but, heaving a great sigh, he said, 'I will go see him.' 'Nay,' answered she, 'thou wouldst mar that which hath been done. Wait; I will go see an thou mayst come in and call thee.'

Meanwhile, Fra Rinaldo, who had heard everything and had dressed himself at his leisure, took the child in his arms and called out, as soon as he had ordered matters to his mind, saying, 'Harkye, gossip, hear I not my gossip your husband there?' 'Ay, sir,' answered the simpleton; whereupon, 'Then,' said the other, 'come hither.' The cuckold went to him and Fra Rinaldo said to him, 'Take your son by the grace of God whole and well, whereas I deemed but now you would not see him alive at vespers; and look you let make a waxen image of his bigness and set it up, to the praise and glory of God, before the statue of our lord St. Ambrose, through whose intercession He hath vouchsafed to restore him unto you.' The child, seeing his father, ran to him and caressed him, as little children used to do, whilst the latter, taking him, weeping, in his arms, no otherwise than as he had brought him forth of the grave, fell to kissing him and returning thanks to his gossip for that he had made him whole.

Meanwhile, Fra Rinaldo's comrade, who had by this taught the serving-wench not one, but maybe more than four paternosters, and had given her a little purse of white thread, which he had from a nun, and made her his devotee, hearing the cuckold call at his wife's chamber-door, had softly betaken himself to a place whence he could, himself unseen, both see and hear what should betide and presently, seeing that all had passed off well, came down and entering the chamber, said, 'Fra Rinaldo, I have despatched all four of the orisons which you bade me say.' 'Brother mine,' answered the friar, 'thou hast a good wind and hast done well; I, for my part, had said but two thereof, when my gossip came; but God the Lord, what with thy pains and mine, hath shown us such favour that the child is healed.' Therewithal the cuckold let bring good wines and confections and entertained his gossip and the latter's comrade with that whereof they had more need than of aught else. Then, attending them to the door, he commended them to God and letting make the waxen image without delay, he sent to hang it up with the others[346] before the statue of St. Ambrose, but not that of Milan."[347]

THE FOURTH STORY

TOFANO ONE NIGHT SHUTTETH HIS WIFE OUT OF DOORS, WHO, AVAILING NOT TO RE-ENTER BY DINT OF ENTREATIES, FEIGNETH TO CAST HERSELF INTO A WELL AND CASTETH THEREIN A GREAT STONE. TOFANO COMETH FORTH OF THE HOUSE AND RUNNETH THITHER, WHEREUPON SHE SLIPPETH IN AND LOCKING HIM OUT, BAWLETH REPROACHES AT HIM FROM THE WINDOW

THE king no sooner perceived Elisa's story to be ended than, turning without delay to Lauretta, he signified to her his pleasure that she should tell; whereupon she, without hesitation, began thus, "O Love, how great and how various is thy might! How many thy resources and thy devices! What philosopher, what craftsman[348] could ever have availed or might avail to teach those shifts, those feints, those subterfuges which thou on the spur of the moment suggestest to whoso ensueth in thy traces! Certes, all others' teaching is halting compared with thine, as may very well have been apprehended by the devices which have already been set forth and to which, lovesome ladies, I will add one practised by a woman of a simple wit enough and such as I know none but Love could have taught her.

There was once, then, in Arezzo, a rich man called Tofano and he was given to wife a very fair lady, by name Madam Ghita, of whom, without knowing why, he quickly waxed jealous. The lady, becoming aware of this, was despited thereat and questioned him once and again of the reason of his jealousy; but he was able to assign her none, save such as were general and naught; wherefore it occurred to her mind to cause him die of the disease whereof he stood without reason in fear. Accordingly, perceiving that a young man, who was much to her taste, sighed for her, she proceeded discreetly to come to an understanding with him and things being so far advanced between them that there lacked but with deeds to give effect to words, she cast about for a means of bringing this also to pass; wherefore, having already remarked, amongst her husband's other ill usances, that he delighted in drinking, she began not only to commend this to him, but would often artfully incite him thereto. This became so much his wont that, well nigh whensoever it pleased her, she led him to drink even to intoxication, and putting him to bed whenas she saw him well drunken, she a first time foregathered with her lover, with whom many a time thereafter she continued to do so in all security. Indeed, she grew to put such trust in her husband's drunkenness that not only did she make bold to bring her gallant into the house, but went whiles to pass a great part of the night with him in his own house, which was not very far distant.

The enamoured lady continuing on this wise, it befell that the wretched husband came to perceive that she, whilst encouraging him to drink, natheless herself drank never; wherefore suspicion took him that it might be as in truth it was, to wit, that she made him drunken, so she might after do her pleasure what while he slept, and wishing to make proof of this, an it were so, he one evening, not having drunken that day, feigned himself, both in words and fashions, the drunkenest man that was aye. The lady, believing this and judging that he needed no more drink, put him to bed in all haste and this done, betook herself, as she was used to do whiles, to the house of her lover, where she abode till midnight. As for Tofano, no sooner did he know the lady to have left the house than he straightway arose and going to the doors, locked them from within; after which he posted himself at the window, so he might see her return and show her that he had gotten wind of her fashions; and there he abode till such time as she came back. The lady, returning home and finding herself locked out, was beyond measure woeful and began to essay an she might avail to open the door by force, which, after Tofano had awhile suffered, 'Wife,' quoth he, 'thou weariest thyself in vain, for thou canst nowise come in here again. Go, get thee back whereas thou hast been till now and be assured that thou shalt never return thither till such time as I shall have done thee, in respect of this affair, such honour as beseemeth thee in the presence of thy kinsfolk and of the neighbours.'

The lady fell to beseeching him for the love of God that it would please him open to her, for that she came not whence he supposed, but from keeping vigil with a she-neighbour of hers, for that the nights were long and she could not sleep them all out nor watch at home alone. However, prayers profited her nought, for that her brute of a husband was minded to have all the Aretines[349] know their shame, whereas none as yet knew it; wherefore, seeing that prayers availed her not, she had recourse to threats and said, 'An thou open not to me, I will make thee the woefullest man alive.' 'And what canst thou do to me?' asked Tofano, and Mistress Tessa, whose wits Love had already whetted with his counsels, replied, 'Rather than brook the shame which thou wouldst wrongfully cause me suffer, I will cast myself into this well that is herenigh, where when I am found dead, there is none will believe otherwise than that thou, for very drunkenness, hast cast me therein; wherefore it will behove thee flee and lose all thou hast and abide in banishment or have thy head cut off for my murderer, as thou wilt in truth have been.'

Tofano was nowise moved by these words from his besotted intent; wherefore quoth she to him, 'Harkye now, I can no longer brook this thy fashery, God pardon it thee! Look thou cause lay up[350] this distaff of mine that I leave here.' So saying, the night being so dark that one might scarce see other by the way, she went up to the well and taking a great stone that lay thereby, cried out, 'God pardon me!' and let it drop into the water. The stone, striking the water, made a very great noise, which when Tofano heard, he verily believed that she had cast herself in; wherefore, snatching up the bucket and the rope, he rushed out of the house and ran to the well to succour her. The lady, who had hidden herself near the door, no sooner saw him run to the well than she slipped into the house and locked herself in; then, getting her to the window, 'You should water your wine, whenas you drink it,' quoth she, 'and not after and by night.' Tofano, hearing this, knew himself to have been fooled and returned to the door, but could get no admission and proceeded to bid her open to him; but she left speaking softly, as she had done till then, and began, well nigh at a scream, to say, 'By Christ His Cross, tiresome sot that thou art, thou shalt not enter here to-night; I cannot brook these thy fashions any longer; needs must I let every one see what manner of man thou art and at what hour thou comest home anights.' Tofano, on his side, flying into a rage, began to rail at her and bawl; whereupon the neighbours, hearing the clamour, arose, both men and women, and coming to the windows, asked what was to do. The lady answered, weeping, 'It is this wretch of a man, who still returneth to me of an evening, drunken, or falleth asleep about the taverns and after cometh home at this hour; the which I have long suffered, but, it availing me not and I being unable to put up with it longer, I have bethought me to shame him therefor by locking him out of doors, to see and he will mend himself thereof.'

Tofano, on the other hand, told them, like an ass as he was, how the case stood and threatened her sore; but she said to the neighbours, 'Look you now what a man he is! What would you say, were I in the street, as he is, and he in the house, as am I? By God His faith, I doubt me you would believe he said sooth. By this you may judge of his wits; he saith I have done just what methinketh he hath himself done. He thought to fear me by casting I know not what into the well; but would God he had cast himself there in good sooth and drowned himself, so he might have well watered the wine which he hath drunken to excess.' The neighbours, both men and women, all fell to blaming Tofano, holding him at fault, and chid him for that which he said against the lady; and in a short time the report was so noised abroad from neighbour to neighbour that it reached the ears of the lady's kinsfolk, who came thither and hearing the thing from one and another of the neighbours, took Tofano and gave him such a drubbing that they broke every bone in his body. Then, entering the house, they took the lady's gear and carried her off home with them, threatening Tofano with worse. The latter, finding himself in ill case and seeing that his jealousy had brought him to a sorry pass, for that he still loved his wife heartily,[351] procured certain friends to intercede for him and so wrought that he made his peace with the lady and had her home again with him, promising her that he would never be jealous again. Moreover, he gave her leave to do her every pleasure, provided she wrought so discreetly that he should know nothing thereof; and on this wise, like a crack-brained churl as he was, he made peace after suffering damage. So long live Love and death to war and all its company!"

THE FIFTH STORY

A JEALOUS HUSBAND, IN THE GUISE OF A PRIEST, CONFESSETH HIS WIFE, WHO GIVETH HIM TO BELIEVE THAT SHE LOVETH A PRIEST, WHO COMETH TO HER EVERY NIGHT; AND WHILST THE HUSBAND SECRETLY KEEPETH WATCH AT THE DOOR FOR THE LATTER, THE LADY BRINGETH IN A LOVER OF HERS BY THE ROOF AND LIETH WITH HIM

LAURETTA having made an end of her story and all having commended the lady for that she had done aright and even as befitted her wretch of a husband, the king, to lose no time, turned to Fiammetta and courteously imposed on her the burden of the story-telling; whereupon she began thus, "Most noble ladies, the foregoing story moveth me to tell you, on like wise, of a jealous husband, accounting, as I do, all that their wives do unto such,—particularly whenas they are jealous without cause,—to be well done and holding that, if the makers of the laws had considered everything, they should have appointed none other penalty unto women who offend in this than that which they appoint unto whoso offendeth against other in self-defence; for that jealous men are plotters against the lives of young women and most diligent procurers of their deaths. Wives abide all the week mewed up at home, occupying themselves with domestic offices and the occasions of their families and households, and after they would fain, like every one else, have some solace and some rest on holidays and be at leisure to take some diversion even as do the tillers of the fields, the artisans of the towns and the administrators of the laws, according to the example of God himself, who rested from all His labours the seventh day, and to the intent of the laws, both human and Divine, which, looking to the honour of God and the common weal of all, have distinguished working days from those of repose. But to this jealous men will on no wise consent; nay, those days which are gladsome for all other women they make wretcheder and more doleful than the others to their wives, keeping them yet closelier straitened and confined; and what a misery and a languishment this is for the poor creatures those only know who have proved it. Wherefore, to conclude, I say that what a woman doth to a husband who is jealous without cause should certes not be condemned, but rather commended.

There was, then, in Arimino a merchant, very rich both in lands and monies, who, having to wife a very fair lady, became beyond measure jealous of her; nor had he other cause for this save that, as he loved her exceedingly and held her very fair and saw that she studied with all her might to please him, even so he imagined that every man loved her and that she appeared fair to all and eke that she studied to please others as she did himself, which was the reasoning of a man of nought and one of little sense. Being grown thus jealous, he kept such strict watch over her and held her in such constraint that belike many there be of those who are condemned to capital punishment who are less straitly guarded of their gaolers; for, far from being at liberty to go to weddings or entertainments or to church or indeed anywise to set foot without the house, she dared not even stand at the window nor look abroad on any occasion; wherefore her life was most wretched and she brooked this annoy with the more impatience as she felt herself the less to blame. Accordingly, seeing herself unjustly suspected of her husband, she determined, for her own solacement, to find a means (an she but might) of doing on such wise that he should have reason for his ill usage of her. And for that she might not station herself at the window and so had no opportunity of showing herself favourable to the suit of any one who might take note of her, as he passed along her street, and pay his court to her,—knowing that in the adjoining house there was a certain young man both handsome and agreeable,—she bethought herself to look if there were any hole in the wall that parted the two houses and therethrough to spy once and again till such time as she should see the youth aforesaid and find an occasion of speaking with him and bestowing on him her love, so he would accept thereof, purposing, if a means could be found, to foregather with him bytimes and on this wise while away her sorry life till such time as the demon [of jealousy] should take leave of her husband.

Accordingly, she went spying about the walls of the house, now in one part and now in another, whenas her husband was abroad, and happened at last upon a very privy place where the wall was somewhat opened by a fissure and looking therethrough, albeit she could ill discover what was on the other side, algates she perceived that the opening gave upon a bedchamber there and said in herself, 'Should this be the chamber of Filippo,' to wit, the youth her neighbour, 'I were half sped.' Then, causing secretly enquire of this by a maid of hers, who had pity upon her, she found that the young man did indeed sleep in that chamber all alone; wherefore, by dint of often visiting the crevice and dropping pebbles and such small matters, whenas she perceived him to be there, she wrought on such wise that he came to the opening, to see what was to do; whereupon she called to him softly. He, knowing her voice, answered her, and she, profiting by the occasion, discovered to him in brief all her mind; whereat the youth was mightily content and made shift to enlarge the hole from his side on such wise that none could perceive it; and therethrough they many a time bespoke one another and touched hands, but could go no farther, for the jealous vigilance of the husband.

After awhile, the Feast of the Nativity drawing near, the lady told her husband that, an it pleased him, she would fain go to church on Christmas morning and confess and take the sacrament, as other Christians did. Quoth he, 'And what sin hast thou committed that thou wouldst confess?' 'How?' answered the lady. 'Thinkest thou that I am a saint, because thou keepest me mewed up? Thou must know well enough that I commit sins like all others that live in this world; but I will not tell them to thee, for that thou art not a priest.' The jealous wretch took suspicion at these words and determined to seek to know what sins she had committed; wherefore, having bethought himself of a means whereby he might gain his end, he answered that he was content, but that he would have her go to no other church than their parish chapel and that thither she must go betimes in the morning and confess herself either to their chaplain or to such priest as the latter should appoint her and to none other and presently return home. Herseemed she half apprehended his meaning; but without saying otherwhat, she answered that she would do as he said.

Accordingly, Christmas Day come, the lady arose at daybreak and attiring herself, repaired to the church appointed her of her husband, who, on his part, betook himself to the same place and reached it before her. Having already taken order with the chaplain of that which he had a mind to do, he hastily donned one of the latter's gowns, with a great flapped cowl, such as we see priests wear, and drawing the hood a little over his face, seated himself in the choir. The lady, entering the chapel, enquired for the chaplain, who came and hearing from her that she would fain confess, said that he could not hear her, but would send her one of his brethren. Accordingly, going away, he sent her the jealous man, in an ill hour for the latter, who came up with a very grave air, and albeit the day was not over bright and he had drawn the cowl far over his eyes, knew not so well to disguise himself but he was readily recognized by the lady, who, seeing this, said in herself, 'Praised be God! From a jealous man he is turned priest; but no matter; I will e'en give him what he goeth seeking.'

Accordingly, feigning not to know him, she seated herself at his feet. My lord Jealousy had put some pebbles in his mouth, to impede his speech somewhat, so his wife might not know him by his voice, himseeming he was in every other particular so thoroughly disguised that he was nowise fearful of being recognized by her. To come to the confession, the lady told him, amongst other things, (having first declared herself to be married,) that she was enamoured of a priest, who came every night to lie with her. When the jealous man heard this, himseemed he had gotten a knife-thrust in the heart, and had not desire constrained him to know more, he had abandoned the confession and gone away. Standing fast, then, he asked the lady, 'How! Doth not your husband lie with you?' 'Ay doth he, sir,' replied she. 'How, then,' asked the jealous man, 'can the priest also lie with you?' 'Sir,' answered she, 'by what art he doth it I know not, but there is not a door in the house so fast locked but it openeth so soon as he toucheth it; and he telleth me that, whenas he cometh to the door of my chamber, before opening it, he pronounceth certain words, by virtue whereof my husband incontinent falleth asleep, and so soon as he perceiveth him to be fast, he openeth the door and cometh in and lieth with me; and this never faileth.' Quoth the mock priest, 'Madam, this is ill done, and it behoveth you altogether to refrain therefrom.' 'Sir,' answered the lady, 'methinketh I could never do that, for that I love him too well.' 'Then,' said the other, 'I cannot shrive you.' Quoth she, 'I am grieved for that; but I came not hither to tell you lies; an I thought I could do it, I would tell you so.' 'In truth, madam,' replied the husband, 'I am concerned for you, for that I see you lose your soul at this game; but, to do you service, I will well to take the pains of putting up my special orisons to God in your name, the which maybe shall profit you, and I will send you bytimes a little clerk of mine, to whom you shall say if they have profited you or not; and if they have profited you, we will proceed farther.' 'Sir,' answered the lady, 'whatever you do, send none to me at home, for, should my husband come to know of it, he is so terribly jealous that nothing in the world would get it out of his head that your messenger came hither for nought[352] but ill, and I should have no peace with him this year to come.' Quoth the other, 'Madam, have no fear of that, for I will certainly contrive it on such wise that you shall never hear a word of the matter from him.' Then said she, 'So but you can engage to do that, I am content.' Then, having made her confession and gotten her penance, she rose to her feet and went off to hear mass; whilst the jealous man, (ill luck go with him!) withdrew, bursting with rage, to put off his priest's habit, and returned home, impatient to find a means of surprising the priest with his wife, so he might play the one and the other an ill turn.

Presently the lady came back from church and saw plainly enough from her husband's looks that she had given him an ill Christmas; albeit he studied, as most he might, to conceal that which he had done and what himseemed he had learned. Then, being inwardly resolved to lie in wait near the street-door that night and watch for the priest's coming, he said to the lady, 'Needs must I sup and lie abroad to-night, wherefore look thou lock the street-door fast, as well as that of the midstair and that of thy chamber, and get thee to bed, whenas it seemeth good to thee.' The lady answered, 'It is well,' and betaking herself, as soon as she had leisure, to the hole in the wall, she made the wonted signal, which when Filippo heard, he came to her forthright. She told him how she had done that morning and what her husband had said to her after dinner and added, 'I am certain he will not leave the house, but will set himself to watch the door; wherefore do thou find means to come hither to me to-night by the roof, so we may lie together.' The young man was mightily rejoiced at this and answered, 'Madam, leave me do.'

Accordingly, the night come, the jealous man took his arms and hid himself by stealth in a room on the ground floor, whilst the lady, whenas it seemed to her time,—having caused lock all the doors and in particular that of the midstair, so he might not avail to come up,— summoned the young man, who came to her from his side by a very privy way. Thereupon they went to bed and gave themselves a good time, taking their pleasure one of the other till daybreak, when the young man returned to his own house. Meanwhile, the jealous man stood to his arms well nigh all night beside the street-door, sorry and supperless and dying of cold, and waited for the priest to come till near upon day, when, unable to watch any longer, he returned to the ground floor room and there fell asleep. Towards tierce he awoke and the street door being now open, he made a show of returning from otherwhere and went up into his house and dined. A little after, he sent a lad, as he were the priest's clerkling that had confessed her, to the lady to ask if she wot of were come thither again. She knew the messenger well enough and answered that he had not come thither that night and that if he did thus, he might haply pass out of her mind, albeit she wished it not. What more should I tell you? The jealous man abode on the watch night after night, looking to catch the priest at his entering in, and the lady still had a merry life with her lover the while.

At length the cuckold, able to contain himself no longer, asked his wife, with an angry air, what she had said to the priest the morning she had confessed herself to him. She answered that she would not tell him, for that it was neither a just thing nor a seemly; whereupon, 'Vile woman that thou art!' cried he. 'In despite of thee I know what thou saidst to him, and needs must I know the priest of whom thou art so mightily enamoured and who, by means of his conjurations, lieth with thee every night; else will I slit thy weasand.' She replied that it was not true that she was enamoured of any priest. 'How?' cried the husband, 'Saidst thou not thus and thus to the priest who confessed thee?' And she, 'Thou couldst not have reported it better, not to say if he had told it thee, but if thou hadst been present; ay, I did tell him this.' 'Then,' rejoined the jealous man, 'tell me who is this priest, and that quickly.'

The lady fell a-smiling and answered, 'It rejoiceth me mightily to see a wise man led by the nose by a woman, even as one leadeth a ram by the horns to the shambles, albeit thou art no longer wise nor hast been since the hour when, unknowing why, thou sufferedst the malignant spirit of jealousy to enter thy breast; and the sillier and more besotted thou art, so much the less is my glory thereof. Deemest thou, husband mine, I am as blind of the eyes of the body as thou of those of the mind? Certes, no; I perceived at first sight who was the priest that confessed me and know that thou wast he; but I had it at heart to give thee that which thou wentest seeking, and in sooth I have done it. Wert thou as wise as thou thinkest to be, thou wouldst not have essayed by this means to learn the secrets of thy good wife, but wouldst, without taking vain suspicion, have recognized that which she confessed to thee to be the very truth, without her having sinned in aught. I told thee that I loved a priest, and wast not thou, whom I am much to blame to love as I do, become a priest? I told thee that no door of my house could abide locked, whenas he had a mind to lie with me; and what door in the house was ever kept against thee, whenas thou wouldst come whereas I might be? I told thee that the priest lay with me every night, and when was it that thou layest not with me? And whenassoever thou sentest thy clerk to me, which was thou knowest, as often as thou layest from me, I sent thee word that the priest had not been with me. What other than a crack-brain like thee, who has suffered thyself to be blinded by thy jealousy, had failed to understand these things? Thou hast abidden in the house, keeping watch anights, and thoughtest to have given me to believe that thou wast gone abroad to sup and sleep. Bethink thee henceforth and become a man again, as thou wast wont to be; and make not thyself a laughing stock to whoso knoweth thy fashions, as do I, and leave this unconscionable watching that thou keepest; for I swear to God that, an the fancy took me to make thee wear the horns, I would engage, haddest thou an hundred eyes, as thou hast but two, to do my pleasure on such wise that thou shouldst not be ware thereof.'

The jealous wretch, who thought to have very adroitly surprised his wife's secrets, hearing this, avouched himself befooled and without answering otherwhat, held the lady for virtuous and discreet; and whenas it behoved him to be jealous, he altogether divested himself of his jealousy, even as he had put it on, what time he had no need thereof. Wherefore the discreet lady, being in a manner licensed to do her pleasures, thenceforward no longer caused her lover to come to her by the roof, as go the cats, but e'en brought him in at the door, and dealing advisedly, many a day thereafter gave herself a good time and led a merry life with him."

THE SIXTH STORY

MADAM ISABELLA, BEING IN COMPANY WITH LEONETTO HER LOVER, IS VISITED BY ONE MESSER LAMBERTUCCIO, OF WHOM SHE IS BELOVED; HER HUSBAND RETURNING, [UNEXPECTED,] SHE SENDETH LAMBERTUCCIO FORTH OF THE HOUSE, WHINGER IN HAND, AND THE HUSBAND AFTER ESCORTETH LEONETTO HOME

THE company were wonder-well pleased with Fiammetta's story, all affirming that the lady had done excellently well and as it behoved unto such a brute of a man, and after it was ended, the king bade Pampinea follow on, who proceeded to say, "There are many who, speaking ignorantly, avouch that love bereaveth folk of their senses and causeth whoso loveth to become witless. Meseemeth this is a foolish opinion, as hath indeed been well enough shown by the things already related, and I purpose yet again to demonstrate it.

In our city, which aboundeth in all good things, there was once a young lady both gently born and very fair, who was the wife of a very worthy and notable gentleman; and as it happeneth often that folk cannot for ever brook one same food, but desire bytimes to vary their diet, this lady, her husband not altogether satisfying her, became enamoured of a young man called Leonetto and very well bred and agreeable, for all he was of no great extraction. He on like wise fell in love with her, and as you know that seldom doth that which both parties desire abide without effect, it was no great while before accomplishment was given to their loves. Now it chanced that, she being a fair and engaging lady, a gentleman called Messer Lambertuccio became sore enamoured of her, whom, for that he seemed to her a disagreeable man and a tiresome, she could not for aught in the world bring herself to love. However, after soliciting her amain with messages and it availing him nought, he sent to her threatening her, for that he was a notable man, to dishonour her, an she did not his pleasure; wherefore she, fearful and knowing his character, submitted herself to do his will.

It chanced one day that the lady, whose name was Madam Isabella, being gone, as is our custom in summer-time, to abide at a very goodly estate she had in the country and her husband having ridden somewhither to pass some days abroad, she sent for Leonetto to come and be with her, whereat he was mightily rejoiced and betook himself thither incontinent. Meanwhile Messer Lambertuccio, hearing that her husband was gone abroad, took horse and repairing, all alone, to her house, knocked at the door. The lady's waiting-woman, seeing him, came straight to her mistress, who was closeted with Leonetto, and called to her, saying, 'Madam, Messer Lambertuccio is below, all alone.' The lady, hearing this, was the woefullest woman in the world, but, as she stood in great fear of Messer Lambertuccio, she besought Leonetto not to take it ill to hide himself awhile behind the curtains of her bed till such time as the other should be gone. Accordingly, Leonetto, who feared him no less than did the lady, hid himself there and she bade the maid go open to Messer Lambertuccio, which being done, he lighted down in the courtyard and making his palfrey fast to a staple there, went up into the house. The lady put on a cheerful countenance and coming to the head of the stair, received him with as good a grace as she might and asked him what brought him thither; whereupon he caught her in his arms and clipped her and kissed her, saying, 'My soul, I understood that your husband was abroad and am come accordingly to be with you awhile.' After these words, they entered a bedchamber, where they locked themselves in, and Messer Lambertuccio fell to taking delight of her.

As they were thus engaged, it befell, altogether out of the lady's expectation, that her husband returned, whom when the maid saw near the house, she ran in haste to the lady's chamber and said, 'Madam, here is my lord come back; methinketh he is already below in the courtyard.' When the lady heard this, bethinking her that she had two men in the house and knowing that there was no hiding Messer Lambertuccio, by reason of his palfrey which was in the courtyard, she gave herself up for lost. Nevertheless, taking a sudden resolution, she sprang hastily down from the bed and said to Messer Lambertuccio, 'Sir, an you wish me anywise well and would save me from death, do that which I shall bid you. Take your hanger naked in your hand and go down the stair with an angry air and all disordered and begone, saying, "I vow to God that I will take him elsewhere." And should my husband offer to detain you or question you of aught, do you say no otherwhat than that which I have told you, but take horse and look you abide not with him on any account.' The gentleman answered that he would well, and accordingly, drawing his hanger, he did as she had enjoined him, with a face all afire what with the swink he had furnished and with anger at the husband's return. The latter was by this dismounted in the courtyard and marvelled to see the palfrey there; then, offering to go up into the house, he saw Messer Lambertuccio come down and wondering both at his words and his air, said, 'What is this, sir?' Messer Lambertuccio putting his foot in the stirrup and mounting to horse, said nought but, 'Cock's body, I shall find him again otherwhere,' and made off.

The gentleman, going up, found his wife at the stairhead, all disordered and fearful, and said to her, 'What is all this? Whom goeth Messer Lambertuccio threatening thus in such a fury?' The lady, withdrawing towards the chamber where Leonetto was, so he might hear her, answered, 'Sir, never had I the like of this fright. There came fleeing hither but now a young man, whom I know not, followed by Messer Lambertuccio, hanger in hand, and finding by chance the door of this chamber open, said to me, all trembling, "For

God's sake, madam, help me, that I be not slain in your arms." I rose to my feet and was about to question him who he was and what ailed him, when, behold, in rushed Messer Lambertuccio, saying, "Where art thou, traitor?" I set myself before the chamber-door and hindered him from entering; and he was in so far courteous that, after many words, seeing it pleased me not that he should enter there, he went his way down, as you have seen.' Quoth the husband, 'Wife, thou didst well, it were too great a reproach to us, had a man been slain in our house, and Messer Lambertuccio did exceeding unmannerly to follow a person who had taken refuge here.'

Then he asked where the young man was, and the lady answered, 'Indeed sir, I know not where he hath hidden himself.' Then said the husband 'Where art thou? Come forth in safety.' Whereupon Leonetto, who had heard everything, came forth all trembling for fear, (as indeed he had had a great fright,) of the place where he had hidden himself, and the gentleman said to him, 'What hast thou to do with Messer Lambertuccio?' 'Sir,' answered he, 'I have nothing in the world to do with him, wherefore methinketh assuredly he is either not in his right wits or he hath mistaken me for another; for that no sooner did he set eyes on me in the road not far from this house than he forthright clapped his hand to his hanger and said, "Traitor, thou art a dead man!" I stayed not to ask why, but took to my heels as best I might and made my way hither, where, thanks to God and to this gentlewoman, I have escaped.' Quoth the husband, 'Go to; have no fears; I will bring thee to thine own house safe and sound, and thou canst after seek out what thou hast to do with him.' Accordingly, when they had supped, he mounted him a-horseback and carrying him back to Florence, left him in his own house. As for Leonetto, that same evening, according as he had been lessoned of the lady, he privily bespoke Messer Lambertuccio and took such order with him, albeit there was much talk of the matter thereafterward, the husband never for all that became aware of the cheat that had been put on him by his wife."

THE SEVENTH STORY

LODOVICO DISCOVERETH TO MADAM BEATRICE THE LOVE HE BEARETH HER, WHEREUPON SHE SENDETH EGANO HER HUSBAND INTO THE GARDEN, IN HER OWN FAVOUR, AND LIETH MEANWHILE WITH LODOVICO, WHO, PRESENTLY ARISING, GOETH AND CUDGELLETH EGANO IN THE GARDEN

MADAM ISABELLA'S presence of mind, as related by Pampinea, was held admirable by all the company; but, whilst they yet marvelled thereat, Filomena, whom the king had appointed to follow on, said, "Lovesome ladies, and I mistake not, methinketh I can tell you no less goodly a story on the same subject, and that forthright.

You must know, then, that there was once in Paris a Florentine gentleman, who was for poverty turned merchant and had thriven so well in commerce that he was grown thereby very rich. He had by his lady one only son, whom he had named Lodovico, and for that he might concern himself with his father's nobility and not with trade, he had willed not to place him in any warehouse, but had sent him to be with other gentlemen in the service of the King of France, where he learned store of goodly manners and other fine things. During his sojourn there, it befell that certain gentlemen, who were returned from visiting the Holy Sepulchre, coming in upon a conversation between certain young men, of whom Lodovico was one, and hearing them discourse among themselves of the fair ladies of France and England and other parts of the world, one of them began to say that assuredly, in all the lands he had traversed and for all the ladies he had seen, he had never beheld the like for beauty of Madam Beatrice, the wife of Messer Egano de' Gulluzzi of Bologna; to which all his companions, who had with him seen her at Bologna, agreed.

Lodovico, who had never yet been enamoured of any woman, hearkening to this, was fired with such longing to see her that he could hold his thought to nothing else and being altogether resolved to journey to Bologna for that purpose and there, if she pleased him, to abide awhile, he feigned to his father that he had a mind to go visit the Holy Sepulchre, the which with great difficulty he obtained of him. Accordingly, taking the name of Anichino, he set out for Bologna, and on the day following [his arrival,] as fortune would have it, he saw the lady in question at an entertainment, where she seemed to him fairer far than he had imagined her; wherefore, falling most ardently enamoured of her, he resolved never to depart Bologna till he should have gained her love. Then, devising in himself what course he should take to this end, he bethought himself, leaving be all other means, that, an he might but avail to become one of her husband's servants, whereof he entertained many, he might peradventure compass that which he desired. Accordingly, having sold his horses and disposed as best might be of his servants, bidding them make a show of knowing him not, he entered into discourse with his host and told him that he would fain engage for a servant with some gentleman of condition, could such an one be found. Quoth the host, 'Thou art the right serving-man to please a gentleman of this city, by name Egano, who keepeth many and will have them all well looking, as thou art. I will bespeak him of the matter.' As he said, so he did, and ere he took leave of Egano, he had brought Anichino to an accord with him, to the exceeding satisfaction of the latter, who, abiding with Egano and having abundant opportunity of seeing his lady often, proceeded to serve him so well and so much to his liking that he set such store by him that he could do nothing without him and committed to him the governance, not of himself alone, but of all his affairs.

It chanced one day that, Egano being gone a-fowling and having left Anichino at home, Madam Beatrice (who was not yet become aware of his love for her, albeit, considering him and his fashions, she had ofttimes much commended him to herself and he pleased her,) fell to playing chess with him and he, desiring to please her, very adroitly contrived to let himself be beaten, whereat the lady was marvellously rejoiced. Presently, all her women having gone away from seeing them play and left them playing alone, Anichino heaved a great sigh, whereupon she looked at him and said, 'What aileth thee, Anichino? Doth it irk thee that I should beat thee?' 'Madam,' answered he, 'a far greater thing than that was the cause of my sighing.' Quoth the lady, 'Prithee, as thou wishest me well, tell it me.' When Anichino heard himself conjured, 'as thou wishest me well,' by her whom he loved over all else, he heaved a sigh yet heavier than the first; wherefore the lady besought him anew that it would please him tell her the cause of his sighing. 'Madam,' replied Anichino, 'I am sore fearful lest it displease you, if I tell it you, and moreover I misdoubt me you will tell it again to others.' Whereto rejoined she, 'Certes, it will not displease me, and thou mayst be assured that, whatsoever thou sayest to me I will never tell to any, save whenas it shall please thee.' Quoth he, 'Since you promise me this, I will e'en tell it you.' Then, with tears in his eyes, he told her who he was and what he had heard of her and when and how he was become enamoured of her and why he had taken service with her husband and after humbly besought her that it would please her have compassion on him and comply with him in that his secret and so fervent desire, and in case she willed not to do this, that she should suffer him to love her, leaving him be in that his then present guise.

O singular blandness of the Bolognese blood! How art thou still to be commended in such circumstance! Never wast thou desirous of tears or sighs; still wast thou compliant unto prayers and amenable unto amorous desires! Had I words worthy to commend thee, my voice should never weary of singing thy praises. The gentle lady, what while Anichino spoke, kept her eyes fixed on him and giving full credence to his words, received, by the prevalence of his prayers, the love of him with such might into her heart that she also fell a-sighing and presently answered, 'Sweet my Anichino, be of good courage; neither presents nor promises nor solicitations of nobleman or gentleman or other (for I have been and am yet courted of many) have ever availed to move my heart to love any one of them; but thou, in this small space of time that thy words have lasted, hast made me far more thine than mine own. Methinketh thou hast right well earned my love, wherefore I give it thee and promise thee that I will cause thee have enjoyment thereof ere this next night be altogether spent. And that this may have effect, look thou come to my chamber about midnight. I will leave the door open; thou knowest which side the bed I lie; do thou come thither and if I sleep, touch me so I may awake, and I will ease thee of this so long desire that thou hast had. And that thou mayst believe this that I say, I will e'en give thee a kiss by way of arles.' Accordingly, throwing her arms about his neck, she kissed him amorously and he on like wise kissed her. These things said, he left her and went to do certain occasions of his, awaiting with the greatest gladness in the world the coming of the night.

Presently, Egano returned from fowling and being weary, betook himself to bed, as soon as he had supper, and after him the lady, who left the chamber-door open, as she had promised. Thither, at the appointed hour, came Anichino and softly entering the chamber, shut the door again from within; then, going up to the bed on the side where the lady lay, he put his hand to her breast and found her awake. As soon as she felt him come, she took his hand in both her own and held it fast; then, turning herself about in the bed, she did on such wise that Egano, who was asleep, awoke; whereupon quoth she to him, 'I would not say aught to thee yestereve, for that meseemed thou was weary; but tell me, Egano, so God save thee, whom holdest thou thy best and trustiest servant and him who most loveth thee of those whom thou hast in the house?' 'Wife,' answered Egano, 'what is this whereof thou askest me? Knowest thou it not? I have not nor had aye any in whom I so trusted and whom I loved as I love and trust in Anichino. But why dost thou ask me thereof?'

Anichino, seeing Egano awake and hearing talk of himself, was sore afraid lest the lady had a mind to cozen him and offered again and again to draw his hand away, so he might begone; but she held it so fast that he could not win free. Then said she to Egano, 'I will tell thee. I also believed till to-day that he was even such as thou sayest and that he was more loyal to thee than any other, but he hath undeceived me; for that, what while thou wentest a-fowling to-day, he abode here, and whenas it seemed to him time, he was not ashamed to solicit me to yield myself to his pleasures, and I, so I might make thee touch and see this thing and that it might not behove me certify thee thereof with too many proofs, replied that I would well and that this very night, after midnight, I would go into our garden and there await him at the foot of the pine. Now for my part I mean not to go thither; but thou, an thou have a mind to know thy servant's fidelity, thou mayst lightly do it by donning a gown and a veil of mine and going down yonder to wait and see if he will come thither, as I am assured he will.' Egano hearing this, answered, 'Certes, needs must I go see,' and rising, donned one of the lady's gowns, as best he knew in the dark; then, covering his head with a veil, he betook himself to the garden and proceeded to await Anichino at the foot of the pine.

As for the lady, as soon as she knew him gone forth of the chamber, she arose and locked the door from within, whilst Anichino, (who had had the greatest fright he had ever known and had enforced himself as most he might to escape from the lady's hands, cursing her and her love and himself who had trusted in her an hundred thousand times,) seeing this that she had done in the end, was the joyfullest man that was aye. Then, she having returned to bed, he, at her bidding, put off his clothes and coming to bed to her, they took delight and pleasure together a pretty while; after which, herseeming he should not abide longer, she caused him arise and dress himself and said to him, 'Sweetheart, do thou take a stout cudgel and get thee to the garden and there, feigning to have solicited me to try me, rate Egano, as he were I, and ring me a good peal of bells on his back with the cudgel, for that thereof will ensue to us marvellous pleasure and delight.' Anichino accordingly repaired to the garden, with a sallow-stick in his hand, and Egano, seeing him draw near the pine, rose up and came to meet him, as he would receive him with the utmost joy; whereupon quoth Anichino, 'Ah, wicked woman, art thou then come hither, and thinkest thou I would do my lord such a wrong? A thousand times ill come to thee!' Then, raising the cudgel, he began to lay on to him.

Egano, hearing this and seeing the cudgel, took to his heels, without saying a word, whilst Anichino still followed after him, saying, 'Go to, God give thee an ill year, vile woman that thou art! I will certainly tell it to Egano to-morrow morning.' Egano made his way back to the chamber as quickliest he might, having gotten sundry good clouts, and being questioned of the lady if Anichino had come to the garden, 'Would God he had not!' answered he. 'For that, taking me for thee, he hath cudgelled me to a mummy and given me the soundest rating that was aye bestowed upon lewd woman. Certes, I marvelled sore at him that he should have said these words to thee, with intent to do aught that might be a shame to me; but, for that he saw thee so blithe and gamesome, he had a mind to try thee.' Then said the lady, 'Praised be God that he hath tried me with words and thee with deeds! Methinketh he may say that I suffered his words more patiently than thou his deeds. But, since he is so loyal to thee, it behoveth thee hold him dear and do him honour.' 'Certes,' answered Egano, 'thou sayst sooth'; and reasoning by this, he concluded that he had the truest wife and the trustiest servant that ever gentleman had; by reason whereof, albeit both he and the lady made merry more than once with Anichino over this adventure, the latter and his mistress had leisure enough of that which belike, but for this, they would not have had, to wit, to do that which afforded them pleasance and delight, that while it pleased Anichino abide with Egano in Bologna."

THE EIGHTH STORY

A MAN WAXETH JEALOUS OF HIS WIFE, WHO BINDETH A PIECE OF PACKTHREAD TO HER GREAT TOE ANIGHTS, SO SHE MAY HAVE NOTICE OF HER LOVER'S COMING. ONE NIGHT HER HUSBAND BECOMETH AWARE OF THIS DEVICE AND WHAT WHILE HE PURSUETH THE LOVER, THE LADY PUTTETH ANOTHER WOMAN TO BED IN HER ROOM. THIS LATTER THE HUSBAND BEATETH AND CUTTETH OFF HER HAIR, THEN FETCHETH HIS WIFE'S BROTHERS, WHO, FINDING HIS STORY [SEEMINGLY] UNTRUE, GIVE HIM HARD WORDS

IT SEEMED to them all that Madam Beatrice had been extraordinarily ingenious in cozening her husband and all agreed that Anichino's fright must have been very great, whenas, being the while held fast by the lady, he heard her say that he had required her of love. But the king, seeing Filomena silent, turned to Neifile and said to her, "Do you tell"; whereupon she, smiling first a little, began, "Fair ladies, I have a hard task before me if I desire to pleasure you with a goodly story, as those of you have done, who have already told; but, with God's aid, I trust to discharge myself thereof well enough.

You must know, then, that there was once in our city a very rich merchant called Arriguccio Berlinghieri, who, foolishly thinking, as merchants yet do every day, to ennoble himself by marriage, took to wife a young gentlewoman ill sorting with himself, by name Madam Sismonda, who, for that he, merchant-like, was much abroad and sojourned little with her, fell in love with a young man called Ruberto, who had long courted her, and clapped up a lover's privacy with him. Using belike over-little discretion in her dealings with her lover, for that they were supremely delightsome to her, it chanced that, whether Arriguccio scented aught of the matter or how else soever it happened, the latter became the most jealous man alive and leaving be his going about and all his other concerns, applied himself well nigh altogether to the keeping good watch over his wife; nor would he ever fall asleep, except he first felt her come into the bed; by reason whereof the lady suffered the utmost chagrin, for that on no wise might she avail to be with her Ruberto.

However, after pondering many devices for finding a means to foregather with him and being to boot continually solicited thereof by him, it presently occurred to her to do on this wise; to wit, having many a time observed that Arriguccio tarried long to fall asleep, but after slept very soundly, she determined to cause Ruberto come about midnight to the door of the house and to go open to him and abide with him what while her husband slept fast. And that she might know when he should be come, she bethought herself to hang a twine out of the window of her bedchamber, which looked upon the street, on such wise that none might perceive it, one end whereof should well nigh reach the ground, whilst she carried the other end along the floor of the room to the bed and hid it under the clothes, meaning to make it fast to her great toe, whenas she should be abed. Accordingly, she sent to acquaint Ruberto with this and charged him, when he came, to pull the twine, whereupon, if her husband slept, she would let it go and come to open to him; but, if he slept not, she would hold it fast and draw it to herself, so he should not wait. The device pleased Ruberto and going thither frequently, he was whiles able to foregather with her and whiles not.

On this wise they continued to do till, one night, the lady being asleep, it chanced that her husband stretched out his foot in bed and felt the twine, whereupon he put his hand to it and finding it made fast to his wife's toe, said in himself, 'This should be some trick'; and presently perceiving that the twine led out of window, he held it for certain. Accordingly, he cut it softly from the lady's toe and making it fast to his own, abode on the watch to see what this might mean. He had not waited long before up came Ruberto and pulled at the twine, as of his wont; whereupon Arriguccio started up; but, he not having made the twine well fast to his toe and Ruberto pulling hard, it came loose in the latter's hand, whereby he understood that he was to wait and did so. As for Arriguccio, he arose in haste and taking his arms, ran to the door, to see who this might be and do him a mischief, for, albeit a merchant, he was a stout fellow and a strong. When he came to the door, he opened it not softly as the lady was used to do, which when Ruberto, who was await, observed, he guessed how the case stood, to wit, that it was Arriguccio who opened the door, and accordingly made off in haste and the other after him. At last, having fled a great way and Arriguccio stinting not from following him, Ruberto, being also armed, drew his sword and turned upon his pursuer, whereupon they fell to blows, the one attacking and the other defending himself.

Meanwhile, the lady, awaking, as Arriguccio opened the chamber-door, and finding the twine cut from her toe, knew incontinent that her device was discovered, whereupon, perceiving that her husband had run after her lover, she arose in haste and foreseeing what might happen, called her maid, who knew all, and conjured her to such purpose that she prevailed with her to take her own place in the bed, beseeching her patiently to endure, without discovering herself, whatsoever buffets Arriguccio might deal her, for that she would requite her therefor on such wise that she should have no cause to complain; after which she did out the light that burnt in the chamber and going forth thereof, hid herself in another part of the house and there began to await what should betide.

Meanwhile, the people of the quarter, aroused by the noise of the affray between Arriguccio and Ruberto, arose and fell a-railing at them; whereupon the husband, fearing to be known, let the youth go, without having availed to learn who he was or to do him any hurt, and returned to his house, full of rage and despite. There, coming into the chamber, he cried out angrily, saying, 'Where art thou, vile woman? Thou hast done out the light, so I may not find thee; but thou art mistaken.' Then, coming to the bedside, he seized upon the maid, thinking to take his wife, and laid on to her so lustily with cuffs and kicks, as long as he could wag his hands and feet, that he bruised all her face, ending by cutting off her hair, still giving her the while the hardest words that were ever said to worthless woman. The maid wept sore, as indeed she had good cause to do, and albeit she said whiles, 'Alas, mercy, for God's sake!' and 'Oh, no more!' her voice was so broken with sobs and Arriguccio was so hindered with his rage that he never discerned it to be that of another woman than his wife.

Having, then, as we have said, beaten her to good purpose and cut off her hair, he said to her, 'Wicked woman that thou art, I mean not to touch thee otherwise, but shall now go fetch thy brothers and acquaint them with thy fine doings and after bid them come for thee and deal with thee as they shall deem may do them honour and carry thee away; for assuredly in this house thou shalt abide no longer.' So saying, he departed the chamber and locking the door from without, went away all alone. As soon as Madam Sismonda, who had heard all, was certified of her husband's departure, she opened the door and rekindling the light, found her maid all bruised and weeping sore; whereupon she comforted her as best she might and carried her back to her own chamber, where she after caused privily tend her and care for her and so rewarded her of Arriguccio's own monies that she avouched herself content. No sooner had she done this than she hastened to make the bed in her own chamber and all restablished it and set it in such order as if none had lain there that night; after which she dressed and tired herself, as if she had not yet gone to bed; then, lighting a lamp, she took her clothes and seated herself at the stairhead, where she proceeded to sew and await the issue of the affair.

Meanwhile Arriguccio betook himself in all haste to the house of his wife's brothers and there knocked so long and so loudly that he was heard and it was opened to him. The lady's three brothers and her mother, hearing that it was Arriguccio, rose all and letting kindle lights, came to him and asked what he went seeking at that hour and alone. Whereupon, beginning from the twine he had found tied to wife's toe, he recounted to them all that he had discovered and done, and to give them entire proof of the truth of his story, he put into their hands the hair he thought to have cut from his wife's head, ending by requiring them to come for her and do with her that which they should judge pertinent to their honour, for that he meant to keep her no longer in his house. The lady's brothers, hearing this and holding it for certain, were sore incensed against her and letting kindle torches, set out to accompany Arriguccio to his house, meaning to do her a mischief; which their mother seeing, she followed after them, weeping and entreating now the one, now the other not to be in such haste to believe these things of their sister, without seeing or knowing more of the matter, for that her husband might have been angered with her for some other cause and have maltreated her and might now allege this in his own excuse, adding that she marvelled exceedingly how this [whereof he accused her] could have happened, for that she knew her daughter well, as having reared her from a little child, with many other words to the like purpose.

When they came to Arriguccio's house, they entered and proceeded to mount the stair, whereupon Madam Sismonda, hearing them come, said, 'Who is there?' To which one of her brothers answered, 'Thou shalt soon know who it is, vile woman that thou art!' 'God aid us!' cried she. 'What meaneth this?' Then, rising to her feet, 'Brothers mine,' quoth she, 'you are welcome; but what go you all three seeking at this hour?' The brothers,—seeing her seated sewing, with no sign of beating on her face, whereas Arriguccio avouched that he had beaten her to a mummy,—began to marvel and curbing the violence of their anger, demanded of her how that had been whereof Arriguccio accused her, threatening her sore, and she told them not all. Quoth she, 'I know not what you would have me say nor of what Arriguccio can have complained to you of me.' Arriguccio, seeing her thus, eyed her as if he had lost his wits, remembering that he had dealt her belike a thousand buffets on the face and scratched her and done her all the ill in the world, and now he beheld her as if nothing of all this had been.

Her brothers told her briefly what they had heard from Arriguccio, twine and beating and all, whereupon she turned to him and said, 'Alack, husband mine, what is this I hear? Why wilt thou make me pass, to thine own great shame, for an ill woman, where as I am none, and thyself for a cruel and wicked man, which thou art not? When wast thou in this house to-night till now, let alone with me? When didst thou beat me? For my part, I have no remembrance of it.' 'How, vile woman that thou art!' cried he. 'Did we not go to bed together here? Did I not return hither, after running after thy lover? Did I not deal thee a thousand buffets and cut off thy hair?' 'Thou wentest not to bed in this house to-night,' replied Sismonda. 'But let that pass, for I can give no proof thereof other than mine own true words, and let us come to that which thou sayest, to wit, that thou didst beat me and cut off my hair. Me thou hast never beaten, and do all who are here and thou thyself take note of me, if I have any mark of beating in any part of my person. Indeed, I should not counsel thee make so bold as to lay a hand on me, for, by Christ His Cross, I would mar thy face for thee! Neither didst thou cut off my hair, for aught that I felt or saw; but haply thou didst it on such wise that I perceived it not; let me see if I have it shorn or no.' Then, putting off her veil from her head, she showed that she had her hair unshorn and whole.

Her mother and brothers, seeing and hearing all this, turned upon her husband and said to him, 'What meanest thou, Arriguccio? This is not that so far which thou camest to tell us thou hadst done, and we know not how thou wilt make good the rest.' Arriguccio stood as one in a trance and would have spoken; but, seeing that it was not as he thought he could show, he dared say nothing; whereupon the lady, turning to her brothers, said to them, 'Brothers mine, I see he hath gone seeking to have me do what I have never yet chosen to do, to wit, that I should acquaint you with his lewdness and his vile fashions, and I will do it. I firmly believe that this he hath told you hath verily befallen him and that he hath done as he saith; and you shall hear how. This worthy man, to whom in an ill hour for me you gave me to wife, who calleth himself a merchant and would be thought a man of credit, this fellow, forsooth, who should be more temperate than a monk and chaster than a maid, there be few nights but he goeth fuddling himself about the taverns, foregathering now with this lewd woman and now with that and keeping me waiting for him, on such wise as you find me, half the night and whiles even till morning. I doubt not but that, having well drunken, he went to bed with some trull of his and waking, found the twine on her foot and after did all these his fine feats whereof he telleth, winding up by returning to her and beating her and cutting off her hair; and not being yet well come to himself, he fancied (and I doubt not yet fancieth) that he did all this to me; and if you look him well in the face, you will see he is yet half fuddled. Algates, whatsoever he may have said of me, I will not have you take it to yourselves except as a drunken man's talk, and since I forgive him, do you also pardon him.'

Her mother, hearing this, began to make an outcry and say, 'By Christ His Cross, daughter mine, it shall not pass thus! Nay, he should rather be slain for a thankless, ill-conditioned dog, who was never worthy to have a girl of thy fashion to wife. Marry, a fine thing, forsooth! He could have used thee no worse, had he picked thee up out of the dirt! Devil take him if thou shalt abide at the mercy of the spite of a paltry little merchant of asses' dung! They come to us out of their pigstyes in the country, clad in homespun frieze, with their bag-breeches and pen in arse, and as soon as they have gotten a leash of groats, they must e'en have the daughters of gentlemen and right ladies to wife and bear arms and say, "I am of such a family" and "Those of my house did thus and thus." Would God my sons had followed my counsel in the matter, for that they might have stablished thee so worshipfully in the family of the Counts Guidi, with a crust of bread to thy dowry! But they must needs give thee to this fine jewel of fellow, who, whereas thou art the best girl in Florence and the modestest, is not ashamed to knock us up in the middle of the night, to tell us that thou art a strumpet, as if we knew thee not. But, by God His faith, an they would be ruled by me, he should get such a trouncing therefor that he should stink for it!' Then, turning to the lady's brothers, 'My sons,' said she, 'I told you this could not be. Have you heard how your fine brother-in-law here entreateth your sister? Four-farthing[353] huckster that he is! Were I in your shoes, he having said what he hath of her and doing that which he doth, I would never hold myself content nor appeased till I had rid the earth of him; and were I a man, as I am a woman, I would trouble none other than myself to despatch his business. Confound him for a sorry drunken beast, that hath no shame!'

The young men, seeing and hearing all this, turned upon Arriguccio and gave him the soundest rating ever losel got; and ultimately they said to him. 'We pardon thee this as to a drunken man; but, as thou tenderest thy life, look henceforward we hear no more news of this kind, for, if aught of the like come ever again to our ears, we will pay thee at once for this and for that.' So saying, they went their ways, leaving Arriguccio all aghast, as it were he had taken leave of his wits, unknowing in himself whether that which he had done had really been or whether he had dreamed it; wherefore he made no more words thereof, but left his wife in peace. Thus the lady, by her ready wit, not only escaped the imminent peril [that threatened her,] but opened herself a way to do her every pleasure in time to come, without evermore having any fear of her husband."

THE NINTH STORY

LYDIA, WIFE OF NICOSTRATUS, LOVETH PYRRHUS, WHO, SO HE MAY BELIEVE IT, REQUIRETH OF HER THREE THINGS, ALL WHICH SHE DOTH. MOREOVER, SHE SOLACETH HERSELF WITH HIM IN THE PRESENCE OF NICOSTRATUS AND MAKETH THE LATTER BELIEVE THAT THAT WHICH HE HATH SEEN IS NOT REAL

NEIFILE'S story so pleased the ladies that they could neither give over to laugh at nor to talk of it, albeit the king, having bidden Pamfilo tell his story, had several times imposed silence upon them. However, after they had held their peace, Pamfilo began thus: "I do not believe, worshipful ladies, that there is anything, how hard and doubtful soever it be, that whoso loveth passionately will not dare to do; the which, albeit it hath already been demonstrated in many stories, methinketh, nevertheless, I shall be able yet more plainly to show forth to you in one which I purpose to tell you and wherein you shall hear of a lady, who was in her actions much more favoured of fortune than well-advised of reason; wherefore I would not counsel any one to adventure herself in the footsteps of her of whom I am to tell, for that fortune is not always well disposed nor are all men in the world equally blind.

In Argos, city of Achia far more famous for its kings of past time than great in itself, there was once a nobleman called Nicostratus, to whom, when already neighbouring on old age, fortune awarded a lady of great family to wife, whose name was Lydia and who was no less high-spirited than fair. Nicostratus, like a nobleman and a man of wealth as he was, kept many servants and hounds and hawks and took the utmost delight in the chase. Among his other servants he had a young man called Pyrrhus, who was sprightly and well bred and comely of his person and adroit in all that he had a mind to do, and him he loved and trusted over all else. Of this Pyrrhus Lydia became so sore enamoured that neither by day nor by night could she have her thought otherwhere than with him; but he, whether it was that he perceived not her liking for him or that he would none of it, appeared to reck nothing thereof, by reason whereof the lady suffered intolerable chagrin in herself and being altogether resolved to give him to know of her passion, called a chamberwoman of hers, Lusca by name, in whom she much trusted, and said to her, 'Lusca, the favours thou hast had of me should make thee faithful and obedient; wherefore look thou none ever know that which I shall presently say to thee, save he to whom I shall charge thee tell it. As thou seest, Lusca, I am a young and lusty lady, abundantly endowed with all those things which any woman can desire; in brief, I can complain of but one thing, to wit, that my husband's years are overmany, an they be measured by mine own, wherefore I fare but ill in the matter of that thing wherein young women take most pleasure, and none the less desiring it, as other women do, I have this long while determined in myself, since fortune hath been thus little my friend in giving me so old a husband, that I will not be so much mine own enemy as not to contrive to find means for my pleasures and my weal; which that I may have as complete in this as in other things, I have bethought myself to will that our Pyrrhus, as being worthier thereof than any other, should furnish them with his embracements; nay, I have vowed him so great a love that I never feel myself at ease save whenas I see him or think of him, and except I foregather with him without delay, methinketh I shall certainly die thereof. Wherefore, if my life be dear to thee, thou wilt, on such wise as shall seem best to thee, signify to him any love and beseech him, on my part, to be pleased to come to me, whenas thou shalt go for him.'

The chamberwoman replied that she would well and taking Pyrrhus apart, whenas first it seemed to her time and place, she did her lady's errand to him as best she knew. Pyrrhus, hearing this, was sore amazed thereat, as one who had never anywise perceived aught of the matter, and misdoubted him the lady had let say this to him to try him; wherefore he answered roughly and hastily, 'Lusca, I cannot believe that these words come from my lady; wherefore, have a care what thou sayst; or, if they do indeed come from her, I do not believe that she caused thee say them with intent, and even if she did so, my lord doth me more honour than I deserve and I would not for my life do him such an outrage; wherefore look thou bespeak me no more of such things.' Lusca, nowise daunted by his austere speech, said to him, 'Pyrrhus, I will e'en bespeak thee both of this and of everything else wherewithal my lady shall charge me when and as often as she shall bid me, whether it cause thee pleasure or annoy; but thou art an ass.' Then, somewhat despited at his words, she returned to her mistress, who, hearing what Pyrrhus had said, wished for death, but, some days after, she again bespoke the chamberwoman of the matter and said to her, 'Lusca, thou knowest that the oak falleth not for the first stroke; wherefore meseemeth well that thou return anew to him who so strangely willeth to abide loyal to my prejudice, and taking a sortable occasion, throughly discover to him my passion and do thine every endeavour that the thing may have effect; for that, an it fall through thus, I shall assuredly die of it. Moreover, he will think to have been befooled, and whereas we seek to have his love, hate will ensue thereof.'

The maid comforted her and going in quest of Pyrrhus found him merry and well-disposed and said to him, 'Pyrrhus I showed thee, a few days agone, in what a fire my lady and thine abideth for the love she beareth thee, and now anew I certify thee thereof, for that, an thou persist in the rigour thou showedst the other day, thou mayst be assured that she will not live long; wherefore I prithee be pleased to satisfy her of her desire, and if thou yet abide fast in thine obstinacy, whereas I have still accounted thee mighty discreet, I shall hold thee a blockhead. What can be a greater glory for thee than that such a lady, so fair and so noble, should love thee over all else? Besides, how greatly shouldst thou acknowledge thyself beholden unto Fortune, seeing that she proffereth thee a thing of such worth and so conformable to the desires of thy youth and to boot, such a resource for thy necessities! Which of thy peers knowest thou who fareth better by way of delight than thou mayst fare, an thou be wise? What other couldst thou find who may fare so well in the matter of arms and horses and apparel and monies as thou mayst do, so thou wilt but vouchsafe thy love to this lady? Open, then, thy mind to my words and return to thy senses; bethink thee that once, and no oftener, it is wont to betide that fortune cometh unto a man with smiling face and open arms, who an he know not then to welcome, if after he find himself poor and beggarly, he hath himself and not her to blame. Besides, there is no call to use that loyalty between servants and masters that behoveth between friends and kinsfolk; nay, servants should use their masters, in so far as they may, like as themselves are used of them. Thinkest thou, an thou hadst a fair wife or mother or daughter or sister, who pleased Nicostratus, that he would go questing after this loyalty that thou wouldst fain observe towards him in respect of this lady? Thou are a fool, if thou think thus; for thou mayst hold it for certain that, if blandishments and prayers sufficed him not, he would not scruple to use force in the matter, whatsoever thou mightest deem thereof. Let us, then, entreat them and their affairs even as they entreat us and ours. Profit by the favour of fortune and drive her not away, but welcome her with open arms and meet her halfway, for assuredly, and thou do it not, thou wilt yet (leave alone the death that will without fail ensue thereof to thy lady) repent thee thereof so many a time thou wilt be fain to die therefor.'

Pyrrhus, who had again and again pondered the words that Lusca had said to him, had determined, and she should return to him, to make her another guess answer and altogether to submit himself to comply with the lady's wishes, so but he might be certified that it was not a trick to try him, and accordingly answered, 'Harkye, Lusca; all that thou sayst to me I allow to be true; but, on the other hand, I know my lord for very discreet and well-advised, and as he committeth all his affairs to my hands, I am sore adread lest Lydia, with his counsel and by his wish, do this to try me; wherefore, an it please her for mine assurance do three things that I shall ask, she shall for certain thereafterward command me nought but I will do it forthright. And the three things I desire are these: first, that in Nicostratus his presence she slay his good hawk; secondly, that she send me a lock of her husband's beard and lastly, one of his best teeth.' These conditions seemed hard unto Lusca and to the lady harder yet; however, Love, who is an excellent comforter[354] and a past master in shifts and devices, made her resolve to do his pleasure and accordingly she sent him word by her chamberwoman that she would punctually do what he required and that quickly, and that over and above this, for that he deemed Nicostratus so well-advised, she would solace herself with him in her husband's presence and make the latter believe that it was not true.

Pyrrhus, accordingly, began to await what the lady should do, and Nicostratus having, a few days after, made, as he oftentimes used to do, a great dinner to certain gentlemen, Madam Lydia, whenas the tables were cleared away, came forth of her chamber, clad in green samite and richly bedecked, and entered the saloon where the guests were. There, in the sight of Pyrrhus and of all the rest, she went up to the perch, whereon was the hawk that Nicostratus held so dear, and cast it loose, as she would set it on her hand; then, taking it by the jesses, she dashed it against the wall and killed it; whereupon Nicostratus cried out at her, saying, 'Alack, wife, what hast thou done?' She answered him nothing, but, turning to the gentlemen who had eaten with him, she said to them, 'Gentlemen, I should ill know how to avenge myself on a king who did me a despite, an I dared not take my wreak of a hawk. You must know that this bird hath long robbed me of all the time which should of men be accorded to the pleasuring of the ladies; for that no sooner is the day risen than Nicostratus is up and drest and away he goeth a-horseback, with his hawk on his fist, to the open plains, to see him fly, whilst I, such as you see me, abide in bed alone and ill-content;

wherefore I have many a time had a mind to do that which I have now done, nor hath aught hindered me therefrom but that I waited to do it in the presence of gentlemen who would be just judges in my quarrel, as methinketh you will be.' The gentlemen, hearing this and believing her affection for Nicostratus to be no otherwise than as her words denoted, turned all to the latter, who was angered, and said, laughing, 'Ecod, how well hath the lady done to avenge herself of her wrong by the death of the hawk!' Then, with divers of pleasantries upon the subject (the lady being now gone back to her chamber), they turned Nicostratus his annoy into laughter; whilst Pyrrhus, seeing all this, said in himself, 'The lady hath given a noble beginning to my happy loves; God grant she persevere!'

Lydia having thus slain the hawk, not many days were passed when, being in her chamber with Nicostratus, she fell to toying and frolicking with him, and he, pulling her somedele by the hair, by way of sport, gave her occasion to accomplish the second thing required of her by Pyrrhus. Accordingly, taking him of a sudden by a lock of his beard, she tugged so hard at it, laughing the while, that she plucked it clean out of his chin; whereof he complaining, 'How now?' quoth she. 'What aileth thee to pull such a face? Is it because I have plucked out maybe half a dozen hairs of thy beard? Thou feltest not that which I suffered, whenas thou pulledst me now by the hair.' On this wise continuing their disport from one word to another, she privily kept the lock of hair that she had plucked from his beard and sent it that same day to her lover.

Anent the last of the three things required by Pyrrhus she was harder put to it for a device; nevertheless, being of a surpassing wit and Love making her yet quicker of invention, she soon bethought herself what means she should use to give it accomplishment. Nicostratus had two boys given him of their father, to the intent that, being of gentle birth, they might learn somewhat of manners and good breeding in his house, of whom, whenas he was at meat, one carved before him and the other gave him to drink. Lydia called them both and giving them to believe that they stank at the mouth, enjoined them that, whenas they served Nicostratus, they should still hold their heads backward as most they might nor ever tell this to any. The boys, believing that which she said, proceeded to do as she had lessoned them, and she after a while said to her husband one day, 'Hast thou noted that which yonder boys do, whenas they serve thee?' 'Ay have I,' replied Nicostratus; 'and indeed I had it in mind to ask them why they did it.' Quoth the lady, 'Do it not, for I can tell thee the reason; and I have kept it silent from thee this long while, not to cause thee annoy; but, now I perceive that others begin to be aware thereof, it skilleth not to hide it from thee longer. This betideth thee for none other what than that thou stinkest terribly at the mouth, and I know not what can be the cause thereof; for that it used not to be thus. Now this is a very unseemly thing for thee who hast to do with gentlemen, and needs must we see for a means of curing it.' Whereupon said he, 'What can this be? Can I have some rotten tooth in my head?' 'Maybe ay,' answered Lydia and carried him to a window, where she made him open his mouth, and after she had viewed it in every part, 'O Nicostratus,' cried she, 'how canst thou have put up with it so long? Thou hast a tooth on this side which meseemth is not only decayed, but altogether rotten, and assuredly, and thou keep it much longer in thy mouth, it will mar thee those which be on either side; wherefore I counsel thee have it drawn, ere the thing go farther.' 'Since it seemeth good to thee,' answered he, 'I will well; let a surgeon be sent for without more delay, who shall draw it for me.' 'God forbid,' rejoined the lady, 'that a surgeon come hither for that! Methinketh it lieth on such wise that I myself, without any surgeon, can very well draw it for thee; more by token that these same surgeons are so barbarous in doing such offices that my heart would on no account suffer me to see or know thee in the hands of any one of them; for, an it irk thee overmuch, I will at least loose thee incontinent, which a surgeon would not do.'

Accordingly, she let fetch the proper instruments and sent every one forth of the chamber, except only Lusca; after which, locking herself in, she made Nicostratus lie down on a table and thrusting the pincers into his mouth, what while the maid held him fast, she pulled out one of his teeth by main force, albeit he roared out lustily for the pain. Then, keeping to herself that which she had drawn, she brought out a frightfully decayed tooth she had ready in her hand and showed it to her husband, half dead as he was for pain, saying, 'See what thou hast had in thy mouth all this while.' Nicostratus believed what she said and now that the tooth was out, for all he had suffered the most grievous pain and made sore complaint thereof, him seemed he was cured; and presently, having comforted himself with one thing and another and the pain being abated, he went forth of the chamber; whereupon his wife took the tooth and straightway despatched it to her gallant, who, being now certified of her love, professed himself ready to do her every pleasure.

The lady, albeit every hour seemed to her a thousand till she should be with him, desiring to give him farther assurance and wishful to perform that which she had promised him, made a show one day of being ailing and being visited after dinner by Nicostratus, with no one in his company but Pyrrhus, she prayed them, by way of allaying her unease, to help her go into the garden. Accordingly, Nicostratus taking her on one side and Pyrrhus on the other, they carried her into the garden and set her down on a grassplot, at the foot of a fine pear-tree; where, after they had sat awhile, the lady, who had already given her gallant to know what he had to do, said, 'Pyrrhus, I have a great desire to eat of yonder pears; do thou climb up and throw us down some of them.' Pyrrhus straightway climbed up into the tree and fell to throwing down of the pears, which as he did, he began to say, 'How now, my lord! What is this you do? And you, madam, are you not ashamed to suffer it in my presence? Think you I am blind? But now you were sore disordered; how cometh it you have so quickly recovered that you do such things? An you have a mind unto this, you have store of goodly chambers; why go you not do it in one of these? It were more seemly than in my presence.'

The lady turned to her husband and said, 'What saith Pyrrhus? Doth he rave?' 'No, madam,' answered the young man, 'I rave not. Think you I cannot see?' As for Nicostratus, he marvelled sore and said, 'Verily, Pyrrhus, methinketh thou dreamest.' 'My lord,' replied Pyrrhus, 'I dream not a jot, neither do you dream; nay, you bestir yourselves on such wise that were this tree to do likewise, there would not be a pear left on it.' Quoth the lady, 'What may this be? Can it be that this he saith appeareth to him to be true? So God save me, and I were whole as I was aforetime, I would climb up into the tree, to see what marvels are those which this fellow saith he seeth.' Meanwhile Pyrrhus from the top of the pear-tree still said the same thing and kept up the pretence; whereupon Nicostratus bade him come down. Accordingly he came down and his master said to him, 'Now, what sayst thou thou sawest?' 'Methinketh,' answered he, 'you take me for a lackwit or a loggerhead. Since I must needs say it, I saw you a-top of your lady, and after, as I came down, I saw you arise and seat yourself where you presently are.' 'Assuredly,' said Nicostratus, 'thou dotest; for we have not stirred a jot, save as thou seest, since thou climbest up into the pear-tree.' Whereupon quoth Pyrrhus, 'What booteth it to make words of the matter? I certainly saw you; and if I did see you, it was a-top of your own.'

Nicostratus waxed momently more and more astonished, insomuch that he said, 'Needs must I see if this pear-tree is enchanted and if whoso is thereon seeth marvels.' Thereupon he climbed up into the tree and no sooner was he come to the top than the lady and Pyrrhus fell to solacing themselves together; which when Nicostratus saw, he began to cry out, saying, 'Ah, vile woman that thou art, what is this thou dost? And thou, Pyrrhus, in whom I most trusted?' So saying, he proceeded to descend the tree, whilst the lovers said, 'We are sitting here'; then, seeing him come down, they reseated themselves whereas he had left them. As soon as he was down and saw his wife and Pyrrhus where he had left them, he fell a-railing at them; whereupon quoth Pyrrhus, 'Now, verily, Nicostratus, I acknowledged that, as you said before, I must have seen falsely what while I was in the pear-tree, nor do I know it otherwise than by this, that I see and know yourself to have seen falsely in the like case. And that I speak the truth nought else should be needful to certify you but that you have regard to the circumstances of the case and consider if it be possible that your lady, who is the most virtuous of women and discreeter than any other of her sex, could, an she had a mind to outrage you on such wise, bring herself to do it before your very eyes. I speak not of myself, who would rather suffer myself to be torn limb-meal than so much as think of such a thing, much more come to do it in your presence. Wherefore the fault of this misseeing must needs proceed from the pear-tree, for that all the world had not made me believe but that you were in act to have carnal knowledge of your lady here, had I not heard you say that it appeared to yourself that I did what I know most certainly I never thought, much less did.'

Thereupon the lady, feigning to be mightily incensed, rose to her feet and said, 'Ill luck betide thee, dost thou hold me so little of wit that, an I had a mind to such filthy fashions as thou wouldst have us believe thou sawest, I should come to do them before thy very eyes? Thou mayst be assured of this that, if ever the fancy took me thereof, I should not come hither; marry, methinketh I should have sense enough to contrive it in one of our chambers, on such wise and after such a fashion that it would seem to me an extraordinary thing if ever thou camest to know of it.' Nicostratus, himseeming that what the lady and Pyrrhus said was true, to wit, that they would never have ventured upon such an act there before himself, gave over words and reproaches and fell to discoursing of the strangeness of the fact and the miracle of the sight, which was thus changed unto whoso climbed up into the pear-tree. But his wife, feigning herself chagrined for the ill thought he had shown of her, said, 'Verily, this pear-tree shall never again, if I can help it, do me nor any other lady the like of this shame; wherefore do thou run, Pyrrhus, and fetch a hatchet and at one stroke avenge both thyself and me by cutting it down; albeit it were better yet lay it about Nicostratus his cosard, who, without any consideration, suffered the eyes of his understanding to be so quickly blinded, whenas, however certain that which thou[355] saidst might seem to those[356] which thou hast in thy head, thou shouldst for nought in the world in the judgment of thy mind have believed or allowed that such a thing could be.'

Pyrrhus very readily fetched the hatchet and cut down the tree, which when the lady saw fallen, she said to Nicostratus, 'Since I see the enemy of mine honour overthrown, my anger is past,' and graciously forgave her husband, who besought her thereof, charging him that it should never again happen to him to presume such a thing of her, who loved him better than herself. Accordingly, the wretched husband, thus befooled, returned with her and her lover to the palace, where many a time thereafterward Pyrrhus took delight and pleasance more at ease of Lydia and she of him. God grant us as much!"

THE TENTH STORY

TWO SIENNESE LOVE A LADY, WHO IS GOSSIP TO ONE OF THEM; THE LATTER DIETH AND RETURNING TO HIS COMPANION, ACCORDING TO PROMISE MADE HIM, RELATETH TO HIM HOW FOLK FARE IN THE OTHER WORLD

IT NOW rested only with the king to tell and he accordingly, as soon as he saw the ladies quieted, who lamented the cutting down of the unoffending pear-tree, began, "It is a very manifest thing that every just king should be the first to observe the laws made by him, and an he do otherwise, he must be adjudged a slave deserving of punishment and not a king, into which offence and under which reproach I, who am your king, am in a manner constrained to fall. True it is that yesterday I laid down the law for to-day's discourses, purposing not this day to make use of my privilege, but, submitting myself to the same obligation as you, to discourse of that whereof you have all discoursed. However, not only hath that story been told which I had thought to tell, but so many other and far finer things have been said upon the matter that, for my part, ransack my memory as I will, I can call nothing to mind and must avouch myself unable to say aught anent such a subject that may compare with those stories which have already been told. Wherefore, it behoving me transgress against the law made by myself, I declare myself in advance ready, as one deserving of punishment, to submit to any forfeit which may be imposed on me, and so have recourse to my wonted privilege. Accordingly, dearest ladies, I say that Elisa's story of Fra Rinaldo and his gossip and eke the simplicity of the Siennese have such efficacy that they induce me, letting be the cheats put upon foolish husbands by their wily wives, to tell you a slight story of them,[357] which though it have in it no little of that which must not be believed, will natheless in part, at least, be pleasing to hear.

There were, then, in Siena two young men of the people, whereof one was called Tingoccio Mini and the other Meuccio di Tura; they abode at Porta Salaja and consorted well nigh never save one with the other. To all appearance they loved each exceedingly and resorting, as men do, to churches and preachings, they had many a time heard tell of the happiness and of the misery that are, according to their deserts, allotted in the next world to the souls of those who die; of which things desiring to have certain news and finding no way thereto, they promised one another that whichever of them died first should, an he might, return to him who abode on life and give him tidings of that which he would fain know; and this they confirmed with an oath. Having come to this accord and companying still together, as hath been said, it chanced that Tingoccio became godfather to a child which one Ambruogio Anselmini, abiding at Campo Reggi, had had of his wife, Mistress Mita by name, and from time to time visiting, together with Meuccio, his gossip who was a very fair and lovesome lady, he became, notwithstanding the gossipship, enamoured of her. Meuccio, on like wise, hearing her mightily commended of his friend and being himself much pleased with her, fell in love with her, and each hid his love from the other, but not for one same reason. Tingoccio was careful not to discover it to Meuccio, on account of the naughty deed which himseemed he did to love his gossip and which he had been ashamed that any should know. Meuccio, on the other hand, kept himself therefrom,[358] for that he had already perceived that the lady pleased Tingoccio; whereupon he said in himself, 'If I discover this to him, he will wax jealous of me and being able, as her gossip, to bespeak her at his every pleasure, he will, inasmuch as he may, bring me in ill savour with her, and so I shall never have of her aught that may please me.'

Things being at this pass, it befell that Tingoccio, having more leisure of discovering his every desire to the lady, contrived with acts and words so to do that he had his will of her, of which Meuccio soon became aware and albeit it sore misliked him, yet, hoping some time or other to compass his desire, he feigned ignorance thereof, so Tingoccio might not have cause or occasion to do him an ill turn or hinder him in any of his affairs. The two friends loving thus, the one more happily than the other, it befell that Tingoccio, finding the soil of his gossip's demesne soft and eath to till, so delved and laboured there that there overcame him thereof a malady, which after some days waxed so heavy upon him that, being unable to brook it, he departed this life. The third day after his death (for that belike he had not before been able) he came by night, according to the promise made, into Meuccio's chamber and called the latter, who slept fast. Meuccio awoke and said, 'Who art thou?' Whereto he answered, 'I am Tingoccio, who, according to the promise which I made thee, am come back to thee to give thee news of the other world.'

Meuccio was somewhat affrighted at seeing him; nevertheless, taking heart, 'Thou art welcome, brother mine,' quoth he, and presently asked him if he were lost. 'Things are lost that are not to be found,' replied Tingoccio; 'and how should I be here, if I were lost?' 'Alack,' cried Meuccio, 'I say not so; nay, I ask thee if thou art among the damned souls in the avenging fire of hell.' Whereto quoth Tingoccio, 'As for that, no; but I am, notwithstanding, in very grievous and anguishful torment for the sins committed by me.' Meuccio then particularly enquired of him what punishments were awarded in the other world for each of the sins that folk use to commit here below, and he told him them all. After this Meuccio asked if there were aught he might do for him in this world, whereto Tingoccio replied that there was, to wit, that he should let say for him masses and orisons and do alms in his name, for that these things were mightily profitable to those who abode yonder. Meuccio said that he would well and Tingoccio offering to take leave of him, he remembered himself of the latter's amour with his gossip and raising his head, said, 'Now that I bethink me, Tingoccio, what punishment is given thee over yonder anent thy gossip, with whom thou layest, whenas thou wast here below?' 'Brother mine,' answered Tingoccio, 'whenas I came yonder, there was one who it seemed knew all my sins by heart and bade me betake myself to a certain place, where I bemoaned my offences in exceeding sore punishment and where I found many companions condemned to the same penance as myself. Being among them and remembering me of that which I had done whilere with my gossip, I looked for a much sorer punishment on account thereof than that which had presently been given me and went all shivering for fear, albeit I was in a great fire and an exceeding hot; which one who was by my side perceiving, he said to me, "What aileth thee more than all the others who are here that thou shiverest, being in the fire?" "Marry," said I, "my friend, I am sore in fear of the sentence I expect for a grievous sin I wrought aforetime." The other asked me what sin this was, and I answered, "It was that I lay with a gossip of mine, and that with such a vengeance that it cost me my life"; whereupon quoth he, making merry over my fear, "Go to, fool; have no fear. Here is no manner of account taken of gossips." Which when I heard, I was altogether reassured.' This said and the day drawing near, 'Meuccio,' quoth he, 'abide with God, for I may no longer be with thee,' and was suddenly gone. Meuccio, hearing that no account was taken of gossips in the world to come, began to make mock of his own simplicity, for that whiles he had spared several of them; wherefore, laying by his ignorance, he became wiser in that respect for the future. Which things if Fra Rinaldo had known, he had not needed to go a-syllogizing,[359] whenas he converted his good gossip to his pleasure."

Zephyr was now arisen, for the sun that drew near unto the setting, when the king, having made an end of his story and there being none other left to tell, put off the crown from his own head and set it on that of Lauretta, saying, "Madam, with yourself[360] I crown you queen of our company; do you then, from this time forth, as sovereign lady, command that which you may deem shall be for the pleasure and solacement of all." This said, he reseated himself, whereupon Lauretta, become queen, let call the seneschal and bade him look that the tables be set in the pleasant valley somewhat earlier than of wont, so they might return to the palace at their leisure; after which she instructed him what he should do what while her sovranty lasted. Then, turning to the company, she said, "Dioneo willed yesterday that we should discourse to-day of the tricks that women play their husbands and but that I am loath to show myself of the tribe of snappish curs, which are fain incontinent to avenge themselves of any affront done them, I would say that to-morrow's discourse should be of the tricks that men play their wives.

But, letting that be, I ordain that each bethink himself to tell OF THE TRICKS THAT ALL DAY LONG WOMEN PLAY MEN OR MEN WOMEN OR MEN ONE ANOTHER; and I doubt not but that in this[361] there will be no less of pleasant discourse than there hath been to-day." So saying, she rose to her feet and dismissed the company till supper-time.

Accordingly, they all, ladies and men alike, arose and some began to go barefoot through the clear water, whilst others went a-pleasuring upon the greensward among the straight and goodly trees. Dioneo and Fiammetta sang together a great while of Arcite and Palemon, and on this wise, taking various and divers delights, they passed the time with the utmost satisfaction until the hour of supper; which being come, they seated themselves at table beside the lakelet and there, to the song of a thousand birds, still refreshed by a gentle breeze, that came from the little hills around, and untroubled of any fly, they supped in peace and cheer. Then, the tables being removed and the sun being yet half-vespers[362] high, after they had gone awhile round about the pleasant valley, they wended their way again, even as it pleased their queen, with slow steps towards their wonted dwelling-place, and jesting and chattering a thousand things, as well of those whereof it had been that day discoursed as of others, they came near upon nightfall to the fair palace, where having with the coolest of wines and confections done away the fatigues of the little journey, they presently fell to dancing about the fair fountain, carolling[363] now to the sound of Tindaro's bagpipe and anon to that of other instruments. But, after awhile, the queen bade Filomena sing a song, whereupon she began thus:

Alack, my life forlorn!
Will't ever chance I may once more regain
Th' estate whence sorry fortune hath me torn?

Certes, I know not, such a wish of fire
I carry in my thought
To find me where, alas! I was whilere.
O dear my treasure, thou my sole desire,
That holdst my heart distraught,
Tell it me, thou; for whom I know nor dare

To ask it otherwhere.
Ah, dear my lord, oh, cause me hope again,
So I may comfort me my spright wayworn.

What was the charm I cannot rightly tell
That kindled in me such
A flame of love that rest nor day nor night
I find; for, by some strong unwonted spell,
Hearing and touch
And seeing each new fires in me did light,
Wherein I burn outright;
Nor other than thyself can soothe my pain
Nor call my senses back, by love o'erborne.

O tell me if and when, then, it shall be
That I shall find thee e'er
Whereas I kissed those eyes that did me slay.
O dear my good, my soul, ah, tell it me,
When thou wilt come back there,
And saying "Quickly," comfort my dismay
Somedele. Short be the stay
Until thou come, and long mayst thou remain!
I'm so love-struck, I reck not of men's scorn.

If once again I chance to hold thee aye,
I will not be so fond
As erst I was to suffer thee to fly;
Nay, fast I'll hold thee, hap of it what may,
And having thee in bond,
Of thy sweet mouth my lust I'll satisfy.
Now of nought else will I
Discourse. Quick, to thy bosom come me strain;
The sheer thought bids me sing like lark at morn.

This song caused all the company conclude that a new and pleasing love held Filomena in bonds, and as by the words it appeared that she had tasted more thereof than sight alone, she was envied of this by certain who were there and who held her therefor so much the happier. But, after her song was ended, the queen, remembering her that the ensuing day was Friday, thus graciously bespoke all, "You know, noble ladies and you also, young men, that to-morrow is the day consecrated to the passion of our Lord, the which, an you remember aright, what time Neifile was queen, we celebrated devoutly and therein gave pause to our delightsome discoursements, and on like wise we did with the following Saturday. Wherefore, being minded to follow the good example given us by Neifile, I hold it seemly that to-morrow and the next day we abstain, even as we did a week agone, from our pleasant story-telling, recalling to memory that which on those days befell whilere for the salvation of our souls." The queen's pious speech was pleasing unto all and a good part of the night being now past, they all, dismissed by her, betook them to repose.

HERE ENDETH THE SEVENTH DAY
OF THE DECAMERON

The Decameron of Giovanni Boccaccio - Part II

Day the Eighth

HERE BEGINNETH THE EIGHTH DAY OF THE DECAMERON WHEREIN UNDER THE GOVERNANCE OF LAURETTA IS DISCOURSED OF THE TRICKS THAT ALL DAY LONG WOMEN PLAY MEN OR MEN WOMEN OR MEN ONE ANOTHER

ALREADY on the Sunday morning the rays of the rising light appeared on the summits of the higher mountains and every shadow having departed, things might manifestly be discerned, when the queen, arising with her company, went wandering first through the dewy grass and after, towards half-tierce,[364] visiting a little neighboring church, heard there divine service; then, returning home, they ate with mirth and joyance and after sang and danced awhile till the queen dismissed them, so whoso would might go rest himself. But, whenas the sun had passed the meridian, they all seated themselves, according as it pleased the queen, near the fair fountain, for the wonted story-telling, and Neifile, by her commandment, began thus:

THE FIRST STORY

GULFARDO BORROWETH OF GUASPARRUOLO CERTAIN MONIES, FOR WHICH HE HATH AGREED WITH HIS WIFE THAT HE SHALL LIE WITH HER, AND ACCORDINGLY GIVETH THEM TO HER; THEN, IN HER PRESENCE, HE TELLETH GUASPARRUOLO THAT HE GAVE THEM TO HER, AND SHE CONFESSETH IT TO BE TRUE

"SINCE God hath so ordered it that I am to give a beginning to the present day's discourses, with my story, I am content, and therefore, lovesome ladies, seeing that much hath been said of the tricks played by women upon men, it is my pleasure to relate one played by a man upon a woman, not that I mean therein to blame that which the man did or to deny that it served the woman aright, nay, rather to commend the man and blame the woman and to show that men also know how to cozen those who put faith in them, even as themselves are cozened by those in whom they believe. Indeed, to speak more precisely, that whereof I have to tell should not be called cozenage; nay, it should rather be styled a just requital; for that, albeit a woman should still be virtuous and guard her chastity as her life nor on any account suffer herself be persuaded to sully it, yet, seeing that, by reason of our frailty, this is not always possible as fully as should be, I affirm that she who consenteth to her own dishonour for a price is worthy of the fire, whereas she who yieldeth for Love's sake, knowing his exceeding great puissance, meriteth forgiveness from a judge not too severe, even as, a few days agone, Filostrato showed it to have been observed towards Madam Filippa at Prato.

There was, then, aforetime at Milan a German, by name Gulfardo, in the pay of the state, a stout fellow of his person and very loyal to those in whose service he engaged himself, which is seldom the case with Germans; and for that he was a very punctual repayer of such loans as were made him, he might always find many merchants ready to lend him any quantity of money at little usance. During his sojourn in Milan, he set his heart upon a very fair lady called Madam Ambruogia, the wife of a rich merchant, by name Guasparruolo Cagastraccio, who was much his acquaintance and friend, and loving her very discreetly, so that neither her husband nor any other suspected it, he sent one day to speak with her, praying her that it would please her vouchsafe him her favours and protesting that he, on his part, was ready to do whatsoever she should command him. The lady, after many parleys, came to this conclusion, that she was ready to do that which Gulfardo wished, provided two things should ensue thereof; one, that this should never be by him discovered to any and the other, that, as she had need of two hundred gold florins for some occasion of hers, he, who was a rich man, should give them to her; after which she would still be at his service.

Gulfardo, hearing this and indignant at the sordidness of her whom he had accounted a lady of worth, was like to exchange his fervent love for hatred and thinking to cheat her, sent back to her, saying that he would very willingly do this and all else in his power that might please her and that therefore she should e'en send him word when she would have him go to her, for that he would carry her the money, nor should any ever hear aught of the matter, save a comrade of his in whom he trusted greatly and who still bore him company in whatsoever he did. The lady, or rather, I should say, the vile woman, hearing this, was well pleased and sent to him, saying that Guasparruolo her husband was to go to Genoa for his occasions a few days hence and that she would presently let him know of this and send for him. Meanwhile, Gulfardo, taking his opportunity, repaired to Guasparruolo and said to him, 'I have present occasion for two hundred gold florins, the which I would have thee lend me at that same usance whereat thou art wont to lend me other monies.' The other replied that he would well and straightway counted out to him the money.

A few days thereafterward Guasparruolo went to Genoa, even as the lady had said, whereupon she sent to Gulfardo to come to her and bring the two hundred gold florins. Accordingly, he took his comrade and repaired to the lady's house, where finding her expecting him, the first thing he did was to put into her hands the two hundred gold florins, in his friend's presence, saying to her, 'Madam, take these monies and give them to your husband, whenas he shall be returned.' The lady took them, never guessing why he said thus, but supposing that he did it so his comrade should not perceive that he gave them to her by way of price, and answered, 'With all my heart; but I would fain see how many they are.' Accordingly, she turned them out upon the table and finding them full two hundred, laid them up, mighty content in herself; then, returning to Gulfardo and carrying him into her chamber, she satisfied him of her person not that night only, but many others before her husband returned from Genoa.

As soon as the latter came back, Gulfardo, having spied out a time when he was in company with his wife, betook himself to him, together with his comrade aforesaid, and said to him, in the lady's presence, 'Guasparruolo, I had no occasion for the monies, to wit, the two hundred gold florins, thou lentest me the other day, for that I could not compass the business for which I borrowed them. Accordingly, I brought them presently back to thy lady here and gave them to her; wherefore look thou cancel my account.' Guasparruolo, turning to his wife, asked her if she had the monies, and she, seeing the witness present, knew not how to deny, but said, 'Ay, I had them and had not yet remembered me to tell thee.' Whereupon quoth Guasparruolo, 'Gulfardo, I am satisfied; get you gone and God go with you: I will settle your account aright.' Gulfardo gone, the lady, finding herself cozened, gave her husband the dishonourable price of her baseness; and on this wise the crafty lover enjoyed his sordid mistress without cost."

THE SECOND STORY

THE PARISH PRIEST OF VARLUNGO LIETH WITH MISTRESS BELCOLORE AND LEAVETH HER A CLOAK OF HIS IN PLEDGE; THEN, BORROWING A MORTAR OF HER, HE SENDETH IT BACK TO HER, DEMANDING IN RETURN THE CLOAK LEFT BY WAY OF TOKEN, WHICH THE GOOD WOMAN GRUDGINGLY GIVETH HIM BACK

MEN and ladies alike commended that which Gulfardo had done to the sordid Milanese lady, and the queen, turning to Pamfilo, smilingly charged him follow on; whereupon quoth he, "Fair ladies, it occurreth to me to tell you a little story against those who continually offend against us, without being open to retaliation on our part, to wit, the clergy, who have proclaimed a crusade against our wives and who, whenas they avail to get one of the latter under them, conceive themselves to have gained forgiveness of fault and pardon of penalty no otherwise than as they had brought the Soldan bound from Alexandria to Avignon.[365] Whereof the wretched laymen cannot return them the like, albeit they wreak their ire upon the priests' mothers and sisters, doxies and daughters, assailing them with no less ardour than the former do their wives. Wherefore I purpose to recount to you a village love-affair, more laughable for its conclusion than long in words, wherefrom you may yet gather, by way of fruit, that priests are not always to be believed in everything.

You must know, then, that there was once at Varlungo,—a village very near here, as each of you ladies either knoweth or may have heard,—a worthy priest and a lusty of his person in the service of the ladies, who, albeit he knew not overwell how to read, natheless regaled his parishioners with store of good and pious saws at the elmfoot on Sundays and visited their women, whenas they went abroad anywhither, more diligently than any priest who had been there aforetime, carrying them fairings and holy water and a stray candle-end or so, whiles even to their houses. Now it chanced that, among other his she-parishioners who were most to his liking, one pleased him over all, by name Mistress Belcolore, the wife of a husbandman who styled himself Bentivegna del Mazzo, a jolly, buxom country wench, brown-favoured and tight-made, as apt at turning the mill[366] as any woman alive. Moreover, it was she who knew how to play the tabret and sing 'The water runneth to the ravine' and lead up the haye and the round, when need was, with a fine muckender in her hand and a quaint, better than any woman of her neighbourhood; by reason of which things my lord priest became so sore enamoured of her that he was like to lose his wits therefor and would prowl about all day long to get a sight of her. Whenas he espied her in church of a Sunday morning, he would say a Kyrie and a Sanctus, studying to show himself a past master in descant, that it seemed as it were an ass a-braying; whereas, when he saw her not there, he passed that part of the service over lightly enough. But yet he made shift to do on such wise that neither Bentivegna nor any of his neighbours suspected aught; and the better to gain Mistress Belcolore's goodwill, he made her presents from time to time, sending her whiles a clove of garlic, which he had the finest of all the countryside in a garden he tilled with his own hands, and otherwhiles a punnet of peascods or a bunch of chives or scallions, and whenas he saw his opportunity, he would ogle her askance and cast a friendly gibe at her; but she, putting on the prude, made a show of not observing it and passed on with a demure air; wherefore my lord priest could not come by his will of her.

It chanced one day that as he sauntered about the quarter on the stroke of noon, he encountered Bentivegna del Mazzo, driving an ass laden with gear, and accosting him, asked whither he went. 'Faith, sir,' answered the husbandman, 'to tell you the truth, I am going to town about a business of mine and am carrying these things to Squire Bonaccorri da Ginestreto, so he may help me in I know not what whereof the police-court judge hath summoned me by his proctor for a peremptory attendance.' The priest was rejoiced to hear this and said, 'Thou dost well, my son; go now with my benison and return speedily; and shouldst thou chance to see Lapuccio or Naldino, forget not to bid them bring me those straps they wot of for my flails.' Bentivegna answered that it should be done and went his way towards Florence, whereupon the priest bethought himself that now was his time to go try his luck with Belcolore. Accordingly, he let not the grass grow under his feet, but set off forthright and stayed not till he came to her house and entering in, said, 'God send us all well! Who is within there?' Belcolore, who was gone up into the hayloft, hearing him, said, 'Marry, sir, you are welcome; but what do you gadding it abroad in this heat?' 'So God give me good luck,' answered he, 'I came to abide with thee awhile, for that I met thy man going to town.'

Belcolore came down and taking a seat, fell to picking over cabbage-seed which her husband had threshed out a while before; whereupon quoth the priest to her, 'Well, Belcolore, wilt thou still cause me die for thee on this wise?' She laughed and answered, 'What is it I do to you?' Quoth he, 'Thou dost nought to me, but thou sufferest me not do to thee that which I would fain do and which God commandeth.' 'Alack!' cried Belcolore, 'Go to, go to. Do priests do such things?' 'Ay do we,' replied he, 'as well as other men; and why not? And I tell thee more, we do far and away better work and knowest thou why? Because we grind with a full head of water. But in good sooth it shall be shrewdly to thy profit, an thou wilt but abide quiet and let me do.' 'And what might this "shrewdly to my profit" be?' asked she. 'For all you priests are stingier than the devil.' Quoth he, 'I know not; ask thou. Wilt have a pair of shoes or a head-lace or a fine stammel waistband or what thou wilt?' 'Pshaw!' cried Belcolore. 'I have enough and to spare of such things; but an you wish me so well, why do you not render me a service, and I will do what you will?' Quoth the priest, 'Say what thou wilt have of me, and I will do it willingly.' Then said she, 'Needs must I go to Florence, come Saturday, to carry back the wool I have spun and get my spinning-wheel mended; and an you will lend me five crowns, which I know you have by you, I can take my watchet gown out of pawn and my Sunday girdle[367] that I brought my husband, for you see I cannot go to church nor to any decent place, because I have them not; and after I will still do what you would have me.' 'So God give me a good year,' replied the priest, 'I have them not about me; but believe me, ere Saturday come, I will contrive that thou shalt have them, and that very willingly.' 'Ay,' said Belcolore, 'you are all like this, great promisers, and after perform nothing to any. Think you to do with me as you did with Biliuzza, who went off with the ghittern-player?[368] Cock's faith, then, you shall not, for that she is turned a common drab only for that. If you have them not about you, go for them.' 'Alack,' cried the priest, 'put me not upon going all the way home. Thou seest that I have the luck just now to find thee alone, but maybe, when I return, there will be some one or other here to hinder us; and I know not when I shall find so good an opportunity again.' Quoth she, 'It is well; an you choose to go, go; if not, go without.'

The priest, seeing that she was not in the humour to do his pleasure without a salvum me fac, whereas he would fain have done it sine custodiâ, said, 'Harkye, thou believest not that I will bring thee the money; but, so thou mayst credit me, I will leave thee this my blue-cloth cloak.' Belcolore raised her eyes and said, 'Eh what! That cloak? What is it worth?' 'Worth?' answered the priest. 'I would have thee know that it is cloth of Douay, nay, Threeay, and there be some of our folk here who hold it for Fouray.[369] It is scarce a fortnight since it cost me seven crowns of hard money to Lotto the broker, and according to what Buglietto telleth me (and thou knowest he is a judge of this kind of cloth), I had it good five shillings overcheap.' 'Indeed!' quoth Belcolore. 'So God be mine aid, I had never thought it. But give it me first of all.' My lord priest, who had his arbalest ready cocked, pulled off the cloak and gave it her; and she, after she had laid it up, said, 'Come, sir, let us go into the barn, for no one ever cometh there.' And so they did. There the priest gave her the heartiest busses in the world and making her sib to God Almighty,[370] solaced himself with her a great while; after which he took leave of her and returned to the parsonage in his cassock, as it were he came from officiating at a wedding.

There, bethinking himself that all the candle-ends he got by way of offertory in all the year were not worth the half of five crowns, himseemed he had done ill and repenting him of having left the cloak, he fell to considering how he might have it again without cost. Being shrewd enough in a small way, he soon hit upon a device and it succeeded to his wish; for that on the morrow, it being a holiday, he sent a neighbour's lad of his to Mistress Belcolore's house, with a message praying her be pleased to lend him her stone mortar, for that Binguccio dal Poggio and Nuto Buglietti were to dine with him that morning and he had a mind to make sauce. She sent it to him and towards dinner-time, the priest, having spied out when Bentivegna and his wife were at meat together, called his clerk and said to him, 'Carry this mortar back to Belcolore and say to her, 'His reverence biddeth you gramercy and prayeth you send him back the cloak that the boy left you by way of token.' The clerk accordingly repaired to her house and there, finding her at table with Bentivegna, set down the mortar and did the priest's errand. Belcolore, hearing require the cloak again, would have answered; but her husband said, with an angry air, 'Takest thou a pledge of his reverence? I vow to Christ, I have a mind to give thee a good clout over the head! Go, give it quickly back to him, pox take thee! And in future, let him ask what he will of ours, (ay, though he should seek our ass,) look that it be not denied him.' Belcolore rose, grumbling, and pulling the cloak out of the chest, gave it to the clerk, saying, 'Tell her reverence from me, Belcolore saith, she voweth to God you shall never again pound sauce in her mortar; you have done her no such fine honour of this bout.'

The clerk made off with the cloak and did her message to the priest, who said, laughing, 'Tell her, when thou seest her, that, an she will not lend me her mortar, I will not lend her my pestle; and so we shall be quits.' Bentivegna concluded that his wife had said this, because he had chidden her, and took no heed thereof; but Belcolore bore the priest a grudge and held him at arm's length till vintage-time; when, he having threatened to cause her go into the mouth of Lucifer the great devil, for very fear she made her peace with him over must and roast chestnuts and they after made merry together time and again. In lieu of the five crowns, the priest let put new parchment to her tabret and string thereto a cast of hawk's bells, and with this she was fain to be content."

THE THIRD STORY

CALANDRINO, BRUNO AND BUFFALMACCO GO COASTING ALONG THE MUGNONE IN SEARCH OF THE HELIOTROPE AND CALANDRINO THINKETH TO HAVE FOUND IT. ACCORDINGLY HE RETURNETH HOME, LADEN WITH STONES, AND HIS WIFE CHIDETH HIM; WHEREUPON, FLYING OUT INTO A RAGE, HE BEATETH HER AND RECOUNTETH TO HIS COMPANIONS THAT WHICH THEY KNOW BETTER THAN HE

PAMFILO having made an end of his story, at which the ladies had laughed so much that they laugh yet, the queen bade Elisa follow on, who, still laughing, began, "I know not, charming ladies, if with a little story of mine, no less true than pleasant, I shall succeed in making you laugh as much as Pamfilo hath done with his; but I will do my endeavor thereof.

In our city, then, which hath ever abounded in various fashions and strange folk, there was once, no great while since, a painter called Calandrino, a simple-witted man and of strange usances. He companied most of his time with other two painters, called the one Bruno and the other Buffalmacco, both very merry men, but otherwise well-advised and shrewd, who consorted with Calandrino for that they ofttimes had great diversion of his fashions and his simplicity. There was then also in Florence a young man of a mighty pleasant humor and marvellously adroit in all he had a mind to do, astute and plausible, who was called Maso del Saggio, and who, hearing certain traits of Calandrino's simplicity, determined to amuse himself at his expense by putting off some cheat on him or causing him believe some strange thing. He chanced one day to come upon him in the church of San Giovanni and seeing him intent upon the carved work and paintings of the pyx, which is upon the altar of the said church and which had then not long been placed there, he judged the place and time opportune for carrying his intent into execution. Accordingly, acquainting a friend of his with that which he purposed to do, they both drew near unto the place where Calandrino sat alone and feigning not to see him, fell a-discoursing together of the virtues of divers stones, whereof Maso spoke as authoritatively as if he had been a great and famous lapidary.

Calandrino gave ear to their talk and presently, seeing that it was no secret, he rose to his feet and joined himself to them, to the no small satisfaction of Maso, who, pursuing his discourse, was asked by Calandrino where these wonder-working stones were to be found. Maso replied that the most of them were found in Berlinzone, a city of the Basques, in a country called Bengodi,[371] where the vines are tied up with sausages and a goose is to be had for a farthing[372] and a gosling into the bargain, and that there was a mountain all of grated Parmesan cheese, whereon abode folk who did nothing but make maccaroni and ravioli[373] and cook them in capon-broth, after which they threw them down thence and whoso got most thereof had most; and that hard by ran a rivulet of vernage,[374] the best ever was drunk, without a drop of water therein. 'Marry,' cried Calandrino, 'that were a fine country; but tell me, what is done with the capons that they boil for broth?' Quoth Maso, 'The Basques eat them all.' Then said Calandrino, 'Wast thou ever there?' 'Was I ever there, quotha!' replied Maso. 'If I have been there once I have been there a thousand times.' 'And how many miles is it distant hence?' asked Calandrino; and Maso, 'How many? a million or more; you might count them all night and not know.' 'Then,' said Calandrino, 'it must be farther off than the Abruzzi?' 'Ay, indeed,' answered Maso; 'it is a trifle farther.'

Calandrino, like a simpleton as he was, hearing Maso tell all this with an assured air and without laughing, gave such credence thereto as can be given to whatsoever verity is most manifest and so, holding it for truth, said, 'That is overfar for my money; though, were it nearer, I tell thee aright I would go thither with thee once upon a time, if but to see the maccaroni come tumbling headlong down and take my fill thereof. But tell me, God keep thee merry, is there none of those wonder-working stones to be found in these parts?' 'Ay is there,' answered Maso; 'there be two kinds of stones of very great virtue found here; the first are the grits of Settignano and Montisci, by virtue whereof, when they are wrought into millstones, flour is made; wherefore it is said in those parts that grace cometh from God and millstones from Montisci; but there is such great plenty of these grits that they are as little prized with us as emeralds with the folk over yonder, where they have mountains of them bigger than Mount Morello, which shine in the middle of the night, I warrant thee. And thou must know that whoso should cause set fine and perfect millstones, before they are pierced, in rings and carry them to the Soldan might have for them what he would. The other is what we lapidaries call Heliotrope, a stone of exceeding great virtue, for that whoso hath it about him is not seen of any other person whereas he is not, what while he holdeth it.' Quoth Calandrino, 'These be indeed great virtues; but where is this second stone found?' To which Maso replied that it was commonly found in the Mugnone. 'What bigness is this stone,' asked Calandrino, 'and what is its colour?' Quoth Maso, 'It is of various sizes, some more and some less; but all are well nigh black of colour.'

Calandrino noted all this in himself and feigning to have otherwhat to do, took leave of Maso, inwardly determined to go seek the stone in question, but bethought himself not to do it without the knowledge of Bruno and Buffalmacco, whom he most particularly affected. Accordingly he addressed himself to seek for them, so they might, without delay and before any else, set about the search, and spent all the rest of the morning seeking them. At last, when it was past none, he remembered him that they were awork in the Ladies' Convent at Faenza and leaving all his other business, he betook himself thither well nigh at a run, notwithstanding the great heat. As soon as he saw them, he called them and bespoke them thus: 'Comrades, an you will hearken to me, we may become the richest men in all Florence, for that I have learned from a man worthy of belief that in the Mugnone is to be found a stone, which whoso carrieth about him is not seen of any; wherefore meseemeth we were best go thither in quest thereof without delay, ere any forestall us. We shall certainly find it, for that I know it well, and when we have gotten it, what have we to do but put it in our poke and getting us to the moneychangers' tables, which you know stand still laden with groats and florins, take as much as we will thereof? None will see us, and so may we grow rich of a sudden, without having to smear walls all day long, snail-fashion.'

Bruno and Buffalmacco, hearing this, fell a-laughing in their sleeves and eyeing each other askance, made a show of exceeding wonderment and praised Calandrino's counsel, but Bruno asked how the stone in question was called. Calandrino, who was a clod-pated fellow, had already forgotten the name, wherefore quoth he, 'What have we to do with the name, since we know the virtue of the stone? Meseemeth we were best go about the quest without more ado.' 'Well, then,' said Bruno, 'how is it fashioned?' 'It is of all fashions,' replied Calandrino; 'but all are well nigh black; wherefore meseemeth that what we have to do is to gather up all the black stones we see, till we happen upon the right. So let us lose no time, but get us gone.' Quoth Bruno, 'Wait awhile,' and turning to his comrade, said, 'Methinketh Calandrino saith well; but meseemeth this is no season for the search, for that the sun is high and shineth full upon the Mugnone, where it hath dried all the stones, so that certain of those that be there appear presently white, which of a morning, ere the sun have dried them, show black; more by token that, to-day being a working day, there be many folk, on one occasion or another abroad along the banks, who, seeing us, may guess what we are about and maybe do likewise, whereby the stone may come to their hands and we shall have lost the trot for the amble. Meseemeth (an you be of the same way of thinking) that this is a business to be undertaken of a morning, whenas the black may be the better known from the white, and of a holiday, when there will be none there to see us.'

Buffalmacco commended Bruno's counsel and Calandrino fell in therewith; wherefore they agreed to go seek for the stone all three on the following Sunday morning, and Calandrino besought them over all else not to say a word of the matter to any one alive, for that it had been imparted to him in confidence, and after told them that which he had heard tell of the land of Bengodi, affirming with an oath that it was as he said. As soon as he had taken his leave, the two others agreed with each other what they should do in the matter and Calandrino impatiently awaited the Sunday morning, which being come, he arose at break of day and called his friends, with whom he sallied forth of the city by the San Gallo gate and descending into the bed of the Mugnone, began to go searching down stream for the stone. Calandrino, as the eagerest of the three, went on before, skipping nimbly hither and thither, and whenever he espied any black stone, he pounced upon it and picking it up, thrust it into his bosom. His comrades followed after him picking up now one stone and now another; but Calandrino had not gone far before he had his bosom full of stones; wherefore, gathering up the skirts of his grown, which was not cut Flanders fashion,[375] he tucked them well into his surcingle all round and made an ample lap thereof. However, it was no great while ere he had filled it, and making a lap on like wise of his mantle, soon filled this also with stones. Presently, the two others seeing that he had gotten his load and that dinner-time drew nigh, quoth Bruno to Buffalmacco, in accordance with the plan concerted between them, 'Where is Calandrino?' Buffalmacco, who saw him hard by, turned about and looking now here and now there, answered, 'I know not; but he was before us but now.' 'But now, quotha!' cried Bruno. 'I warrant you he is presently at home at dinner and hath left us to play the fool here, seeking black stones down the Mugnone.' 'Egad,' rejoined Buffalmacco 'he hath done well to make mock of us and leave us here, since we were fools enough to credit him. Marry, who but we had been simple enough to believe that a stone of such virtue was to be found in the Mugnone?'

Calandrino, hearing this, concluded that the heliotrope had fallen into his hands and that by virtue thereof they saw him not, albeit he was present with them, and rejoiced beyond measure at such a piece of good luck, answered them not a word, but determined to return; wherefore, turning back, he set off homeward. Buffalmacco, seeing this, said to Bruno, 'What shall we do? Why do we not get us gone?' Whereto Bruno answered, 'Let us begone; but I vow to God that Calandrino shall never again serve me thus, and were I presently near him as I have been all the morning, I would give him such a clout on the shins with this stone that he should have cause to remember this trick for maybe a month to come.' To say this and to let fly at Calandrino's shins with the stone were one and the same thing; and the latter, feeling the pain, lifted up his leg and began to puff and blow, but yet held his peace and fared on. Presently

Buffalmacco took one of the flints he had picked up and said to Bruno, 'Look at this fine flint; here should go for Calandrino's loins!' So saying, he let fly and dealt him a sore rap in the small of the back with the stone. Brief, on this wise, now with one word and now with another, they went pelting him up the Mugnone till they came to the San Gallo gate, where they threw down the stones they had gathered and halted awhile at the custom house.

The officers, forewarned by them, feigned not to see Calandrino and let him pass, laughing heartily at the jest, whilst he, without stopping, made straight for his house, which was near the Canto alla Macina, and fortune so far favoured the cheat that none accosted him, as he came up the stream and after through the city, as, indeed, he met with few, for that well nigh every one was at dinner. Accordingly, he reached his house, thus laden, and as chance would have it, his wife, a fair and virtuous lady, by name Mistress Tessa, was at the stairhead. Seeing him come and somewhat provoked at his long tarriance, she began to rail at him, saying, 'Devil take the man! Wilt thou never think to come home betimes? All the folk have already dined whenas thou comest back to dinner.' Calandrino, hearing this and finding that he was seen, was overwhelmed with chagrin and vexation and cried out, 'Alack, wicked woman that thou art, wast thou there? Thou hast undone me; but, by God His faith, I will pay thee therefor!' Therewithal he ran up to a little saloon he had and there disburdened himself of the mass of stones he had brought home; then, running in a fury at his wife, he laid hold of her by the hair and throwing her down at his feet, cuffed and kicked her in every part as long as he could wag his arms and legs, without leaving a hair on her head or a bone in her body that was not beaten to a mash, nor did it avail her aught to cry him mercy with clasped hands.

Meanwhile Bruno and Buffalmacco, after laughing awhile with the keepers of the gate, proceeded with slow step to follow Calandrino afar off and presently coming to the door of his house, heard the cruel beating he was in act to give his wife; whereupon, making a show of having but then come back, they called Calandrino, who came to the window, all asweat and red with anger and vexation, and prayed them come up to him. Accordingly, they went up, making believe to be somewhat vexed, and seeing the room full of stones and the lady, all torn and dishevelled and black and blue in the face for bruises, weeping piteously in one corner of the room, whilst Calandrino sat in another, untrussed and panting like one forspent, eyed them awhile, then said, 'What is this, Calandrino? Art thou for building, that we see all these stones here? And Mistress Tessa, what aileth her? It seemeth thou hast beaten her. What is all this ado?' Calandrino, outwearied with the weight of the stones and the fury with which he had beaten his wife, no less than with chagrin for the luck which himseemed he had lost, could not muster breath to give them aught but broken words in reply; wherefore, as he delayed to answer, Buffalmacco went on, 'Harkye, Calandrino, whatever other cause for anger thou mightest have had, thou shouldst not have fooled us as thou hast done, in that, after thou hadst carried us off to seek with thee for the wonder-working stone, thou leftest us in the Mugnone, like a couple of gulls, and madest off home, without saying so much as God be with you or devil; the which we take exceeding ill; but assuredly this shall be the last trick thou shalt ever play us.'

Therewithal, Calandrino enforcing himself,[376] answered, 'Comrades, be not angered; the case standeth otherwise than as you deem. I (unlucky wretch that I am!) had found the stone in question, and you shall hear if I tell truth. When first you questioned one another of me, I was less than half a score yards distant from you; but, seeing that you made off and saw me not, I went on before you and came back hither, still keeping a little in front of you.' Then, beginning from the beginning, he recounted to them all that they had said and done, first and last, and showed them how the stones had served his back and shins; after which, 'And I may tell you,' continued he, 'that, whenas I entered in at the gate, with all these stones about me which you see here, there was nothing said to me, albeit you know how vexatious and tiresome these gatekeepers use to be in wanting to see everything; more by token that I met by the way several of my friends and gossips, who are still wont to accost me and invite me to drink; but none of them said a word to me, no, nor half a word, as those who saw me not. At last, being come home hither, this accursed devil of a woman presented herself before me, for that, as you know, women cause everything lose its virtue, wherefore I, who might else have called myself the luckiest man in Florence, am become the most unlucky. For this I have beaten her as long as I could wag my fists and I know not what hindereth me from slitting her weasand, accursed be the hour when first I saw her and when she came to me in this house.' Then, flaming out into fresh anger, he offered to rise and beat her anew.

Bruno and Buffalmacco, hearing all this, made believe to marvel exceedingly and often confirmed that which Calandrino said, albeit they had the while so great a mind to laugh that they were like to burst; but, seeing him start up in a rage to beat his wife again, they rose upon him and withheld him, avouching that the lady was nowise at fault, but that he had only himself to blame for that which had377 happened, since he knew that women caused things to lose their virtue and had not bidden her beware of appearing before him that day, and that God had bereft him of foresight to provide against this, either for that the adventure was not to be his or because he had had it in mind to cozen his comrades, to whom he should have discovered the matter, as soon as he perceived that he had found the stone. Brief, after many words, they made peace, not without much ado, between him and the woebegone lady and went their ways, leaving him disconsolate, with the house full of stones."

THE FOURTH STORY

THE RECTOR OF FIESOLE LOVETH A WIDOW LADY, BUT IS NOT LOVED BY HER AND THINKING TO LIE WITH HER, LIETH WITH A SERVING-WENCH OF HERS, WHILST THE LADY'S BROTHERS CAUSE THE BISHOP FIND HIM IN THIS CASE

ELISA being come to the end of her story, which she had related to the no small pleasure of all the company, the queen turned to Emilia, and signified to her her wish that she should follow after with her story, whereupon she promptly began thus: "I have not forgotten, noble ladies, that it hath already been shown, in sundry of the foregoing stories, how much we women are exposed to the importunities of the priests and friars and clergy of every kind; but, seeing that so much cannot be said thereof but that yet more will remain to say, I purpose, to boot, to tell you a story of a rector, who, maugre all the world, would e'en have a gentlewoman wish him well,[377] whether she would or not; whereupon she, like a very discreet woman as she was, used him as he deserved.

As all of you know, Fiesole, whose hill we can see hence, was once a very great and ancient city, nor, albeit it is nowadays all undone, hath it ever ceased to be, as it is yet, the seat of a bishop. Near the cathedral church there a widow lady of noble birth, by name Madam Piccarda, had an estate, where, for that she was not overwell to do, she abode the most part of the year in a house of hers that was not very big, and with her, two brothers of hers, very courteous and worthy youths. It chanced that, the lady frequenting the cathedral church and being yet very young and fair and agreeable, the rector of the church became so sore enamoured of her that he could think of nothing else, and after awhile, making bold to discover his mind to her, he prayed her accept of his love and love him as he loved her. Now he was already old in years, but very young in wit, malapert and arrogant and presumptuous in the extreme, with manners and fashions full of conceit and ill grace, and withal so froward and ill-conditioned that there was none who wished him well; and if any had scant regard for him, it was the lady in question, who not only wished him no whit of good, but hated him worse than the megrims; wherefore, like a discreet woman as she was, she answered him, 'Sir, that you love me should be mighty pleasing to me, who am bound to love you and will gladly do so; but between your love and mine nothing unseemly should ever befall. You are my spiritual father and a priest and are presently well stricken in years, all which things should make you both modest and chaste; whilst I, on the other hand, am no girl, nor do these amorous toys beseem my present condition, for that I am a widow and you well know what discretion is required in widows; wherefore I pray you hold me excused, for that I shall never love you after the fashion whereof you require me; nor do I wish to be thus loved of you.'

The rector could get of her no other answer for that time, but, nowise daunted or disheartened by the first rebuff, solicited her again and again with the most overweening importunity, both by letter and message, nay, even by word of mouth, whenas he saw her come into the church. Wherefor, herseeming that this was too great and too grievous an annoy, she cast about to rid herself of him after such a fashion as he deserved, since she could no otherwise, but would do nought ere she had taken counsel with her brothers. Accordingly, she acquainted them with the rector's behaviour towards her and that which she purposed to do, and having therein full license from them, went a few days after to the church, as was her wont. As soon as the rector saw her, he came up to her and with his usual assurance, accosted her familiarly. The lady received him with a cheerful countenance and withdrawing apart with him, after he had said many words to her in his wonted style, she heaved a great sigh and said, 'Sir, I have heard that there is no fortalice so strong but that, being every day assaulted, it cometh at last to be taken, and this I can very well see to have happened to myself; for that you have so closely beset me with soft words and with one complaisance and another, that you have made me break my resolve, and I am now disposed, since I please you thus, to consent to be yours.' 'Gramercy, madam,' answered the rector, overjoyed, 'to tell you the truth, I have often wondered how you could hold out so long, considering that never did the like betide me with any woman; nay, I have said whiles, "Were women of silver, they would not be worth a farthing, for that not one of them would stand the hammer." But let that pass for the present. When and where can we be together?' Whereto quoth the lady, 'Sweet my lord, as for the when, it may be what time soever most pleaseth us, for that I have no husband to whom it behoveth me render an account of my nights; but for the where I know not how to contrive.' 'How?' cried the priest. 'Why, in your house to be sure.' 'Sir,' answered the lady, 'you know I have two young brothers, who come and go about the house with their companions day and night, and my house is not overbig; wherefore it may not be there, except one chose to abide there mute-fashion, without saying a word or making the least sound, and be in the dark, after the manner of the blind. An you be content to do this, it might be, for they meddle not with379 my bedchamber; but their own is so close to mine that one cannot whisper the least word, without its being heard.' 'Madam,' answered the rector, 'this shall not hinder us for a night or two, against I bethink me where we may foregather more at ease.' Quoth she, 'Sir, let that rest with you; but of one thing I pray you, that this abide secret, so no word be ever known thereof.' 'Madam,' replied he, 'have no fear for that; but, an it may be, make shift that we shall foregather this evening.' 'With all my heart,' said the lady; and appointing him how and when he should come, she took leave of him and returned home.

Now she had a serving-wench, who was not overyoung, but had the foulest and worst-favoured visnomy was ever seen; for she had a nose flattened sore, a mouth all awry, thick lips and great ill-set teeth; moreover, she inclined to squint, nor was ever without sore eyes, and had a green and yellow complexion, which gave her the air of having passed the summer not at Fiesole, but at Sinigaglia.[378] Besides all this, she was hipshot and a thought crooked on the right side. Her name was Ciuta, but, for that she had such a dog's visnomy of her own, she was called of every one Ciutazza;[379] and for all she was misshapen of her person, she was not without a spice of roguishness. The lady called her and said to her, 'Harkye, Ciutazza, an thou wilt do me a service this night. I will give thee a fine new shift.' Ciutazza, hearing speak of the shift, answered, 'Madam, so you give me a shift, I will cast myself into the fire, let alone otherwhat.' 'Well, then,' said her mistress, 'I would have thee lie to-night with a man in my bed and load him with caresses, but take good care not to say a word, lest thou be heard by my brothers, who, as thou knowest, sleep in the next room; and after I will give thee the shift.' Quoth Ciutazza, 'With all my heart. I will lie with half a dozen men, if need be, let alone one.' Accordingly, at nightfall, my lord the rector made his appearance, according to agreement, whilst the two young men, by the lady's appointment, were in their bedchamber and took good care to make themselves heard; wherefore he entered the lady's chamber in silence and darkness and betook himself, as she had bidden him, straight to the bed, whither on her part came Ciutazza, who had been well lessoned by the lady of that which she had to do. My lord rector, thinking he had his mistress beside him, caught Ciutazza in his arms and fell to kissing her, without saying a word, and she him; whereupon he proceeded to solace himself with her, taking, as he thought, possession of the long-desired good.

The lady, having done this, charged her brothers carry the rest of the plot into execution, wherefore, stealing softly out of the chamber, they made for the great square and fortune was more favorable to them than they themselves asked in that which they had a mind to do, inasmuch as, the heat being great, the bishop had enquired for the two young gentlemen, so he might go a-pleasuring to their house and drink with them. But, seeing them coming, he acquainted them with his wish and returned with them to their house, where, entering a cool little courtyard380 of theirs, in which were many flambeaux alight, he drank with great pleasure of an excellent wine of theirs. When he had drunken, the young men said to him, 'My lord, since you have done us so much favour as to deign to visit this our poor house, whereto we came to invite you, we would have you be pleased to view a small matter with which we would fain show you.' The bishop answered that he would well; whereupon one of the young men, taking a lighted flambeau in his hand, made for the chamber where my lord rector lay with Ciutazza, followed by the bishop and all the rest. The rector, to arrive the quicklier at his journey's end, had hastened to take horse and had already ridden more than three miles before they came thither; wherefore, being somewhat weary, he had, notwithstanding the heat, fallen asleep with Ciutazza in his arms. Accordingly, when the young man entered the chamber, light in hand, and after him the bishop and all the others, he was shown to the prelate in this plight; whereupon he awoke and seeing the light and the folk about him, was sore abashed and hid his head for fear under the bed-clothes. The bishop gave him a sound rating and made him put out his head and see with whom he had lain; whereupon the rector, understanding the trick that had been played him of the lady, what with this and what with the disgrace himseemed he had gotten, became of a sudden the woefullest man that was aye. Then, having, by the bishop's commandment, reclad himself, he was despatched to his house under good guard, to suffer sore penance for the sin he had committed. The bishop presently enquiring how it came to pass that he had gone thither to lie with Ciutazza, the young men orderly related everything to him, which having heard, he greatly commended both the lady and her brothers for that, without choosing to imbrue their hands in the blood of a priest, they had entreated him as he deserved. As for the rector, he caused him bewail his offence forty days' space; but love and despite made him rue it for more than nine-and-forty,[380] more by token that, for a great while after, he could never go abroad but the children would point at him and say, 'See, there is he who lay with Ciutazza'; the which was so sore an annoy to him that he was like to go mad therefor. On such wise did the worthy lady rid herself of the importunity of the malapert rector and Ciutazza gained the shift and a merry night."

THE FIFTH STORY

THREE YOUNG MEN PULL THE BREECHES OFF A MARCHEGAN JUDGE IN FLORENCE, WHAT WHILE HE IS ON THE BENCH, ADMINISTERING JUSTICE

EMILIA having made an end of her story and the widow lady having been commended of all, the queen looked to Filostrato and said, "It is now thy turn to tell." He answered promptly that he was ready and began, "Delightsome ladies, the mention by Elisa a little before of a certain young man, to381 wit, Maso del Saggio, hath caused me leave a story I purposed to tell you, so I may relate to you one of him and certain companions of his, which, if (albeit it is nowise unseemly) it offer certain expressions which you think shame to use, is natheless so laughable that I will e'en tell it.

As you may all have heard, there come oftentimes to our city governors from the Marches of Ancona, who are commonly meanspirited folk and so paltry and sordid of life that their every fashion seemeth nought other than a lousy cadger's trick; and of this innate paltriness and avarice, they bring with them judges and notaries, who seem men taken from the plough-tail or the cobbler's stall rather than from the schools of law. Now, one of these being come hither for Provost, among the many judges whom he brought with him was one who styled himself Messer Niccola da San Lepidio and who had more the air of a tinker than of aught else, and he was set with other judges to hear criminal causes. As it oft happeneth that, for all the townsfolk have nought in the world to do at the courts of law, yet bytimes they go thither, it befell that Maso del Saggio went thither one morning, in quest of a friend of his, and chancing to cast his eyes whereas this said Messer Niccola sat, himseemed that here was a rare outlandish kind of wild fowl. Accordingly, he went on to examine him from head to foot, and albeit he saw him with the miniver bonnet on his head all black with smoke and grease and a paltry inkhorn at his girdle, a gown longer than his mantle and store of other things all foreign to a man of good breeding and manners, yet of all these the most notable, to his thinking, was a pair of breeches, the backside whereof, as the judge sat, with his clothes standing open in front for straitness, he perceived came halfway down his legs. Thereupon, without tarrying longer to look upon him, he left him with whom he went seeking and beginning a new quest, presently found two comrades of his, called one Ribi and the other Matteuzzo, men much of the same mad humour as himself, and said to them, 'As you tender me, come with me to the law courts, for I wish to show you the rarest scarecrow you ever saw.'

Accordingly, carrying them to the court house, he showed them the aforesaid judge and his breeches, whereat they fell a-laughing, as soon as they caught sight of him afar off; then, drawing nearer to the platform whereon my lord judge sat, they saw that one might lightly pass thereunder and that, moreover, the boards under his feet were so broken that one might with great ease thrust his hand and arm between them; whereupon quoth Maso to his comrades, 'Needs must we pull him off those breeches of his altogether, for that it may very well be done.' Each of the others had already seen how;[381] wherefore, having agreed among themselves what they should say and do, they returned thither next morning, when, the court being very full of folk, Matteuzzo, without being seen of any, crept under the bench and posted himself immediately beneath the judge's feet. Meanwhile, Maso came up to my lord judge on one side and taking him by the skirt of his gown, whilst382 Ribi did the like on the other side, began to say, 'My lord, my lord, I pray you for God's sake, ere yonder scurvy thief on the other side of you go elsewhere, make him restore me a pair of saddle-bags whereof he hath saith indeed he did it not; but I saw him, not a month ago, in act to have them resoled.' Ribi on his side cried out with all his might, 'Believe him not, my lord; he is an arrant knave, and for that he knoweth I am come to lay a complaint against him for a pair of saddle-bags whereof he hath robbed me, he cometh now with his story of the boothose, which I have had in my house this many a day. An you believe me not, I can bring you to witness my next-door neighbor Trecca and Grassa the tripewoman and one who goeth gathering the sweepings from Santa Masia at Verjaza, who saw him when he came back from the country.

Maso on the other hand suffered not Ribi to speak, but bawled his loudest, whereupon the other but shouted the more. The judge stood up and leaned towards them, so he might the better apprehend what they had to say, wherefore Matteuzzo, watching his opportunity, thrust his hand between the crack of the boards and laying hold of Messer Niccola's galligaskins by the breech, tugged at them amain. The breeches came down incontinent, for that the judge was lean and lank of the crupper; whereupon, feeling this and knowing not what it might be, he would have sat down again and pulled his skirts forward to cover himself; but Maso on the one side and Ribi on the other still held him fast and cried out, 'My lord, you do ill not to do me justice and to seek to avoid hearing me and get you gone otherwhere; there be no writs granted in this city for such small matters as this.' So saying, they held him fast by the clothes on such wise that all who were in the court perceived that his breeches had been pulled down. However, Matteuzzo, after he had held them awhile, let them go and coming forth from under the platform, made off out of the court and went his way without being seen; whereupon quoth Ribi, himseeming he had done enough, 'I vow to God I will appeal to the syndicate!' Whilst Maso, on his part, let go the mantle and said, 'Nay, I will e'en come hither again and again until such time as I find you not hindered as you seem to be this morning.' So saying, they both made off as quickliest they might, each on his own side, whilst my lord judge pulled up his breeches in every one's presence, as if he were arisen from sleep; then, perceiving how the case stood, he enquired whither they were gone who were at difference anent the boothose and the saddle-bags; but they were not to be found, whereupon he began to swear by Cock's bowels that need must he know and learn if it were the wont at Florence to pull down the judges' breeches, whenas they sat on the judicial bench. The Provost, on his part, hearing of this, made a great stir; but, his friends having shown him that this had only been done to give him notice that the Florentines right well understood how, whereas he should have brought judges, he had brought them sorry patches, to have them better cheap, he thought it best to hold his peace, and so the thing went no farther for the nonce."

THE SIXTH STORY

BRUNO AND BUFFALMACCO, HAVING STOLEN A PIG FROM CALANDRINO, MAKE HIM TRY THE ORDEAL WITH GINGER BOLUSES AND SACK AND GIVE HIM (INSTEAD OF THE GINGER) TWO DOG-BALLS COMPOUNDED WITH ALOES, WHEREBY IT APPEARETH THAT HE HIMSELF HATH HAD THE PIG AND THEY MAKE HIM PAY BLACKMAIL, AN HE WOULD NOT HAVE THEM TELL HIS WIFE

NO SOONER had Filostrato despatched his story, which had given rise to many a laugh, than the queen bade Filomena follow on, whereupon she began: "Gracious ladies, even as Filostrato was led by the mention of Maso to tell the story which you have just heard from him, so neither more nor less am I moved by that of Calandrino and his friends to tell you another of them, which methinketh will please you.

Who Calandrino, Bruno and Buffalmacco were I need not explain to you, for that you have already heard it well enough; wherefore, to proceed with my story, I must tell you that Calandrino owned a little farm at no great distance from Florence, that he had had to his wife's dowry. From this farm, amongst other things that he got thence, he had every year a pig, and it was his wont still to betake himself thither, he and his wife, and kill the pig and have it salted on the spot. It chanced one year that, his wife being somewhat ailing, he went himself to kill the pig, which Bruno and Buffalmacco hearing and knowing that his wife was not gone to the farm with him, they repaired to a priest, very great friend of theirs and a neighbor of

Calandrino, to sojourn some days with him. Now Calandrino had that very morning killed the pig and seeing them with the priest, called to them saying, 'You are welcome. I would fain have you see what a good husband[382] I am.' Then carrying them into the house, he showed them the pig, which they seeing to be a very fine one and understanding from Calandrino that he meant to salt it down for his family, 'Good lack,' quoth Bruno to him, 'what a ninny thou art! Sell it and let us make merry with the price, and tell thy wife that it hath been stolen from thee.' 'Nay, answered Calandrino, 'she would never believe it and would drive me out of the house. Spare your pains, for I will never do it.' And many were the words, but they availed nothing.

Calandrino invited them to supper, but with so ill a grace that they refused to sup there and took their leave of him; whereupon quoth Bruno and Buffalmacco, 'What sayest thou to stealing yonder pig from him to-night?' 'Marry,' replied the other, 'how can we do it?' Quoth Bruno, 'I can see how well enough, an he remove it not from where it was but now.' 'Then,' rejoined his companion, 'let us do it. Why should we not? And after we will make merry over it with the parson here.' The priest answered that he would well, and Bruno said, 'Here must some little art be used. Thou knowest, Buffalmacco, how niggardly384 Calandrino is and how gladly he drinketh when others pay; let us go and carry him to the tavern, where the priest shall make believe to pay the whole scot in our honor nor suffer him to pay aught. Calandrino will soon grow fuddled and then we can manage it lightly enough, for that he is alone in the house.' As he said, so they did and Calandrino seeing that the priest suffered none to pay, gave himself up to drinking and took in a good load, albeit it needed no great matter to make him drunk. It was pretty late at night when they left the tavern and Calandrino, without troubling himself about supper, went straight home, where, thinking to have shut the door, he left it open and betook himself to bed. Buffalmacco and Bruno went off to sup with the priest and after supper repaired quietly to Calandrino's house, carrying with them certain implements wherewithal to break in whereas Bruno had appointed it; but, finding the door open, they entered and unhooking the pig, carried it off to the priest's house, where they laid it up and betook themselves to sleep.

On the morrow, Calandrino, having slept off the fumes of the wine, arose in the morning and going down, missed his pig and saw the door open; whereupon he questioned this one and that if they knew who had taken it and getting no news of it, began to make a great outcry, saying, 'Woe is me, miserable wretch that I am!' for that the pig had been stolen from him. As soon as Bruno and Buffalmacco were risen, they repaired to Calandrino's house, to hear what he would say anent the pig, and he no sooner saw them than he called out to them, well nigh weeping, and said, 'Woe's me, comrades mine; my pig hath been stolen from me!' Whereupon Bruno came up to him and said softly, 'It is a marvel that thou hast been wise for once.' 'Alack,' replied Calandrino, 'indeed I say sooth.' 'That's the thing to say,' quoth Bruno. 'Make a great outcry, so it may well appear that it is e'en as thou sayst.' Therewithal Calandrino bawled out yet loudlier, saying, 'Cock's body, I tell thee it hath been stolen from me in good earnest!' 'Good, good,' replied Bruno; 'that's the way to speak; cry out lustily, make thyself well heard, so it may seem true.' Quoth Calandrino, 'Thou wouldst make me give my soul to the Fiend! I tell thee and thou believest me not. May I be strung up by the neck an it have not been stolen from me!' 'Good lack!' cried Bruno. 'How can that be? I saw it here but yesterday. Thinkest thou to make me believe that it hath flown away?' Quoth Calandrino, 'It is as I tell thee.' 'Good lack,' repeated Bruno, 'can it be?' 'Certes,' replied Calandrino, 'it is so, more by token that I am undone and know not how I shall return home. My wife will never believe me; or even if she do, I shall have no peace with her this year to come.' Quoth Bruno, 'So God save me, this is ill done, if it be true; but thou knowest, Calandrino, I lessoned thee yesterday to say thus and I would not have thee at once cozen thy wife and us.' Therewithal Calandrino fell to crying out and saying, 'Alack, why will you drive me to desperation and make me blaspheme God and the Saints? I tell you the pig was stolen from me yesternight.'

Then said Buffalmacco, 'If it be so385 indeed, we must cast about for a means of having it again, an we may contrive it.' 'But what means,' asked Calandrino, 'can we find?' Quoth Buffalmacco, 'We may be sure that there hath come none from the Indies to rob thee of thy pig; the thief must have been some one of thy neighbors. An thou canst make shift to assemble them, I know how to work the ordeal by bread and cheese and we will presently see for certain who hath had it.' 'Ay,' put in Bruno, 'thou wouldst make a fine thing of bread and cheese with such gentry as we have about here, for one of them I am certain hath had the pig, and he would smoke the trap and would not come.' 'How, then, shall we do?' asked Buffalmacco, and Bruno said, 'We must e'en do it with ginger boluses and good vernage[383] and invite them to drink. They will suspect nothing and come, and the ginger boluses can be blessed even as the bread and cheese.' Quoth Buffalmacco, 'Indeed, thou sayst sooth. What sayst thou, Calandrino? Shall's do 't?' 'Nay,' replied the gull, 'I pray you thereof for the love of God; for, did I but know who hath had it, I should hold myself half consoled.' 'Marry, then,' said Bruno, 'I am ready to go to Florence, to oblige thee, for the things aforesaid, so thou wilt give me the money.' Now Calandrino had maybe forty shillings, which he gave him, and Bruno accordingly repaired to Florence to a friend of his, a druggist, of whom he bought a pound of fine ginger boluses and caused compound a couple of dogballs with fresh confect of hepatic aloes; after which he let cover these latter with sugar, like the others, and set thereon a privy mark by which he might very well know them, so he should not mistake them nor change them. Then, buying a flask of good vernage, he returned to Calandrino in the country and said to him, 'Do thou to-morrow morning invite those whom thou suspectest to drink with thee; it is a holiday and all will willingly come. Meanwhile, Buffalmacco and I will to-night make the conjuration over the pills and bring them to thee to-morrow morning at home; and for the love of thee I will administer them myself and do and say that which is to be said and done.'

Calandrino did as he said and assembled on the following morning a goodly company of such young Florentines as were presently about the village and of husbandmen; whereupon Bruno and Buffalmacco came with a box of pills and the flask of wine and made the folk stand in a ring. Then said Bruno, 'Gentlemen, needs must I tell you the reason wherefore you are here, so that, if aught betide that please you not, you may have no cause to complain of me. Calandrino here was robbed yesternight of a fine pig, nor can he find who hath had it; and for that none other than some one of us who are here can have stolen it from him, he proffereth each of you, that he may discover who hath had it, one of these pills to eat and a draught of wine. Now you must know that he who hath had the pig will not be able to swallow the pill; nay, it will seem to him more bitter than poison and he will spit it out; wherefore, rather than that shame be done him in the presence of so many, he were better tell it to the parson by way of confession and I386 will proceed no farther with this matter.'

All who were there declared that they would willingly eat of the pills, whereupon Bruno ranged them in order and set Calandrino among them; then, beginning at one end of the line, he proceeded to give each his bolus, and whenas he came over against Calandrino, he took one of the dogballs and put it into his hand. Calandrino clapped it incontinent into his mouth and began to chew it; but no sooner did his tongue taste the aloes, than he spat it out again, being unable to brook the bitterness. Meanwhile, each was looking other in the face, to see who should spit out his bolus, and whilst Bruno, not having made an end of serving them out, went on to do so, feigning to pay no heed to Calandrino's doing, he heard say behind him, 'How now, Calandrino? What meaneth this?' Whereupon he turned suddenly round and seeing that Calandrino had spat out his bolus, said, 'Stay, maybe somewhat else hath caused him spit it out. Take another of them.' Then, taking the other dogball, he thrust it into Calandrino's mouth and went on to finish giving out the rest. If the first ball seemed bitter to Calandrino, the second was bitterer yet; but, being ashamed to spit it out, he kept it awhile in his mouth, chewing it and shedding tears that seemed hazel-nuts so big they were, till at last, unable to hold out longer, he cast it forth, like as he had the first. Meanwhile Buffalmacco and Bruno gave the company to drink, and all, seeing this, declared that Calandrino had certainly stolen the pig from himself; nay, there were those there who rated him roundly.

After they were all gone, and the two rogues left alone with Calandrino, Buffalmacco said to him, 'I still had it for certain that it was thou tookst the pig thyself and wouldst fain make us believe that it had been stolen from thee, to escape giving us one poor while to drink of the monies thou hadst for it.' Calandrino, who was not yet quit of the bitter taste of the aloes, began to swear that he had not had it, and Buffalmacco said, 'But in good earnest, comrade, what gottest thou for it? Was it six florins?' Calandrino, hearing this, began to wax desperate, and Bruno said, 'Harkye, Calandrino, there was such an one in the company that ate and drank with us, who told me that thou hast a wench over yonder, whom thou keepest for thy pleasure and to whom thou givest whatsoever thou canst scrape together, and that he held it for certain that thou hadst sent her the pig. Thou hast learned of late to play pranks of this kind; thou carriedst us off t'other day down the Mugnone, picking up black stones, and whenas thou hadst gotten us aboard ship without biscuit,[384] thou madest off and wouldst after have us believe that thou hadst found the magic stone; and now on like wise thou thinkest, by dint of oaths, to make us believe that the pig, which thou hast given away or more like sold, hath been stolen from thee. But we are used to thy tricks and know them; thou shalt not avail to play us any more of them, and to be plain with thee, since we have been at pains to make the conjuration, we mean that thou shalt give us two pairs of capons;387 else will we tell Mistress Tessa everything.' Calandrino, seeing that he was not believed and himseeming he had had vexation enough, without having his wife's scolding into the bargain, gave them two pairs of capons, which they carried off to Florence, after they had salted the pig, leaving Calandrino to digest the loss and the flouting as best he might."

THE SEVENTH STORY

A SCHOLAR LOVETH A WIDOW LADY, WHO, BEING ENAMOURED OF ANOTHER, CAUSETH HIM SPEND ONE WINTER'S NIGHT IN THE SNOW AWAITING HER, AND HE AFTER CONTRIVETH, BY HIS SLEIGHT, TO HAVE HER ABIDE NAKED, ALL ONE MID-JULY DAY, ON THE SUMMIT OF A TOWER, EXPOSED TO FLIES AND GADS AND SUN

THE ladies laughed amain at the unhappy Calandrino and would have laughed yet more, but that it irked them to see him fleeced of the capons, to boot, by those who had already robbed him of the pig. But, as soon as the end of the story was come, the queen charged

Pampinea tell hers, and she promptly began thus: "It chanceth oft, dearest ladies, that craft is put to scorn by craft and it is therefore a sign of little wit to delight in making mock of others. We have, for several stories, laughed amain at tricks that have been played upon folk and whereof no vengeance is recorded to have been taken; but I purpose now to cause you have some compassion of a just retribution wreaked upon a townswoman of ours, on whose head her own cheat recoiled and was retorted well nigh unto death; and the hearing of this will not be without profit unto you, for that henceforward you will the better keep yourselves from making mock of others, and in this you will show great good sense.

Not many years ago there was in Florence, a young lady, by name Elena, fair of favour and haughty of humour, of very gentle lineage and endowed with sufficient abundance of the goods of fortune, who, being widowed of her husband, chose never to marry again, for that she was enamoured of a handsome and agreeable youth of her own choice, and with the aid of a maid of hers, in whom she put great trust, being quit of every other care, she often with marvellous delight gave herself a good time with him. In these days it chanced that a young gentleman of our city, by name Rinieri, having long studied in Paris, not for the sake of after selling his knowledge by retail, as many do, but to know the nature of things and their causes, the which excellently becometh a gentleman, returned thence to Florence and there lived citizen-fashion, much honoured as well for his nobility as for his learning. But, as it chanceth often that those, who have the most experience of things profound, are the soonest snared of love, even so it befell this Rinieri; for, having one day repaired, by way of diversion, to an entertainment, there presented herself before his eyes the aforesaid Elena, clad all in black, as our widows go, and full, to his judgment, of such beauty and pleasantness as himseemed he had never beheld in any other woman; and in his heart he deemed that he might call himself blest whom God should vouchsafe to hold her naked in his arms. Then, furtively considering her once and again and knowing that great things and precious were not to be acquired without travail, he altogether determined in himself to devote all his pains and all his diligence to the pleasing her, to the end that thereby he might gain her love and so avail to have his fill of her.

The young lady, (who kept not her eyes fixed upon the nether world, but, conceiting herself as much and more than as much as she was, moved them artfully hither and thither, gazing all about, and was quick to note who delighted to look upon her,) soon became aware of Rinieri and said, laughing, in herself, 'I have not come hither in vain to-day; for, an I mistake not, I have caught a woodcock by the bill.' Accordingly, she fell to ogling him from time to time with the tail of her eye and studied, inasmuch as she might, to let him see that she took note of him, thinking that the more men she allured and ensnared with her charms, so much the more of price would her beauty be, especially to him on whom she had bestowed it, together with her love. The learned scholar, laying aside philosophical speculations, turned all his thoughts to her and thinking to please her, enquired where she lived and proceeded to pass to and fro before her house, colouring his comings and goings with various pretexts, whilst the lady, idly glorying in this, for the reason already set out, made believe to take great pleasure in seeing him. Accordingly, he found means to clap up an acquaintance with her maid and discovering to her his love, prayed her make interest for him with her mistress, so he might avail to have her favour. The maid promised freely and told the lady, who hearkened with the heartiest laughter in the world and said, 'Seest thou where yonder man cometh to lose the wit he hath brought back from Paris? Marry, we will give him that which he goeth seeking. An he bespeak thee again, do thou tell him that I love him far more than he loveth me; but that it behoveth me look to mine honour, so I may hold up my head with the other ladies; whereof and he be as wise as folk say, he will hold me so much the dearer.' Alack, poor silly soul, she knew not aright, ladies mine, what it is to try conclusions with scholars. The maid went in search of Rinieri and finding him, did that which had been enjoined her of her mistress, whereat he was overjoyed and proceeded to use more urgent entreaties, writing letters and sending presents, all of which were accepted, but he got nothing but vague and general answers; and on this wise she held him in play a great while.

At last, to show her lover, to whom she had discovered everything and who was whiles somewhat vexed with her for this and had conceived some jealousy of Rinieri, that he did wrong to suspect her thereof, she despatched to the scholar, now grown very pressing, her maid, who told him, on her mistress's part, that she had never yet had an opportunity to do aught that might pleasure him since he had certified her of his love, but that on the occasion of the festival of the Nativity she hoped to be able to be with him; wherefore, an it liked him, he was on the evening of the feast to come by night to her courtyard, whither she would go for him as first she might. At this the scholar was the gladdest man alive and betook himself at the appointed time to his mistress's house, where he was carried by the maid into a courtyard and being there locked in, proceeded to wait the lady's coming. The latter had that evening sent for her lover and after she had supped merrily with him, she told him that which she purposed to do that night, adding, 'And thou mayst see for thyself what and how great is the love I have borne and bear him of whom thou hast taken a jealousy.' The lover heard these words with great satisfaction and was impatient to see by the fact that which the lady gave him to understand with words.

It had by chance snowed hard during the day and everything was covered with snow, wherefore the scholar had not long abidden in the courtyard before he began to feel colder than he could have wished; but, looking to recruit himself speedily, he was fain to endure it with patience. Presently, the lady said to her lover, 'Let us go look from a lattice what yonder fellow, of whom thou art waxed jealous, doth and hear what he shall answer the maid, whom I have sent to parley with him.' Accordingly, they betook themselves to a lattice and thence, seeing, without being seen, they heard the maid from another lattice bespeak the scholar and say, 'Rinieri, my lady is the woefullest woman that was aye, for that there is one of her brothers come hither to-night, who hath talked much with her and after must needs sup with her, nor is yet gone away; but methinketh he will soon be gone; wherefore she hath not been able to come to thee, but will soon come now and prayeth thee not to take the waiting in ill part.' Rinieri, believing this to be true, replied, 'Tell my lady to give herself no concern for me till such time as she can at her commodity come to me, but bid her do this as quickliest she may.' The maid turned back into the house and betook herself to bed, whilst the lady said to her gallant, 'Well, how sayst thou? Thinkest thou that, an I wished him such weal as thou fearest, I would suffer him stand a-freezing down yonder?' So saying, she betook herself to bed with her lover, who was now in part satisfied, and there they abode a great while in joyance and liesse, laughing and making mock of the wretched scholar, who fared to and fro the while in the courtyard, making shift to warm himself with exercise, nor had whereas he might seat himself or shelter from the night-damp. He cursed her brother's long stay with the lady and took everything he heard for the opening of a door to him by her, but hoped in vain.

The lady, having solaced herself with her lover till near upon midnight, said to him, 'How deemest thou, my soul, of our scholar? Whether seemeth to thee the greater, his wit or the love I bear him? Will the cold which I presently cause him suffer do away from thy mind the doubts which my pleasantries aroused therein the other day?' Whereto he replied, 'Heart of my body, yes, I know right well that, like as thou art my good and my peace and my delight and all my hope, even so am I thine.' 'Then,' rejoined she, 'kiss me a thousand times, so I may see if thou say sooth.' Whereupon he clipped her fast in his arms and kissed her not a thousand, but more than an hundred thousand times. Then, after they had abidden awhile in such discourse, the lady said, 'Marry, let us arise a little and go see if the fire is anydele spent, wherein this my new lover wrote me that he burnt all day long.' Accordingly, they arose and getting them to the accustomed lattice, looked out into the courtyard, where they saw the scholar dancing a right merry jig on the snow, so fast and brisk that never had they seen the like, to the sound of the chattering of the teeth that he made for excess of cold; whereupon quoth the lady, 'How sayst thou, sweet my hope? Seemeth to thee that I know how to make folk jig it without sound of trump or bagpipe?' Whereto he answered, laughing, 'Ay dost thou, my chief delight.' Quoth the lady, 'I will that we go down to the door; thou shalt abide quiet, whilst I bespeak him, and we shall hear what he will say; belike we shall have no less diversion thereof than we had from seeing him.'

Accordingly, they softly opened the chamber and stole down to the door, where, without opening it anydele, the lady called to the scholar in a low voice by a little hole that was there. Rinieri hearing himself called, praised God, taking it oversoon for granted that he was to be presently admitted, and coming up to the door, said, 'Here am I, madam; open for God's sake, for I die of cold.' 'O ay,' replied the lady, 'I know thou art a chilly one; is then the cold so exceeding great, because, forsooth, there is a little snow about? I wot the nights are much colder in Paris. I cannot open to thee yet, for that accursed brother of mine, who came to sup with me to-night, is not yet gone; but he will soon begone and I will come incontinent to open to thee. I have but now very hardly stolen away from him, that I might come to exhort thee not to wax weary of waiting.' 'Alack, madam,' cried the scholar, 'I pray you for God's sake open to me, so I may abide within under cover, for that this little while past there is come on the thickest snow in the world and it yet snoweth, and I will wait for you as long as it shall please you.' 'Woe's me, sweet my treasure,' replied the lady, 'that cannot I; for this door maketh so great a noise, whenas it is opened, that it would lightly be heard of my brother, if I should open to thee; but I will go bid him begone, so I may after come back and open to thee.' 'Then go quickly,' rejoined he; 'and I prithee let make a good fire, so I may warm me as soon as I come in, for that I am grown so cold I can scarce feel myself.' Quoth the lady, 'That should not be possible, an that be true which thou hast many a time written me, to wit, that thou burnest for the love of me. Now, I must go, wait and be of good heart.' Then, with her lover, who had heard all this with the utmost pleasure, she went back to bed, and that night they slept little, nay, they spent it well nigh all in dalliance and delight and in making mock of Rinieri.

Meanwhile, the unhappy scholar (now well nigh grown a stork, so sore did his teeth chatter,) perceiving at last that he was befooled, essayed again and again to open the door and sought an he might not avail to issue thence by another way; but, finding no means thereunto, he fell a-ranging to and fro like a lion, cursing the foulness of the weather and the lady's malignity and the length of the night, together with his own credulity; wherefore, being sore despited against his mistress, the long and ardent love he had borne her was suddenly changed to fierce and bitter hatred and he revolved in himself many and various things, so he might find a means of revenge, the which he now desired far more eagerly than he had before desired to be with the lady. At last, after much long tarriance, the night drew near unto day and the dawn began to appear;

whereupon the maid, who had been lessoned by the lady, coming down, opened the courtyard door and feigning to have compassion of Rinieri, said, 'Bad luck may he have who came hither yestereve! He hath kept us all night upon thorns and hath caused thee freeze; but knowest thou what? Bear it with patience, for that which could not be to-night shall be another time. Indeed, I know nought could have happened that had been so displeasing to my lady.'

The despiteful scholar, like a wise man as he was, who knew that threats are but arms for the threatened, locked up in his breast that which untempered will would fain have vented and said in a low voice, without anywise showing himself vexed, 'In truth I have had the worst night I ever had; but I have well apprehended that the lady is nowise to blame for this, inasmuch as she herself of her compassion for me, came down hither to excuse herself and to hearten me; and as thou sayest, that which hath not been to-night shall be another time. Commend me to her and God be with thee.' Therewithal, well nigh stark with cold, he made his way, as best he might, back to his house, where, being drowsed to death, he cast himself upon his bed to sleep and awoke well nigh crippled of his arms and legs; wherefore, sending for sundry physicians and acquainting them with the cold he had suffered, he caused take order for his cure. The leaches, plying him with prompt and very potent remedies, hardly, after some time, availed to recover him of the shrinking of the sinews and cause them relax; and but that he was young and that the warm season came on, he had overmuch to suffer. However, being restored to health and lustihead, he kept his hate to himself and feigned himself more than ever enamoured of his widow.

Now it befell, after a certain space of time, that fortune furnished him with an occasion of satisfying his desire [for vengeance], for that the youth beloved of the widow being, without any regard for the love she bore him, fallen enamoured of another lady, would have nor little nor much to say to her nor do aught to pleasure her, wherefore she pined in tears and bitterness. But her maid, who had great compassion of her, finding no way of rousing her mistress from the chagrin into which the loss of her lover had cast her and seeing the scholar pass along the street, after the wonted manner, entered into a fond conceit, to wit, that the lady's lover might be brought by some necromantic operation or other to love her as he had been wont to do and that the scholar should be a past master in this manner of thing, and told her thought to her mistress. The latter, little wise, without considering that, had the scholar been acquainted with the black art, he would have practised it for himself, lent her mind to her maid's words and bade her forthright learn from him if he would do it and give him all assurance that, in requital thereof, she would do whatsoever pleased him. The maid did her errand well and diligently, which when the scholar heard, he was overjoyed and said in himself, 'Praised be Thou, my God! The time is come when with Thine aid I may avail to make yonder wicked woman pay the penalty of the harm she did me in requital of the great love I bore her.' Then to the maid, 'Tell my lady,' quoth he, 'that she need be in no concern for this, for that, were her lover in the Indies, I would speedily cause him come to her and crave pardon of that which he hath done to displeasure her; but the means she must take to this end I purpose to impart to herself, when and where it shall most please her. So say to her and hearten her on my part.'

The maid carried his answer to her mistress and it was agreed that they should foregather at Santa Lucia del Prato, whither, accordingly, the lady, and the scholar being come and speaking together alone, she, remembering her not that she had aforetime brought him well nigh to death's door, openly discovered to him her case and that which she desired and besought him to succour her. 'Madam,' answered he, 'it is true that amongst the other things I learned at Paris was necromancy, whereof for certain I know that which is extant thereof; but for that the thing is supremely displeasing unto God, I had sworn never to practise it either for myself or for others. Nevertheless, the love I bear you is of such potency that I know not how I may deny you aught that you would have me do; wherefore, though it should behove me for this alone go to the devil's stead, I am yet ready to do it, since it is your pleasure. But I must forewarn you that the thing is more uneath to do than you perchance imagine, especially whenas a woman would recall a man to loving her or a man a woman, for that this cannot be done save by the very person unto whom it pertaineth; and it behoveth that whoso doth it be of an assured mind, seeing it must be done anights and in solitary places without company; which things I know not how you are disposed to do.' The lady, more enamoured than discreet, replied, 'Love spurreth me on such wise that there is nothing I would not do to have again him who hath wrongfully forsaken me. Algates, an it please you, show me in what I must approve myself assured of mind.' 'Madam,' replied the scholar, who had a patch of ill hair to his tail,[385] 'I must make an image of pewter in his name whom you desire to get again, which whenas I shall send you, it will behove you seven times bathe yourself therewith, all naked, in a running stream, at the hour of the first sleep, what time the moon is far on the wane. Thereafter, naked as you are, you must get you up into a tree or to the top of some uninhabited house and turning to the north, with the image in your hand, seven times running say certain words which I shall give you written; which when you shall have done, there will come to you two of the fairest damsels you ever beheld, who will salute you and ask you courteously what you would have done. Do you well and throughly discover to them your desires and look it betide you not to name one for another. As soon as you have told them, they will depart and you may then come down to the place where you shall have left your clothes and re-clothe yourself and return home; and for certain, ere it be the middle of the ensuing night, your lover will come, weeping, to crave you pardon and mercy; and know that from that time forth he will never again leave you for any other.'

The lady, hearing all this and lending entire faith thereto, was half comforted, herseeming she already had her lover again in her arms, and said, 'Never fear; I will very well do these things, and I have therefor the finest commodity in the world; for I have, towards the upper end of the Val d'Arno, a farm, which is very near the riverbank, and it is now July, so that bathing will be pleasant; more by token that I mind me there is, not far from the stream, a little uninhabited tower, save that the shepherds climb up bytimes, by a ladder of chestnut-wood that is there, to a sollar at the top, to look for their strayed beasts: otherwise it is a very solitary out-of-the-way[386] place. Thither will I betake myself and there I hope to do that which you shall enjoin me the best in the world.' The scholar, who very well knew both the place and the tower mentioned by the lady, was rejoiced to be certified of her intent and said, 'Madam, I was never in these part and therefore know neither the farm nor the tower; but, an it be as you say, nothing in the world can be better. Wherefore, whenas it shall be time, I will send you the image and the conjuration; but I pray you instantly, whenas you shall have gotten your desire and shall know I have served you well, that you be mindful of me and remember to keep your promise to me.' She answered that she would without fail do it and taking leave of him, returned to her house; whilst the scholar, rejoiced for that himseemed his desire was like to have effect, made an image with certain talismanic characters of his own devising, and wrote a rigmarole of his fashion, by way of conjuration; the which, whenas it seemed to him time, he despatched to the lady and sent to tell her that she must that very night, without more tarriance, do that which he had enjoined her; after which he secretly betook himself, with a servant of his, to the house of one of his friends who abode very near the tower, so he might give effect to his design.

The lady, on her part, set out with her maid and repaired to her farm, where, as soon as the night was come, she made a show of going to bed and sent the maid away to sleep, but towards the hour of the first sleep, she issued quietly forth of the house and betook herself to the bank of the Arno hard by the tower, where, looking first well all about and seeing nor hearing any, she put off her clothes and hiding them under a bush, bathed seven times with the image; after which, naked as she was, she made for the tower, image in hand. The scholar, who had, at the coming on of the night, hidden himself with his servant among the willows and other trees near the tower and had witnessed all this, seeing her, as she passed thus naked close to him, overcome the darkness of the night with the whiteness of her body and after considering her breast and the other parts of her person and seeing them fair, bethought himself what they should become in a little while and felt some compassion of her; whilst, on the other hand, the pricks of the flesh assailed him of a sudden and caused that stand on end which erst lay prone, inciting him to issue forth of his ambush and go take her and do his will of her. Between the one and the other he was like to be overcome; but, calling to mind who he was and what the injury he had suffered and wherefore and at whose hands and he being thereby rekindled in despite and compassion and carnal appetite banished, he abode firm in his purpose and let her go.

The lady, going up on to the tower and turning to the north, began to repeat the words given her by the scholar, who, coming quietly into the tower awhile after, little by little removed the ladder, which led to the sollar where she was, and after awaited that which she should do and say. Meanwhile, the lady, having seven times said her conjuration, began to look for the two damsels and so long was her waiting (more by token that she felt it cooler than she could have wished) that she saw the dawn appear; whereupon, woeful that it had not befallen as the scholar had told her, she said in herself, 'I fear me yonder man hath had a mind to give me a night such as that which I gave him; but, an that be his intent, he hath ill known to avenge himself, for that this night hath not been as long by a third as was his, forbye that the cold was of anothergates sort.' Then, so the day might not surprise her there, she proceeded to seek to go down from the tower, but found the ladder gone; whereupon her courage forsook her, as it were the world had failed beneath her feet, and she fell down aswoon upon the platform of the tower. As soon as her sense returned to her, she fell to weeping piteously and bemoaning herself, and perceiving but too well that this must have been the scholar's doing, she went on to blame herself for having affronted others and after for having overmuch trusted in him whom she had good reason to believe her enemy; and on this wise she abode a great while. Then, looking if there were no way of descending and seeing none, she fell again to her lamentation and gave herself up to bitter thought, saying in herself, 'Alas, unhappy woman! What will be said of thy brothers and kinsfolk and neighbours and generally of all the people of Florence, when it shall be known that thou has been found here naked? Thy repute, that hath hitherto been so great, will be known to have been false; and shouldst thou seek to frame lying excuses for thyself, (if indeed there are any to be found) the accursed scholar, who knoweth all thine affairs, will not suffer thee lie. Oh wretched woman, that wilt at one stroke have lost the youth so ill-fatedly beloved and thine own honour!'

Therewithal she fell into such a passion of woe that she was like to cast herself down from the tower to the ground; but, the sun being now risen and she drawing near to one side of the walls of the tower, to look if any boy should pass with cattle, whom she might send for her maid, it chanced that the scholar, who had slept awhile at the foot of a bush, awaking, saw her and she him; whereupon quoth he to her, 'Good day, madam; are the damsels come yet?' The lady, seeing and hearing him, began afresh to weep sore and besought him to come within the tower, so she might speak with him. In this he was courteous enough to comply with her and she laying herself prone on the platform and showing only her head at the opening, said, weeping, 'Assuredly, Rinieri, if I gave thee an ill night, thou hast well avenged thyself of me, for that, albeit it is July, I have thought to freeze this night, naked as I am, more by token that I have so sore bewept both the trick I put upon thee and mine own folly in believing thee that it is a wonder I have any eyes left in my head. Wherefore I entreat thee, not for the love of me, whom thou hast no call to love, but for the love of thyself, who are a gentleman, that thou be content, for vengeance of the injury I did thee, with that which thou hast already done and cause fetch me my clothes and suffer me come down hence, nor seek to take from me that which thou couldst not after restore me, an thou wouldst, to wit, my honour; for, if I took from thee the being with me that night, I can render thee many nights for that one, whenassoever it liketh thee. Let this, then, suffice and let it content thee, as a man of honour, to have availed to avenge thyself and to have caused me confess it. Seek not to use thy strength against a woman; no glory is it for an eagle to have overcome a dove, wherefore, for the love of God and thine own honour, have pity on me.'

The scholar, with stern mind revolving in himself the injury suffered and seeing her weep and beseech, felt at once both pleasure and annoy; pleasure in the revenge which he had desired more than aught else, and annoy he felt, for that his humanity moved him to compassion of the unhappy woman. However, humanity availing not to overcome the fierceness of his appetite [for vengeance], 'Madam Elena,' answered he, 'if my prayers (which, it is true, I knew not to bathe with tears nor to make honeyed, as thou presently knowest to proffer thine,) had availed, the night when I was dying of cold in thy snow-filled courtyard, to procure me to be put of thee but a little under cover, it were a light matter to me to hearken now unto thine; but, if thou be presently so much more concerned for thine honour than in the past and it be grievous to thee to abide up there naked, address these thy prayers to him in whose arms thou didst not scruple, that night which thou thyself recallest, to abide naked, hearing me the while go about thy courtyard, chattering with my teeth and trampling the snow, and get thee succour of him; cause him fetch thee thy clothes and set thee the ladder, whereby thou mayest descend, and study to inform him with tenderness for thine honour, the which thou hast not scrupled both now and a thousand other times to imperil for him. Why dost thou not call him to come help thee? To whom pertaineth it more than unto him? Thou art his; and what should he regard or succour, an he regard not neither succour thee? Call him, silly woman that thou art, and prove if the love thou bearest him and thy wits and his together can avail to deliver thee from my folly, whereof, dallying with him the while, thou questionedst aforetime whether himseemed the greater, my folly or the love thou borest him.[387] Thou canst not now be lavish to me of that which I desire not, nor couldst thou deny it to me, an I desired it; keep thy nights for thy lover, an it chance that thou come off hence alive; be they thine and his. I had overmuch of one of them and it sufficeth me to have been once befooled. Again, using thy craft and wiliness in speech, thou studiest, by extolling me, to gain my goodwill and callest me a gentleman and a man of honour, thinking thus to cajole me into playing the magnanimous and forebearing to punish thee for thy wickedness; but thy blandishments shall not now darken me the eyes of the understanding, as did thy disloyal promises whilere. I know myself, nor did I learn so much of myself what while I sojourned at Paris as thou taughtest me in one single night of thine. But, granted I were indeed magnanimous, thou art none of those towards whom magnanimity should be shown; the issue of punishment, as likewise of vengeance, in the case of wild beasts such as thou art, behoveth to be death, whereas for human beings that should suffice whereof thou speakest. Wherefore, albeit I am no eagle, knowing thee to be no dove, but a venomous serpent, I mean to pursue thee, as an immemorial enemy, with every hate and all my might, albeit this that I do to thee can scarce properly be styled vengeance, but rather chastisement, inasmuch as vengeance should overpass the offence and this will not attain thereto; for that, an I sought to avenge myself, considering to what a pass thou broughtest my soul, thy life, should I take it from thee, would not suffice me, no, nor the lives of an hundred others such as thou, since, slaying thee, I should but slay a vile, wicked and worthless trull of a woman. And what a devil more account (setting aside this thy scantling of fair favour,[388] which a few years will mar, filling it with wrinkles,) art thou than whatsoever other sorry serving-drab? Whereas it was no fault of thine that thou failedst of causing the death of a man of honour, as thou styledst me but now, whose life may yet in one day be of more service to the world than an hundred thousand of thy like could be what while the world endureth. I will teach thee, then, by means of this annoy that thou sufferest, what it is to flout men of sense, and particularly scholars, and will give thee cause never more, an thou comest off alive, to fall into such a folly. But, an thou have so great a wish to descend, why dost thou not cast thyself down? On this wise, with God's help, thou wilt, by breaking thy neck, at once deliver thyself from the torment, wherein it seemeth to thee thou art, and make me the joyfullest man in the world. Now, I have no more to say to thee. I knew to contrive on such wise that I caused thee go up thither; do thou now contrive to come down thence, even as thou knewest to befool me.'

What while the scholar spoke thus, the wretched lady wept without ceasing and the time lapsed by, the sun still rising high and higher; but, when she saw that he was silent, she said, 'Alack, cruel man, if the accursed night was so grievous to thee and if my default seem to thee so heinous a thing that neither my young beauty nor my bitter tears and humble prayers may avail to move thee to any pity, at least let this act of mine alone some little move thee and abate the rigour of thy rancour, to wit, that I but now trusted in thee and discovered to thee mine every secret, opening withal to thy desire a way whereby thou mightest avail to make me cognizant of my sin; more by token that, except I had trusted in thee, thou hadst had no means of availing to take of me that vengeance, which thou seemest to have so ardently desired. For God's sake, leave thine anger and pardon me henceforth; I am ready, so thou wilt but forgive me and bring me down hence, altogether to renounce yonder faithless youth and to have thee alone to lover and lord, albeit thou decriest my beauty, avouching it short-lived and little worth; natheless, whatever it be, compared with that of other women, yet this I know, that, if for nought else, it is to be prized for that it is the desire and pastime and delight of men's youth, and thou art not old. And albeit I am cruelly entreated of thee, I cannot believe withal that thou wouldst fain see me die so unseemly a death as were the casting myself down from this tower, as in desperation, before thine eyes, wherein, an thou was not a liar as thou are since become, I was erst so pleasing. Alack, have ruth on me for God's sake and pity's! The sun beginneth to wax hot, and like as the overmuch cold irked me this night, even so doth the heat begin to do me sore annoy.'

The scholar, who held her in parley for his diversion, answered, 'Madam, thou hast not presently trusted thine honour in my hands for any love that thou borest me, but to regain him whom thou hast lost, wherefore it meriteth but greater severity, and if thou think that this way alone was apt and opportune unto the vengeance desired of me, thou thinkest foolishly; I had a thousand others; nay, whilst feigning to love thee, I had spread a thousand snares about thy feet, and it would not have been long, had this not chanced, ere thou must of necessity have fallen into one of them, nor couldst thou have fallen into any but it had caused thee greater torment and shame than this present, the which I took, not to ease thee, but to be the quicklier satisfied. And though all else should have failed me, the pen had still been left me, wherewithal I would have written such and so many things of thee and after such a fashion that, whenas thou camest (as thou wouldst have come) to know of them, thou wouldst a thousand times a day have wished thyself never born. The power of the pen is far greater than they imagine who have not proved it with experience. I swear to God (so may He gladden me to the end of this vengeance that I take of thee, even as He hath made me glad thereof in the beginning!) that I would have written such things of thee, that, being ashamed, not to say before other folk, but before thine own self, thou shouldst have put out thine own eyes, not to see thyself in the glass; wherefore let not the little rivulet twit the sea with having caused it wax. Of thy love or that thou be mine, I reck not, as I have already said, a jot; be thou e'en his, an thou may, whose thou wast erst and whom, as I once hated, so at this present I love, having regard unto that which he hath wrought towards thee of late. You women go falling enamoured of young springalds and covet their love, for that you see them somewhat fresher of colour and blacker of beard and they go erect and jaunty and dance and joust, all which things they have had who are somewhat more in years, ay, and these know that which those have yet to learn. Moreover, you hold them better cavaliers and deem that they fare more miles in a day than men of riper age. Certes, I confess that they jumble a wench's furbelows more briskly; but those more in years, being men of experience, know better where the fleas stick, and little meat and savoury is far and away rather to be chosen than much and insipid, more by token that hard trotting undoth and wearieth folk, how young soever they be, whereas easy going, though belike it bring one somewhat later to the inn, at the least carrieth him thither unfatigued. You women perceive not, animals without understanding that you are, how much ill lieth hid under this scantling of fair seeming. Young fellows are not content with one woman; nay, as many as they see, so many do they covet and of so many themseemeth they are worthy; wherefore their love cannot be stable, and of this thou mayst presently of thine own experience bear very true witness. Themseemeth they are worthy to be worshipped and caressed of their mistresses and they have no greater glory than to vaunt them of those whom they have had; the which default of theirs hath aforetime cast many a woman into the arms of the monks, who tell no tales. Albeit thou sayst that never did any know of thine amours, save thy maid and myself, thou knowest it ill and believest awry, an thou think thus. His[389] quarter talketh well nigh of nothing else, and thine likewise; but most times the last to whose ears such things come is he to whom they pertain. Young men, to boot, despoil you, whereas it is given you[390] of men of riper years. Since, then, thou hast ill chosen, be thou his to whom thou gavest thyself and leave me, of whom thou madest mock, to others, for that I have found a mistress of much more account than thou, who hath been wise enough to know me better than thou didst. And that thou mayst carry into the other world greater assurance of the desire of mine eyes than meseemeth thou gatherest from my words, do but cast thyself down forthright and thy soul, being, as I doubt not it will be, straightway received into the arms of the devil, will be able to see if mine eyes be troubled or not at seeing thee fall headlong. But, as medoubteth thou wilt not consent to do me so much pleasure, I counsel thee, if the sun begin to scorch thee, remember thee of the cold thou madest me suffer, which an thou mingle with the heat aforesaid, thou wilt without fail feel the sun attempered.'

The disconsolate lady, seeing that the scholar's words tended to a cruel end, fell again to weeping and said, 'Harkye, since nothing I can say availeth to move thee to pity of me, let the love move thee, which thou bearest that lady whom thou hast found wiser than I and of whom thou sayst thou art beloved, and for the love of her pardon me and fetch me my clothes, so I may dress myself, and cause me descend hence.' Therewith the scholar began to laugh and seeing that tierce was now passed by a good hour, replied, 'Marry, I know not how to say thee nay, since thou conjurest me by such a lady; tell me where thy clothes are and I will go for them and help thee come down from up yonder.' The lady, believing this, was somewhat comforted and showed him where she had laid her clothes; whereupon he went forth of the tower and bidding his servant not depart thence, but abide near at hand and watch as most he might that none should enter there till such time as he should return, went off to his friend's house, where he dined at his ease and after, whenas himseemed time, betook himself to sleep; whilst the lady, left upon the tower, albeit some little heartened with fond hope, natheless beyond measure woebegone, sat up and creeping close to that part of the wall where there was a little shade, fell a-waiting, in company of very bitter thoughts. There she abode, now hoping and now despairing of the scholar's return with her clothes, and passing from one thought to another, she presently fell asleep, as one who was overcome of dolour and who had slept no whit the past night.

The sun, which was exceeding hot, being now risen to the meridian, beat full and straight upon her tender and delicate body and upon her head, which was all uncovered, with such force that not only did it burn her flesh, wherever it touched it, but cracked and opened it all over little by little, and such was the pain of the burning that it constrained her to awake, albeit she slept fast. Feeling herself on the roast and moving somewhat, it seemed as if all her scorched skin cracked and clove asunder for the motion, as we see happen with a scorched sheepskin, if any stretch it, and to boot her head irked her so sore that it seemed it would burst, which was no wonder. And the platform of the tower was so burning hot that she could find no restingplace there either for her feet or for otherwhat; wherefore, without standing fast, she still removed now hither and now thither, weeping. Moreover, there being not a breath of wind, the flies and gads flocked thither in swarms and settling upon her cracked flesh, stung her so cruelly that each prick seemed to her a pike-stab; wherefore she stinted not to fling her hands about, still cursing herself, her life, her lover and the scholar.

Being thus by the inexpressible heat of the sun, by the flies and the gads and likewise by hunger, but much more by thirst, and by a thousand irksome thoughts, to boot, tortured and stung and pierced to the quick, she started to her feet and addressed herself to look if she might see or hear any one near at hand, resolved, whatever might betide thereof, to call him and crave aid. But of this resource also had her unfriendly fortune deprived her. The husbandmen were all departed from the fields for the heat, more by token that none had come that day to work therenigh, they being all engaged in threshing out their sheaves beside their houses; wherefore she heard nought but crickets and saw the Arno, which latter sight, provoking in her desire of its waters, abated not her thirst, but rather increased it. In several places also she saw thickets and shady places and houses here and there, which were all alike to her an anguish for desire of them. What more shall we say of the ill-starred lady? The sun overhead and the heat of the platform underfoot and the stings of the flies and gads on every side had so entreated her that, whereas with her whiteness she had overcome the darkness of the foregoing night, she was presently grown red as ruddle,[391] and all bescabbed as she was with blood, had seemed to whoso saw her the foulest thing in the world.

As she abode on this wise, without aught of hope or counsel,[392] expecting death more than otherwhat, it being now past half none, the scholar, arising from sleep and remembering him of his mistress, returned to the tower, to see what was come of her, and sent his servant, who was yet fasting, to eat. The lady, hearing him, came, all weak and anguishful as she was for the grievous annoy she had suffered, overagainst the trap-door and seating herself there, began, weeping, to say, 'Indeed, Rinieri, thou hast beyond measure avenged thyself, for, if I made thee freeze in my courtyard by night, thou hast made me roast, nay burn, on this tower by day and die of hunger and thirst to boot; wherefore I pray thee by the One only God that thou come up hither and since my heart suffereth me not give myself death with mine own hands, give it me thou, for that I desire it more than aught else, such and so great are the torments I endure. Or, an thou wilt not do me that favour, let bring me, at the least, a cup of water, so I may wet my mouth, whereunto my tears suffice not; so sore is the drouth and the burning that I have therein.'

The scholar knew her weakness by her voice and eke saw, in part, her body all burnt up of the sun; wherefore and for her humble prayers there overcame him a little compassion of her; but none the less he answered, 'Wicked woman, thou shalt not die by my hands; nay, by thine own shalt thou die, an thou have a mind thereto; and thou shalt have of me as much water for the allaying of thy heat as I had fire of thee for the comforting of my cold. This much I sore regret that, whereas it behoved me heal the infirmity of my cold with the heat of stinking dung, that of thy heat will be healed with the coolth of odoriferous rose-water; and whereas I was like to lose both limbs and life, thou, flayed by this heat, wilt abide fair none otherwise than doth the snake, casting its old skin.' 'Alack, wretch that I am,' cried the lady, 'God give beauties on such wise acquired to those who wish me ill! But thou, that are more cruel than any wild beast, how couldst thou have the heart to torture me after this fashion? What more could I expect from thee or any other, if I had done all thy kinsfolk to death with the cruellest torments? Certes, meknoweth not what greater cruelty could be wreaked upon a traitor who had brought a whole city to slaughter than that whereto thou hast exposed me in causing me to be roasted of the sun and devoured of the flies and withal denying me a cup of water, whenas to murderers condemned of justice is oftentimes, as they go to their death, given to drink of wine, so but they ask it. Nay, since I see thee abide firm in thy savage cruelty and that my sufferance availeth not anywise to move thee, I will resign myself with patience to receive death, so God, whom I beseech to look with equitable eyes upon this thy dealing, may have mercy upon my soul.'

So saying, she dragged herself painfully to the midward of the platform, despairing to escape alive from so fierce a heat; and not once, but a thousand times, over and above her other torments, she thought to swoon for thirst, still weeping and bemoaning her illhap. However, it being now vespers and it seeming to the scholar he had done enough, he caused his servant take up the unhappy lady's clothes and wrap them in his cloak; then, betaking himself to her house, he found her maid seated before the door, sad and disconsolate and unknowing what to do, and said to her, 'Good woman, what is come of thy mistress?' 'Sir,' replied she, 'I know not. I thought to find her this morning in the bed whither meseemed I saw her betake herself yesternight; but I can find her neither there nor otherwhere and know not what is come of her; wherefore I suffer the utmost concern. But you, sir, can you not tell me aught of her?' Quoth he, 'Would I had had thee together with her whereas I have had her, so I might have punished thee of thy default, like as I have punished her for hers! But assuredly thou shalt not escape from my hands, ere I have so paid thee for thy dealings that thou shalt never more make mock of any man, without remembering thee of me.' Then to his servant, 'Give her the clothes,' quoth he, 'and bid her go to her mistress, an she will.' The man did his bidding and gave the clothes to the maid, who, knowing them and hearing what Rinieri said, was sore afraid lest they should have slain her mistress and scarce refrained from crying out; then, the scholar being done, she set out with the clothes for the tower, weeping the while.

Now it chanced that one of the lady's husbandmen had that day lost two of his swine and going in search of them, came, a little after the scholar's departure, to the tower. As he went spying about everywhere if he should see his hogs, he heard the piteous lamentation made of the miserable lady and climbing up as most he might, cried out, 'Who maketh moan there aloft?' The lady knew her husbandman's voice and calling him by name, said to him, 'For God's sake, fetch me my maid and contrive so she may come up hither to me.' Whereupon quoth the man, recognizing her, 'Alack, madam, who hath brought you up yonder? Your maid hath gone seeking you all day; but who had ever thought you could be here?' Then, taking the ladder-poles, he set them up in their place and addressed himself to bind the cross-staves thereto with withy bands.[393] Meanwhile, up came the maid, who no sooner entered the tower than, unable any longer to hold her tongue, she fell to crying out, buffeting herself the while with her hands, 'Alack, sweet my lady, where are you?' The lady, hearing her, answered as loudliest she might, 'O sister mine, I am here aloft. Weep not, but fetch me my clothes quickly.' When the maid heard her speak, she was in a manner all recomforted and with the husbandman's aid, mounting the ladder, which was now well nigh repaired, reached the sollar, where, whenas she saw her lady lying naked on the ground, all forspent and wan, more as she were a half-burnt log than a human being, she thrust her nails into her own face and fell a-weeping over her, no otherwise than as she had been dead.

The lady besought her for God's sake be silent and help her dress herself, and learning from her that none knew where she had been save those who had carried her the clothes and the husbandman there present, was somewhat comforted and prayed them for God's sake never to say aught of the matter to any one. Then, after much parley, the husbandman, taking the lady in his arms, for that she could not walk, brought her safely without the tower; but the unlucky maid, who had remained behind, descending less circumspectly, made a slip of the foot and falling from the ladder to the ground, broke her thigh, whereupon she fell a-roaring for the pain, that it seemed a lion. The husbandman, setting the lady down on a plot of grass, went to see what ailed the maid and finding her with her thigh broken, carried her also to the grass-plat and laid her beside her mistress, who, seeing this befallen in addition to her other troubles and that she had broken her thigh by whom she looked to have been succoured more than by any else, was beyond measure woebegone and fell a-weeping afresh and so piteously that not only could the husbandman not avail to comfort her, but himself fell a-weeping like wise. But presently, the sun being now low, he repaired, at the instance of the disconsolate lady, lest the night should overtake them there, to his own house, and there called his wife and two brothers of his, who returned to the tower with a plank and setting the maid thereon, carried her home, whilst he himself, having comforted the lady with a little cold water and kind words, took her up in his arms and brought her to her own chamber.

His wife gave her a wine-sop to eat and after, undressing her, put her to bed; and they contrived that night to have her and her maid carried to Florence. There, the lady, who had shifts and devices great plenty, framed a story of her fashion, altogether out of conformity with that which had passed, and gave her brothers and sisters and every one else to believe that this had befallen herself and her maid by dint of diabolical bewitchments. Physicians were quickly at hand, who, not without putting her to very great anguish and vexation, recovered the lady of a sore fever, after she had once and again left her skin sticking to the sheets, and on like wise healed the maid of her broken thigh. Wherefore, forgetting her lover, from that time forth she discreetly forbore both from making mock of others and from loving, whilst the scholar, hearing that the maid had broken her thigh, held himself fully avenged and passed on, content, without saying otherwhat thereof. Thus, then, did it befall the foolish young lady of her pranks, for that she thought to fool it with a scholar as she would have done with another, unknowing that scholars,—I will not say all, but the most part of them,—know where the devil keepeth his tail. Wherefore, ladies, beware of making mock of folk, and especially of scholars."

THE EIGHTH STORY

TWO MEN CONSORTING TOGETHER, ONE LIETH WITH THE WIFE OF HIS COMRADE, WHO, BECOMING AWARE THEREOF, DOTH WITH HER ON SUCH WISE THAT THE OTHER IS SHUT UP IN A CHEST, UPON WHICH HE LIETH WITH HIS WIFE, HE BEING INSIDE THE WHILE

ELENA'S troubles had been irksome and grievous to the ladies to hear; natheless, for that they deemed them in part justly befallen her, they passed them over with more moderate compassion, albeit they held the scholar to have been terribly stern and obdurate, nay, cruel. But, Pampinea being now come to the end of her story, the queen charged Fiammetta follow on, who, nothing loath to obey, said,

"Charming ladies, for that meseemeth the severity of the offended scholar hath somedele distressed you, I deem it well to solace your ruffled spirits with somewhat more diverting; wherefore I purpose to tell you a little story of a young man who received an injury in a milder spirit and avenged it after a more moderate fashion, by which you may understand that, whenas a man goeth about to avenge an injury suffered, it should suffice him to give as good as he hath gotten, without seeking to do hurt overpassing the behoof of the feud.

You must know, then, that there were once in Siena, as I have understood aforetime, two young men in easy enough case and of good city families, whereof one was named Spinelloccio Tanena and the other Zeppa di Mino, and they were next-door neighbours in Camollia.[394] These two young men still companied together and loved each other, to all appearance, as they had been brothers, or better; and each of them had a very fair wife. It chanced that Spinelloccio, by dint of much frequenting Zeppa's house, both when the latter was at home and when he was abroad, grew so private with his wife that he ended by lying with her, and on this wise they abode a pretty while, before any became aware thereof. However, at last, one day, Zeppa being at home, unknown to his wife, Spinelloccio came to call him and the lady said that he was abroad; whereupon the other came straightway up into the house and finding her in the saloon and seeing none else there, he took her in his arms and fell to kissing her and she him. Zeppa, who saw this, made no sign, but abode hidden to see in what the game should result and presently saw his wife and Spinelloccio betake themselves, thus embraced, to a chamber and there lock themselves in; whereat he was sore angered. But, knowing that his injury would not become less for making an outcry nor for otherwhat, nay, that shame would but wax therefor, he set himself to think what revenge he should take thereof, so his soul might abide content, without the thing being known all about, and himseeming, after long consideration, he had found the means, he abode hidden so long as Spinelloccio remained with his wife.

As soon as the other was gone away, he entered the chamber and there finding the lady, who had not yet made an end of adjusting her head-veils, which Spinelloccio had plucked down in dallying with her, said to her, 'Wife, what dost thou?' Quoth she, 'Seest thou not?' And Zeppa answered, 'Ay, indeed, I have seen more than I could wish.' So saying, he taxed her with that which had passed and she, in sore affright, confessed to him, after much parley, that which she could not aptly deny of her familiarity with Spinelloccio. Then she began to crave him pardon, weeping, and Zeppa said to her, 'Harkye, wife, thou hast done ill, and if thou wilt have me pardon it to thee, bethink thee punctually to do that which I shall enjoin thee, which is this; I will have thee bid Spinelloccio find an occasion to part company with me to-morrow morning, towards tierce, and come hither to thee. When he is here I will come back and so soon as thou hearest me, do thou make him enter this chest here and lock him therein. Then, when thou shalt have done this, I will tell thee what else thou shalt do; and have thou no fear of doing this, for that I promise thee I will do him no manner of hurt.' The lady, to satisfy him, promised to do his bidding, and so she did.

The morrow come and Zeppa and Spinelloccio being together towards tierce, the latter, who had promised the lady to be with her at that hour, said to the former, 'I am to dine this morning with a friend, whom I would not keep waiting for me; wherefore God be with thee.' Quoth Zeppa, 'It is not dinner-time yet awhile'; but Spinelloccio answered, 'No matter; I am to speak with him also of an affair of mine, so that needs must I be there betimes.' Accordingly, taking leave of him, he fetched a compass and making for Zeppa's house, entered a chamber with the latter's wife. He had not been there long ere Zeppa returned, whom when the lady heard, feigning to be mightily affrighted, she made him take refuge in the chest, as her husband had bidden her, and locking him therein, went forth of the chamber. Zeppa, coming up, said, 'Wife, is it dinner-time?' 'Ay,' answered she, 'forthright.' Quoth he, 'Spinelloccio is gone to dine this morning with a friend of his and hath left his wife alone; get thee to the window and call her and bid her come dine with us.' The lady, fearing for herself and grown therefor mighty obedient, did as he bade her and Spinelloccio's wife, being much pressed by her and hearing that her own husband was to dine abroad, came hither.

Zeppa made much of her and whispering his wife begone into the kitchen, took her familiarly by the hand and carried her into the chamber, wherein no sooner were they come than, turning back, he locked the door within. When the lady saw him do this, she said, 'Alack, Zeppa, what meaneth this? Have you then brought me hither for this? Is this the love you bear Spinelloccio and the loyal companionship you practise towards him?' Whereupon quoth Zeppa, drawing near to the chest wherein was her husband locked up and holding her fast, 'Madam, ere thou complainest, hearken to that which I have to say to thee. I have loved and love Spinelloccio as a brother, and yesterday, albeit he knoweth it not, I found that the trust I had in him was come to this, that he lieth with my wife even as with thee. Now, for that I love him, I purpose not to take vengeance of him, save on such wise as the offence hath been; he hath had my wife and I mean to have thee. An thou wilt not, needs must I take him here and for that I mean not to let this affront go unpunished, I will play him such a turn that neither thou nor he shall ever again be glad.' The lady, hearing this and believing what Zeppa said, after many affirmations made her of him, replied, 'Zeppa mine, since this vengeance is to fall on me, I am content, so but thou wilt contrive, notwithstanding what we are to do, that I may abide at peace with thy wife, even as I intend to abide with her, notwithstanding this that she hath done to me.' 'Assuredly,' rejoined Zeppa, 'I will do it; and to boot, I will give thee a precious and fine jewel as none other thou hast.' So saying, he embraced her; then, laying her flat on the chest, there to his heart's content, he solaced himself with her, and she with him.

Spinelloccio, hearing from within the chest all that Zeppa said his wife's answer and feeling the morrisdance[395] that was toward over his head, was at first so sore despited that himseemed he should die; and but that he stood in fear of Zeppa, he had rated his wife finely, shut up as he was. However, bethinking himself that the offence had begun with him and that Zeppa was in his right to do as he did and had indeed borne himself towards him humanely and like a comrade, he presently resolved in himself to be, an he would, more than ever his friend. Zeppa, having been with the lady so long as it pleased him, dismounted from the chest, and she asking for the promised jewel, he opened the chamber-door and called his wife, who said nought else than 'Madam, you have given me a loaf for my bannock'; and this she said laughing. To her quoth Zeppa, 'Open this chest.' Accordingly she opened it and therein Zeppa showed the lady her husband, saying, 'Here is the jewel I promised thee.' It were hard to say which was the more abashed of the twain, Spinelloccio, seeing Zeppa and knowing that he knew what he had done, or his wife, seeing her husband and knowing that he had both heard and felt that which she had done over his head. But Spinelloccio, coming forth of the chest, said, without more parley, 'Zeppa, we are quits; wherefore it is well, as thou saidst but now to my wife, that we be still friends as we were, and that, since there is nothing unshared between us two but our wives, we have these also in common.' Zeppa was content and they all four dined together in the utmost possible harmony; and thenceforward each of the two ladies had two husbands and each of the latter two wives, without ever having any strife or grudge anent the matter."

THE NINTH STORY

MASTER SIMONE THE PHYSICIAN, HAVING BEEN INDUCED BY BRUNO AND BUFFALMACCO TO REPAIR TO A CERTAIN PLACE BY NIGHT, THERE TO BE MADE A MEMBER OF A COMPANY THAT GOETH A-ROVING, IS CAST BY BUFFALMACCO INTO A TRENCH FULL OF ORDURE AND THERE LEFT

AFTER the ladies had chatted awhile over the community of wives practised by the two Siennese, the queen, with whom alone it rested to tell, so she would not do Dioneo an unright, began on this wise: "Right well, lovesome ladies, did Spinelloccio deserve the cheat put upon him by Zeppa; wherefore meseemeth he is not severely to be blamed (as Pampinea sought awhile ago to show), who putteth a cheat on those who go seeking it or deserve it. Now Spinelloccio deserved it, and I mean to tell you of one who went seeking it for himself. Those who tricked him, I hold not to be blameworthy, but rather commendable, and he to whom it was done was a physician, who, having set out for Bologna a sheepshead, returned to Florence all covered with miniver.[396]

As we see daily, our townsmen return hither from Bologna, this a judge, that a physician and a third a notary, tricked out with robes long and large and scarlets and minivers and store of other fine paraphernalia, and make a mighty brave show, to which how far the effects conform we may still see all day long. Among the rest a certain Master Simone da Villa, richer in inherited goods than in learning, returned hither, no great while since, a doctor of medicine, according to his own account, clad all in scarlet[397] and with a great miniver hood, and took a house in the street which we call nowadays the Via del Cocomero. This said Master Simone, being thus newly returned, as hath been said, had, amongst other his notable customs, a trick of asking whosoever was with him who was no matter what man he saw pass in the street, and as if of the doings and fashions of men he should compound the medicines he gave his patients, he took note of all and laid them all up in his memory. Amongst others on whom it occurred to him more particularly to cast his eyes were two painters of whom it hath already twice to-day been discoursed, namely, Bruno and Buffalmacco, who were neighbours of his and still went in company. Himseeming they recked less of the world and lived more merrily than other folk, as was indeed the case, he questioned divers persons of their condition and hearing from all that they were poor men and painters, he took it into his head that it might not be they lived so blithely of their poverty, but concluded, for that he had heard they were shrewd fellows, that they must needs derive very great profits from some source unknown to the general; wherefore he was taken with a desire to clap up an acquaintance, an he might, with them both, or at least with one of them, and succeeded in making friends with Bruno. The latter, perceiving, after he had been with him a few times, that the physician was a very jackass, began to give himself the finest time in the world with him and to be hugely diverted with his extraordinary humours, whilst Master Simone in like manner took a marvellous delight in his company.

After a while, having sundry times bidden him to dinner and thinking himself entitled in consequence to discourse familiarly with him, he discovered to him the wonderment that he felt at him and Buffalmacco, how, being poor men, they lived so merrily, and besought him to apprise him how they did. Bruno, hearing this talk from the physician and himseeing the question was one of his wonted witless impertinences, fell a-laughing in his sleeve, and bethinking himself to answer him according as his folly deserved, said, 'Doctor, there are not many whom I would tell how we do; but you I shall not scruple to tell, for that you are a friend and I know you will not repeat it to any. It is true we live, my friend and I, as merrily and as well as it appeareth to you, nay, more so, albeit neither of our craft nor of revenues we derive from any possessions might we have enough to pay for the very water we consume. Yet I would not, for all that, have you think that we go steal; nay, we go a-roving, and thence, without hurt unto any, we get us all to which we have a mind or for which we have occasion; hence the merry life you see us lead.'

The physician, hearing this and believing it, without knowing what it was, marvelled exceedingly and forthright conceiving an ardent desire to know what manner of thing this going a-roving might be, besought him very urgently to tell him, affirming that he would assuredly never discover it to any. 'Alack, doctor,' cried Bruno, 'what is this you ask me? This you would know is too great a secret and a thing to undo me and drive me from the world, nay, to bring me into the mouth of the Lucifer of San Gallo,[398] should any come to know it. But so great is the love I bear your right worshipful pumpkinheadship of Legnaja[399] and the confidence I have in you that I can deny you nothing you would have; wherefore I will tell it you, on condition that you swear to me by the cross at Montesone, never, as you have promised, to tell it to any one.

The physician declared that he would never repeat what he should tell him, and Bruno said, 'You must know, then, honey doctor mine, that not long since there was in this city a great master in necromancy, who was called Michael Scott, for that he was of Scotland, and who received the greatest hospitality from many gentlemen, of whom few are nowadays alive; wherefore, being minded to depart hence, he left them, at their instant prayers, two of his ablest disciples, whom he enjoined still to hold themselves in readiness to satisfy every wish of the gentlemen who had so worshipfully entertained him. These two, then, freely served the aforesaid gentlemen in certain amours of theirs and other small matters, and afterward, the city and the usages of the folk pleasing them, they determined to abide there always. Accordingly, they contracted great and strait friendship with certain of the townfolk, regarding not who they were, whether gentle or simple, rich or poor, but solely if they were men comfortable to their own usances; and to pleasure these who were thus become their friends, they founded a company of maybe five-and-twenty men, who should foregather twice at the least in the month in some place appointed of them, where being assembled, each should tell them his desire, which they would forthright accomplish unto him for that night. Buffalmacco and I, having an especial friendship and intimacy with these two, were put of them on the roll of the aforesaid company and are still thereof. And I may tell you that, what time it chanceth that we assemble together, it is a marvellous thing to see the hangings about the saloon where we eat and the tables spread on royal wise and the multitude of noble and goodly servants, as well female as male, at the pleasure of each one who is of the company, and the basons and ewers and flagons and goblets and the vessels of gold and silver, wherein we eat and drink, more by token of the many and various viands that are set before us, each in its season, according to that which each one desireth. I could never avail to set out to you what and how many are the sweet sounds of innumerable instruments and the songs full of melody that are heard there; nor might I tell you how much wax is burned at these suppers nor what and how many are the confections that are consumed there nor how costly are the wines that are drunken. But I would not have you believe, good saltless pumpkinhead mine, that we abide there in this habit and with these clothes that you see us wear every day; nay, there is none of us of so little account but would seem to you an emperor, so richly are we adorned with vestments of price and fine things. But, over all the other pleasures that be there is that of fair ladies, who, so one but will it, are incontinent brought thither from the four quarters of the world. There might you see the Sovereign Lady of the Rascal-Roughs, the Queen of the Basques, the wife of the Soldan, the Empress of the Usbeg Tartars, the Driggledraggletail of Norroway, the Moll-a-green of Flapdoodleland and the Madkate of Woolgathergreen. But why need I enumerate them to you? There be all the queens in the world, even, I may say, to the Sirreverence of Prester John, who hath his horns amiddleward his arse; see you now? There, after we have drunken and eaten confections and walked a dance or two, each lady betaketh herself to her bedchamber with him at whose instance she hath been brought thither. And you must know that these bedchambers are a very paradise to behold, so goodly they are; ay, and they are no less odoriferous than are the spice-boxes of your shop, whenas you let bray cummin-seed, and therein are beds that would seem to you goodlier than that of the Doge of Venice, and in these they betake themselves to rest. Marry, what a working of the treadles, what a hauling-to of the battens to make the cloth close, these weaveresses keep up, I will e'en leave you to imagine; but of those who fare best, to my seeming, are Buffalmacco and myself, for that he most times letteth come thither the Queen of France for himself, whilst I send for her of England, the which are two of the fairest ladies in the world, and we have known so to do that they have none other eye in their head than us.[400] Wherefore you may judge for yourself if we can and should live and go more merrily than other men, seeing we have the love of two such queens, more by token that, whenas we would have a thousand or two thousand florins of them, we get them not. This, then, we commonly style going a-roving, for that, like as the rovers take every man's good, even so do we, save that we are in this much different from them that they never restore that which they take, whereas we return it again, whenas we have used it. Now, worthy doctor mine, you have heard what it is we call going a-roving; but how strictly this requireth to be kept secret you can see for yourself, and therefore I say no more to you nor pray you thereof.'

The physician, whose science reached no farther belike than the curing children of the scald-head, gave as much credit to Bruno's story as had been due to the most manifest truth and was inflamed with as great desire to be received into that company as might be kindled in any for the most desirable thing in the world; wherefore he made answer to him that assuredly it was no marvel if they went merry and hardly constrained himself to defer requesting him to bring him to be there until such time as, having done him further hospitality, he might with more confidence proffer his request to him. Accordingly, reserving this unto a more favourable season, he proceeded to keep straiter usance with Bruno, having him morning and evening to eat with him and showing him an inordinate affection; and indeed so great and so constant was this their commerce that it seemed as if the physician could not nor knew how to live without the painter. The latter, finding himself in good case, so he might not appear ungrateful for the hospitality shown him, had painted Master Simone a picture of Lent in his saloon, besides an Agnus Dei at the entering in of his chamber and a chamber-pot over the street-door, so those who had occasion for his advice might know how to distinguish him from the others; and in a little gallery he had, he had depictured him the battle of the rats and the cats, which appeared to the physician a very fine thing. Moreover, he said whiles to him, whenas he had not supper with him overnight, 'I was at the society yesternight and being a trifle tired of the Queen of England, I caused fetch me the Dolladoxy of the Grand Cham of Tartary.' 'What meaneth Dolladoxy?' asked Master Simone. 'I do not understand these names.' 'Marry, doctor mine,' replied Bruno, 'I marvel not thereat, for I have right well heard that Porcograsso and Vannacena[401] say nought thereof.' Quoth the physician. 'Thou meanest Ipocrasso and Avicenna.' 'I' faith,' answered Bruno, 'I know not; I understand your names as ill as you do mine; but Dolladoxy in the Grand Cham's lingo meaneth as much as to say Empress in our tongue. Egad, you would think her a plaguy fine woman! I dare well say she would make you forget your drugs and your clysters and all your plasters.'

On this wise he bespoke him at one time and another, to enkindle him the more, till one night, what while it chanced my lord doctor held the light to Bruno, who was in act to paint the battle of the rats and the cats, the former, himseeming he had now well taken him with his hospitalities, determined to open his mind to him, and accordingly, they being alone together, he said to him, 'God knoweth, Bruno, there is no one alive for whom I would do everything as I would for thee; indeed, shouldst thou bid me go hence to Peretola, methinketh it would take little to make me go thither; wherefore I would not have thee marvel if I require thee of somewhat familiarly and with confidence. As thou knowest, it is no great while since thou bespokest me of the fashions of your merry company, wherefore so great a longing hath taken me to be one of you that never did I desire aught so much. Nor is this my desire without cause, as thou shalt see, if ever it chance that I be of your company; for I give thee leave to make mock of me an I cause not come thither the finest serving-wench thou ever setst eyes on. I saw her but last year at Cacavincigli and wish her all my weal;[402] and by the body of Christ, I had e'en given her half a score Bolognese groats, so she would but have consented to me; but she would not. Wherefore, as most I may, I prithee teach me what I must do to avail to be of your company and do thou also do and contrive so I may be thereof. Indeed, you will have in me a good and loyal comrade, ay, and a worshipful. Thou seest, to begin with, what a fine man I am and how well I am set up on my legs. Ay, and I have a face as it were a rose, more by token that I am a doctor of medicine, such as I believe you have none among you. Moreover, I know many fine things and goodly canzonets; marry, I will sing you one.' And incontinent he fell a-singing.

Bruno had so great a mind to laugh that he was like to burst; however he contained himself and the physician, having made an end of his song, said, 'How deemedst thou thereof?' 'Certes,' answered Bruno, 'there's no Jew's harp but would lose with you, so archigothically do you caterwarble it.' Quoth Master Simone, 'I tell thee thou wouldst never have believed it, hadst thou not heard me.' 'Certes,' replied Bruno, 'you say sooth!' and the physician went on, 'I know store of others; but let that be for the present. Such as thou seest me, my father was a gentleman, albeit he abode in the country, and I myself come by my mother of the Vallecchio family. Moreover, as thou mayst have seen, I have the finest books and gowns of any physician in Florence. Cock's faith, I have a gown that stood me, all reckoned, in nigh upon an hundred pounds of doits, more than half a score years ago; wherefore I pray thee as most I may, to bring me to be of your company, and by Cock's faith, an thou do it, thou mayst be as ill as thou wilt, for I will never take a farthing of thee for my services.'

Bruno, hearing this and the physician seeming to him a greater numskull than ever, said, 'Doctor, hold the light a thought more this way and take patience till I have made these rats their tails, and after I will answer you.' The tails being finished, Bruno made believe that the physician's request was exceeding irksome to him and said, 'Doctor mine, these be great things you would do for me and I acknowledge it; nevertheless, that which you ask of me, little as it may be for the greatness of your brain, is yet to me a very grave matter, nor know I any one in the world for whom, it being in my power, I would do it, an I did it not for you, both because I love you as it behoveth and on account of your words, which are seasoned with so much wit that they would draw the straps out of a pair of boots, much more me from my purpose; for the more I consort with you, the wiser you appear to me. And I may tell you this, to boot, that, though I had none other reason, yet do I wish you well, for that I see you enamoured of so fair a creature as is she of whom you speak. But this much I will say to you; I have no such power in this matter as you suppose and cannot therefore do for you that which were behoving; however, an you will promise me, upon your solemn and surbated[403] faith, to keep it me secret, I will tell you the means you must use and meseemeth certain that, with such fine books and other gear as you tell me you have, you will gain your end.'

Quoth the doctor, 'Say on in all assurance; I see thou art not yet well acquainted with me and knowest not how I can keep a secret. There be few things indeed that Messer Guasparruolo da Saliceto did, whenas he was judge of the Provostry at Forlimpopoli, but he sent to tell me, for that he found me so good a secret-keeper.[404] And wilt thou judge an I say sooth? I was the first man whom he told that he was to marry Bergamina: seest thou now?' 'Marry, then,' rejoined Bruno, 'all is well; if such a man trusted in you, I may well do so. The course you must take is on this wise. You must know that we still have to this our company a captain and two counsellors, who are changed from six months to six months, and without fail, at the first of the month, Buffalmacco will be captain and I shall be counsellor; for so it is settled. Now whoso is captain can do much by way of procuring whomsoever he will to be admitted into the company; wherefore meseemeth you should seek, inasmuch as you may, to gain Buffalmacco's friendship and do him honour. He is a man, seeing you so wise, to fall in love with you incontinent, and whenas with your wit and with these fine things you have you shall have somedele ingratiated yourself with him, you can make your request to him; he will not know how to say you nay. I have already bespoken him of you and he wisheth you all the weal in the world; and whenas you shall have done this, leave me do with him.' Quoth the physician, 'That which thou counsellest liketh me well. Indeed, an he be a man who delighteth in men of learning and talketh but with me a little, I will engage to make him go still seeking my company, for that, as for wit, I have so much thereof that I could stock a city withal and yet abide exceeding wise.'

This being settled, Bruno imparted the whole matter to Buffalmacco, wherefore it seemed to the latter a thousand years till they should come to do that which this arch-zany went seeking. The physician, who longed beyond measure to go a-roving, rested not till he made friends with Buffalmacco, which he easily succeeded in doing, and therewithal he fell to giving him, and Bruno with him, the finest suppers and dinners in the world. The two painters, like the accommodating gentlemen they were, were nothing loath to engage with him and having once tasted the excellent wines and fat capons and other good things galore, with which he plied them, stuck very close to him and ended by quartering themselves upon him, without awaiting overmuch invitation, still declaring that they would not do this for another. Presently, whenas it seemed to him time, the physician made the same request to Buffalmacco as he had made Bruno aforetime; whereupon Buffalmacco feigned himself sore chagrined and made a great outcry against Bruno, saying, 'I vow to the High God of Pasignano that I can scarce withhold myself from giving thee such a clout over the head as should cause thy nose drop to thy heels, traitor that thou art; for none other than thou hath discovered these matters to the doctor.'

Master Simone did his utmost to excuse Bruno, saying and swearing that he had learned the thing from another quarter, and after many of his wise words, he succeeded in pacifying Buffalmacco; whereupon the latter turned to him and said, 'Doctor mine, it is very evident that you have been at Bologna and have brought back a close mouth to these parts; and I tell you moreover that you have not learnt your A B C on the apple as many blockheads are fain to do; nay, you have learned it aright on the pumpkin, that is so long;[405]

and if I mistake not, you were baptized on a Sunday.[406] And albeit Bruno hath told me that you told me that you studied medicine there, meseemeth you studied rather to learn to catch men, the which you, with your wit and your fine talk, know better to do than any man I ever set eyes on.' Here the physician took the words out of his mouth and breaking in, said to Bruno, 'What a thing it is to talk and consort with learned men! Who would so have quickly apprehended every particular of my intelligence as hath this worthy man? Thou didst not half so speedily become aware of my value as he; but, at the least, that which I told thee, whenas thou saidst to me that Buffalmacco delighted in learned men, seemeth it to thee I have done it?' 'Ay hast thou,' replied Bruno, 'and better.'

Then said the doctor to Buffalmacco, 'Thou wouldst have told another tale, hadst thou seen me at Bologna, where there was none, great or small, doctor or scholar, but wished me all the weal in the world, so well did I know to content them all with my discourse and my wit. And what is more, I never said a word there, but I made every one laugh, so hugely did I please them; and whenas I departed thence, they all set up the greatest lament in the world and would all have had me remain there; nay, to such a pass came it for that I should abide there, that they would have left it to me alone to lecture on medicine to as many students as were there; but I would not, for that I was e'en minded to come hither to certain very great heritages which I have here and which have still been in my family; and so I did.' Quoth Bruno to Buffalmacco, 'How deemest thou? Thou believedst me not, whenas I told it thee. By the Evangels, there is not a leach in these parts who is versed in asses' water to compare with this one, and assuredly thou wouldst not find another of him from here to Paris gates. Marry, hold yourself henceforth [if you can,] from doing that which he will.' Quoth Master Simone, 'Bruno saith sooth; but I am not understood here. You Florentines are somewhat dull of wit; but I would have you see me among the doctors, as I am used to be.' 'Verily, doctor,' said Buffalmacco, 'you are far wiser than I could ever have believed; wherefore to speak to you as it should be spoken to scholars such as you are, I tell you, cut-and-slash fashion,[407] I will without fail procure you to be of our company.'

After this promise the physician redoubled in his hospitalities to the two rogues, who enjoyed themselves [at his expense,] what while they crammed him with the greatest extravagances in the world and fooled him to the top of his bent, promising him to give him to mistress the Countess of Jakes,[408]who was the fairest creature to be found in all the back-settlements of the human generation. The physician enquired who this countess was, whereto quoth Buffalmacco, 'Good my seed-pumpkin, she is a very great lady and there be few houses in the world wherein she hath not some jurisdiction. To say nothing of others, the Minor Friars themselves render her tribute, to the sound of kettle-drums.[409] And I can assure you that, whenas she goeth abroad, she maketh herself well felt,[410] albeit she abideth for the most part shut up. Natheless, it is no great while since she passed by your door, one night that she repaired to the Arno, to wash her feet and take the air a little; but her most continual abiding-place is in Draughthouseland.[411] There go ofttimes about store of her serjeants, who all in token of her supremacy, bear the staff and the plummet, and of her barons many are everywhere to be seen, such as Sirreverence of the Gate, Goodman Turd, Hardcake,[412] Squitterbreech and others, who methinketh are your familiars, albeit you call them not presently to mind. In the soft arms, then, of this great lady, leaving be her of Cacavincigli, we will, an expectation cheat us not, bestow you.'

The physician, who had been born and bred at Bologna, understood not their canting terms and accordingly avouched himself well pleased with the lady in question. Not long after this talk, the painters brought him news that he was accepted to member of the company and the day being come before the night appointed for their assembly, he had them both to dinner. When they had dined, he asked them what means it behoved him take to come thither; whereupon quoth Buffalmacco, 'Look you, doctor, it behoveth you have plenty of assurance; for that, an you be not mighty resolute, you may chance to suffer hindrance and do us very great hurt; and in what it behoveth you to approve yourself very stout-hearted you shall hear. You must find means to be this evening, at the season of the first sleep, on one of the raised tombs which have been lately made without Santa Maria Novella, with one of your finest gowns on your back, so you may make an honourable figure for your first appearance before the company and also because, according to what was told us (we were not there after) the Countess is minded, for that you are a man of gentle birth, to make you a Knight of the Bath at her own proper costs and charges; and there you must wait till there cometh for you he whom we shall send. And so you may be apprised of everything, there will come for you a black horned beast, not overbig, which will go capering about the piazza before you and making a great whistling and bounding, to terrify you; but, when he seeth that you are not to be daunted, he will come up to you quietly. Then do you, without any fear, come down from the tomb and mount the beast, naming neither God nor the Saints; and as soon as you are settled on his back, you must cross your hands upon your breast, in the attitude of obeisance, and touch him no more. He will then set off softly and bring you to us; but if you call upon God or the Saints or show fear, I must tell you that he may chance to cast you off or strike you into some place where you are like to stink for it; wherefore, an your heart misgive you and unless you can make sure of being mighty resolute, come not thither, for you would but do us a mischief, without doing yourself any good.'[413]

Quoth the physician, 'I see you know me not yet; maybe you judge of me by my gloves and long gown. If you knew what I did aforetimes at Bologna anights, when I went a-wenching whiles with my comrades, you would marvel. Cock's faith, there was such and such a night when, one of them refusing to come with us, (more by token that she was a scurvy little baggage, no higher than my fist,) I dealt her, to begin with, good store of cuffs, then, taking her up bodily, I dare say I carried her a crossbowshot and wrought so that needs must she come with us. Another time I remember me that, without any other in my company than a serving-man of mine, I passed yonder alongside the Cemetery of the Minor Friars, a little after the Ave Maria, albeit there had been a woman buried there that very day, and felt no whit of fear; wherefore misdoubt you not of this, for I am but too stout of heart and lusty. Moreover, I tell you that, to do you credit at my coming thither, I will don my gown of scarlet, wherein I was admitted doctor, and we shall see if the company rejoice not at my sight and an I be not made captain out of hand. You shall e'en see how the thing will go, once I am there, since, without having yet set eyes on me, this countess hath fallen so enamoured of me that she is minded to make me a Knight of the Bath. It may be knighthood will not sit so ill on me nor shall I be at a loss to carry it off with worship! Marry, only leave me do.' 'You say very well,' answered Buffalmacco; 'but look you leave us not in the lurch and not come or not be found at the trysting-place, whenas we shall send for you; and this I say for that the weather is cold and you gentlemen doctors are very careful of yourselves thereanent.' 'God forbid!' cried Master Simone. 'I am none of your chilly ones. I reck not of the cold; seldom or never, whenas I rise of a night for my bodily occasions, as a man will bytimes, do I put me on more than my fur gown over my doublet. Wherefore I will certainly be there.'

Thereupon they took leave of him and whenas it began to grow towards night, Master Simone contrived to make some excuse or other to his wife and secretly got out his fine gown; then, whenas it seemed to him time, he donned it and betook himself to Santa Maria Novella, where he mounted one of the aforesaid tombs and huddling himself up on the marble, for that the cold was great, he proceeded to wait the coming of the beast. Meanwhile Buffalmacco, who was tall and robust of his person, made shift to have one of those masks that were wont to be used for certain games which are not held nowadays, and donning a black fur pelisse, inside out, arrayed himself therein on such wise that he seemed a very bear, save that his mask had a devil's face and was horned. Thus accoutred, he betook himself to the new Piazza of Santa Maria, Bruno following him to see how the thing should go. As soon as he perceived that the physician was there, he fell a-capering and caracoling and made a terrible great blustering about the piazza, whistling and howling and bellowing as he were possessed of the devil. When Master Simone, who was more fearful than a woman, heard and saw this, every hair of his body stood on end and he fell a-trembling all over, and it was now he had liefer been at home than there. Nevertheless, since he was e'en there, he enforced himself to take heart, so overcome was he with desire to see the marvels whereof the painters had told him.

After Buffalmacco had raged about awhile, as hath been said, he made a show of growing pacified and coming up to the tomb whereon was the physician, stood stock-still. Master Simone, who was all a-tremble for fear, knew not what to do, whether to mount or abide where he was. However, at last, fearing that the beast should do him a mischief, an he mounted him not, he did away the first fear with the second and coming down from the tomb, mounted on his back, saying softly, 'God aid me!' Then he settled himself as best he might and still trembling in every limb, crossed his hands upon his breast, as it had been enjoined him; whereupon Buffalmacco set off at an amble towards Santa Maria della Scala and going on all fours, brought him hard by the Nunnery of Ripole. In those days there were dykes in that quarter, wherein the tillers of the neighbouring lands let empty the jakes, to manure their fields withal; whereto whenas Buffalmacco came nigh, he went up to the brink of one of them and taking the opportunity, laid hold of one of the physician's legs and jerking him off his back, pitched him clean in, head foremost. Then he fell a-snorting and snarling and capering and raged about awhile; after which he made off alongside Santa Maria della Scala till he came to Allhallows Fields. There he found Bruno, who had taken to flight, for that he was unable to restrain his laughter; and with him, after they had made merry together at Master Simone's expense, he addressed himself to see from afar what the bemoiled physician should do.

My lord leech, finding himself in that abominable place, struggled to arise and strove as best he might to win forth thereof; and after falling in again and again, now here and now there, and swallowing some drachms of the filth, he at last succeeded in making his way out of the dyke, in the woefullest of plights, bewrayed from head to foot and leaving his bonnet behind him. Then, having wiped himself as best he might with his hands and knowing not what other course to take, he returned home and knocked till it was opened to him. Hardly was he entered, stinking as he did, and the door shut again ere up came Bruno and Buffalmacco, to hear how he should be received of his wife, and standing hearkening, they heard the lady give him the foulest rating was ever given poor devil, saying, 'Good lack, what a pickle thou art in! Thou hast been gallanting it to some other woman and must needs seek to cut a figure with thy gown of scarlet! What, was not I enough for thee? Why, man alive, I could suffice to a whole people, let alone thee. Would God they had choked thee, like as they cast thee whereas thou deservedst to be thrown! Here's a fine physician for you, to have a wife of his own and go a-gadding anights after other folk's womankind!' And with these and many other words of the same fashion she gave not over tormenting him till midnight, what while the physician let wash himself from head to foot.

Next morning up came Bruno and Buffalmacco, who had painted all their flesh under their clothes with livid blotches, such as beatings use to make, and entering the physician's house, found him already arisen. Accordingly they went in to him and found the whole place full of stench, for that they had not yet been able so to clean everything that it should not stink there. Master Simone, seeing them enter, came to meet them and bade God give them good day; whereto the two rogues, as they had agreed beforehand, replied with an angry air, saying, 'That say we not to you; nay, rather, we pray God give you so many ill years that you may die a dog's death, as the most disloyal man and the vilest traitor alive; for it was no thanks to you that, whereas we studied to do you pleasure and worship, we were not slain like dogs. As it is, thanks to your disloyalty, we have gotten so many buffets this past night that an ass would go to Rome for less, without reckoning that we have gone in danger of being expelled the company into which we had taken order for having you received. An you believe us not, look at our bodies and see how they have fared.' Then, opening their clothes in front, they showed him, by an uncertain light, their breasts all painted and covered them up again in haste.

The physician would have excused himself and told of his mishaps and how and where he had been cast; but Buffalmacco said, 'Would he had thrown you off the bridge into the Arno! Why did you call on God and the Saints? Were you not forewarned of this?' 'By God His faith,' replied the physician, 'I did it not.' 'How?' cried Buffalmacco. 'You did not call on them? Egad, you did it again and again; for our messenger told us that you shook like a reed and knew not where you were. Marry, for the nonce you have befooled us finely; but never again shall any one serve us thus, and we will yet do you such honour thereof as you merit.' The physician fell to craving pardon and conjuring them for God's sake not to dishonour him and studied to appease them with the best words he could command. And if aforetime he had entreated them with honour, from that time forth he honoured them yet more and made much of them, entertaining them with banquets and otherwhat, for fear lest they should publish his shame. Thus, then, as you have heard, is sense taught to whoso hath learned no great store thereof at Bologna."

THE TENTH STORY

A CERTAIN WOMAN OF SICILY ARTFULLY DESPOILETH A MERCHANT OF THAT WHICH HE HAD BROUGHT TO PALERMO; BUT HE, MAKING BELIEVE TO HAVE RETURNED THITHER WITH MUCH GREATER PLENTY OF MERCHANDISE THAN BEFORE, BORROWETH MONEY OF HER AND LEAVETH HER WATER AND TOW IN PAYMENT

How much the queen's story in divers places made the ladies laugh, it needed not to ask; suffice it to say that there was none of them to whose eyes the tears had not come a dozen times for excess of laughter: but, after it had an end, Dioneo, knowing that it was come to his turn to tell, said, "Gracious ladies, it is a manifest thing that sleights and devices are the more pleasing, the subtler the trickster who is thereby artfully outwitted. Wherefore, albeit you have related very fine stories, I mean to tell you one, which should please you more than any other that hath been told upon the same subject, inasmuch as she who was cheated was a greater mistress of the art of cheating others than was any of the men or women who were cozened by those of whom you have told.

There used to be, and belike is yet, a custom, in all maritime places which have a port, that all merchants who come thither with merchandise, having unloaded it, should carry it all into a warehouse, which is in many places called a customhouse, kept by the commonality or by the lord of the place. There they give unto those who are deputed to that end a note in writing of all their merchandise and the value thereof, and they thereupon make over to each merchant a storehouse, wherein he layeth up his goods under lock and key. Moreover, the said officers enter in the book of the Customs, to each merchant's credit, all his merchandise, causing themselves after he paid their dues of the merchants, whether for all his said merchandise or for such part thereof as he withdraweth from the customhouse. By this book of the Customs the brokers mostly inform themselves of the quality and the quantity of the goods that are in bond there and also who are the merchants that own them; and with these latter, as occasion serveth them, they treat of exchanges and barters and sales and other transactions. This usance, amongst many other places, was current at Palermo in Sicily, where likewise there were and are yet many women, very fair of their person, but sworn enemies to honesty, who would be and are by those who know them not held great ladies and passing virtuous and who, being given not to shave, but altogether to flay men, no sooner espy a merchant there than they inform themselves by the book of the Customs of that which he hath there and how much he can do;[414] after which by their lovesome and engaging fashions and with the most dulcet words, they study to allure the said merchants and draw them into the snare of their love; and many an one have they aforetime lured thereinto, from whom they have wiled great part of their merchandise; nay, many have they despoiled of all, and of these there be some who have left goods and ship and flesh and bones in their hands, so sweetly hath the barberess known to ply the razor.

It chanced, not long since, that there came thither, sent by his masters, one of our young Florentines, by name Niccolo da Cignano, though more commonly called Salabaetto, with as many woollen cloths, left on his hands from the Salerno fair, as might be worth some five hundred gold florins, which having given the customhouse officers the invoice thereof, he laid up in a magazine and began, without showing overmuch haste to dispose of them, to go bytimes a-pleasuring about the city. He being of a fair complexion and yellow-haired and withal very sprightly and personable, it chanced that one of these same barberesses, who styled herself Madam Biancofiore, having heard somewhat of his affairs, cast her eyes on him; which he perceiving and taking her for some great lady, concluded that he pleased her for his good looks and bethought himself to order this amour with the utmost secrecy; wherefore, without saying aught thereof to any, he fell to passing and repassing before her house. She, noting this, after she had for some days well enkindled him with her eyes, making believe to languish for him, privily despatched to him one of her women, who was a past mistress in the procuring art and who, after much parley, told him, well nigh with tears in her eyes, that he had so taken her mistress with his comeliness and his pleasing fashions that she could find no rest day or night; wherefore, whenas it pleased him, she desired, more than aught else, to avail to foregather with him privily in a bagnio; then, pulling a ring from her pouch, she gave it to him on the part of her mistress. Salabaetto, hearing this, was the joyfullest man that was aye and taking the ring, rubbed it against his eyes and kissed it; after which he set it on his finger and replied to the good woman that, if Madam Biancofiore loved him, she was well requited it, for that he loved her more than his proper life and was ready to go whereassoever it should please her and at any hour. The messenger returned to her mistress with this answer and it was appointed Salabaetto out of hand at what bagnio he should expect her on the ensuing day after vespers.

Accordingly, without saying aught of the matter to any, he punctually repaired thither at the hour appointed him and found the bagnio taken by the lady; nor had he waited long ere there came two slave-girls laden with gear and bearing on their heads, the one a fine large mattress of cotton wool and the other a great basket full of gear. The mattress they set on a bedstead in one of the chambers of the bagnio and spread thereon a pair of very fine sheets, laced with silk, together with a counterpane of snow-white Cyprus buckram[415] and two pillows wonder-curiously wrought.[416] Then, putting off their clothes they entered the bath and swept it all and washed it excellent well. Nor was it long ere the lady herself came thither, with other two slave-girls, and accosted Salabaetto with the utmost joy; then, as first she had commodity, after she had both clipped and kissed him amain, heaving the heaviest sighs in the world, she said to him, 'I know not who could have brought me to this pass, other than thou; thou hast kindled a fire in my vitals, little dog of a Tuscan!' Then, at her instance, they entered the bath, both naked, and with them two of the slave-girls; and there, without letting any else lay a finger on him, she with her own hands washed Salabaetto all wonder-well with musk and clove-scented soap; after which she let herself be washed and rubbed of the slave-girls. This done, the latter brought two very white and fine sheets, whence came so great a scent of roses that everything there seemed roses, in one of which they wrapped Salabaetto and in the other the lady and taking them in their arms, carried them both to the bed prepared for them. There, whenas they had left sweating, the slave-girls did them loose from the sheets wherein they were wrapped and they abode naked in the others, whilst the girls brought out of the basket wonder-goodly casting-bottles of silver, full of sweet waters, rose and jessamine and orange and citron-flower scented, and sprinkled them all therewith; after which boxes of succades and wines of great price were produced and they refreshed themselves awhile.

It seemed to Salabaetto as he were in Paradise and he cast a thousand glances at the lady, who was certes very handsome, himseeming each hour was an hundred years till the slave-girls should begone and he should find himself in her arms. Presently, at her commandment, the girls departed the chamber, leaving a flambeau alight there; whereupon she embraced Salabaetto and he her, and they abode together a great while, to the exceeding pleasure of the Florentine, to whom it seemed she was all afire for love of him. Whenas it seemed to her time to rise, she called the slave-girls and they clad themselves; then they recruited themselves somedele with a second collation of wine and sweetmeats and washed their hands and faces with odoriferous waters; after which, being about to depart, the lady said to Salabaetto, 'So it be agreeable to thee, it were doing me a very great favour an thou camest this evening to sup and lie the night with me.' Salabaetto, who was by this time altogether captivated by her beauty and the artful pleasantness of her fashions and firmly believed himself to be loved of her as he were the heart out of her body, replied, 'Madam, your every pleasure is supremely agreeable to me, wherefore both to-night and at all times I mean to do that which shall please you and that which shall be commanded me of you.'

Accordingly the lady returned to her house, where she caused well bedeck her bedchamber with her dresses and gear and letting make ready a splendid supper, awaited Salabaetto, who, as soon as it was grown somewhat dark, betook himself thither and being received with open arms, supped with all cheer and commodity of service. Thereafter they betook themselves into the bedchamber, where he smelt a marvellous fragrance of aloes-wood and saw the bed very richly adorned with Cyprian singing-birds[417] and store of fine dresses upon the pegs, all which things together and each of itself made him conclude that this must be some great and rich lady. And although he had heard some whispers to the contrary anent her manner of life, he would not anywise believe it; or, if he e'en gave so much credit thereto as to allow that she might erst have cozened others, for nothing in the world could he have believed that this might possibly happen to himself. He lay that night with her in the utmost delight, still waxing more enamoured, and in the morning she girt him on a quaint and goodly girdle of silver, with a fine purse thereto, saying, 'Sweet my Salabaetto, I commend myself to thy remembrance, and like as my person is at thy pleasure, even so is all that is here and all that dependeth upon me at thy service and commandment.' Salabaetto, rejoiced, embraced and kissed her; then, going forth of her house, he betook himself whereas the other merchants were used to resort.

On this wise consorting with her at one time and another, without its costing him aught in the world, and growing every hour more entangled, it befell that he sold his stuffs for ready money and made a good profit thereby; of which the lady incontinent heard, not from him, but from others, and Salabaetto being come one night to visit her, she fell to prattling and wantoning with him, kissing and clipping him and feigning herself so enamoured of him that it seemed she must die of love in his arms. Moreover, she would fain have given him two very fine hanaps of silver that she had; but he would not take them, for that he had had of her, at one time and another, what was worth a good thirty gold florins, without availing to have her take of him so much as a groat's worth. At last, whenas she had well enkindled him by showing herself so enamoured and freehanded, one of her slave-girls called her, as she had ordained beforehand; whereupon she left the chamber and coming back, after awhile, in tears cast herself face downward on the bed and fell to making the woefullest lamentation ever woman made. Salabaetto, marvelling at this, caught her in his arms and fell a-weeping with her and saying, 'Alack, heart of my body, what aileth thee thus suddenly? What is the cause of this grief? For God's sake, tell it me, my soul.' The lady, after letting herself be long entreated, answered, 'Woe's me, sweet my lord, I know not what to say or to do; I have but now received letters from Messina and my brother writeth me that, should I sell or pawn all that is here,[418] I must without fail send him a thousand gold florins within eight days from this time, else will his head be cut off; and I know not how I shall do to get this sum so suddenly. Had I but fifteen days' grace, I would find a means of procuring it from a certain quarter whence I am to have much more, or I would sell one of our farms; but, as this may not be, I had liefer be dead than that this ill news should have come to me.'

So saying, she made a show of being sore afflicted and stinted not from weeping; whereupon quoth Salabaetto, whom the flames of love had bereft of great part of his wonted good sense, so that he believed her tears to be true and her words truer yet, 'Madam, I cannot oblige you with a thousand florins, but five hundred I can very well advance you, since you believe you will be able to return them to me within a fortnight from this time; and this is of your good fortune that I chanced but yesterday to sell my stuffs; for, had it not been so, I could not have lent you a groat.' 'Alack,' cried the lady, 'hast thou then been straitened for lack of money? Marry, why didst thou not require me thereof? Though I have not a thousand, I had an hundred and even two hundred to give thee. Thou hast deprived me of all heart to accept of thee the service thou profferest me.' Salabaetto was more than ever taken with these words and said, 'Madam, I would not have you refrain on that account, for, had I had such an occasion therefor as you presently have, I would assuredly have asked you.' 'Alack, Salabaetto mine,' replied the lady, 'now know I aright that thine is a true and perfect love for me, since, without waiting to be required, thou freely succoureth me, in such a strait, with so great a sum of money. Certes, I was all thine without this, but with this I shall be far more so; nor shall I ever forget that I owe thee my brother's life. But God knoweth I take it sore unwillingly, seeing that thou art a merchant and that with money merchants transact all their affairs; however, since need constraineth me, and I have certain assurance of speedily restoring it to thee, I will e'en take it; and for the rest, an I find no readier means, I will pawn all these my possessions.' So saying, she let herself fall, weeping, on Salabaetto's neck. He fell to comforting her and after abiding the night with her, he, next morning, to approve himself her most liberal servant, without waiting to be asked by her, carried her five hundred right gold florins, which she received with tears in her eyes, but laughter in her heart, Salabaetto contenting himself with her simple promise.

As soon as the lady had the money, the signs began to change, and whereas before he had free access to her whenassoever it pleased him, reasons now began to crop up, whereby it betided him not to win admission there once out of seven times, nor was he received with the same countenance nor the same caresses and rejoicings as before. And the term at which he was to have had his monies again being, not to say come, but past by a month or two and he requiring them, words were given him in payment. Thereupon his eyes were opened to the wicked woman's arts and his own lack of wit, wherefore, feeling that he could say nought of her beyond that which might please her concerning the matter, since he had neither script nor other evidence thereof, and being ashamed to complain to any, as well for that he had been forewarned thereof as for fear of the scoffs which he might reasonably expect for his folly, he was beyond measure woeful and inwardly bewailed his credulity.

At last, having had divers letters from his masters, requiring him to change[419] the monies in question and remit them to them, he determined to depart, lest, an he did it not, his default should be discovered there, and accordingly, going aboard a little ship, he betook himself, not to Pisa, as he should have done, but to Naples. There at that time was our gossip Pietro dello Canigiano, treasurer to the Empress of Constantinople, a man of great understanding and subtle wit and a fast friend of Salabaetto and his family; and to him, as to a very discreet man, the disconsolate Florentine recounted that which he had done and the mischance that had befallen him, requiring him of aid and counsel, so he might contrive to gain his living there, and avouching his intention nevermore to return to Florence. Canigiano was concerned for this and said, 'Ill hast thou done and ill hast thou carried thyself; thou hast disobeyed thy masters and hast, at one cast, spent a great sum of money in wantonness; but, since it is done, we must look for otherwhat.'[420] Accordingly, like a shrewd man as he was, he speedily bethought himself what was to be done and told it to Salabaetto, who was pleased with the device and set about putting it in execution. He had some money and Canigiano having lent him other some, he made up a number of bales well packed and corded; then, buying a score of oil-casks and filling them, he embarked the whole and returned to Palermo, where, having given the customhouse officers the bill of lading and the value of the casks and let enter everything to his account, he laid the whole up in the magazines, saying that he meant not to touch them till such time as certain other merchandise which he expected should be come.

Biancofiore, getting wind of this and hearing that the merchandise he had presently brought with him was worth good two thousand florins, without reckoning what he looked for, which was valued at more than three thousand, bethought herself that she had flown at too small game and determined to restore him the five hundred florins, so she might avail to have the greater part of the five thousand. Accordingly, she sent for him and Salabaetto, grown cunning, went to her; whereupon, making believe to know nothing of that which he had brought with him, she received him with a great show of fondness and said to him, 'Harkye, if thou wast vexed with me, for that I repaid thee not thy monies on the very day....' Salabaetto fell a-laughing and answered; 'In truth, madam, it did somewhat displease me, seeing I would have torn out my very heart to give it you, an I thought to pleasure you withal; but I will have you hear how I am vexed with you. Such and so great is the love I bear you, that I have sold the most part of my possessions and have presently brought hither merchandise to the value of more than two thousand florins and expect from the westward as much more as will be worth over three thousand, with which I mean to stock me a warehouse in this city and take up my sojourn here, so I may still be near you, meseeming I fare better of your love than ever lover of his lady.'

'Look you, Salabaetto,' answered the lady, 'every commodity of thine is mighty pleasing to me, as that of him whom I love more than my life, and it pleaseth me amain that thou art returned hither with intent to sojourn here, for that I hope yet to have good time galore with thee; but I would fain excuse myself somedele to thee for that, whenas thou wast about to depart, thou wouldst bytimes have come hither and couldst not, and whiles thou camest and wast not so gladly seen as thou wast used to be, more by token that I returned thee not thy monies at the time promised. Thou must know that I was then in very great concern and sore affliction, and whoso is in such case, how much soever he may love another, cannot always show him so cheerful a countenance or pay him such attention as he might wish. Moreover, thou must know that it is mighty uneasy for a woman to avail to find a thousand gold florins; all day long we are put off with lies and that which is promised us is not performed unto us; wherefore needs must we in our turn lie unto others. Hence cometh it, and not of my default, that I gave thee not back thy monies. However, I had them a little after thy departure, and had I known whither to send them, thou mayst be assured that I would have remitted them to thee; but, not knowing this, I kept them for thee.' Then, letting fetch a purse wherein were the very monies he had brought her, she put it into his hand, saying, 'Count them if there be five hundred.' Never was Salabaetto so glad; he counted them and finding them five hundred, put them up and said, 'Madam, I am assured that you say sooth; but you have done enough [to convince me of your love for me,] and I tell you that, for this and for the love I bear you, you could never require me, for any your occasion, of whatsoever sum I might command, but I would oblige you therewith; and whenas I am established here, you may put this to the proof.'

Having again on this wise renewed his loves with her in words, he fell again to using amically with her, whilst she made much of him and showed him the greatest goodwill and honour in the world, feigning the utmost love for him. But he, having a mind to return her cheat for cheat, being one day sent for by her to sup and sleep with her, went thither so chapfallen and so woebegone that it seemed as he would die. Biancofiore, embracing him and kissing him, began to question him of what ailed him to be thus melancholy, and he, after letting himself be importuned a good while, answered, 'I am a ruined man, for that the ship, wherein is the merchandise I expected, hath been taken by the corsairs of Monaco and held to ransom in ten thousand gold florins, whereof it falleth to me to pay a thousand, and I have not a farthing, for that the five hundred pieces thou returnedst to me I sent incontinent to Naples to lay out in cloths to be brought hither; and should I go about at this present to sell the merchandise I have here, I should scarce get a penny for two pennyworth, for that it is no time for selling. Nor am I yet so well known that I could find any here to help me to this, wherefore I know not what to do or to say; for, if I send not the monies speedily, the merchandise will be carried off to Monaco and I shall never again have aught thereof.'

The lady was mightily concerned at this, fearing to lose him altogether, and considering how she should do, so he might not go to Monaco, said, 'God knoweth I am sore concerned for the love of thee; but what availeth it to afflict oneself thus? If I had the monies, God knoweth I would lend them to thee incontinent; but I have them not. True, there is a certain person here who obliged me the other day with the five hundred florins that I lacked; but he will have heavy usance for his monies; nay, he requireth no less than thirty in the hundred, and if thou wilt borrow of him, needs must he be made secure with a good pledge. For my part, I am ready to engage for thee all these my goods and my person, to boot, for as much as he will lend thereon; but how wilt thou assure him of the rest?' Salabaetto readily apprehended the reason that moved her to do him this service and divined that it was she herself who was to lend him the money; wherewith he was well pleased and thanking her, answered that he would not be put off for exorbitant usance, need constraining him. Moreover, he said that he would give assurance of the merchandise he had in the customhouse, letting inscribe it to him who should lend him the money; but that needs must be kept the key of the magazines, as well that he might be able to show his wares, an it were required of him, as that nothing might be touched or changed or tampered withal.

The lady answered that it was well said and that this was good enough assurance; wherefore, as soon as the day was come, she sent for a broker, in whom she trusted greatly, and taking order with him of the matter, gave him a thousand gold florins, which he lent to Salabaetto, letting inscribe in his own name at the customhouse that which the latter had there; then, having made their writings and counter-writings together and being come to an accord,[421] they occupied themselves with their other affairs. Salabaetto, as soonest he might, embarked, with the fifteen hundred gold florins, on board a little ship and returned to Pietro dello Canigiano at Naples, whence he remitted to his masters, who had despatched him with the stuffs, a good and entire account thereof. Then, having repaid Pietro and every other to whom he owed aught, he made merry several days with Canigiano over the cheat he had put upon the Sicilian trickstress; after which, resolved to be no more a merchant, he betook himself to Ferrara.

Meanwhile, Biancofiore, finding that Salabaetto had left Palermo, began to marvel and wax misdoubtful and after having awaited him good two months, seeing that he came not, she caused the broker force open the magazines. Trying first the casks, which she believed to be filled with oil, she found them full of seawater, save that there was in each maybe a runlet of oil at the top near the bunghole. Then, undoing the bales, she found them all full of tow, with the exception of two, which were stuffs; and in brief, with all that was there, there was not more than two hundred florins' worth. Wherefore Biancofiore, confessing herself outwitted, long lamented the five hundred florins repaid and yet more the thousand lent, saying often, 'Who with a Tuscan hath to do, Must nor be blind nor see askew.' On this wise, having gotten nothing for her pains but loss and scorn, she found, to her cost, that some folk know as much as others."

No sooner had Dioneo made an end of his story than Lauretta, knowing the term to be come beyond which she was not to reign and having commended Canigiano's counsel (which was approved good by its effect) and Salabaetto's shrewdness (which was no less commendable) in carrying it into execution, lifted the laurel from her own head and set it on that of Emilia, saying, with womanly grace, "Madam, I know not how pleasant a queen we shall have of you; but, at the least, we shall have a fair one. Look, then, that your actions be conformable to your beauties." So saying, she returned to her seat, whilst Emilia, a thought abashed, not so much at being made queen as to see herself publicly commended of that which women use most to covet, waxed such in face as are the new-blown roses in the dawning. However, after she had kept her eyes awhile lowered, till the redness had given place, she took order with the seneschal of that which concerned the general entertainment and presently said, "Delightsome ladies, it is common, after oxen have toiled some part of the day, confined under the yoke, to see them loosed and eased thereof and freely suffered to go a-pasturing, where most it liketh them, about the woods; and it is manifest also that leafy gardens, embowered with various plants, are not less, but much more fair than groves wherein one seeth only oaks. Wherefore, seeing how many days we have discoursed, under the restraint of a fixed law, I opine that, as well unto us as to those whom need constraineth to labour for their daily bread, it is not only useful, but necessary, to play the truant awhile and wandering thus afield, to regain strength to enter anew under the yoke. Wherefore, for that which is to be related to-morrow, ensuing your delectable usance of discourse, I purpose not to restrict you to any special subject, but will have each discourse according as it pleaseth him, holding it for certain that the variety of the things which will be said will afford us no less entertainment than to have discoursed of one alone; and having done thus, whoso shall come after me in the sovranty may, as stronger than I, avail with greater assurance to restrict us within the limits of the wonted laws." So saying, she set every one at liberty till supper-time.

All commended the queen of that which she had said, holding it sagely spoken, and rising to their feet, addressed themselves, this to one kind of diversion and that to another, the ladies to weaving garlands and to gambolling and the young men to gaming and singing. On this wise they passed the time until the supper-hour, which being come, they supped with mirth and good cheer about the fair fountain and after diverted themselves with singing and dancing according to the wonted usance. At last, the queen, to ensue the fashion of her predecessors, commanded Pamfilo to sing a song, notwithstanding those which sundry of the company had already sung of their freewill; and he readily began thus:

Such is thy pleasure, Love
And such the allegresse I feel thereby
That happy, burning in thy fire, am I.

The abounding gladness in my heart that glows,
For the high joy and dear
Whereto thou hast me led,
Unable to contain there, overflows
And in my face's cheer
Displays my happihead;
For being enamouréd
In such a worship-worthy place and high
Makes eath to me the burning I aby.

I cannot with my finger what I feel
Limn, Love, nor do I know
My bliss in song to vent;
Nay, though I knew it, needs must I conceal,
For, once divulged, I trow
'Twould turn to dreariment.
Yet am I so content,
All speech were halt and feeble, did I try
The least thereof with words to signify.

Who might conceive it that these arms of mine
Should anywise attain
Whereas I've held them aye,
Or that my face should reach so fair a shrine
As that, of favour fain
And grace, I've won to? Nay,
Such fortune ne'er a day

Believed me were; whence all afire am I,
Hiding the source of my liesse thereby.

This was the end of Pamfilo's song, whereto albeit it had been completely responded of all, there was none but noted the words thereof with more attent solicitude than pertained unto him, studying to divine that which, as he sang, it behoved him to keep hidden from them; and although sundry went imagining various things, nevertheless none happened upon the truth of the case.[422] But the queen, seeing that the song was ended and that both young ladies and men would gladly rest themselves, commanded that all should betake themselves to bed.

HERE ENDETH THE EIGHTH DAY
OF THE DECAMERON

Day the Ninth

HERE BEGINNETH THE NINTH DAY OF THE DECAMERON WHEREIN UNDER THE GOVERNANCE OF EMILIA EACH DISCOURSETH ACCORDING AS IT PLEASETH HIM AND OF THAT WHICH IS MOST TO HIS LIKING

THE light, from whose resplendence the night fleeth, had already changed all the eighth heaven[423] from azure to watchet-colour[424] and the flowerets began to lift their heads along the meads, when Emilia, uprising, let call the ladies her comrades and on like wise the young men, who, being come, fared forth, ensuing the slow steps of the queen, and betook themselves to a coppice but little distant from the palace. Therein entering, they saw the animals, wild goats and deer and others, as if assured of security from the hunters by reason of the prevailing pestilence, stand awaiting them no otherwise than as they were grown without fear or tame, and diverted themselves awhile with them, drawing near, now to this one and now to that, as if they would fain lay hands on them, and making them run and skip. But, the sun now waxing high, they deemed it well to turn back. They were all garlanded with oak leaves, with their hands full of flowers and sweet-scented herbs, and whoso encountered them had said no otherwhat than "Or these shall not be overcome of death or it will slay them merry." On this wise, then, they fared on, step by step, singing and chatting and laughing, till they came to the palace, where they found everything orderly disposed and their servants full of mirth and joyous cheer. There having rested awhile, they went not to dinner till half a dozen canzonets, each merrier than other, had been carolled by the young men and the ladies; then, water being given to their hands, the seneschal seated them all at table, according to the queen's pleasure, and the viands being brought, they all ate blithely. Rising thence, they gave themselves awhile to dancing and music-making, and after, by the queen's commandment, whoso would betook himself to rest. But presently, the wonted hour being come, all in the accustomed place assembled to discourse, whereupon the queen, looking at Filomena, bade her give commencement to the stories of that day, and she, smiling, began on this wise:

THE FIRST STORY

MADAM FRANCESCA, BEING COURTED BY ONE RINUCCIO PALERMINI AND ONE ALESSANDRO CHIARMONTESI AND LOVING NEITHER THE ONE NOR THE OTHER, ADROITLY RIDDETH HERSELF OF BOTH BY CAUSING ONE ENTER FOR DEAD INTO A SEPULCHRE AND THE OTHER BRING HIM FORTH THEREOF FOR DEAD, ON SUCH WISE THAT THEY CANNOT AVAIL TO ACCOMPLISH THE CONDITION IMPOSED

"SINCE it is your pleasure, madam, I am well pleased to be she who shall run the first ring in this open and free field of story-telling, wherein your magnificence hath set us; the which an I do well, I doubt not but that those who shall come after will do well and better. Many a time, charming ladies, hath it been shown in our discourses what and how great is the power of love; natheless, for that medeemeth not it hath been fully spoken thereof (no, nor would be, though we should speak of nothing else for a year to come,) and that not only doth love bring lovers into divers dangers of death, but causeth them even to enter for dead into the abiding-places of the dead, it is my pleasure to relate to you a story thereof, over and above those which have been told, whereby not only will you apprehend the puissance of love, but will know the wit used by a worthy lady in ridding herself of two who loved her against her will.

You must know, then, that there was once in the city of Pistoia a very fair widow lady, of whom two of our townsmen, called the one Rinuccio Palermini and the other Alessandro Chiarmontesi, there abiding by reason of banishment from Florence, were, without knowing one of other, passionately enamoured, having by chance fallen in love with her and doing privily each his utmost endeavour to win her favour. The gentlewoman in question, whose name was Madam Francesca de' Lazzari, being still importuned of the one and the other with messages and entreaties, to which she had whiles somewhat unwisely given ear, and desiring, but in vain, discreetly to retract, bethought herself how she might avail to rid herself of their importunity by requiring them of a service, which, albeit it was possible, she conceived that neither of them would render her, to the intent that, they not doing that which she required, she might have a fair and colourable occasion of refusing to hearken more to their messages; and the device which occurred to her was on this wise.

There had died that very day at Pistoia, one, who, albeit his ancestors were gentlemen, was reputed the worst man that was, not only in Pistoia, but in all the world; more by token that he was in his lifetime so misshapen and of so monstrous a favour that whoso knew him not, seeing him for the first time, had been affeared of him; and he had been buried in a tomb without the church of the Minor Friars. This circumstance she bethought herself would in part be very apt to her purpose and accordingly she said to a maid of hers, 'Thou knowest the annoy and the vexation I suffer all day long by the messages of yonder two Florentines, Rinuccio and Alessandro. Now I am not disposed to gratify [either of] them with my love, and to rid myself of them, I have bethought myself, for the great proffers that they make, to seek to make proof of them in somewhat which I am certain they will not do; so shall I do away from me this their importunity, and thou shalt see how. Thou knowest that Scannadio,[425] for so was the wicked man called of whom we have already spoken, 'was this morning buried in the burial-place of the Minor Brethren, Scannadio, of whom, whenas they saw him alive, let alone dead, the doughtiest men of this city went in fear; wherefore go thou privily first to Alessandro and bespeak him, saying, "Madam Francesca giveth thee to know that now is the time come whenas thou mayst have her love, which thou hast so much desired, and be with her, an thou wilt, on this wise. This night, for a reason which thou shalt know after, the body of Scannadio, who was this morning buried, is to be brought to her house by a kinsman of hers, and she, being in great fear of him, dead though he be, would fain not have him there; wherefore she prayeth thee that it please thee, by way of doing her a great service, go this evening, at the time of the first sleep, to the tomb wherein he is buried, and donning the dead man's clothes, abide as thou wert he until such time as they shall come for thee. Then, without moving or speaking, thou must suffer thyself be taken up out of the tomb and carried to her house, where she will receive thee, and thou mayst after abide with her and depart at thy leisure, leaving to her the care of the rest." An he say that he will do it, well and good; but, should he refuse, bid him on my part, never more show himself whereas I may be and look, as he valueth his life, that he send me no more letters or messages. Then shalt thou betake thee to Rinuccio Palermini and say to him, "Madam Francesca saith that she is ready to do thine every pleasure, an thou wilt render her a great service, to wit, that to-night, towards the middle hour, thou get thee to the tomb wherein Scannadio was this morning buried and take him up softly thence and bring him to her at her house, without saying a word of aught thou mayst hear or feel. There shalt thou learn what she would with him and have of her thy pleasure; but, an it please thee not to do this, she chargeth thee never more send her writ nor message."'

The maid betook herself to the two lovers and did her errand punctually to each, saying as it had been enjoined her; whereto each made answer that, an it pleased her, they would go, not only into a tomb, but into hell itself. The maid carried their reply to the lady and she waited to see if they would be mad enough to do it. The night come, whenas it was the season of the first sleep, Alessandro Chiarmontesi, having stripped himself to his doublet, went forth of his house to take Scannadio's place in the tomb; but, by the way, there came a very frightful thought into his head and he fell a-saying in himself, 'Good lack, what a fool I am! Whither go I? How know I but yonder woman's kinsfolk, having maybe perceived that I love her and believing that which is not, have caused me do this, so they may slaughter me in yonder tomb? An it should happen thus, I should suffer for it nor would aught in the world be ever known thereof to their detriment. Or what know I but maybe some enemy of mine hath procured me this, whom she belike loveth and seeketh to oblige therein?' Then said he, 'But, grant that neither of these things be and that her kinsfolk are e'en for carrying me to her house, I must believe that they want not Scannadio's body to hold it in their arms or to put it in hers; nay, it is rather to be conceived that they mean to do it some mischief, as the body of one who maybe disobliged them in somewhat aforetime. She saith that I am not to say a word for aught that I may feel. But, should they put out mine eyes or draw my teeth or lop off my hands or play me any other such trick, how shall I do? How could I abide quiet? And if I speak, they will know me and mayhap do me a mischief, or, though they do me no hurt, yet shall I have accomplished nothing, for that they will not leave me with the lady; whereupon she will say that I have broken her commandment and will never do aught to pleasure me.' So saying, he had well nigh returned home; but, nevertheless, his great love urged him on with counter arguments of such potency that they brought him to the tomb, which he opened and entering therein, stripped Scannadio of his clothes; then, donning them and shutting the tomb upon himself, he laid himself in the dead man's place. Thereupon he began to call to mind what manner of man the latter had been and remembering him of all the things whereof he had aforetime heard tell as having befallen by night, not to say in the sepulchres of the dead, but even otherwise, his every hair began to stand on end and himseemed each moment as if Scannadio should rise upright and butcher him then and there. However, aided by his ardent love, he got the better of these and the other fearful thoughts that beset him and abiding as he were the dead man, he fell to awaiting that which should betide him.

Meanwhile, Rinuccio, midnight being now at hand, departed his house, to do that which had been enjoined him of his mistress, and as he went, he entered into many and various thoughts of the things which might possibly betide him; as, to wit, that he might fall into the hands of the police, with Scannadio's body on his shoulders, and be doomed to the fire as a sorcerer, and that he should, an the thing came to be known, incur the ill-will of his kinsfolk, and other like thoughts, whereby he was like to have been deterred. But after, bethinking himself again, 'Alack,' quoth he, 'shall I deny this gentlewoman, whom I have so loved and love, the first thing she requireth of me, especially as I am thereby to gain her favour? God forbid, though I were certainly to die thereof, but I should set myself to do that which I have promised!' Accordingly, he went on and presently coming to the sepulchre, opened it easily; which Alessandro hearing, abode still, albeit he was in great fear. Rinuccio, entering in and thinking to take Scannadio's body, laid hold of Alessandro's feet and drew him forth of the tomb; then, hoisting him on his shoulders, he made off towards the lady's house.

Going thus and taking no manner of heed to his burden, he jolted it many a time now against one corner and now another of certain benches that were beside the way, more by token that the night was so cloudy and so dark he could not see whither he went. He was already well nigh at the door of the gentlewoman, who had posted herself at the window with her maid, to see if he would bring Alessandro, and was ready armed with an excuse to send them both away, when it chanced that the officers of the watch, who were ambushed in the street and abode silently on the watch to lay hands upon a certain outlaw, hearing the scuffling that Rinuccio made with his feet, suddenly put out a light, to see what was to do and whither to go, and rattled their targets and halberds, crying, 'Who goeth there?' Rinuccio, seeing this and having scant time for deliberation, let fall his burden and made off as fast as his legs would carry him; whereupon Alessandro arose in haste and made off in his turn, for all he was hampered with the dead man's clothes, which were very long. The lady, by the light of the lantern put out by the police, had plainly recognized Rinuccio, with Alessandro on his shoulders, and perceiving the latter to be clad in Scannadio's clothes, marvelled amain at the exceeding hardihood of both; but, for all her wonderment, she laughed heartily to see Alessandro cast down on the ground and to see him after take to flight. Then, rejoiced at this accident and praising God that He had rid her of the annoy of these twain, she turned back into the house and betook herself to her chamber, avouching to her maid that without doubt they both loved her greatly, since, as it appeared, they had done that which she had enjoined them.

Meanwhile Rinuccio, woeful and cursing his ill fortune, for all that returned not home, but, as soon as the watch had departed the neighbourhood, he came back whereas he had dropped Alessandro and groped about, to see if he could find him again, so he might make an end of his service; but, finding him not and concluding that the police had carried him off, he returned to his own house, woebegone, whilst Alessandro, unknowing what else to do, made off home on like wise, chagrined at such a misadventure and without having recognized him who had borne him thither. On the morrow, Scannadio's tomb being found open and his body not to be seen, for that Alessandro had rolled it to the bottom of the vault, all Pistoia was busy with various conjectures anent the matter, and the simpler sort concluded that he had been carried off by the devils. Nevertheless, each of the two lovers signified to the lady that which he had done and what had befallen and excusing himself withal for not having full accomplished her commandment, claimed her favour and her love; but she, making believe to credit neither of this, rid herself of them with a curt response to the effect that she would never consent to do aught for them, since they had not done that which she had required of them."

THE SECOND STORY

AN ABBESS, ARISING IN HASTE AND IN THE DARK TO FIND ONE OF HER NUNS, WHO HAD BEEN DENOUNCED TO HER, IN BED WITH HER LOVER AND THINKING TO COVER HER HEAD WITH HER COIF, DONNETH INSTEAD THEREOF THE BREECHES OF A PRIEST WHO IS ABED WITH HER; THE WHICH THE ACCUSED NUN OBSERVING AND MAKING HER AWARE THEREOF, SHE IS ACQUITTED AND HATH LEISURE TO BE WITH HER LOVER

FILOMENA was now silent and the lady's address in ridding herself of those whom she chose not to love having been commended of all, whilst, on the other hand, the presumptuous hardihood of the two gallants was held of them to be not love, but madness, the queen said gaily to Elisa, "Elisa, follow on." Accordingly, she promptly began, "Adroitly, indeed, dearest ladies, did Madam Francesca contrive to rid herself of her annoy, as hath been told; but a young nun, fortune aiding her, delivered herself with an apt speech from an imminent peril. As you know, there be many very dull folk, who set up for teachers and censors of others, but whom, as you may apprehend from my story, fortune bytimes deservedly putteth to shame, as befell the abbess, under whose governance was the nun of whom I have to tell.

You must know, then, that there was once in Lombardy a convent, very famous for sanctity and religion, wherein, amongst the other nuns who were there, was a young lady of noble birth and gifted with marvellous beauty, who was called Isabetta and who, coming one day to the grate to speak with a kinsman of hers, fell in love with a handsome young man who accompanied him. The latter, seeing her very fair and divining her wishes with his eyes, became on like wise enamoured of her, and this love they suffered a great while without fruit, to the no small unease of each. At last, each being solicited by a like desire, the young man hit upon a means of coming at his nun in all secrecy, and she consenting thereto, he visited her, not once, but many times, to the great contentment of both. But, this continuing, it chanced one night that he was, without the knowledge of himself or his mistress, seen of one of the ladies of the convent to take leave of Isabetta and go his ways. The nun communicated her discovery to divers others and they were minded at first to denounce Isabetta to the abbess, who was called Madam Usimbalda and who, in the opinion of the nuns and of whosoever knew her, was a good and pious lady; but, on consideration, they bethought themselves to seek to have the abbess take her with the young man, so there might be no room for denial. Accordingly, they held their peace and kept watch by turns in secret to surprise her.

Now it chanced that Isabetta, suspecting nothing of this nor being on her guard, caused her lover come thither one night, which was forthright known to those who were on the watch for this and who, whenas it seemed to them time, a good part of the night being spent, divided themselves into two parties, whereof one abode on guard at the door of her cell, whilst the other ran to the abbess's chamber and knocking at the door, till she answered, said to her, 'Up, madam; arise quickly, for we have discovered that Isabetta hath a young man in her cell.' Now the abbess was that night in company with a priest, whom she ofttimes let come to her in a chest; but, hearing the nuns' outcry and fearing lest, of their overhaste and eagerness, they should push open the door, she hurriedly arose and dressed herself as best she might in the dark. Thinking to take certain plaited veils, which nuns wear on their heads and call a psalter, she caught up by chance the priest's breeches, and such was her haste that, without remarking what she did, she threw them over her head, in lieu of the psalter, and going forth, hurriedly locked the door after her, saying, 'Where is this accursed one of God?' Then, in company with the others, who were so ardent and so intent upon having Isabetta taken in default that they noted not that which the abbess had on her head, she came to the cell-door and breaking it open, with the aid of the others, entered and found the two lovers abed in each other's arms, who, all confounded at such a surprise, abode fast, unknowing what to do.

The young lady was incontinent seized by the other nuns and haled off, by command of the abbess, to the chapter-house, whilst her gallant dressed himself and abode await to see what should be the issue of the adventure, resolved, if any hurt were offered to his mistress, to do a mischief to as many nuns as he could come at and carry her off. The abbess, sitting in chapter, proceeded, in the presence of all the nuns, who had no eyes but for the culprit, to give the latter the foulest rating that ever woman had, as having by her lewd and filthy practices (an the thing should come to be known without the walls) sullied the sanctity, the honour and the fair fame of the convent; and to this she added very grievous menaces. The young lady, shamefast and fearful, as feeling herself guilty, knew not what to answer and keeping silence, possessed the other nuns with compassion for her. However, after a while, the abbess multiplying words, she chanced to raise her eyes and espied that which the former had on her head and the hose-points that hung down therefrom on either side; whereupon, guessing how the matter stood, she was all reassured and said, 'Madam, God aid you, tie up your coif and after say what you will to me.'

The abbess, taking not her meaning, answered, 'What coif, vile woman that thou art? Hast thou the face to bandy pleasantries at such a time? Thinkest thou this that thou hast done is a jesting matter?' 'Prithee, madam,' answered Isabetta, 'tie up your coif and after say what you will to me.' Thereupon many of the nuns raised their eyes to the abbess's head and she also, putting her hand thereto, perceived, as did the others, why Isabetta spoke thus; wherefore the abbess, becoming aware of her own default and perceiving that it was seen of all, past hope of recoverance, changed her note and proceeding to speak after a fashion altogether different from her beginning, came to the conclusion that it is impossible to withstand the pricks of the flesh, wherefore she said that each should, whenas she might, privily give herself a good time, even as it had been done until that day. Accordingly, setting the young lady free, she went back to sleep with her priest and Isabetta returned to her lover, whom many a time thereafter she let come thither, in despite of those who envied her, whilst those of the others who were loverless pushed their fortunes in secret, as best they knew."

THE THIRD STORY

MASTER SIMONE, AT THE INSTANCE OF BRUNO AND BUFFALMACCO AND NELLO, MAKETH CALANDRINO BELIEVE THAT HE IS WITH CHILD; WHEREFORE HE GIVETH THEM CAPONS AND MONEY FOR MEDICINES AND RECOVERETH WITHOUT BRINGING FORTH

AFTER Elisa had finished her story and all the ladies had returned thanks to God, who had with a happy issue delivered the young nun from the claws of her envious companions, the queen bade Filostrato follow on, and he, without awaiting further commandment, began, "Fairest ladies, the unmannerly lout of a Marchegan judge, of whom I told you yesterday, took out of my mouth a story of Calandrino and his companions, which I was about to relate; and for that, albeit it hath been much discoursed of him and them, aught that is told of him cannot do otherwise than add to our merriment, I will e'en tell you that which I had then in mind.

It hath already been clearly enough shown who Calandrino was and who were the others of whom I am to speak in this story, wherefore, without further preface, I shall tell you that an aunt of his chanced to die and left him two hundred crowns in small coin; whereupon he fell a-talking of wishing to buy an estate and entered into treaty with all the brokers in Florence, as if he had ten thousand gold florins to expend; but the matter still fell through, when they came to the price of the estate in question. Bruno and Buffalmacco, knowing all this, had told him once and again that he were better spend the money in making merry together with them than go buy land, as if he had had to make pellets;[426] but, far from this, they had never even availed to bring him to give them once to eat. One day, as they were complaining of this, there came up a comrade of theirs, a painter by name Nello, and they all three took counsel together how they might find a means of greasing their gullets at Calandrino's expense; wherefore, without more delay, having agreed among themselves of that which was to do, they watched next morning for his coming forth of his house, nor had he gone far when Nello accosted him, saying, 'Good-day, Calandrino.' Calandrino answered God give him good day and good year, and Nello, halting awhile, fell to looking him in the face; whereupon Calandrino asked him, 'At what lookest thou?' Quoth the painter, 'Hath aught ailed thee this night? Meseemeth thou are not thyself this morning.' Calandrino incontinent began to quake and said, 'Alack, how so? What deemest thou aileth me?' 'Egad,' answered Nello, 'as for that I can't say; but thou seemest to me all changed; belike it is nothing.' So saying, he let him pass, and Calandrino fared on, all misdoubtful, albeit he felt no whit ailing; but Buffalmacco, who was not far off, seeing him quit of Nello, made for him and saluting him, enquired if aught ailed him. Quoth Calandrino, 'I know not; nay, Nello told me but now that I seemed to him all changed. Can it be that aught aileth me?' 'Ay,' rejoined Buffalmacco, 'there must e'en be something or other amiss with thee, for thou appearest half dead.'

By this time it seemed to Calandrino that he had the fevers, when, lo, up came Bruno and the first thing he said was, 'Calandrino, what manner of face is this?' Calandrino, hearing them all in the same tale, held it for certain that he was in an ill way and asked them, all aghast, 'what shall I do?' Quoth Bruno, 'Methinketh thou wert best return home and get thee to bed and cover thyself well and send thy water to Master Simone the doctor, who is, as thou knowest, as our very creature and will tell thee incontinent what thou must do. We will go with thee and if it behoveth to do aught, we will do it.' Accordingly, Nello having joined himself to them, they returned home with Calandrino, who betook himself, all dejected, into the bedchamber and said to his wife, 'Come, cover me well, for I feel myself sore disordered.' Then, laying himself down, he despatched his water by a little maid to Master Simone, who then kept shop in the Old Market, at the sign of the Pumpkin, whilst Bruno said to his comrades, 'Abide you here with him, whilst I go hear what the doctor saith and bring him hither, if need be.' 'Ay, for God's sake, comrade mine,' cried Calandrino, 'go thither and bring me back word how the case standeth, for I feel I know not what within me.'

Accordingly, Bruno posted off to Master Simone and coming thither before the girl who brought the water, acquainted him with the case; wherefore, the maid being come and the physician, having seen the water, he said to her, 'Begone and bid Calandrino keep himself well warm, and I will come to him incontinent and tell him that which aileth him and what he must do.' The maid reported this to her master nor was it long before the physician and Bruno came, whereupon the former, seating himself beside Calandrino, fell to feeling his pulse and presently, the patient's wife being there present, he said, 'Harkye, Calandrino, to speak to thee as a friend, there aileth thee nought but that thou art with child.' When Calandrino heard this, he fell a-roaring for dolour and said, 'Woe's me! Tessa, this is thy doing, for that thou wilt still be uppermost; I told thee how it would be.' The lady, who was a very modest person, hearing her husband speak thus, blushed all red for shamefastness and hanging her head, went out of the room, without answering a word; whilst Calandrino, pursuing his complaint, said, 'Alack, wretch that I am! How shall I do? How shall I bring forth this child? Whence shall he issue? I see plainly I am a dead man, through the mad lust of yonder wife of mine, whom God make as woeful as I would fain be glad! Were I as well as I am not, I would arise and deal her so many and such buffets that I would break every bone in her body; albeit it e'en serveth me right, for that I should never have suffered her get the upper hand; but, for certain, an I come off alive this time, she may die of desire ere she do it again.'

Bruno and Buffalmacco and Nello were like to burst with laughter, hearing Calandrino's words; however, they contained themselves, but Doctor Simple-Simon[427] laughed so immoderately that you might have drawn every tooth in his head. Finally, Calandrino commending himself to the physician and praying him give him aid and counsel in this his strait, the latter said to him, 'Calandrino, I will not have thee lose heart; for, praised be God, we have taken the case so betimes that, in a few days and with a little trouble, I will deliver thee thereof; but it will cost thee some little expense.' 'Alack, doctor mine,' cried Calandrino, 'ay, for the love of God, do it! I have here two hundred crowns, wherewith I was minded to buy me an estate; take them all, if need be, so I be not brought to bed; for I know not how I should do, seeing I hear women make such a terrible outcry, whereas they are about to bear child, for all they have ample commodity therefor, that methinketh, if I had that pain to suffer, I should die ere I came to the bringing forth.' Quoth the doctor, 'Have no fear of that; I will let make thee a certain ptisan of distilled waters, very good and pleasant to drink, which will in three mornings' time carry off everything and leave thee sounder than a fish; but look thou be more discreet for the future and suffer not thyself fall again into these follies. Now for this water it behoveth us have three pairs of fine fat capons, and for other things that are required thereanent, do thou give one of these (thy comrades) five silver crowns, so he may buy them, and let carry everything to my shop; and to-morrow, in God's name, I will send thee the distilled water aforesaid, whereof thou shalt proceed to drink a good beakerful at a time.' 'Doctor mine,' replied Calandrino, 'I put myself in your hands'; and giving Bruno five crowns and money for three pairs of capons, he besought him to oblige him by taking the pains to buy these things.

The physician then took his leave and letting make a little clary,[428] despatched it to Calandrino, whilst Bruno, buying the capons and other things necessary for making good cheer, ate them in company with his comrades and Master Simone. Calandrino drank of his clary three mornings, after which the doctor came to him, together with his comrades, and feeling his pulse, said to him, 'Calandrino, thou art certainly cured; wherefore henceforth thou mayst safely go about thine every business nor abide longer at home for this.' Accordingly, Calandrino arose, overjoyed, and went about his occasions, mightily extolling, as often as he happened to speak with any one, the fine cure that Master Simone had wrought of him, in that he had unbegotten him with child in three days' time, without any pain; whilst Bruno and Buffalmacco and Nello abode well pleased at having contrived with this device to overreach his niggardliness, albeit Dame Tessa, smoking the cheat, rated her husband amain thereanent."

THE FOURTH STORY

CECCO FORTARRIGO GAMETH AWAY AT BUONCONVENTO ALL HIS GOOD AND THE MONIES OF CECCO ANGIOLIERI [HIS MASTER;] MOREOVER, RUNNING AFTER THE LATTER, IN HIS SHIRT, AND AVOUCHING THAT HE HATH ROBBED HIM, HE CAUSETH HIM BE TAKEN OF THE COUNTRYFOLK; THEN, DONNING ANGIOLIERI'S CLOTHES AND MOUNTING HIS PALFREY, HE MAKETH OFF AND LEAVETH THE OTHER IN HIS SHIRT

CALANDRINO'S speech concerning his wife had been hearkened of all the company with the utmost laughter; then, Filostrato being silent, Neifile, as the queen willed it, began, "Noble ladies, were it not uneather for men to show forth unto others their wit and their worth than it is for them to exhibit their folly and their vice, many would weary themselves in vain to put a bridle on their tongues; and this hath right well been made manifest to you by the folly of Calandrino, who had no call, in seeking to be made whole of the ailment in which his simplicity caused him believe, to publish the privy diversions of his wife; and this hath brought to my mind somewhat of contrary purport to itself, to wit, a story of how one man's knavery got the better of another's wit, to the grievous hurt and confusion of the over-reached one, the which it pleaseth me to relate to you.

There were, then, in Siena, not many years ago, two (as far as age went) full-grown men, each of whom was called Cecco. One was the son of Messer Angiolieri and the other of Messer Fortarrigo, and albeit in most other things they sorted ill of fashions one with the other, they were natheless so far of accord in one particular, to wit, that they were both hated of their fathers, that they were by reason thereof grown friends and companied often together. After awhile, Angiolieri, who was both a handsome man and a well-mannered, himseeming he could ill live at Siena of the provision assigned him of his father and hearing that a certain cardinal, a great patron of his, was come into the Marches of Ancona as the Pope's Legate, determined to betake himself to him, thinking thus to better his condition. Accordingly, acquainting his father with his purpose, he took order with him to have at once that which he was to give him in six months, so he might clothe and horse himself and make an honourable figure. As he went seeking some one whom he might carry with him for his service, the thing came to Fortarrigo's knowledge, whereupon he presently repaired to Angiolieri and besought him, as best he knew, to carry him with him, offering himself to be to him lackey and serving-man and all, without any wage beyond his expenses paid. Angiolieri answered that he would nowise take him, not but he knew him to be right well sufficient unto every manner of service, but for that he was a gambler and bytimes a drunkard, to boot. But the other replied that he would without fail keep himself from both of these defaults and affirmed it unto him with oaths galore, adding so many prayers that Angiolieri was prevailed upon and said that he was content.

Accordingly, they both set out one morning and went to dine at Buonconvento, where, after dinner, the heat being great, Angiolieri let make ready a bed at the inn and undressing himself, with Fortarrigo's aid, went to sleep, charging the latter call him at the stroke of none. As soon as his master was asleep, Fortarrigo betook himself to the tavern and there, after drinking awhile, he fell to gaming with certain men, who in a trice won of him some money he had and after, the very clothes he had on his back; whereupon, desirous of retrieving himself, he repaired, in his shirt as he was, to Angiolieri's chamber and seeing him fast asleep, took from his purse what monies he had and returning to play, lost these as he had lost the others. Presently, Angiolieri awoke and arising, dressed himself and enquired for Fortarrigo. The latter was not to be found and Angiolieri, concluding him to be asleep, drunken, somewhere, as was bytimes his wont, determined to leave him be and get himself another servant at Corsignano. Accordingly, he caused put his saddle and his valise on a palfrey he had and thinking to pay the reckoning, so he might get him gone, found himself without a penny; whereupon great was the outcry and all the hostelry was in an uproar, Angiolieri declaring that he had been robbed there and threatening to have the host and all his household carried prisoners to Siena.

At this moment up came Fortarrigo in his shirt, thinking to take his master's clothes, as he had taken his money, and seeing the latter ready to mount, said, 'What is this, Angiolieri? Must we needs be gone already? Good lack, wait awhile; there will be one here forthwith who hath my doublet in pawn for eight-and-thirty shillings; and I am certain that he will render it up for five-and-thirty, money down.' As he spoke, there came one who certified Angiolieri that it was Fortarrigo who had robbed him of his monies, by showing him the sum of those which the latter had lost at play; wherefore he was sore incensed and loaded Fortarrigo with reproaches; and had he not feared others more than he feared God, he had done him a mischief; then, threatening to have him strung up by the neck or outlawed from Siena, he mounted to horse. Fortarrigo, as if he spoke not to him, but to another, said, 'Good lack, Angiolieri, let be for the nonce this talk that skilleth not a straw, and have regard unto this; by redeeming it[429] forthright, we may have it again for five-and-thirty shillings; whereas, if we tarry but till tomorrow, he will not take less than the eight-and-thirty he lent me thereon; and this favour he doth me for that I staked it after his counsel. Marry, why should we not better ourselves by these three shillings?'

Angiolieri, hearing him talk thus, lost all patience (more by token that he saw himself eyed askance by the bystanders, who manifestly believed, not that Fortarrigo had gamed away his monies, but that he had yet monies of Fortarrigo's in hand) and said to him, 'What have I to do with thy doublet? Mayst thou be strung up by the neck, since not only hast thou robbed me and gambled away my money, but hinderest me to boot in my journey, and now thou makest mock of me.' However, Fortarrigo still stood to it, as it were not spoken to him and said, 'Ecod, why wilt thou not better me these three shillings? Thinkest thou I shall not be able to oblige thee therewith another time? Prithee, do it, an thou have any regard for me. Why all this haste? We shall yet reach Torrenieri betimes this evening. Come, find the purse; thou knowest I might ransack all Siena and not find a doublet to suit me so well as this; and to think I should let yonder fellow have it for eight-and-thirty shillings! It is worth yet forty shillings or more, so that thou wouldst worsen me in two ways.'[430]

Angiolieri, beyond measure exasperated to see himself first robbed and now held in parley after this fashion, made him no further answer, but, turning his palfrey's head, took the road to Torrenieri, whilst Fortarrigo, bethinking himself of a subtle piece of knavery, proceeded to trot after him in his shirt good two miles, still requiring him of his doublet. Presently, Angiolieri pricking on amain, to rid his ears of the annoy, Fortarrigo espied some husbandmen in a field, adjoining the highway in advance of him, and cried out to them, saying, 'Stop him, stop him!' Accordingly, they ran up, some with spades and others with mattocks, and presenting themselves in the road before Angiolieri, concluding that he had robbed him who came crying after him in his shirt, stopped and took him. It availed him little to tell them who he was and how the case stood, and Fortarrigo, coming up, said with an angry air, 'I know not what hindereth me from slaying thee, disloyal thief that thou wast to make off with my gear!' Then, turning to the countrymen, 'See, gentlemen,' quoth he, 'in what a plight he left me at the inn, having first gamed away all his own! I may well say by God and by you have I gotten back this much, and thereof I shall still be beholden to you.'

Angiolieri told them his own story, but his words were not heeded; nay, Fortarrigo, with the aid of the countrymen, pulled him off his palfrey and stripping him, clad himself in his clothes; then, mounting to horse, he left him in his shirt and barefoot and returned to Siena, avouching everywhere that he had won the horse and clothes of Angiolieri, whilst the latter, who had thought to go, as a rich man, to the cardinal in the Marches, returned to Buonconvento, poor and in his shirt, nor dared for shamefastness go straight back to Siena, but, some clothes being lent him, he mounted the rouncey that Fortarrigo had ridden and betook himself to his kinsfolk at Corsignano, with whom he abode till such time as he was furnished anew by his father. On this wise Fortarrigo's knavery baffled

Angiolieri's fair advisement,[431] albeit his villainy was not left by the latter unpunished in due time and place."

THE FIFTH STORY

CALANDRINO FALLETH IN LOVE WITH A WENCH AND BRUNO WRITETH HIM A TALISMAN, WHEREWITH WHEN HE TOUCHETH HER, SHE GOETH WITH HIM; AND HIS WIFE FINDING THEM TOGETHER, THERE BETIDETH HIM GRIEVOUS TROUBLE AND ANNOY

NEIFILE'S short story being finished and the company having passed it over without overmuch talk or laughter, the queen turned to Fiammetta and bade her follow on, to which she replied all blithely that she would well and began, "Gentlest ladies, there is, as methinketh you may know, nothing, how much soever it may have been talked thereof, but will still please, provided whoso is minded to speak of it know duly to choose the time and the place that befit it. Wherefore, having regard to our intent in being here (for that we are here to make merry and divert ourselves and not for otherwhat), meseemeth that everything which may afford mirth and pleasance hath here both due place and due time; and albeit it may have been a thousand times discoursed thereof, it should natheless be none the less pleasing, though one speak of it as much again. Wherefore, notwithstanding it hath been many times spoken among us of the sayings and doings of Calandrino, I will make bold, considering, as Filostrato said awhile ago, that these are all diverting, to tell you yet another story thereof, wherein were I minded to swerve from the fact, I had very well known to disguise and recount it under other names; but, for that, in the telling of a story, to depart from the truth of things betided detracteth greatly from the listener's pleasure, I will e'en tell it you in its true shape, moved by the reason aforesaid.

Niccolo Cornacchini was a townsman of ours and a rich man and had, among his other possessions, a fine estate at Camerata, whereon he let build a magnificent mansion and agreed with Bruno and Buffalmacco to paint it all for him; and they, for that the work was great, joined to themselves Nello and Calandrino and fell to work. Thither, for that there was none of the family in the house, although there were one or two chambers furnished with beds and other things needful and an old serving-woman abode there, as guardian of the place, a son of the said Niccolo, by name Filippo, being young and without a wife, was wont bytimes to bring some wench or other for his diversion and keep her there a day or two and after send her away. It chanced once, among other times, that he brought thither one called Niccolosa, whom a lewd fellow, by name Mangione, kept at his disposal in a house at Camaldoli and let out on hire. She was a woman of a fine person and well clad and for her kind well enough mannered and spoken.

One day at noontide, she having come forth her chamber in a white petticoat, with her hair twisted about her head, and being in act to wash her hands and face at a well that was in the courtyard of the mansion, it chanced that Calandrino came thither for water and saluted her familiarly. She returned him his greeting and fell to eying him, more because he seemed to her an odd sort of fellow than for any fancy she had for him; whereupon he likewise fell a-considering her and himseeming she was handsome, he began to find his occasions for abiding there and returned not to his comrades with the water, but, knowing her not, dared not say aught to her. She, who had noted his looking, glanced at him from time to time, to make game of him, heaving some small matter of sighs the while; wherefore Calandrino fell suddenly over head and ears in love with her and left not the courtyard till she was recalled by Filippo into the chamber. Therewithal he returned to work, but did nought but sigh, which Bruno, who had still an eye to his doings, for that he took great delight in his fashions, remarking, 'What a devil aileth thee, friend Calandrino?' quoth he. 'Thou dost nought but sigh.' 'Comrade,' answered Calandrino, 'had I but some one to help me, I should fare well.' 'How so?' enquired Bruno; and Calandrino replied, 'It must not be told to any; but there is a lass down yonder, fairer than a fairy, who hath fallen so mightily in love with me that 'twould seem to thee a grave matter. I noted it but now, whenas I went for the water.' 'Ecod,' cried Bruno, 'look she be not Filippo's wife.' Quoth Calandrino, 'Methinketh it is she, for that he called her and she went to him in the chamber; but what of that? In matters of this kind I would jockey Christ himself, let alone Filippo; and to tell thee the truth, comrade, she pleaseth me more than I can tell thee.' 'Comrade,' answered Bruno, 'I will spy thee out who she is, and if she be Filippo's wife, I will order thine affairs for thee in a brace of words, for she is a great friend of mine. But how shall we do, so Buffalmacco may not know? I can never get a word with her, but he is with me.' Quoth Calandrino, 'Of Buffalmacco I reck not; but we must beware of Nello, for that he is Tessa's kinsman and would mar us everything.' And Bruno said, 'True.'

Now he knew very well who the wench was, for that he had seen her come and moreover Filippo had told him. Accordingly, Calandrino having left work awhile and gone to get a sight of her, Bruno told Nello and Buffalmacco everything and they took order together in secret what they should do with him in the matter of this his enamourment. When he came back, Bruno said to him softly, 'Hast seen her?' 'Alack, yes,' replied Calandrino; 'she hath slain me.' Quoth Bruno, 'I must go see an it be she I suppose; and if it be so, leave me do.' Accordingly, he went down into the courtyard and finding Filippo and Niccolosa there, told them precisely what manner of man Calandrino was and took order with them of that which each of them should do and say, so they might divert themselves with the lovesick gull and make merry over his passion. Then, returning to Calandrino, he said, 'It is indeed she; wherefore needs must the thing be very discreetly managed, for, should Filippo get wind of it, all the water in the Arno would not wash us. But what wouldst thou have me say to her on thy part, if I should chance to get speech of her?' 'Faith,' answered Calandrino, 'thou shalt tell her, to begin with, that I will her a thousand measures of that good stuff that getteth with child, and after, that I am her servant and if she would have aught.... Thou takest me?' 'Ay,' said Bruno, 'leave me do.'

Presently, supper-time being come, the painters left work and went down into the courtyard, where they found Filippo and Niccolosa and tarried there awhile, to oblige Calandrino. The latter fell to ogling Niccolosa and making the oddest grimaces in the world, such and so many that a blind man would have remarked them. She on her side did everything that she thought apt to inflame him, and Filippo, in accordance with the instructions he had of Bruno, made believe to talk with Buffalmacco and the others and to have no heed of this, whilst taking the utmost diversion in Calandrino's fashions. However, after a while, to the latter's exceeding chagrin, they took their leave and as they returned to Florence, Bruno said to Calandrino, 'I can tell thee thou makest her melt like ice in the sun. Cock's body, wert thou to fetch thy rebeck and warble thereto some of those amorous ditties of thine, thou wouldst cause her cast herself out of window to come to thee.' Quoth Calandrino, 'Deemest thou, gossip? Deemest thou I should do well to fetch it?' 'Ay, do I,' answered Bruno; and Calandrino went on, 'Thou wouldst not credit me this morning, whenas I told it thee; but, for certain, gossip, methinketh I know better than any man alive to do what I will. Who, other than I, had known to make such a lady so quickly in love with me? Not your trumpeting young braggarts,[432] I warrant you, who are up and down all day long and could not make shift, in a thousand years, to get together three handsful of cherry stones. I would fain have thee see me with the rebeck; 'twould be fine sport for thee. I will have thee to understand once for all that I am no dotard, as thou deemest me, and this she hath right well perceived, she; but I will make her feel it othergates fashion, so once I get my claw into her back; by the very body of Christ, I will lead her such a dance that she will run after me, as the madwoman after her child.' 'Ay,' rejoined Bruno, 'I warrant me thou wilt rummage her; methinketh I see thee, with those teeth of thine that were made for virginal jacks,[433] bite that little vermeil mouth of hers and those her cheeks, that show like two roses, and after eat her all up.'

Calandrino, hearing this, fancied himself already at it and went singing and skipping, so overjoyed that he was like to jump out of his skin. On the morrow, having brought the rebeck, he, to the great diversion of all the company, sang sundry songs thereto; and in brief, he was taken with such an itch for the frequent seeing of her that he wrought not a whit, but ran a thousand times a day, now to the window, now to the door and anon into the courtyard, to get a look at her, whereof she, adroitly carrying out Bruno's instructions, afforded him ample occasion. Bruno, on his side, answered his messages in her name and bytimes brought him others as from her; and whenas she was not there, which was mostly the case, he carried him letters from her, wherein she gave him great hopes of compassing his desire, feigning herself at home with her kinsfolk, where he might not presently see her. On this wise, Bruno, with the aid of Buffalmacco, who had a hand in the matter, kept the game afoot and had the greatest sport in the world with Calandrino's antics, causing him give them bytimes, as at his mistress's request, now an ivory comb, now a purse and anon a knife and such like toys, for which they brought him in return divers paltry counterfeit rings of no value, with which he was vastly delighted; and to boot, they had of him, for their pains, store of dainty collations and other small matters of entertainment, so they might be diligent about his affairs.

On this wise they kept him in play good two months, without getting a step farther, at the end of which time, seeing the work draw to an end and bethinking himself that, an he brought not his amours to an issue in the meantime, he might never have another chance thereof, he began to urge and importune Bruno amain; wherefore, when next the girl came to the mansion, Bruno, having first taken order with her and Filippo of what was to be done, said to Calandrino, 'Harkye, gossip, yonder lady hath promised me a good thousand times to do that which thou wouldst have and yet doth nought thereof, and meseemeth she leadeth thee by the nose; wherefore, since she doth it not as she promiseth, we will an it like thee, make her do it, will she, nill she.' 'Ecod, ay!' answered Calandrino. 'For the love of God let it be done speedily.' Quoth Bruno, 'Will thy heart serve thee to touch her with a script I shall give thee?' 'Ay, sure,' replied Calandrino; and the other, 'Then do thou make shift to bring me a piece of virgin parchment and a live bat, together with three grains of frankincense and a candle that hath been blessed by the priest, and leave me do.' Accordingly, Calandrino lay in wait all the next night with his engines to catch a bat and having at last taken one, carried it to Bruno, with the other things required; whereupon the latter, withdrawing to a chamber, scribbled divers toys of his fashion upon the parchment, in characters of his own devising, and brought it to him, saying, 'Know, Calandrino, that, if thou touch her with this script, she will incontinent follow thee and do what thou wilt. Wherefore, if Filippo should go abroad anywhither to-day, do thou contrive to accost her on some pretext or other and touch her; then betake thyself to the barn yonder, which is the best place here for thy purpose, for that no one ever frequenteth there. Thou wilt find she will come thither, and when she is there, thou knowest well what thou hast to do.' Calandrino was the joyfullest man alive and took the script, saying, 'Gossip, leave me do.'

Now Nello, whom Calandrino mistrusted, had as much diversion of the matter as the others and bore a hand with them in making sport of him: wherefore, of accord with Bruno, he betook himself to Florence to Calandrino's wife and said to her, 'Tessa, thou knowest what a beating Calandrino gave thee without cause the day he came back, laden with stones from the Mugnone; wherefore I mean to have thee avenge thyself on him; and if thou do it not, hold me no more for kinsman or for friend. He hath fallen in love with a woman over yonder, and she is lewd enough to go very often closeting herself with him. A little while agone, they appointed each other to foregather together this very day; wherefore I would have thee come thither and lie in wait for him and chastise him well.' When the lady heard this, it seemed to her no jesting matter, but, starting to her feet, she fell a-saying, 'Alack, common thief that thou art, is it thus that thou usest me? By Christ His Cross, it shall not pass thus, but I will pay thee therefor!' Then, taking her mantle and a little maid to bear her company, she started off at a good round pace for the mansion, together with Nello.

As soon as Bruno saw the latter afar off, he said to Filippo, 'Here cometh our friend'; whereupon the latter, betaking himself whereas Calandrino and the others were at work, said, 'Masters, needs must I go presently to Florence; work with a will.' Then, going away, he hid himself in a place when he could, without being seen, see what Calandrino should do. The latter, as soon as he deemed Filippo somewhat removed, came down into the courtyard and finding Niccolosa there alone, entered into talk with her, whilst she, who knew well enough what she had to do, drew near him and entreated him somewhat more familiarly than of wont. Thereupon he touched her with the script and no sooner had he done so than he turned, without saying a word, and made for the barn, whither she followed him. As soon as she was within, she shut the door and taking him in her arms, threw him down on the straw that was on the floor; then, mounting astride of him and holding him with her hands on his shoulders, without letting him draw near her face, she gazed at him, as he were her utmost desire, and said, 'O sweet my Calandrino, heart of my body, my soul, my treasure, my comfort, how long have I desired to have thee and to be able to hold thee at my wish! Thou hast drawn all the thread out of my shift with thy gentilesse; thou hast tickled my heart with thy rebeck. Can it be true that I hold thee?' Calandrino, who could scarce stir, said, 'For God's sake, sweet my soul, let me buss thee.' 'Marry,' answered she, 'thou art in a mighty hurry. Let me first take my fill of looking upon thee; let me sate mine eyes with that sweet face of thine.'

Now Bruno and Buffalmacco were come to join Filippo and all three heard and saw all this. As Calandrino was now offering to kiss Niccolosa perforce, up came Nello with Dame Tessa and said, as soon as he reached the place, 'I vow to God they are together.' Then, coming up to the door of the barn, the lady, who was all a-fume with rage, dealt it such a push with her hands that she sent it flying, and entering, saw Niccolosa astride of Calandrino. The former, seeing the lady, started up in haste and taking to flight, made off to join Filippo, whilst Dame Tessa fell tooth and nail upon Calandrino, who was still on his back, and clawed all his face; then, clutching him by the hair and haling him hither and thither, 'Thou sorry shitten cur,' quoth she, 'dost thou then use me thus? Besotted dotard that thou art, accursed be the weal I have willed thee! Marry, seemeth it to thee thou hast not enough to do at home, that thou must go wantoning it in other folk's preserves? A fine gallant, i'faith! Dost thou not know thyself, losel that thou art? Dost thou not know thyself, good for nought? Wert thou to be squeezed dry, there would not come as much juice from thee as might suffice for a sauce. Cock's faith, thou canst not say it was Tessa that was presently in act to get thee with child, God make her sorry, who ever she is, for a scurvy trull as she must be to have a mind to so fine a jewel as thou!'

Calandrino, seeing his wife come, abode neither dead nor alive and had not the hardihood to make any defence against her; but, rising, all scratched and flayed and baffled as he was, and picking up his bonnet, he fell to humbly beseeching her leave crying out, an she would not have him cut in pieces, for that she who had been with him was the wife of the master of the house; whereupon quoth she, 'So be it, God give her an ill year.' At this moment, Bruno and Buffalmacco, having laughed their fill at all this, in company with Filippo and Niccolosa, came up, feigning to be attracted by the clamour, and having with no little ado appeased the lady, counselled Calandrino betake himself to Florence and return thither no more, lest Filippo should get wind of the matter and do him a mischief. Accordingly he returned to Florence, chapfallen and woebegone, all flayed and scratched, and never ventured to go thither again; but, being plagued and harassed night and day with his wife's reproaches, he made an end of his fervent love, having given much cause for laughter to his companions, no less than to Niccolosa and Filippo."

THE SIXTH STORY

TWO YOUNG GENTLEMEN LODGE THE NIGHT WITH AN INNKEEPER, WHEREOF ONE GOETH TO LIE WITH THE HOST'S DAUGHTER, WHILST HIS WIFE UNWITTINGLY COUCHETH WITH THE OTHER; AFTER WHICH HE WHO LAY WITH THE GIRL GETTETH HIM TO BED WITH HER FATHER AND TELLETH HIM ALL, THINKING TO BESPEAK HIS COMRADE. THEREWITHAL THEY COME TO WORDS, BUT THE WIFE, PERCEIVING HER MISTAKE, ENTERETH HER DAUGHTER'S BED AND THENCE WITH CERTAIN WORDS APPEASETH EVERYTHING

CALANDRINO, who had otherwhiles afforded the company matter for laughter, made them laugh this time also, and whenas the ladies had left devising of his fashions, the queen bade Pamfilo tell, whereupon quoth he, "Laudable ladies, the name of Niccolosa, Calandrino's mistress, hath brought me back to mind a story of another Niccolosa, which it pleaseth me to tell you, for that therein you shall see how a goodwife's ready wit did away a great scandal.

In the plain of Mugnone there was not long since a good man who gave wayfarers to eat and drink for their money, and although he was poor and had but a small house, he bytimes at a pinch gave, not every one, but sundry acquaintances, a night's lodging. He had a wife, a very handsome woman, by whom he had two children, whereof one was a fine buxom lass of some fifteen or sixteen years of age, who was not yet married, and the other a little child, not yet a year old, whom his mother herself suckled. Now a young gentleman of our city, a sprightly and pleasant youth, who was often in those parts, had cast his eyes on the girl and loved her ardently; and she, who gloried greatly in being beloved of a youth of his quality, whilst studying with pleasing fashions to maintain him in her love, became no less enamoured of him, and more than once, by mutual accord, this their love had had the desired effect, but that Pinuccio (for such was the young man's name) feared to bring reproach upon his mistress and himself. However, his ardour waxing from day to day, he could no longer master his desire to foregather with her and bethought himself to find a means of harbouring with her father, doubting not, from his acquaintance with the ordinance of the latter's house, but he might in that event contrive to pass the night in her company, without any being the wiser; and no sooner had he conceived this design than he proceeded without delay to carry it into execution.

Accordingly, in company with a trusty friend of his called Adriano, who knew his love, he late one evening hired a couple of hackneys and set thereon two pairs of saddle-bags, filled belike with straw, with which they set out from Florence and fetching a compass, rode till they came overagainst the plain of Mugnone, it being by this night; then, turning about, as they were on their way back from Romagna, they made for the good man's house and knocked at the door. The host, being very familiar with both of them, promptly opened the door and Pinuccio said to him, 'Look you, thou must needs harbour us this night. We thought to reach Florence before dark, but have not availed to make such haste but that we find ourselves here, as thou seest at this hour.' 'Pinuccio,' answered the host, 'thou well knowest how little commodity I have to lodge such men as you are; however, since the night hath e'en overtaken you here and there is no time for you to go otherwhere, I will gladly harbour you as I may.' The two young men accordingly alighted and entered the inn, where they first eased[434] their hackneys and after supper with the host, having taken good care to bring provision with them.

Now the good man had but one very small bedchamber, wherein were three pallet-beds set as best he knew, two at one end of the room and the third overagainst them at the other end; nor for all that was there so much space left that one could go there otherwise than straitly. The least ill of the three the host let make ready for the two friends and put them to lie there; then, after a while neither of the gentlemen being asleep, though both made a show thereof, he caused his daughter betake herself to bed in one of the two others and lay down himself in the third, with his wife, who set by the bedside the cradle wherein she had her little son. Things being ordered after this fashion and Pinuccio having seen everything, after a while, himseeming that every one was asleep, he arose softly and going to the bed where slept the girl beloved of him, laid himself beside the latter, by whom, for all she did it timorously, he was joyfully received, and with her he proceeded to take of that pleasure which both most desired. Whilst Pinuccio abode thus with his mistress, it chanced that a cat caused certain things fall, which the good wife, awaking, heard; whereupon, fearing lest it were otherwhat, she arose, as she was, in the dark and betook herself whereas she had heard the noise.

Meanwhile, Adriano, without intent aforethought, arose by chance for some natural occasion and going to despatch this, came upon the cradle, whereas it had been set by the good wife, and unable to pass without moving it, took it up and set it down beside his own bed; then, having accomplished that for which he had arisen, he returned and betook himself to bed again, without recking of the cradle. The good wife, having searched and found the thing which had fallen was not what she thought, never troubled herself to kindle a light, to see it, but, chiding the cat, returned to the chamber and groped her way to the bed where her husband lay. Finding the cradle not there, 'Mercy o' me!' quoth she in herself. 'See what I was about to do! As I am a Christian, I had well nigh gone straight to our guest's bed.' Then, going a little farther and finding the cradle, she entered the bed whereby it stood and laid herself down beside Adriano, thinking to couch with her husband. Adriano, who was not yet asleep, feeling this, received her well and joyously and laying her aboard in a trice, clapped on all sail, to the no small contentment of the lady.

Meanwhile, Pinuccio, fearing lest sleep should surprise him with his lass and having taken of her his fill of pleasure, arose from her, to return to his own bed, to sleep, and finding the cradle in his way, took the adjoining bed for that of his host; wherefore, going a little farther, he lay down with the latter, who awoke at his coming. Pinuccio, deeming himself beside Adriano, said, 'I tell thee there never was so sweet a creature as is Niccolosa. Cock's body, I have had with her the rarest sport ever man had with woman, more by token that I have gone upwards of six times into the country, since I left thee.' The host, hearing this talk and being not overwell pleased therewith, said first in himself, 'What a devil doth this fellow here?' Then, more angered than well-advised, 'Pinuccio,' quoth he, 'this hath been a great piece of villainy of thine, and I know not why thou shouldst have used me thus; but, by the body of God, I will pay thee for it!!' Pinuccio, who was not the wisest lad in the world, seeing his mistake, addressed not himself to mend it as best he might, but said, 'Of what wilt thou pay me? What canst thou do to me?' Therewithal the hostess, who thought herself with her husband, said to Adriano, 'Good lack, hark to our guests how they are at I know not what words together!' Quoth Adriano, laughing, 'Leave them do, God land them in an ill year! They drank overmuch yesternight.'

The good wife, herseeming she had heard her husband scold and hearing Adriano speak, incontinent perceived where and with whom she had been; whereupon, like a wise woman as she was, she arose forthright, without saying a word, and taking her little son's cradle, carried it at a guess, for that there was no jot of light to be seen in the chamber, to the side of the bed where her daughter slept and lay down with the latter; then, as if she had been aroused by her husband's clamour, she called him and enquired what was to do between himself and Pinuccio. He answered, 'Hearest thou not what he saith he hath done this night unto Niccolosa?' 'Marry,' quoth she, 'he lieth in his throat, for he was never abed with Niccolosa, seeing that I have lain here all night; more by token that I have not been able to sleep a wink; and thou art an ass to believe him. You men drink so much of an evening that you do nothing but dream all night and fare hither and thither, without knowing it, and fancy you do wonders. 'Tis a thousand pities you don't break your necks. But what doth Pinuccio yonder? Why bideth he not in his own bed?' Adriano, on his part, seeing how adroitly the good wife went about to cover her own shame and that of her daughter, chimed in with, 'Pinuccio, I have told thee an hundred times not to go abroad, for that this thy trick of arising in thy sleep and telling for true the extravagances thou dreamest will bring thee into trouble some day or other. Come back here, God give thee an ill night!'

The host, hearing what his wife and Adriano said, began to believe in good earnest that Pinuccio was dreaming; and accordingly, taking him by the shoulders, he fell to shaking and calling him, saying, 'Pinuccio, awake; return to thine own bed.' Pinuccio having apprehended all that had been said began to wander off into other extravagances, after the fashion of a man a-dream; whereat the host set up the heartiest laughter in the world. At last, he made believe to awake for stress of shaking, and calling to Adriano, said, 'Is it already day, that thou callest me?' 'Ay,' answered the other, 'come hither.' Accordingly, Pinuccio, dissembling and making a show of being sleepy-eyed, arose at last from beside the host and went back to bed with Adriano. The day come and they being risen, the host fell to laughing and mocking at Pinuccio and his dreams; and so they passed from one jest to another, till the young men, having saddled their rounceys and strapped on their valises and drunken with the host, remounted to horse and rode away to Florence, no less content with the manner in which the thing had betided than with the effect itself thereof. Thereafter Pinuccio found other means of foregathering with Niccolosa, who vowed to her mother that he had certainly dreamt the thing; wherefore the goodwife, remembering her of Adriano's embracements, inwardly avouched herself alone to have waked."

THE SEVENTH STORY

TALANO DI MOLESE DREAMETH THAT A WOLF MANGLETH ALL HIS WIFE'S NECK AND FACE AND BIDDETH HER BEWARE THEREOF; BUT SHE PAYETH NO HEED TO HIS WARNING AND IT BEFALLETH HER EVEN AS HE HAD DREAMED

PAMFILO'S story being ended and the goodwife's presence of mind having been commended of all, the queen bade Pampinea tell hers and she thereupon began, "It hath been otherwhile discoursed among us, charming ladies, of the truths foreshown by dreams, the which many of our sex scoff at; wherefore, notwithstanding that which hath been said thereof, I shall not scruple to tell you, in a very few words, that which no great while ago befell a she-neighbour of mine for not giving credit to a dream of herself seen by her husband.

I know not if you were acquainted with Talano di Molese, a very worshipful man, who took to wife a young lady called Margarita, fair over all others, but so humoursome, ill-conditioned and froward that she would do nought of other folk's judgment, nor could others do aught to her liking; the which, irksome as it was to Talano to endure, natheless, as he could no otherwise, needs must he put up with. It chanced one night that, being with this Margarita of his at an estate he had in the country, himseemed in his sleep he saw his wife go walking in a very fair wood which they had not far from their house, and as she went, himseemed there came forth of a thicket a great and fierce wolf, which sprang straight at her throat and pulling her to the ground, enforced himself to carry her off, whilst she screamed for aid; and after, she winning free of his fangs, it seemed he had marred all her throat and face. Accordingly, when he arose in the morning, he said to the lady, 'Wife, albeit thy frowardness hath never suffered me to have a good day with thee, yet it would grieve me should ill betide thee; wherefore, an thou wilt hearken to my counsel, thou wilt not go forth the house to-day'; and being asked of her why, he orderly recounted to her his dream.

The lady shook her head and said, 'Who willeth thee ill, dreameth thee ill. Thou feignest thyself mighty careful of me; but thou dreamest of me that which thou wouldst fain see come to pass; and thou mayst be assured that I will be careful both to-day and always not to gladden thee with this or other mischance of mine.' Quoth Talano, 'I knew thou wouldst say thus; for that such thanks still hath he who combeth a scald-head; but, believe as thou listeth, I for my part tell it to thee for good, and once more I counsel thee abide at home to-day or at least beware of going into our wood.' 'Good,' answered the lady, 'I will do it'; and after fell a-saying to herself, 'Sawest thou how artfully yonder man thinketh to have feared me from going to our wood to-day? Doubtless he hath given some trull or other tryst there and would not have me find him with her. Marry, it were fine eating for him with blind folk and I should be a right simpleton an I saw not his drift and if I believed him! But certes he shall not have his will; nay, though I abide there all day, needs must I see what traffic is this that he hath in hand to-day.'

Accordingly, her husband being gone out at one door, she went out at the other and betook herself as most secretly she might straight to the wood and hid herself in the thickest part thereof, standing attent and looking now here and now there, an she should see any one come. As she abode on this wise, without any thought of danger, behold, there sallied forth of a thick coppice hard by a terrible great wolf, and scarce could she say, 'Lord, aid me!' when it flew at her throat and laying fast hold of her, proceeded to carry her off, as she were a lambkin. She could neither cry nor aid herself on other wise, so sore was her gullet straitened; wherefore the wolf, carrying her off, would assuredly have throttled her, had he not encountered certain shepherds, who shouted at him and constrained him to loose her. The shepherds knew her and carried her home, in a piteous plight, where, after long tending by the physicians, she was healed, yet not so wholly but she had all her throat and a part of her face marred on such wise that, whereas before she was fair, she ever after appeared misfeatured and very foul of favour; wherefore, being ashamed to appear whereas she might be seen, she many a time bitterly repented her of her frowardness and her perverse denial to put faith, in a matter which cost her nothing, in her husband's true dream."

THE EIGHTH STORY

BIONDELLO CHEATETH CIACCO OF A DINNER, WHEREOF THE OTHER CRAFTILY AVENGETH HIMSELF, PROCURING HIM TO BE SHAMEFULLY BEATEN

THE merry company with one accord avouched that which Talano had seen in sleep to have been no dream, but a vision, so punctually, without there failing aught thereof, had it come to pass. But, all being silent the queen charged Lauretta follow on, who said, "Like as those, most discreet ladies, who have to-day foregone me in speech, have been well nigh all moved to discourse by something already said, even so the stern vengeance wreaked by the scholar, of whom Pampinea told us yesterday, moveth me to tell of a piece of revenge, which, without being so barbarous as the former, was nevertheless grievous unto him who brooked it.

I must tell you, then, that there was once in Florence a man whom all called Ciacco,[435] as great a glutton as ever lived. His means sufficing him not to support the expense that his gluttony required and he being, for the rest, a very well-mannered man and full of goodly and pleasant sayings, he addressed himself to be, not altogether a buffoon, but a spunger[436] and to company with those who were rich and delighted to eat of good things; and with these he went often to dine and sup, albeit he was not always bidden. There was likewise at Florence, in those days, a man called Biondello, a little dapper fellow of his person, very quaint of his dress and sprucer than a fly, with his coif on his head and his yellow periwig still drest to a nicety, without a hair awry, who plied the same trade as Ciacco. Going one morning in Lent whereas they sell the fish and cheapening two very fine lampreys for Messer Vieri de' Cerchj, he was seen by Ciacco, who accosted him and said, 'What meaneth this?' Whereto Biondello made answer, 'Yestereve there were sent unto Messer Corso Donati three lampreys, much finer than these, and a sturgeon; to which sufficing him not for a dinner he is minded to give certain gentlemen, he would have me buy these other two. Wilt thou not come thither, thou?' Quoth Ciacco, 'Thou knowest well that I shall be there.'

. Accordingly, whenas it seemed to him time, he betook himself to Messer Corso's house, where he found him with sundry neighbours of his, not yet gone to dinner, and being asked of him what he went doing, answered, 'Sir, I am come to dine with you and your company.' Quoth Messer Corso, 'Thou art welcome; and as it is time, let us to table.' Thereupon they seated themselves at table and had, to begin with, chickpease and pickled tunny, and after a dish of fried fish from the Arno, and no more, Ciacco, perceiving the cheat that Biondello had put upon him, was inwardly no little angered thereat and resolved to pay him for it; nor had many days passed ere he again encountered the other, who had by this time made many folk merry with the trick he had played him. Biondello, seeing him, saluted him and asked him, laughing, how he had found Messer Corso's lampreys; to which Ciacco answered, 'That shalt thou know much better than I, ere eight days be past.'

Then, without wasting time over the matter, he took leave of Biondello and agreeing for a price with a shrewd huckster, carried him near to the Cavicciuoli Gallery and showing him a gentleman there, called Messer Filippo Argenti, a big burly rawboned fellow and the most despiteful, choleric and humoursome man alive, gave him a great glass flagon and said to him, 'Go to yonder gentleman with this flask in hand and say to him, "Sir Biondello sendeth me to you and prayeth you be pleased to rubify him this flask with your good red wine, for that he would fain make merry somedele with his minions." But take good care he lay not his hands on thee; else will he give thee an ill morrow and thou wilt have marred my plans.' 'Have I aught else to say,' asked the huckster; and Ciacco answered, 'No; do but go and say this and after come back to me here with the flask and I will pay thee.' The huckster accordingly set off and did his errand to Messer Filippo, who, hearing the message and being lightly ruffled, concluded that Biondello, whom he knew, had a mind to make mock of him, and waxing all red in the face, said, 'What "rubify me" and what "minions" be these? God land thee and him an ill year!' Then, starting to his feet, he put out his hand to lay hold of the huckster; but the latter, who was on his guard, promptly took to his heels and returning by another way to Ciacco, who had seen all that had passed, told him what Messer Filippo had said to him. Ciacco, well pleased, paid him and rested not till he found Biondello, to whom quoth he, 'Hast thou been late at the Cavicciuoli Gallery?' 'Nay,' answered the other. 'Why dost thou ask me?' 'Because,' replied Ciacco, 'I must tell thee that Messer Filippo enquireth for thee; I know not what he would have.' 'Good,' rejoined Biondello; 'I am going that way and will speak with him.' Accordingly, he made off, and Ciacco followed him, to see how the thing should pass.

Meanwhile Messer Filippo, having failed to come at the huckster, abode sore disordered and was inwardly all a-fume with rage, being unable to make anything in the world of the huckster's words, if not that Biondello, at whosesoever instance, was minded to make mock of him. As he fretted himself thus, up came Biondello, whom no sooner did he espy than he made for him and dealt him a sore buffet in the face. 'Alack, sir,' cried Biondello, 'what is this?' Whereupon Messer Filippo, clutching him by the hair and tearing his coif, cast his bonnet to the ground and said, laying on to him amain the while, 'Knave that thou art, thou shalt soon see what it is! What is this thou sendest to say to me with thy "rubify me" and thy "minions"? Deemest thou me a child, to be flouted on this wise?' So saying, he battered his whole face with his fists, which were like very iron, nor left him a hair on his head unruffled; then, rolling him in the mire, he tore all the clothes off his back; and to this he applied himself with such a will that Biondello could not avail to say a word to him nor ask why he served him thus. He had heard him indeed speak of 'rubify me' and 'minions,' but knew not what this meant.

At last, Messer Filippo having beaten him soundly, the bystanders, whereof many had by this time gathered about them, dragged him, with the utmost difficulty, out of the other's clutches, all bruised and battered as he was, and told him why the gentleman had done this, blaming him for that which he had sent to say to him and telling him that he should by that time have known Messer Filippo better and that he was not a man to jest withal. Biondello, all in tears protested his innocence, declaring that he had never sent to Messer Filippo for wine, and as soon as he was somewhat recovered, he returned home, sick and sorry, divining that this must have been Ciacco's doing. When, after many days, the bruises being gone, he began to go abroad again, it chanced that Ciacco encountered him and asked him, laughing, 'Harkye, Biondello, how deemest thou of Messer Filippo's wine?' 'Even as thou of Messer Corso's lampreys,' replied the other; and Ciacco said, 'The thing resteth with thee henceforth. Whenever thou goest about to give me to eat as thou didst, I will give thee in return to drink after t'other day's fashion.' Biondello, knowing full well that it was easier to wish Ciacco ill than to put it in practise, besought God of his peace[437] and thenceforth was careful to affront him no more."

THE NINTH STORY

TWO YOUNG MEN SEEK COUNSEL OF SOLOMON, ONE HOW HE MAY BE LOVED AND THE OTHER HOW HE MAY AMEND HIS FROWARD WIFE, AND IN ANSWER HE BIDDETH THE ONE LOVE AND THE OTHER GET HIM TO GOOSEBRIDGE

NONE other than the queen remaining to tell, so she would maintain Dioneo his privilege, she, after the ladies had laughed at the unlucky Biondello, began blithely to speak thus: "Lovesome ladies, if the ordinance of created things be considered with a whole mind, it will lightly enough be seen that the general multitude of women are by nature, by custom and by law subjected unto men and that it behoveth them order and govern themselves according to the discretion of these latter; wherefore each woman, who would have quiet and ease and solace with those men to whom she pertaineth, should be humble, patient and obedient, besides being virtuous, which latter is the supreme and especial treasure of every wise woman. Nay, though the laws, which in all things regard the general weal, and usance or (let us say) custom, whose puissance is both great and worship-worth, taught us not this, nature very manifestly showeth it unto us, inasmuch as she hath made us women tender and delicate of body and timid and fearful of spirit and hath given us little bodily strength, sweet voices and soft and graceful movements, all things testifying that we have need of the governance of others. Now, those who have need to be helped and governed, all reason requireth that they be obedient and submissive and reverent to their governors; and whom have we to governors and helpers, if not men? To men, therefore, it behoveth us submit ourselves, honouring them supremely; and whoso departeth from this, I hold her deserving, not only of grave reprehension, but of severe punishment. To these considerations I was lead, though not for the first time, by that which Pampinea told us a while ago of Talano's froward wife, upon whom God sent that chastisement which her husband had not known to give her; wherefore, as I have already said, all those women who depart from being loving, compliant and amenable, as nature, usance and law will it, are, in my judgment, worthy of stern and severe chastisement. It pleaseth me, therefore, to recount to you a counsel given by Solomon, as a salutary medicine for curing women who are thus made of that malady; which counsel let none, who meriteth not such treatment, repute to have been said for her, albeit men have a byword which saith, 'Good horse and bad horse both the spur need still, And women need the stick, both good and ill.' Which words, an one seek to interpret them by way of pleasantry, all women will lightly allow to be true; nay, but considering them morally,[438] I say that the same must be conceded of them; for that women are all naturally unstable and prone [to frailty,] wherefore, to correct the iniquity of those who allow themselves too far to overpass the limits appointed them, there needeth the stick which punisheth them, and to support the virtue of others who suffer not themselves to transgress, there needeth the stick which sustaineth and affeareth them. But, to leave be preaching for the nonce and come to that which I have it in mind to tell.

You must know that, the high renown of Solomon's miraculous wisdom being bruited abroad well nigh throughout the whole world, no less than the liberality with which he dispensed it unto whoso would fain be certified thereof by experience, there flocked many to him from divers parts of the world for counsel in their straitest and most urgent occasions. Amongst others who thus resorted to him was a young man, Melisso by name, a gentleman of noble birth and great wealth, who set out from the city of Lajazzo,[439] whence he was and where he dwelt; and as he journeyed towards Jerusalem, it chanced that, coming forth of Antioch, he rode for some distance with a young man called Giosefo, who held the same course as himself. As the custom is of wayfarers, he entered into discourse with him and having learned from him what and whence he was, he asked him whither he went and upon what occasion; to which Giosefo replied that he was on his way to Solomon, to have counsel of him what course he should take with a wife he had, the most froward and perverse woman alive, whom neither with prayers nor with blandishments nor on any other wise could he avail to correct of her waywardness. Then he in his turn questioned Melisso whence he was and whither he went and on what errand, and he answered, 'I am of Lajazzo, and like as thou hast a grievance, even so have I one; I am young and rich and spend my substance in keeping open house and entertaining my fellow-townsmen, and yet, strange to say, I cannot for all that find one who wisheth me well; wherefore I go whither thou goest, to have counsel how I may win to be beloved.'

Accordingly, they joined company and journeyed till they came to Jerusalem, where, by the introduction of one of Solomon's barons, they were admitted to the presence of the king, to whom Melisso briefly set forth his occasion. Solomon answered him, 'Love'; and this said, Melisso was straightway put forth and Giosefo told that for which he was there. Solomon made him no other answer than 'Get thee to Goosebridge'; which said, Giosefo was on like wise removed, without delay, from the king's presence and finding Melisso awaiting him without, told him that which he had had for answer. Thereupon, pondering Solomon's words and availing to apprehend therefrom neither significance nor profit whatsoever for their occasions, they set out to return home, as deeming themselves flouted. After journeying for some days, they came to a river, over which was a fine bridge, and a caravan of pack-mules and sumpter-horses being in act to pass, it behoved them tarry till such time as these should be crossed over. Presently, the beasts having well nigh all crossed, it chanced that one of the mules took umbrage, as oftentimes we see them do, and would by no means pass on; whereupon a muleteer, taking a stick, began to beat it at first moderately enough to make it go on; but the mule shied now to this and now to that side of the road and whiles turned back altogether, but would on no wise pass on; whereupon the man, incensed beyond measure, fell to dealing it with the stick the heaviest blows in the world, now on the head, now on the flanks and anon on the crupper, but all to no purpose.

Melisso and Giosefo stood watching this and said often to the muleteer, 'Alack, wretch that thou art, what dost thou? Wilt thou kill the beast? Why studiest thou not to manage him by fair means and gentle dealing? He will come quicklier than for cudgeling him as thou dost.' To which the man answered, 'You know your horses and I know my mule; leave me do with him.' So saying, he fell again to cudgelling him and belaboured him to such purpose on one side and on the other, that the mule passed on and the muleteer won the bout. Then, the two young men being now about to depart, Giosefo asked a poor man, who sat at the bridge-head, how the place was called, and he answered, 'Sir, this is called Goosebridge.' When Giosefo heard this, he straightway called to mind Solomon's words and said to Melisso, 'Marry, I tell thee, comrade, that the counsel given me by Solomon may well prove good and true, for I perceive very plainly that I knew not how to beat my wife; but this muleteer hath shown me what I have to do.'

Accordingly, they fared on and came, after some days, to Antioch, where Giosefo kept Melisso with him, that he might rest himself a day or two, and being scurvily enough received of his wife, he bade her prepare supper according as Melisso should ordain; whereof the latter, seeing that it was his friend's pleasure, acquitted himself in a few words. The lady, as her usance had been in the past, did not as Melisso had ordained, but well nigh altogether the contrary; which Giosefo seeing, he was vexed and said, 'Was it not told thee on what wise thou shouldst prepare the supper?' The lady, turning round haughtily, answered, 'What meaneth this? Good lack, why dost thou not sup, an thou have a mind to sup? An if it were told me otherwise, it seemed good to me to do thus. If it please thee, so be it; if not, leave it be.' Melisso marvelled at the lady's answer and blamed her exceedingly; whilst Giosefo, hearing this, said, 'Wife, thou art still what thou wast wont to be; but, trust me, I will make thee change thy fashion.' Then turning to Melisso, 'Friend,' said he, 'we shall soon see what manner of counsel was Solomon's; but I prithee let it not irk thee to stand to see it and hold that which I shall do for a sport. And that thou mayest not hinder me, bethink thee of the answer the muleteer made us, when we pitied his mule.' Quoth Melisso, 'I am in thy house, where I purpose not to depart from thy good pleasure.'

Giosefo then took a round stick, made of a young oak, and repaired a chamber, whither the lady, having arisen from table for despite, had betaken herself, grumbling; then, laying hold of her by the hair, he threw her down at his feet and proceeded to give her a sore beating with the stick. The lady at first cried out and after fell to threats; but, seeing that Giosefo for all that stinted not and being by this time all bruised, she began to cry him mercy for God's sake and besought him not to kill her, declaring that she would never more depart from his pleasure. Nevertheless, he held not his hand; nay, he continued to baste her more furiously than ever on all her seams, belabouring her amain now on the ribs, now on the haunches and now about the shoulder, nor stinted till he was weary and there was not a place left unbruised on the good lady's back. This done, he returned to his friend and said to him, 'To-morrow we shall see what will be the issue of the counsel to go to Goosebridge.' Then, after he had rested awhile and they had washed their hands, he supped with Melisso and in due season they betook themselves to bed.

Meanwhile the wretched lady arose with great pain from the ground and casting herself on the bed, there rested as best she might until the morning, when she arose betimes and let ask Giosefo what he would have dressed for dinner. The latter, making merry over this with Melisso, appointed it in due course, and after, whenas it was time, returning, they found everything excellently well done and in accordance with the ordinance given; wherefore they mightily commended the counsel at first so ill apprehended of them. After some days, Melisso took leave of Giosefo and returning to his own house, told one, who was a man of understanding, the answer he had had from Solomon; whereupon quoth the other, 'He could have given thee no truer nor better counsel. Thou knowest thou lovest no one, and the honours and services thou renderest others, thou dost not for love that thou bearest them, but for pomp and ostentation. Love, then, as Solomon bade thee, and thou shalt be loved.' On this wise, then, was the froward wife corrected and the young man, loving, was beloved."

THE TENTH STORY

DOM GIANNI, AT THE INSTANCE OF HIS GOSSIP PIETRO, PERFORMETH A CONJURATION FOR THE PURPOSE OF CAUSING THE LATTER'S WIFE TO BECOME A MARE; BUT, WHENAS HE COMETH TO PUT ON THE TAIL, PIETRO MARRETH THE WHOLE CONJURATION, SAYING THAT HE WILL NOT HAVE A TAIL

THE queen's story made the young men laugh and gave rise to some murmurs on the part of the ladies; then, as soon as the latter were quiet, Dioneo began to speak thus, "Sprightly ladies, a black crow amongst a multitude of white doves addeth more beauty than would a snow-white swan, and in like manner among many sages one less wise is not only an augmentation of splendour and goodliness to

The Decameron of Giovanni Boccaccio - Part II

their maturity, but eke a source of diversion and solace. Wherefore, you ladies being all exceeding discreet and modest, I, who savour somewhat of the scatterbrain, should be dearer to you, causing, as I do, your worth to shine the brightlier for my default, than if with my greater merit I made this of yours wax dimmer; and consequently, I should have larger license to show you myself such as I am and should more patiently be suffered of you, in saying that which I shall say, than if I were wiser. I will, therefore, tell you a story not overlong, whereby you may apprehend how diligently it behoveth to observe the conditions imposed by those who do aught by means of enchantment and how slight a default thereof sufficeth to mar everything done by the magician.

A year or two agone there was at Barletta a priest called Dom Gianni di Barolo, who, for that he had but a poor cure, took to eking out his livelihood by hawking merchandise hither and thither about the fairs of Apulia with a mare of his and buying and selling. In the course of his travels he contracted a strait friendship with one who styled himself Pietro da Tresanti and plied the same trade with the aid of an ass he had. In token of friendship and affection, he called him still Gossip Pietro, after the Apulian fashion, and whenassoever he visited Barletta, he carried him to his parsonage and there lodged him with himself and entertained him to the best of his power. Gossip Pietro, on his part, albeit he was very poor and had but a sorry little house at Tresanti, scarce sufficing for himself and a young and buxom wife he had and his ass, as often as Dom Gianni came to Tresanti, carried him home with him and entertained him as best he might, in requital of the hospitality received from him at Barletta. Nevertheless, in the matter of lodging, having but one sorry little bed, in which he slept with his handsome wife, he could not entertain him as he would, but, Dom Gianni's mare being lodged with Pietro's ass in a little stable he had, needs must the priest himself lie by her side on a truss of straw.

The goodwife, knowing the hospitality which the latter did her husband at Barletta, would more than once, whenas the priest came thither, have gone to lie with a neighbor of hers, by name Zita Caraprese, [daughter] of Giudice Leo, so he might sleep in the bed with her husband, and had many a time proposed it to Dom Gianni, but he would never hear of it; and once, amongst other times, he said to her, 'Gossip Gemmata, fret not thyself for me; I fare very well, for that, whenas it pleaseth me, I cause this mare of mine become a handsome wench and couch with her, and after, when I will, I change her into a mare again; wherefore I care not to part from her.'

The young woman marvelled, but believed his tale and told her husband, saying, 'If he is so much thy friend as thou sayest, why dost thou not make him teach thee his charm, so thou mayst avail to make of me a mare and do thine affairs with the ass and the mare? So should we gain two for one; and when we were back at home, thou couldst make me a woman again, as I am.' Pietro, who was somewhat dull of wit, believed what she said and falling in with her counsel, began, as best he knew, to importune Dom Gianni to teach him the trick. The latter did his best to cure him of that folly, but availing not thereto, he said, 'Harkye, since you will e'en have it so, we will arise to-morrow morning before day, as of our wont, and I will show you how it is done. To tell thee the truth, the uneathest part of the matter is the putting on of the tail, as thou shalt see.'

Accordingly, whenas it drew near unto day, Goodman Pietro and Gossip Gemmata, who had scarce slept that night, with such impatience did they await the accomplishment of the matter, arose and called Dom Gianni, who, arising in his shirt, betook himself to Pietro's little chamber and said to him, 'I know none in the world, except you, for whom I would do this; wherefore since it pleaseth you, I will e'en do it; but needs must you do as I shall bid you, an you would have the thing succeed.' They answered that they would do that which he should say; whereupon, taking the light, he put it into Pietro's hand and said to him, 'Mark how I shall do and keep well in mind that which I shall say. Above all, have a care, an thou wouldst not mar everything, that, whatsoever thou hearest or seest, thou say not a single word, and pray God that the tail may stick fast.' Pietro took the light, promising to do exactly as he said, whereupon Dom Gianni let strip Gemmata naked as she was born and caused her stand on all fours, mare-fashion, enjoining herself likewise not to utter a word for aught that should betide. Then, passing his hand over her face and her head, he proceeded to say, 'Be this a fine mare's head,' and touching her hair, said, 'Be this a fine mare's mane'; after which he touched her arms, saying, 'Be these fine mare's legs and feet,' and coming presently to her breast and finding it round and firm, such an one awoke that was not called and started up on end,[440] whereupon quoth he, 'Be this a fine mare's chest.' And on like wise he did with her back and belly and crupper and thighs and legs. Ultimately, nothing remaining to do but the tail, he pulled up his shirt and taking the dibble with which he planted men, he thrust it hastily into the furrow made therefor and said, 'And be this a fine mare's tail.'

Pietro, who had thitherto watched everything intently, seeing this last proceeding and himseeming it was ill done, said, 'Ho there, Dom Gianni, I won't have a tail there, I won't have a tail there!' The radical moisture, wherewith all plants are made fast, was by this come, and Dom Gianni drew it forth, saying, 'Alack, gossip Pietro, what hast thou done? Did I not bid thee say not a word for aught that thou shouldst see? The mare was all made; but thou hast marred everything by talking, nor is there any means of doing it over again henceforth.' Quoth Pietro, 'Marry, I did not want that tail there. Why did you not say to me, "Make it thou"? More by token that you were for setting it too low.' 'Because,' answered Dom Gianni, 'thou hadst not known for the first time to set it on so well as I.' The young woman, hearing all this, stood up and said to her husband, in all good faith, 'Dolt that thou art, why hast thou marred thine affairs and mine? What mare sawest thou ever without a tail? So God aid me, thou art poor, but it would serve thee right, wert thou much poorer.' Then, there being now, by reason of the words that Pietro had spoken, no longer any means of making a mare of the young woman, she donned her clothes, woebegone and disconsolate, and Pietro, continuing to ply his old trade with an ass, as he was used, betook himself, in company with Dom Gianni, to the Bitonto fair, nor ever again required him of such a service."

How much the company laughed at this story, which was better understood of the ladies than Dioneo willed, let her who shall yet laugh thereat imagine for herself. But, the day's stories being now ended and the sun beginning to abate of its heat, the queen, knowing the end of her seignory to be come, rose to her feet and putting off the crown, set it on the head of Pamfilo, whom alone it remained to honour after such a fashion, and said, smiling, "My lord, there devolveth on thee a great burden, inasmuch as with thee it resteth, thou being the last, to make amends for my default and that of those who have foregone me in the dignity which thou presently holdest; whereof God lend thee grace, even as He hath vouchsafed it unto me to make thee king." Pamfilo blithely received the honour done him and answered, "Your merit and that of my other subjects will do on such wise that I shall be adjudged deserving of commendation, even as the others have been." Then, having, according to the usance of his predecessors, taken order with the seneschal of the things that were needful, he turned to the expectant ladies and said to them, "Lovesome ladies, it was the pleasure of Emilia, who hath this day been our queen, to give you, for the purpose of affording some rest to your powers, license to discourse of that which should most please you; wherefore, you being now rested, I hold it well to return to the wonted ordinance, and accordingly I will that each of you bethink herself to discourse to-morrow of this, to wit, OF WHOSO HATH ANYWISE WROUGHT GENEROUSLY OR MAGNIFICENTLY IN MATTERS OF LOVE OR OTHERWHAT. The telling and doing of these things will doubtless fire your well-disposed minds to do worthily; so will our life, which may not be other than brief in this mortal body, be made perpetual in laudatory renown; a thing which all, who serve not the belly only, as do the beasts, should not only desire, but with all diligence seek and endeavour after."

The theme pleased the joyous company, who having all, with the new king's license, arisen from session, gave themselves to their wonted diversions, according to that unto which each was most drawn by desire; and on this wise they did until the hour of supper, whereunto they came joyously and were served with diligence and fair ordinance. Supper at an end, they arose to the wonted dances, and after they had sung a thousand canzonets, more diverting of words than masterly of music, the king bade Neifile sing one in her own name; whereupon, with clear and blithesome voice, she cheerfully and without delay began thus:

A youngling maid am I and full of glee,
Am fain to carol in the new-blown May,
Love and sweet thoughts-a-mercy, blithe and free.

I go about the meads, considering
The vermeil flowers and golden and the white,
Roses thorn-set and lilies snowy-bright,
And one and all I fare a-likening
Unto his face who hath with love-liking
Ta'en and will hold me ever, having aye
None other wish than as his pleasures be;

Whereof when one I find me that doth show,
Unto my seeming, likest him, full fain
I cull and kiss and talk with it amain
And all my heart to it, as best I know,
Discover, with its store of wish and woe,
Then it with others in a wreath I lay,
Bound with my hair so golden-bright of blee.

Ay, and that pleasure which the eye doth prove,
By nature, of the flower's view, like delight
Doth give me as I saw the very wight
Who hath inflamed me of his dulcet love,
And what its scent thereover and above
Worketh in me, no words indeed can say;
But sighs thereof bear witness true for me,

The which from out my bosom day nor night
Ne'er, as with other ladies, fierce and wild,
Storm up; nay, thence they issue warm and mild
And straight betake them to my loved one's sight,
Who, hearing, moveth of himself, delight
To give me; ay, and when I'm like to say
"Ah come, lest I despair," still cometh he.

Neifile's canzonet was much commended both of the king and of the other ladies; after which, for that a great part of the night was now spent, the king commanded that all should betake themselves to rest until the day.

HERE ENDETH THE NINTH DAY
OF THE DECAMERON

Day the Tenth

HERE BEGINNETH THE TENTH AND LAST DAY OF THE DECAMERON WHEREIN UNDER THE GOVERNANCE OF PAMFILO IS DISCOURSED OF WHOSO HATH ANYWISE WROUGHT GENEROUSLY OR MAGNIFICENTLY IN MATTERS OF LOVE OR OTHERWHAT

CERTAIN cloudlets in the West were yet vermeil, what time those of the East were already at their marges grown lucent like unto very gold, when Pamfilo, arising, let call his comrades and the ladies, who being all come, he took counsel with them of whither they should go for their diversion and fared forth with slow step, accompanied by Filomena and Fiammetta, whilst all the others followed after. On this wise, devising and telling and answering many things of their future life together, they went a great while a-pleasuring; then, having made a pretty long circuit and the sun beginning to wax overhot, they returned to the palace. There they let rinse the beakers in the clear fountain and whoso would drank somewhat; after which they went frolicking among the pleasant shades of the garden until the eating-hour. Then, having eaten and slept, as of their wont, they assembled whereas it pleased the king and there he called upon Neifile for the first discourse, who blithely began thus:

THE FIRST STORY

A KNIGHT IN THE KING'S SERVICE OF SPAIN THINKING HIMSELF ILL GUERDONED, THE KING BY VERY CERTAIN PROOF SHOWETH HIM THAT THIS IS NOT HIS FAULT, BUT THAT OF HIS OWN PERVERSE FORTUNE, AND AFTER LARGESSETH HIM MAGNIFICENTLY

"NEEDS, honourable ladies, must I repute it a singular favour to myself that our king hath preferred me unto such an honour as it is to be the first to tell of magnificence, the which, even as the sun is the glory and adornment of all the heaven, is the light and lustre of every other virtue. I will, therefore, tell you a little story thereof, quaint and pleasant enough to my thinking, which to recall can certes be none other than useful.

You must know, then, that, among the other gallant gentlemen who have from time immemorial graced our city, there was one (and maybe the most of worth) by name Messer Ruggieri de' Figiovanni, who, being both rich and high-spirited and seeing that, in view of the way of living and of the usages of Tuscany, he might, if he tarried there, avail to display little or nothing of his merit, resolved to seek service awhile with Alfonso, King of Spain, the renown of whose valiance transcended that of every other prince of his time; wherefore he betook himself, very honourably furnished with arms and horses and followers, to Alfonso in Spain and was by him graciously received. Accordingly, he took up his abode there and living splendidly and doing marvellous deeds of arms, he very soon made himself known for a man of worth and valour.

When he had sojourned there a pretty while and had taken particular note of the king's fashions, himseemed he bestowed castles and cities and baronies now upon one and now upon another with little enough discretion, as giving them to those who were unworthy thereof, and for that to him, who held himself for that which he was, nothing was given, he conceived that his repute would be much abated by reason thereof; wherefore he determined to depart and craved leave of the king. The latter granted him the leave he sought and gave him one of the best and finest mules that ever was ridden, the which, for the long journey he had to make, was very acceptable to Messer Ruggieri. Moreover, he charged a discreet servant of his that he should study, by such means as seemed to him best, to ride with Messer Ruggieri on such wise that he should not appear to have been sent by the king, and note everything he should say of him, so as he might avail to repeat it to him, and that on the ensuing morning he should command him return to the court. Accordingly, the servant, lying in wait for Messer Ruggieri's departure, accosted him, as he came forth the city, and very aptly joined company with him, giving him to understand that he also was bound for Italy. Messer Ruggieri, then, fared on, riding the mule given him by the king and devising of one thing and another with the latter's servant, till hard upon tierce, when he said, 'Methinketh it were well done to let our beasts stale.' Accordingly, they put them up in a stable and they all staled, except the mule; then they rode on again, whilst the squire still took note of the gentleman's words, and came presently to a river, where, as they watered their cattle, the mule staled in the stream; which Messer Ruggieri seeing, 'Marry,' quoth he, 'God confound thee, beast, for that thou art made after the same fashion as the prince who gave thee to me!' The squire noted these words and albeit he took store of many others, as he journeyed with him all that day, he heard him say nought else but what was to the highest praise of the king.

Next morning, they being mounted and Ruggieri offering to ride towards Tuscany, the squire imparted to him the king's commandment, whereupon he incontinent turned back. When he arrived at court, the king, learning what he had said of the mule, let call him to himself and receiving him with a cheerful favour, asked him why he had likened him to his mule, or rather why he had likened the mule to him. 'My lord,' replied Ruggieri frankly, 'I likened her to you for that, like as you give whereas it behoveth not and give not whereas it behoveth, even so she staled not whereas it behoved, but staled whereas it behoved not.' Then said the king, 'Messer Ruggieri, if I have not given to you, as I have given unto many who are of no account in comparison with you, it happened not because I knew you not for a most valiant cavalier and worthy of every great gift; nay, but it is your fortune, which hath not suffered me guerdon you according to your deserts, that hath sinned in this, and not I; and that I may say sooth I will manifestly prove to you.' 'My lord,' replied Ruggieri, 'I was not chagrined because I have gotten no largesse of you, for that I desire not to be richer than I am, but because you have on no wise borne witness to my merit. Natheless, I hold your excuse for good and honourable and am ready to see that which it shall please you show me, albeit I believe you without proof.' The king then carried him into a great hall of his, where, as he had ordered it beforehand, were two great locked coffers, and said to him, in presence of many, 'Messer Ruggieri, in one of these coffers is my crown, the royal sceptre and the orb, together with many goodly girdles and ouches and rings of mine, and in fine every precious jewel I have; and the other is full of earth.

Take, then, one and be that which you shall take yours; and you may thus see whether of the twain hath been ungrateful to your worth, myself of your ill fortune.'

Messer Ruggieri, seeing that it was the king's pleasure, took one of the coffers, which, being opened by Alfonso's commandment, was found to be that which was full of earth; whereupon quoth the king, laughing, 'Now can you see, Messer Ruggieri, that this that I tell you of your fortune is true; but certes your worth meriteth that I should oppose myself to her might. I know you have no mind to turn Spaniard and therefore I will bestow upon you neither castle nor city in these parts; but this coffer, of which fortune deprived you, I will in her despite shall be yours, so you may carry it off to your own country and justly glorify yourself of your worth in the sight of your countrymen by the witness of my gifts.' Messer Ruggieri accordingly took the coffer and having rendered the king those thanks which sorted with such a gift, joyfully returned therewith to Tuscany."

THE SECOND STORY

GHINO DI TACCO TAKETH THE ABBOT OF CLUNY AND HAVING CURED HIM OF THE STOMACH-COMPLAINT, LETTETH HIM GO; WHEREUPON THE ABBOT, RETURNING TO THE COURT OF ROME, RECONCILETH HIM WITH POPE BONIFACE AND MAKETH HIM A PRIOR OF THE HOSPITALLERS

THE magnificence shown by King Alfonso to the Florentine cavalier having been duly commended, the king, who had been mightily pleased therewith, enjoined Elisa to follow on, and she straightway began thus: "Dainty dames, it cannot be denied that for a king to be munificent and to have shown his munificence to him who had served him is a great and a praiseworthy thing; but what shall we say if a churchman be related to have practised marvellous magnanimity towards one, whom if he had used as an enemy, he had of none been blamed therefor? Certes, we can say none otherwise than that the king's magnificence was a virtue, whilst that of the churchman was a miracle, inasmuch as the clergy are all exceeding niggardly, nay, far more so than women, and sworn enemies of all manner of liberality; and albeit all men naturally hunger after vengeance for affronts received, we see churchmen, for all they preach patience and especially commend the remission of offences, pursue it more eagerly than other folk. This, then, to wit, how a churchman was magnanimous, you may manifestly learn from the following story of mine.

Ghino di Tacco, a man very famous for his cruelty and his robberies, being expelled Siena and at feud with the Counts of Santa Fiore, raised Radicofani against the Church of Rome and taking up his sojourn there, caused his swashbucklers despoil whosoever passed through the surrounding country. Now, Boniface the Eighth being pope in Rome, there came to court the Abbot of Cluny, who is believed to be one of the richest prelates in the world, and having there marred his stomach, he was advised by the physicians to repair to the baths of Siena and he would without fail be cured. Accordingly, having gotten the pope's leave, he set out on his way thither in great pomp of gear and baggage and horses and servitors, unrecking of Ghino's [ill] report. The latter, hearing of his coming, spread his nets and hemmed him and all his household and gear about in a strait place, without letting a single footboy escape. This done, he despatched to the abbot one, the most sufficient, of his men, well accompanied, who in his name very lovingly prayed him be pleased to light down and sojourn with the aforesaid Ghino in his castle. The abbot, hearing this, answered furiously that he would nowise do it, having nought to do with Ghino, but that he would fare on and would fain see who should forbid his passage. Whereto quoth the messenger on humble wise, 'Sir, you are come into parts where, barring God His might, there is nothing to fear for us and where excommunications and interdicts are all excommunicated; wherefore, may it please you, you were best comply with Ghino in this.'

During this parley, the whole place had been encompassed about with men-at-arms; wherefore the abbot, seeing himself taken with his men, betook himself, sore against his will, to the castle, in company with the ambassador, and with him all his household and gear, and alighting there, was, by Ghino's orders, lodged all alone in a very dark and mean little chamber in one of the pavilions, whilst every one else was well enough accommodated, according to his quality, about the castle and the horses and all the gear put in safety, without aught thereof being touched. This done, Ghino betook himself to the abbot and said to him, 'Sir, Ghino, whose guest you are, sendeth to you, praying you acquaint him whither you are bound and on what occasion.' The abbot, like a wise man, had by this laid by his pride and told him whither he went and why. Ghino, hearing this, took his leave and bethought himself to go about to cure him without baths. Accordingly, he let keep a great fire still burning in the little room and causing guard the place well, returned not to the abbot till the following morning, when he brought him, in a very white napkin, two slices of toasted bread and a great beaker of his own Corniglia vernage[441] and bespoke him thus, 'Sir, when Ghino was young, he studied medicine and saith that he learned there was no better remedy for the stomach-complaint than that which he purposeth to apply to you and of which these things that I bring you are the beginning; wherefore do you take them and refresh yourself.'

The abbot, whose hunger was greater than his desire to bandy words, ate the bread and drank the wine, though he did it with an ill will, and after made many haughty speeches, asking and counselling of many things and demanding in particular to see Ghino. The latter, hearing this talk, let part of it pass as idle and answered the rest very courteously, avouching that Ghino would visit him as quickliest he might. This said, he took his leave of him and returned not until the ensuing day, when he brought him as much toasted bread and as much malmsey; and so he kept him several days, till such time as he perceived that he had eaten some dried beans, which he had of intent aforethought brought secretly thither and left there; whereupon he asked him, on Ghino's part, how he found himself about the stomach. The abbot answered, 'Meseemeth I should fare well, were I but out of his hands; and after that, I have no greater desire than to eat, so well have his remedies cured me.' Thereupon Ghino caused the abbot's own people array him a goodly chamber with his own gear and let make ready a magnificent banquet, to which he bade the prelate's whole household, together with many folk of the burgh. Next morning, he betook himself to the abbot and said to him, 'Sir, since you feel yourself well, it is time to leave the infirmary.' Then, taking him by the hand, he brought him to the chamber prepared for him and leaving him there in company of his own people, occupied himself with caring that the banquet should be a magnificent one.

The abbot solaced himself awhile with his men and told them what his life had been since his capture, whilst they, on the other hand, avouched themselves all to have been wonder-well entreated of Ghino. The eating-hour come, the abbot and the rest were well and orderly served with goodly viands and fine wines, without Ghino yet letting himself be known of the prelate; but, after the latter had abidden some days on this wise, the outlaw, having let bring all his gear into one saloon and all his horses, down to the sorriest rouncey, into a courtyard that was under the windows thereof, betook himself to him and asked him how he did and if he deemed himself strong enough to take horse. The abbot answered that he was strong enough and quite recovered of his stomach-complaint and that he should fare perfectly well, once he should be out of Ghino's hands. Ghino then brought him into the saloon, wherein was his gear and all his train, and carrying him to a window, whence he might see all his horses, said, 'My lord abbot, you must know that it was the being a gentleman and expelled from his house and poor and having many and puissant enemies, and not evilness of mind, that brought Ghino di Tacco (who is none other than myself) to be, for the defence of his life and his nobility, a highway-robber and an enemy of the court of Rome. Nevertheless, for that you seem to me a worthy gentleman, I purpose not, now that I have cured you of your stomach-complaint, to use you as I would another, from whom, he being in my hands as you are, I would take for myself such part of his goods as seemed well to me; nay, it is my intent that you, having regard to my need, shall appoint to me such part of your good as you yourself will. It is all here before you in its entirety and your horses you may from this window see in the courtyard; take, therefore, both part and all, as it pleaseth you, and from this time forth be it at your pleasure to go or to stay.'

The abbot marvelled to hear such generous words from a highway-robber and was exceeding well pleased therewith, insomuch that, his anger and despite being of a sudden fallen, nay, changed into goodwill, he became Ghino's hearty friend and ran to embrace him, saying, 'I vow to God that, to gain the friendship of a man such as I presently judge thee to be, I would gladly consent to suffer a far greater affront than that which meseemed but now thou hadst done me. Accursed be fortune that constrained thee to so damnable a trade!' Then, letting take of his many goods but a very few necessary things, and the like of his horses, he left all the rest to Ghino and returned to Rome. The pope had had news of the taking of the abbot and albeit it had given him sore concern, he asked him, when he saw him, how the baths had profited him; whereto he replied, smiling, 'Holy Father, I found a worthy physician nearer than at the baths, who hath excellently well cured me'; and told him how, whereat the pope laughed, and the abbot, following on his speech and moved by a magnanimous spirit, craved a boon of him. The pope, thinking he would demand otherwhat, freely offered to do that which he should ask; and the abbot said, 'Holy Father, that which I mean to ask of you is that you restore your favour to Ghino di Tacco, my physician, for that, of all the men of worth and high account whom I ever knew, he is certes one of the most deserving; and for this ill that he doth, I hold it much more fortune's fault than his; the which[442] if you change by bestowing on him somewhat whereby he may live according to his condition, I doubt not anywise but you will, in brief space of time, deem of him even as I do.' The pope, who was great of soul and a lover of men of worth, hearing this, replied that he would gladly do it, an Ghino were indeed of such account as the abbot avouched, and bade the latter cause him come thither in all security. Accordingly, Ghino, at the abbot's instance, came to court, upon that assurance, nor had he been long about the pope's person ere the latter reputed him a man of worth and taking him into favour, bestowed on him a grand priory of those of the Hospitallers, having first let make him a knight of that order; which office he held whilst he lived, still approving himself a loyal friend and servant of Holy Church and of the Abbot of Cluny."

THE THIRD STORY

MITHRIDANES, ENVYING NATHAN HIS HOSPITALITY AND GENEROSITY AND GOING TO KILL HIM, FALLETH IN WITH HIMSELF, WITHOUT KNOWING HIM, AND IS BY HIM INSTRUCTED OF THE COURSE HE SHALL TAKE TO ACCOMPLISH HIS PURPOSE; BY MEANS WHEREOF HE FINDETH HIM, AS HE HIMSELF HAD ORDERED IT, IN A COPPICE AND RECOGNIZING HIM, IS ASHAMED AND BECOMETH HIS FRIEND

THEMSEEMED all they had heard what was like unto a miracle, to wit, that a churchman should have wrought anywhat magnificently; but, as soon as the ladies had left discoursing thereof, the king bade Filostrato proceed, who forthright began, "Noble ladies, great was the magnificence of the King of Spain and that of the Abbot of Cluny a thing belike never yet heard of; but maybe it will seem to you no less marvellous a thing to hear how a man, that he might do generosity to another who thirsted for his blood, nay, for the very breath of his nostrils, privily bethought himself to give them to him, ay, and would have done it, had the other willed to take them, even as I purpose to show you in a little story of mine.

It is a very certain thing (if credit may be given to the report of divers Genoese and others who have been in those countries) that there was aforetime in the parts of Cattajo[443] a man of noble lineage and rich beyond compare, called Nathan, who, having an estate adjoining a highway whereby as of necessity passed all who sought to go from the Ponant to the Levant or from the Levant to the Ponant, and being a man of great and generous soul and desirous that it should be known by his works, assembled a great multitude of artificers and let build there, in a little space of time, one of the fairest and greatest and richest palaces that had ever been seen, the which he caused excellently well furnished with all that was apt unto the reception and entertainment of gentlemen. Then, having a great and goodly household, he there received and honourably entertained, with joyance and good cheer, whosoever came and went; and in this praiseworthy usance he persevered insomuch that not only the

Levant, but well nigh all the Ponant, knew him by report. He was already full of years nor was therefore grown weary of the practice of hospitality, when it chanced that his fame reached the ears of a young man of a country not far from his own, by name Mithridanes, who, knowing himself no less rich than Nathan and waxing envious of his renown and his virtues, bethought himself to eclipse or shadow them with greater liberality. Accordingly, letting build a palace like unto that of Nathan, he proceeded to do the most unbounded courtesies[444] that ever any did whosoever came or went about those parts, and in a short time he became without doubt very famous.

It chanced one day that, as he abode all alone in the midcourt of his palace, there came in, by one of the gates, a poor woman, who sought of him an alms and had it; then, coming in again to him by the second, she had of him another alms, and so on for twelve times in succession; but, whenas she returned for the thirteenth time, he said to her, 'Good woman, thou art very diligent in this thine asking,' and natheless gave her an alms. The old crone, hearing these words, exclaimed, 'O liberality of Nathan, how marvellous art thou! For that, entering in by each of the two-and-thirty gates which his palace hath, and asking of him an alms, never, for all that he showed, was I recognized of him, and still I had it; whilst here, having as yet come in but at thirteen gates, I have been both recognized and chidden.' So saying, she went her ways and returned thither no more. Mithridanes, hearing the old woman's words, flamed up into a furious rage, as he who held that which he heard of Nathan's fame a diminishment of his own, and fell to saying, 'Alack, woe is me! When shall I attain to Nathan's liberality in great things, let alone overpass it, as I seek to do, seeing that I cannot approach him in the smallest? Verily, I weary myself in vain, an I remove him not from the earth; wherefore, since eld carrieth him not off, needs must I with mine own hands do it without delay.'

Accordingly, rising upon that motion, he took horse with a small company, without communicating his design to any, and came after three days whereas Nathan abode. He arrived there at eventide and bidding his followers make a show of not being with him and provide themselves with lodging, against they should hear farther from him, abode alone at no great distance from the fair palace, where he found Nathan all unattended, as he went walking for his diversion, without any pomp of apparel, and knowing him not, asked him if he could inform him where Nathan dwelt. 'My son,' answered the latter cheerfully, 'there is none in these parts who is better able than I to show thee that; wherefore, whenas it pleaseth thee, I will carry thee thither.' Mithridanes rejoined that this would be very acceptable to him, but that, an it might be, he would fain be neither seen nor known of Nathan; and the latter said, 'That also will I do, since it pleaseth thee.' Mithridanes accordingly dismounted and repaired to the goodly palace, in company with Nathan, who quickly engaged him in most pleasant discourse. There he caused one of his servants take the young man's horse and putting his mouth to his ear, charged him take order with all those of the house, so none should tell the youth that he was Nathan; and so was it done. Moreover, he lodged him in a very goodly chamber, where none saw him, save those whom he had deputed to this service, and let entertain him with the utmost honour, himself bearing him company.

After Mithridanes had abidden with him awhile on this wise, he asked him (albeit he held him in reverence as a father) who he was; to which Nathan answered, 'I am an unworthy servant of Nathan, who have grown old with him from my childhood, nor hath he ever advanced me to otherwhat than that which thou seest me; wherefore, albeit every one else is mighty well pleased with him, I for my part have little cause to thank him.' These words afforded Mithridanes some hope of availing with more certitude and more safety to give effect to his perverse design, and Nathan very courteously asking him who he was and what occasion brought him into those parts and proffering him his advice and assistance insomuch as lay in his power, he hesitated awhile to reply, but, presently, resolving to trust himself to him, he with a long circuit of words[445] required him first of secrecy and after of aid and counsel and entirely discovered to him who he was and wherefore and on what motion he came. Nathan, hearing his discourse and his cruel design, was inwardly all disordered; but nevertheless, without much hesitation, he answered him with an undaunted mind and a firm countenance, saying, 'Mithridanes, thy father was a noble man and thou showest thyself minded not to degenerate from him, in having entered upon so high an emprise as this thou hast undertaken, to wit, to be liberal unto all; and greatly do I commend the jealousy thou bearest unto Nathan's virtues, for that, were there many such,[446] the world, that is most wretched, would soon become good. The design that thou hast discovered to me I will without fail keep secret; but for the accomplishment thereof I can rather give thee useful counsel than great help; the which is this. Thou mayst from here see a coppice, maybe half a mile hence, wherein Nathan well nigh every morning walketh all alone, taking his pleasure there a pretty long while; and there it will be a light matter to thee to find him and do thy will of him. If thou slay him, thou must, so thou mayst return home without hindrance, get thee gone, not by that way thou camest, but by that which thou wilt see issue forth of the coppice on the left hand, for that, albeit it is somewhat wilder, it is nearer to thy country and safer for thee.'

Mithridanes, having received this information and Nathan having taken leave of him, privily let his companions, who had, like himself, taken up their sojourn in the palace, know where they should look for him on the morrow; and the new day came, Nathan, whose intent was nowise at variance with the counsel he had given Mithridanes nor was anywise changed, betook himself alone to the coppice, there to die. Meanwhile, Mithridanes arose and taking his bow and his sword, for other arms he had not, mounted to horse and made for the coppice, where he saw Nathan from afar go walking all alone. Being resolved, ere he attacked him, to seek to see him and hear him speak, he ran towards him and seizing him by the fillet he had about his head, said, 'Old man, thou art dead.' Whereto Nathan answered no otherwhat than, 'Then have I merited it.' Mithridanes, hearing his voice and looking him in the face, knew him forthright for him who had so lovingly received him and familiarly companied with him and faithfully counselled him; whereupon his fury incontinent subsided and his rage was changed into shame. Accordingly, casting away the sword, which he had already pulled out to smite him, and lighting down from his horse, he ran, weeping, to throw himself at Nathan's feet and said to him, 'Now, dearest father, do I manifestly recognize your liberality, considering with what secrecy you are come hither to give me your life, whereof, without any reason, I showed myself desirous, and that to yourself; but God, more careful of mine honour than I myself, hath, in the extremest hour of need, opened the eyes of my understanding, which vile envy had closed. Wherefore, the readier you have been to comply with me, so much the more do I confess myself beholden to do penance for my default. Take, then, of me the vengeance which you deem conformable to my sin.'

Nathan raised Mithridanes to his feet and tenderly embraced and kissed him, saying, 'My son, it needeth not that thou shouldst ask nor that I should grant forgiveness of thine emprise, whatever thou choosest to style it, whether wicked or otherwise; for that thou pursuedst it, not of hatred, but to win to be held better. Live, then, secure from me and be assured that there is no man alive who loveth thee as I do, having regard to the loftiness of thy soul, which hath given itself, not to the amassing of monies, as do the covetous, but to the expenditure of those that have been amassed. Neither be thou ashamed of having sought to slay me, so though mightest become famous, nor think that I marvel thereat. The greatest emperors and the most illustrious kings have, with well nigh none other art than that of slaying, not one man, as thou wouldst have done, but an infinite multitude of men, and burning countries and razing cities, enlarged their realms and consequently their fame; wherefore, an thou wouldst, to make thyself more famous, have slain me only, thou diddest no new nor extraordinary thing, but one much used.'

Mithridanes, without holding himself excused of his perverse design, commended the honourable excuse found by Nathan and came, in course of converse with him, to say that he marvelled beyond measure how he could have brought himself to meet his death and have gone so far as even to give him means and counsel to that end; whereto quoth Nathan, 'Mithridanes, I would not have thee marvel at my resolution nor at the counsel I gave thee, for that, since I have been mine own master and have addressed myself to do that same thing which thou hast undertaken to do, there came never any to my house but I contented him, so far as in me lay, of that which was required of me by him. Thou camest hither, desirous of my life; wherefore, learning that thou soughtest it, I straightway determined to give it thee, so thou mightest not be the only one to depart hence without his wish; and in order that thou mightest have thy desire, I gave thee such counsel as I thought apt to enable thee to have my life and not lose thine own; and therefore I tell thee once more and pray thee, an it please thee, take it and satisfy thyself thereof. I know not how I may better bestow it. These fourscore years have I occupied it and used it about my pleasures and my diversions, and I know that in the course of nature, according as it fareth with other men and with things in general, it can now be left me but a little while longer; wherefore I hold it far better to bestow it by way of gift, like as I have still given and expended my [other] treasures, than to seek to keep it until such times as it shall be taken from me by nature against my will. To give an hundred years is no great boon; how much less, then, is it to give the six or eight I have yet to abide here? Take it, then, an it like thee. Prithee, then, take it, an thou have a mind thereto; for that never yet, what while I have lived here, have I found any who hath desired it, nor know I when I may find any such, an thou, who demandest it, take it not. And even should I chance to find any one, I know that, the longer I keep it, the less worth will it be; therefore, ere it wax sorrier, take it, I beseech thee.'

Mithridanes was sore abashed and replied, 'God forbid I should, let alone take and sever from you a thing of such price as your life, but even desire to do so, as but late I did,—your life, whose years far from seeking to lessen, I would willingly add thereto of mine own!' Whereto Nathan straightway rejoined, 'And art thou indeed willing, it being in thy power to do it, to add of thy years unto mine and in so doing, to cause me do for thee that which I never yet did for any man, to wit, take of thy good, I who never yet took aught of others?' 'Ay am I,' answered Mithridanes in haste. 'Then,' said Nathan, 'thou must do as I shall bid thee. Thou shalt take up thine abode, young as thou art, here in my house and bear the name of Nathan, whilst I will betake myself to thy house and let still call myself Mithridanes.' Quoth Mithridanes, 'An I knew how to do as well as you have done and do, I would, without hesitation, take that which you proffer me; but, since meseemeth very certain that my actions would be a diminishment of Nathan's fame and as I purpose not to mar in another that which I know not how to order in myself, I will not take it.' These and many other courteous discourses having passed between them, they returned, at Nathan's instance, to the latter's palace, where he entertained Mithridanes with the utmost honour sundry days, heartening him in his great and noble purpose with all manner of wit and wisdom. Then, Mithridanes desiring to return to his own house with his company, he dismissed him, having throughly given him to know that he might never avail to outdo him in liberality."

THE FOURTH STORY

MESSER GENTILE DE' CARISENDI, COMING FROM MODONA, TAKETH FORTH OF THE SEPULCHRE A LADY WHOM HE LOVETH AND WHO HATH BEEN BURIED FOR DEAD. THE LADY, RESTORED TO LIFE, BEARETH A MALE CHILD AND MESSER GENTILE RESTORETH HER AND HER SON TO NICCOLUCCIO CACCIANIMICO, HER HUSBAND

IT SEEMED to all a marvellous thing that a man should be lavish of his own blood and they declared Nathan's liberality to have verily transcended that of the King of Spain and the Abbot of Cluny. But, after enough to one and the other effect had been said thereof, the king, looking towards Lauretta, signed to her that he would have her tell, whereupon she straightway began, "Young ladies, magnificent and goodly are the things that have been recounted, nor meseemeth is there aught left unto us who have yet to tell, wherethrough we may range a story-telling, so throughly have they all[447] been occupied with the loftiness of the magnificences related, except we have recourse to the affairs of love, which latter afford a great abundance of matter for discourse on every subject; wherefore, at once on this account and for that the theme is one to which our age must needs especially incline us, it pleaseth me to relate to you an act of magnanimity done by a lover, which, all things considered, will peradventure appear to you nowise inferior to any of those already set forth, if it be true that treasures are lavished, enmities forgotten and life itself, nay, what is far more, honour and renown, exposed to a thousand perils, so we may avail to possess the thing beloved.

There was, then, in Bologna, a very noble city of Lombardy, a gentleman very notable for virtue and nobility of blood, called Messer Gentile Carisendi, who, being young, became enamoured of a noble lady called Madam Catalina, the wife of one Niccoluccio Caccianimico; and for that he was ill repaid of his love by the lady, being named provost of Modona, he betook himself thither, as in despair of her. Meanwhile, Niccoluccio being absent from Bologna and the lady having, for that she was with child, gone to abide at a country house she had maybe three miles distant from the city, she was suddenly seized with a grievous fit of sickness,[448] which overcame her with such violence that it extinguished in her all sign of life, so that she was even adjudged dead of divers physicians; and for that her nearest kinswomen declared themselves to have had it from herself that she had not been so long pregnant that the child could be fully formed, without giving themselves farther concern, they buried her, such as she was, after much lamentation, in one of the vaults of a neighbouring church.

The thing was forthright signified by a friend of his to Messer Gentile, who, poor as he had still been of her favour, grieved sore therefor and ultimately said in himself, 'Harkye, Madam Catalina, thou art dead, thou of whom, what while thou livedst, I could never avail to have so much as a look; wherefore, now thou canst not defend thyself, needs must I take of thee a kiss or two, all dead as thou art.' This said, he took order so his going should be secret and it being presently night, he mounted to horse with one of his servants and rode, without halting, till he came whereas the lady was buried and opened the sepulchre with all despatch. Then, entering therein, he laid himself beside her and putting his face to hers, kissed her again and again with many tears. But presently,—as we see men's appetites never abide content within any limit, but still desire farther, and especially those of lovers,—having bethought himself to tarry there no longer, he said, 'Marry, now that I am here, why should I not touch her somedele on the breast? I may never touch her more, nor have I ever yet done so.' Accordingly, overcome with this desire, he put his hand into her bosom and holding it there awhile, himseemed he felt her heart beat somewhat. Thereupon, putting aside all fear, he sought more diligently and found that she was certainly not dead, scant and feeble as he deemed the life [that lingered in her;] wherefore, with the help of his servant, he brought her forth of the tomb, as softliest he might, and setting her before him on his horse, carried her privily to his house in Bologna.

There was his mother, a worthy and discreet gentlewoman, and she, after she had heard everything at large from her son, moved to compassion, quietly addressed herself by means of hot baths and great fires to recall the strayed life to the lady, who, coming presently to herself, heaved a great sigh and said, 'Ah me, where am I?' To which the good lady replied, 'Be of good comfort; thou art in safety.' Madam Catalina, collecting herself, looked about her and knew not aright where she was; but, seeing Messer Gentile before her, she was filled with wonderment and besought his mother to tell her how she came thither; whereupon Messer Gentile related to her everything in order. At this she was sore afflicted, but presently rendered him such thanks as she might and after conjured him, by the love he had erst borne her and of his courtesy, that she might not in his house suffer at his hands aught that should be anywise contrary to her honour and that of her husband and that, as soon as the day should be come, he would suffer her return to her own house. 'Madam,' answered Messer Gentile, 'whatsoever may have been my desire of time past, I purpose not, either at this present or ever henceforth, (since God hath vouchsafed me this grace that He hath restored you to me from death to life, and that by means of the love I have hitherto borne you,) to use you either here or elsewhere otherwise than as a dear sister; but this my service that I have done you to-night meriteth some recompense; wherefore I would have you deny me not a favour that I shall ask you.'

The lady very graciously replied that she was ready to do his desire, so but she might and it were honourable. Then said he, 'Madam, your kinsfolk and all the Bolognese believe and hold you for certain to be dead, wherefore there is no one who looketh for you more at home, and therefore I would have you of your favour be pleased to abide quietly here with my mother till such time as I shall return from Modona, which will be soon. And the reason for which I require you of this is that I purpose to make a dear and solemn present of you to your husband in the presence of the most notable citizens of this place.' The lady, confessing herself beholden to the gentleman and that his request was an honourable one, determined to do as he asked, how much soever she desired to gladden her kinsfolk of her life,[449] and so she promised it to him upon her faith. Hardly had she made an end of her reply, when she felt the time of her delivery to be come and not long after, being lovingly tended of Messer Gentile's mother, she gave birth to a goodly male child, which manifold redoubled his gladness and her own. Messer Gentile took order that all things needful should be forthcoming and that she should be tended as she were his proper wife and presently returned in secret to Modona. There, having served the term of his office and being about to return to Bologna, he took order for the holding of a great and goodly banquet at his house on the morning he was to enter the city, and thereto he bade many gentlemen of the place, amongst whom was Niccoluccio Caccianimico. Accordingly, when he returned and dismounted, he found them all awaiting him, as likewise the lady, fairer and sounder than ever, and her little son in good case, and with inexpressible joy seating his guests at table, he let serve them magnificently with various meats.

Whenas the repast was near its end, having first told the lady what he meant to do and taken order with her of the course that she should hold, he began to speak thus: 'Gentlemen, I remember to have heard whiles that there is in Persia a custom and to my thinking a pleasant one, to wit, that, whenas any is minded supremely to honour a friend of his, he biddeth him to his house and there showeth him the thing, be it wife or mistress or daughter or whatsoever else, he holdeth most dear, avouching that, like as he showeth him this, even so, an he might, would he yet more willingly show him his very heart; which custom I purpose to observe in Bologna. You, of your favour, have honoured my banquet with your presence, and I in turn mean to honour you, after the Persian fashion, by showing you the most precious thing I have or may ever have in the world. But, ere I proceed to do this, I pray you tell me what you deem of a doubt[450] which I shall broach to you and which is this. A certain person hath in his house a very faithful and good servant, who falleth grievously sick, whereupon the former, without awaiting the sick man's end, letteth carry him into the middle street and hath no more heed of him. Cometh a stranger, who, moved to compassion of the sick man, carrieth him off to his own house and with great diligence and expense bringeth him again to his former health. Now I would fain know whether, if he keep him and make use of his services, his former master can in equity complain of or blame the second, if, he demanding him again, the latter refuse to restore him.'

The gentlemen, after various discourse among themselves, concurring all in one opinion, committed the response to Niccoluccio Caccianimico, for that he was a goodly and eloquent speaker; whereupon the latter, having first commended the Persian usage, declared that he and all the rest were of opinion that the first master had no longer any right in his servant, since he had, in such a circumstance, not only abandoned him, but cast him away, and that, for the kind offices done him by the second, themseemed the servant was justly become his; wherefore, in keeping him, he did the first no hurt, no violence, no unright whatsoever. The other guests at table (and there were men there of worth and worship) said all of one accord that they held to that which had been answered by Niccoluccio; and Messer Gentile, well pleased with this response and that Niccoluccio had made it, avouched himself also to be of the same opinion. Then said he, 'It is now time that I honour you according to promise,' and calling two of his servants, despatched them to the lady, whom he had let magnificently dress and adorn, praying her be pleased to come gladden the company with her presence. Accordingly, she took her little son, who was very handsome, in her arms and coming into the banqueting-hall, attended by two serving-men seated herself, as Messer Gentile willed it, by the side of a gentleman of high standing. Then said he, 'Gentlemen, this is the thing which I hold and purpose to hold dearer than any other; look if it seem to you that I have reason to do so.'

The guests, having paid her the utmost honour, commending her amain and declaring to Messer Gentile that he might well hold her dear, fell to looking upon her; and there were many there who had avouched her to be herself,[451] had they not held her for dead. But Niccoluccio gazed upon her above all and unable to contain himself, asked her, (Messer Gentile having withdrawn awhile,) as one who burned to know who she was, if she were a Bolognese lady or a foreigner. The lady, seeing herself questioned of her husband, hardly restrained herself from answering; but yet, to observe the appointed ordinance, she held her peace. Another asked her if the child was hers and a third if she were Messer Gentile's wife or anywise akin to him; but she made them no reply. Presently, Messer Gentile coming up, one of his guests said to him, 'Sir, this is a fair creature of yours, but she seemeth to us mute; is she so?' 'Gentlemen,' replied he, 'her not having spoken at this present is no small proof of her virtue.' And the other said, 'Tell us, then, who she is.' Quoth Messer Gentile, 'That will I gladly, so but you will promise me that none, for aught that I shall say, will budge from his place till such time as I shall have made an end of my story.'

All promised this and the tables being presently removed, Messer Gentile, seating himself beside the lady, said, 'Gentlemen, this lady is that loyal and faithful servant, of whom I questioned you awhile agone and who, being held little dear of her folk and so, as a thing without worth and no longer useful, cast out into the midward of the street, was by me taken up; yea, by my solicitude and of my handiwork I brought her forth of the jaws of death, and God, having regard to my good intent, hath caused her, by my means, from a frightful corpse become thus beautiful. But, that you may more manifestly apprehend how this betided me, I will briefly declare it to you.' Then, beginning from his falling enamoured of her, he particularly related to them that which had passed until that time, to the great wonderment of the hearers, and added, 'By reason of which things, an you, and especially Niccoluccio, have not changed counsel since awhile ago, the lady is fairly mine, nor can any with just title demand her again of me.' To this none made answer; nay, all awaited that which he should say farther; whilst Niccoluccio and the lady and certain of the others who were there wept for compassion.[452]

Then Messer Gentile, rising to his feet and taking the little child in his arms and the lady by the hand, made for Niccoluccio and said to him, 'Rise up, gossip; I do not restore thee thy wife, whom thy kinsfolk and hers cast away; nay, but I will well bestow on thee this lady my gossip, with this her little son, who I am assured, was begotten of thee and whom I held at baptism and named Gentile;

and I pray thee that she be none the less dear to thee for that she hath abidden near upon three months in my house; for I swear to thee, — by that God who belike caused me aforetime fall in love with her, to the intent that my love might be, as in effect it hath been, the occasion of her deliverance, —that never, whether with father or mother or with thee, hath she lived more chastely than she hath done with my mother in my house.' So saying, he turned to the lady and said to her, 'Madam, from this time forth I absolve you of every promise made me and leave you free [to return] to Niccoluccio.'[453] Then, giving the lady and the child into Niccoluccio's arms, he returned to his seat. Niccoluccio received them with the utmost eagerness, so much the more rejoiced as he was the farther removed from hope thereof, and thanked Messer Gentile, as best he might and knew; whilst the others, who all wept for compassion, commended the latter amain of this; yea, and he was commended of whosoever heard it. The lady was received in her house with marvellous rejoicing and long beheld with amazement by the Bolognese, as one raised from the dead; whilst Messer Gentile ever after abode a friend of Niccoluccio and of his kinsfolk and those of the lady.

What, then, gentle ladies, will you say [of this case]? Is, think you, a king's having given away his sceptre and his crown or an abbot's having, without cost to himself, reconciled an evildoer with the pope or an old man's having proffered his weasand to the enemy's knife to be evened with this deed of Messer Gentile, who, being young and ardent and himseeming he had a just title to that which the heedlessness of others had cast away and he of his good fortune had taken up, not only honourably tempered his ardour, but, having in his possession that which he was still wont with all his thoughts to covet and to seek to steal away, freely restored it [to its owner]? Certes, meseemeth none of the magnificences already recounted can compare with this."

The Decameron of Giovanni Boccaccio - Part II

THE FIFTH STORY

MADAM DIANORA REQUIRETH OF MESSER ANSALDO A GARDEN AS FAIR IN JANUARY AS IN MAY, AND HE BY BINDING HIMSELF [TO PAY A GREAT SUM OF MONEY] TO A NIGROMANCER, GIVETH IT TO HER. HER HUSBAND GRANTETH HER LEAVE TO DO MESSER ANSALDO'S PLEASURE, BUT HE, HEARING OF THE FORMER'S GENEROSITY, ABSOLVETH HER OF HER PROMISE, WHEREUPON THE NIGROMANCER, IN HIS TURN, ACQUITTETH MESSER ANSALDO OF HIS BOND, WITHOUT WILLING AUGHT OF HIS

MESSER GENTILE having by each of the merry company been extolled to the very skies with the highest praise, the king charged Emilia follow on, who confidently, as if eager to speak, began as follows: "Dainty dames, none can with reason deny that Messer Gentile wrought magnificently; but, if it be sought to say that his magnanimity might not be overpassed, it will not belike be uneath to show that more is possible, as I purpose to set out to you in a little story of mine.

In Friuli, a country, though cold, glad with goodly mountains and store of rivers and clear springs, is a city called Udine, wherein was aforetime a fair and noble lady called Madam Dianora, the wife of a wealthy gentleman named Gilberto, who was very debonair and easy of composition. The lady's charm procured her to be passionately loved of a noble and great baron by name Messer Ansaldo Gradense, a man of high condition and everywhere renowned for prowess and courtesy. He loved her fervently and did all that lay in his power to be beloved of her, to which end he frequently solicited her with messages, but wearied himself in vain. At last, his importunities being irksome to the lady and she seeing that, for all she denied him everything he sought of her, he stinted not therefor to love and solicit her, she determined to seek to rid herself of him by means of an extraordinary and in her judgment an impossible demand; wherefore she said one day to a woman, who came often to her on his part, 'Good woman, thou hast many times avouched to me that Messer Ansaldo loveth me over all things and hast proffered me marvellous great gifts on his part, which I would have him keep to himself, seeing that never thereby might I be prevailed upon to love him or comply with his wishes; but, an I could be certified that he loveth me in very deed as much as thou sayest, I might doubtless bring myself to love him and do that which he willeth; wherefore, an he choose to certify me of this with that which I shall require of him, I shall be ready to do his commandments.' Quoth the good woman, 'And what is that, madam, which you would have him do?' 'That which I desire,' replied the lady, 'is this; I will have, for this coming month of January, a garden, near this city, full of green grass and flowers and trees in full leaf, no otherwise than as it were May; the which if he contrive not, let him never more send me thee nor any other, for that, an he importune me more, so surely as I have hitherto kept his pursuit hidden from my husband and my kinsfolk, I will study to rid myself of him by complaining to them.'

The gentleman, hearing the demand and the offer of his mistress, for all it seemed to him a hard thing and in a manner impossible to do and he knew it to be required of the lady for none otherwhat than to bereave him of all hope, determined nevertheless to essay whatsoever might be done thereof and sent into various parts about the world, enquiring if there were any to be found who would give him aid and counsel in the matter. At last, he happened upon one who offered, so he were well guerdoned, to do the thing by nigromantic art, and having agreed with him for a great sum of money, he joyfully awaited the appointed time, which come and the cold being extreme and everything full of snow and ice, the learned man, the night before the calends of January, so wrought by his arts in a very goodly meadow adjoining the city, that it appeared in the morning (according to the testimony of those who saw it) one of the goodliest gardens was ever seen of any, with grass and trees and fruits of every kind. Messer Ansaldo, after viewing this with the utmost gladness, let cull of the finest fruits and the fairest flowers that were there and caused privily present them to his mistress, bidding her come and see the garden required by her, so thereby she might know how he loved her and after, remembering her of the promise made him and sealed with an oath, bethink herself, as a loyal lady, to accomplish it to him.

The lady, seeing the fruits and flowers and having already from many heard tell of the miraculous garden, began to repent of her promise. Natheless, curious, for all her repentance, of seeing strange things, she went with many other ladies of the city to view the garden and having with no little wonderment commended it amain, returned home, the woefullest woman alive, bethinking her of that to which she was bounden thereby. Such was her chagrin that she availed not so well to dissemble it but needs must it appear, and her husband, perceiving it, was urgent to know the reason. The lady, for shamefastness, kept silence thereof a great while; but at last, constrained to speak, she orderly discovered to him everything; which Gilberto, hearing, was at the first sore incensed, but presently, considering the purity of the lady's intent and chasing away anger with better counsel, he said, 'Dianora, it is not the part of a discreet nor of a virtuous woman to give ear unto any message of this sort nor to compound with any for her chastity under whatsoever condition. Words received into the heart by the channel of the ears have more potency than many conceive and well nigh every thing becometh possible to lovers. Thou didst ill, then, first to hearken and after to enter into terms of composition; but, for that I know the purity of thine intent, I will, to absolve thee of the bond of the promise, concede thee that which peradventure none other would do, being thereto the more induced by fear of the nigromancer, whom Messer Ansaldo, an thou cheat him, will maybe cause make us woeful. I will, then, that thou go to him and study to have thyself absolved of this thy promise, preserving thy chastity, if thou mayst anywise contrive it; but, an it may not be otherwise, thou shalt, for this once, yield him thy body, but not thy soul.'

The lady, hearing her husband's speech, wept and denied herself willing to receive such a favour from him; but, for all her much denial, he would e'en have it be so. Accordingly, next morning, at daybreak, the lady, without overmuch adorning herself, repaired to Messer Ansaldo's house, with two of her serving-men before and a chamberwoman after her. Ansaldo, hearing that his mistress was come to him, marvelled sore and letting call the nigromancer, said to him, 'I will have thee see what a treasure thy skill hath gotten me.' Then, going to meet her, he received her with decency and reverence, without ensuing any disorderly appetite, and they entered all[454] into a goodly chamber, wherein was a great fire. There he caused set her a seat and said, 'Madam, I prithee, if the long love I have borne you merit any recompense, let it not irk you to discover to me the true cause which hath brought you hither at such an hour and in such company.' The lady, shamefast and well nigh with tears in her eyes, answered, 'Sir, neither love that I bear you nor plighted faith bringeth me hither, but the commandment of my husband, who, having more regard to the travails of your disorderly passion than to his honour and mine own, hath caused me come hither; and by his behest I am for this once disposed to do your every pleasure.' If Messer Ansaldo had marvelled at the sight of the lady, far more did he marvel, when he heard her words, and moved by Gilberto's generosity, his heat began to change to compassion and he said, 'God forbid, madam, an it be as you say, that I should be a marrer of his honour who hath compassion of my love; wherefore you shall, what while it is your pleasure to abide here, be no otherwise entreated than as you were my sister; and whenas it shall be agreeable to you, you are free to depart, so but you will render your husband, on my part, those thanks which you shall deem befitting unto courtesy such as his hath been and have me ever, in time to come, for brother and for servant.'

The lady, hearing these words, was the joyfullest woman in the world and answered, saying, 'Nothing, having regard to your fashions, could ever make me believe that aught should ensue to me of my coming other than this that I see you do in the matter; whereof I shall still be beholden to you.' Then, taking leave, she returned, under honourable escort, to Messer Gilberto and told him that which had passed, of which there came about a very strait and loyal friendship between him and Messer Ansaldo. Moreover, the nigromancer, to whom the gentleman was for giving the promised guerdon, seeing Gilberto's generosity towards his wife's lover and that of the latter towards the lady, said, 'God forbid, since I have seen Gilberto liberal of his honour and you of your love, that I should not on like wise be liberal of my hire; wherefore, knowing it[455] will stand you in good stead, I intend that it shall be yours.'

At this the gentleman was ashamed and studied to make him take or all or part; but, seeing that he wearied himself in vain and it pleasing the nigromancer (who had, after three days, done away his garden) to depart, he commended him to God and having extinguished from his heart his lustful love for the lady, he abode fired with honourable affection for her. How say you now, lovesome ladies? Shall we prefer [Gentile's resignation of] the in a manner dead lady and of his love already cooled for hope forspent, before the generosity of Messer Ansaldo, whose love was more ardent than ever and who was in a manner fired with new hope, holding in his hands the prey so long pursued? Meseemeth it were folly to pretend that this generosity can be evened with that."

THE SIXTH STORY

KING CHARLES THE OLD, THE VICTORIOUS, FALLETH ENAMOURED OF A YOUNG GIRL, BUT AFTER, ASHAMED OF HIS FOND THOUGHT, HONOURABLY MARRIETH BOTH HER AND HER SISTER

IT WERE over longsome fully to recount the various discourse that had place among the ladies of who used the greatest generosity, Gilberto or Messer Ansaldo or the nigromancer, in Madam Dianora's affairs; but, after the king had suffered them debate awhile, he looked at Fiammetta and bade her, telling a story, put an end to their contention; whereupon she, without hesitation, began as follows: "Illustrious ladies, I was ever of opinion that, in companies such as ours, it should still be discoursed so much at large that the overstraitness[456] of intent of the things said be not unto any matter for debate, the which is far more sortable among students in the schools than among us [women,] who scarce suffice unto the distaff and the spindle. Wherefore, seeing that you are presently at cross-purposes by reason of the things already said, I, who had in mind a thing maybe somewhat doubtful [of meaning,] will leave that be and tell you a story, treating nowise of a man of little account, but of a valiant king, who therein wrought knightly, in nothing attainting his honour.

Each one of you must many a time have heard tell of King Charles the Old or First, by whose magnanimous emprise, and after by the glorious victory gained by him over King Manfred, the Ghibellines were expelled from Florence and the Guelphs returned thither. In consequence of this a certain gentleman, called Messer Neri degli Uberti, departing the city with all his household and much monies and being minded to take refuge no otherwhere than under the hand of King Charles, betook himself to Castellamare di Stabia.[457] There, belike a crossbowshot removed from the other habitations of the place, among olive-trees and walnuts and chestnuts, wherewith the country aboundeth, he bought him an estate and built thereon a goodly and commodious dwelling-house, with a delightsome garden thereby, amiddleward which, having great plenty of running water, he made, after our country fashion, a goodly and clear fishpond and lightly filled it with good store of fish. Whilst he concerned himself to make his garden goodlier every day, it befell that King Charles repaired to Castellamare, to rest himself awhile in the hot season, and there hearing tell of the beauty of Messer Neri's garden, he desired to behold it. Hearing, moreover, to whom it belonged, he bethought himself that, as the gentleman was of the party adverse to his own, it behoved to deal the more familiarly with him, and accordingly sent to him to say that he purposed to sup with him privily in his garden that evening, he and four companions. This was very agreeable to Messer Neri, and having made magnificent preparation and taken order with his household of that which was to do, he received the king in his fair garden as gladliest he might and knew. The latter, after having viewed and commended all the garden and Messer Neri's house and washed, seated himself at one of the tables, which were set beside the fishpond, and seating Count Guy de Montfort, who was of his company, on one side of him and Messer Neri on the other, commanded other three, who were come thither with them, to serve according to the order appointed of his host. Thereupon there came dainty meats and there were wines of the best and costliest and the ordinance was exceeding goodly and praiseworthy, without noise or annoy whatsoever, the which the king much commended.

Presently, as he sat blithely at meat, enjoying the solitary place, there entered the garden two young damsels of maybe fifteen years of age, with hair like threads of gold, all ringleted and hanging loose, whereon was a light chaplet of pervinck-blossoms. Their faces bespoke them rather angels than otherwhat, so delicately fair they were, and they were clad each upon her skin in a garment of the finest linen and white as snow, the which from the waist upward was very strait and thence hung down in ample folds, pavilionwise, to the feet. She who came first bore on her left shoulder a pair of hand-nets and in her right hand a long pole, and the other had on her left shoulder a frying-pan and under the same arm a faggot of wood, whilst in her left hand she held a trivet and in the other a flask of oil and a lighted flambeau. The king, seeing them, marvelled and in suspense awaited what this should mean. The damsels came forward modestly and blushingly did obeisance to him, then, betaking themselves whereas one went down into the fishpond, she who bore the frying-pan set it down and the other things by it and taking the pole that the other carried, they both entered the water, which came up to their breasts. Meanwhile, one of Messer Neri's servants deftly kindled fire under the trivet and setting the pan thereon, poured therein oil and waited for the damsels to throw him fish. The latter, the one groping with the pole in those parts whereas she knew the fish lay hid and the other standing ready with the net, in a short space of time took fish galore, to the exceeding pleasure of the king, who eyed them attently; then, throwing some thereof to the servant, who put them in the pan, well nigh alive, they proceeded, as they had been lessoned, to take of the finest and cast them on the table before the king and his table-fellows. The fish wriggled about the table, to the marvellous diversion of the king, who took of them in his turn and sportively cast them back to the damsels; and on this wise they frolicked awhile, till such time as the servant had cooked the fish which had been given him and which, Messer Neri having so ordered it, were now set before the king, more as a relish than as any very rare and delectable dish.

The damsels, seeing the fish cooked and having taken enough, came forth of the water, their thin white garments all clinging to their skins and hiding well nigh nought of their delicate bodies, and passing shamefastly before the king, returned to the house. The latter and the count and the others who served had well considered the damsels and each inwardly greatly commended them for fair and well shapen, no less than for agreeable and well mannered. But above all they pleased the king, who had so intently eyed every part of their bodies, as they came forth of the water, that, had any then pricked him, he would not have felt it, and as he called them more particularly to mind, unknowing who they were, he felt a very fervent desire awaken in his heart to please them, whereby he right well perceived himself to be in danger of becoming enamoured, an he took no heed to himself thereagainst; nor knew he indeed whether of the twain it was the more pleased him, so like in all things was the one to the other. After he had abidden awhile in this thought, he turned to Messer Neri and asked him who were the two damsels, to which the gentleman answered, 'My lord, these are my daughters born at a birth, whereof the one is called Ginevra the Fair and the other Isotta the Blonde.' The king commended them greatly and exhorted him to marry them, whereof Messer Neri excused himself, for that he was no more able thereunto. Meanwhile, nothing now remaining to be served of the supper but the fruits, there came the two damsels in very goodly gowns of sendal, with two great silver platters in their hands, full of various fruits, such as the season afforded, and these they set on the table before the king; which done, they withdrew a little apart and fell to singing a canzonet, whereof the words began thus:

Whereas I'm come, O Love,
It might not be, indeed, at length recounted, etc.

This song they carolled on such dulcet wise and so delightsomely that to the king, who beheld and hearkened to them with ravishment, it seemed as if all the hierarchies of the angels were lighted there to sing. The song sung, they fell on their knees and respectfully craved of him leave to depart, who, albeit their departure was grievous to him, yet with a show of blitheness accorded it to them. The supper being now at an end, the king remounted to horse with his company and leaving Messer Neri, returned to the royal lodging, devising of one thing and another. There, holding his passion hidden, but availing not, for whatsoever great affair might supervene, to forget the beauty and grace of

Ginevra the Fair, (for love of whom he loved her sister also, who was like unto her,) he became so fast entangled in the amorous snares that he could think of well nigh nought else and feigning other occasions, kept a strait intimacy with Messer Neri and very often visited his fair garden, to see Ginevra.

At last, unable to endure longer and bethinking himself, in default of other means of compassing his desire, to take not one alone, but both of the damsels from their father, he discovered both his passion and his intent to Count Guy, who, for that he was an honourable man, said to him, 'My lord, I marvel greatly at that which you tell me, and that more than would another, inasmuch as meseemeth I have from your childhood to this day known your fashions better than any other; wherefore, meseeming never to have known such a passion in your youth, wherein Love might lightlier have fixed his talons, and seeing you presently hard upon old age, it is so new and so strange to me that you should love by way of enamourment[458] that it seemeth to me well nigh a miracle, and were it my office to reprove you thereof, I know well that which I should say to you thereanent, having in regard that you are yet with your harness on your back in a kingdom newly gained, amidst a people unknown and full of wiles and treasons, and are all occupied with very grave cares and matters of high moment, nor have you yet availed to seat yourself [in security;] and yet, among such and so many affairs, you have made place for the allurements of love. This is not the fashion of a magnanimous king; nay, but rather that of a pusillanimous boy. Moreover, what is far worse, you say that you are resolved to take his two daughters from a gentleman who hath entertained you in his house beyond his means and who, to do you the more honour, hath shown you these twain in a manner naked, thereby attesting how great is the faith he hath in you and that he firmly believeth you to be a king and not a ravening wolf. Again, hath it so soon dropped your memory that it was the violences done of Manfred to women that opened you the entry into this kingdom? What treason was ever wroughten more deserving of eternal punishment than this would be, that you should take from him who hospitably entreateth you his honour and hope and comfort? What would be said of you, an you should do it? You think, maybe, it were a sufficient excuse to say, "I did it for that he is a Ghibelline." Is this of the justice of kings, that they who resort on such wise to their arms should be entreated after such a fashion, be they who they may? Let me tell you, king, that it was an exceedingly great glory to you to have overcome Manfred, but a far greater one it is to overcome one's self; wherefore do you, who have to correct others, conquer yourself and curb this appetite, nor offer with such a blot to mar that which you have so gloriously gained.'

These words stung the king's conscience to the quick and afflicted him the more inasmuch as he knew them for true; wherefore, after sundry heavy sighs, he said, 'Certes, Count, I hold every other enemy, however strong, weak and eath enough to the well-lessoned warrior to overcome in comparison with his own appetites; natheless, great as is the travail and inexpressible as is the might it requireth, your words have so stirred me that needs must I, ere many days be past, cause you see by deed that, like as I know how to conquer others, even so do I know how to overcome myself.' Nor had many days passed after this discourse when the king, having returned to Naples, determined, as well to deprive himself of occasion to do dishonourably as to requite the gentleman the hospitality received from him, to go about (grievous as it was to him to make others possessors of that which he coveted over all for himself) to marry the two young ladies, and that not as Messer Neri's daughters, but as his own. Accordingly, with Messer Neri's accord, he dowered them magnificently and gave Ginevra the Fair to Messer Maffeo da Palizzi and Isotta the Blonde to Messer Guglielmo della Magna, both noble cavaliers and great barons, to whom with inexpressible chagrin consigning them, he betook himself into Apulia, where with continual fatigues he so mortified the fierceness of his appetite that, having burst and broken the chains of love, he abode free of such passion for the rest of his life. There are some belike who will say that it was a little thing for a king to have married two young ladies, and that I will allow; but a great and a very great thing I call it, if we consider that it was a king enamoured who did this and who married to another her whom he loved, without having gotten or taking of his love leaf or flower or fruit. On this wise, then, did this magnanimous king, at once magnificently guerdoning the noble gentleman, laudably honouring the young ladies whom he loved and bravely overcoming himself."

THE SEVENTH STORY

KING PEDRO OF ARRAGON, COMING TO KNOW THE FERVENT LOVE BORNE HIM BY LISA, COMFORTETH THE LOVE-SICK MAID AND PRESENTLY MARRIETH HER TO A NOBLE YOUNG GENTLEMAN; THEN, KISSING HER ON THE BROW, HE EVER AFTER AVOUCHETH HIMSELF HER KNIGHT

FIAMMETTA having made an end of her story and the manful magnanimity of King Charles having been much commended, albeit there was one lady there who, being a Ghibelline, was loath to praise him, Pampinea, by the king's commandment, began thus, "There is no one of understanding, worshipful ladies, but would say that which you say of good King Charles, except she bear him ill-will for otherwhat; but, for that there occurreth to my memory a thing, belike no less commendable than this, done of one his adversary to one of our Florentine damsels, it pleaseth me to relate it to you.

At the time of the expulsion of the French from Sicily, one of our Florentines was an apothecary at Palermo, a very rich man called Bernardo Puccini, who had by his wife an only daughter, a very fair damsel and already apt for marriage. Now King Pedro of Arragon, become lord of the island, held high festival with his barons at Palermo, wherein he tilting after the Catalan fashion, it chanced that Bernardo's daughter, whose name was Lisa, saw him running [at the ring] from a window where she was with other ladies, and he so marvellously pleased her that, looking upon him once and again, she fell passionately in love with him; and the festival ended and she abiding in her father's house, she could think of nothing but of this her illustrious and exalted love. And what most irked her in this was the consciousness of her own mean condition, which scarce suffered her to cherish any hope of a happy issue; natheless, she could not therefor bring herself to leave loving the king, albeit, for fear of greater annoy, she dared not discover her passion. The king had not perceived this thing and recked not of her, wherefor she suffered intolerable chagrin, past all that can be imagined. Thus it befell that, love still waxing in her and melancholy redoubling upon melancholy, the fair maid, unable to endure more, fell sick and wasted visibly away from day to day, like snow in the sun. Her father and mother, sore concerned for this that befell her, studied with assiduous tenderness to hearten her and succoured her in as much as might be with physicians and medicines, but it availed nothing, for that, despairing of her love, she had elected to live no longer.

It chanced one day that, her father offering to do her every pleasure, she bethought herself, and she might aptly, to seek, before she died, to make the king acquainted with her love and her intent, and accordingly she prayed him bring her Minuccio d'Arezzo. Now this Minuccio was in those days held a very quaint and subtle singer and player and was gladly seen of the king; and Bernardo concluded that Lisa had a mind to hear him sing and play awhile. Accordingly, he sent to tell him, and Minuccio, who was a man of a debonair humour, incontinent came to her and having somedele comforted her with kindly speech, softly played her a fit or two on a viol he had with him and after sang her sundry songs, the which were fire and flame unto the damsel's passion, whereas he thought to solace her. Presently she told him that she would fain speak some words with him alone, wherefore, all else having withdrawn, she said to him, 'Minuccio, I have chosen thee to keep me very faithfully a secret of mine, hoping in the first place that thou wilt never discover it to any one, save to him of whom I shall tell thee, and after that thou wilt help me in that which lieth in thy power; and of this I pray thee Thou must know, then, Minuccio mine, that the day our lord King Pedro held the great festival in honour of his exaltation to the throne, it befell me, as he tilted, to espy him at so dour a point[459] that for the love of him there was kindled in my heart a fire that hath brought me to this pass wherein thou seest me, and knowing how ill my love beseemeth to a king, yet availing not, let alone to drive it away, but even to abate it, and it being beyond measure grievous to me to bear, I have as a lesser evil elected to die, as I shall do. True it is that I should begone hence cruelly disconsolate, an he first knew it not; wherefore, unknowing by whom I could more aptly acquaint him with this my resolution than by thyself, I desire to commit it to thee and pray thee that thou refuse not to do it, and whenas thou shalt have done it, that thou give me to know thereof, so that, dying comforted, I may be assoiled of these my pains.' And this said, she stinted, weeping.

Minuccio marvelled at the greatness of the damsel's soul and at her cruel resolve and was sore concerned for her; then, it suddenly occurring to his mind how he might honourably oblige her, he said to her, 'Lisa, I pledge thee my faith, whereof thou mayst live assured that thou wilt never find thyself deceived, and after, commending thee of so high an emprise as it is to have set thy mind upon so great a king, I proffer thee mine aid, by means whereof I hope, an thou wilt but take comfort, so to do that, ere three days be past, I doubt not to bring thee news that will be exceeding grateful to thee; and to lose no time, I mean to go about it forthright.' Lisa, having anew besought him amain thereof and promised him to take comfort, bade him God speed; whereupon Minuccio, taking his leave, betook himself to one Mico da Siena, a mighty good rhymer of those days, and constrained him with prayers to make the following canzonet:

Bestir thee, Love, and get thee to my Sire
And tell him all the torments I aby;
Tell him I'm like to die,
For fearfulness concealing my desire.

Love, with clasped hands I cry thee mercy, so
Thou mayst betake thee where my lord doth dwell.
Say that I love and long for him, for lo,
My heart he hath inflamed so sadly well;
Yea, for the fire wherewith I'm all aglow,
I fear to die nor yet the hour can tell
When I shall part from pain so fierce and fell
As that which, longing, for his sake I dree
In shame and fear; ah me,
For God's sake, cause him know my torment dire.

Since first enamoured, Love, of him I grew,
Thou hast not given me the heart to dare
So much as one poor once my lord unto
My love and longing plainly to declare,

My lord who maketh me so sore to rue;
Death, dying thus, were hard to me to bear.
Belike, indeed, for he is debonair,
'Twould not displease him, did he know what pain
I feel and didst thou deign
Me daring to make known to him my fire.

Yet, since 'twas not thy pleasure to impart,
Love, such assurance to me that by glance
Or sign or writ I might make known my heart
Unto my lord, for my deliverance
I prithee, sweet my master, of thine art
Get thee to him and give him souvenance
Of that fair day I saw him shield and lance
Bear with the other knights and looking more,
Enamoured fell so sore
My heart thereof doth perish and expire.

These words Minuccio forthwith set to a soft and plaintive air, such as the matter thereof required, and on the third day he betook himself to court, where, King Pedro being yet at meat, he was bidden by him sing somewhat to his viol. Thereupon he fell to singing the song aforesaid on such dulcet wise that all who were in the royal hall appeared men astonied, so still and attent stood they all to hearken, and the king maybe more than the others. Minuccio having made an end of his singing, the king enquired whence came this song that himseemed he had never before heard. 'My lord,' replied the minstrel, 'it is not yet three days since the words were made and the air.' The king asked for whom it had been made; and Minuccio answered, 'I dare not discover it save to you alone.' The king, desirous to hear it, as soon as the tables were removed, sent for Minuccio into his chamber and the latter orderly recounted to him all that he had heard from Lisa; wherewith Don Pedro was exceeding well pleased and much commended the damsel, avouching himself resolved to have compassion of so worthful a young lady and bidding him therefore go comfort her on his part and tell her that he would without fail come to visit her that day towards vespers. Minuccio, overjoyed to be the bearer of such pleasing news, betook himself incontinent, viol and all, to the damsel and bespeaking her in private, recounted to her all that had passed and after sang her the song to his viol; whereat she was so rejoiced and so content that she straightway showed manifest signs of great amendment and longingly awaited the hour of vespers, whenas her lord should come, without any of the household knowing or guessing how the case stood.

Meanwhile, the king, who was a debonair and generous prince, having sundry times taken thought to the things heard from Minuccio and very well knowing the damsel and her beauty, waxed yet more pitiful over her and mounting to horse towards vespers, under colour of going abroad for his diversion, betook himself to the apothecary's house, where, having required a very goodly garden which he had to be opened to him, he alighted therein and presently asked Bernardo what was come of his daughter and if he had yet married her. 'My lord,' replied the apothecary, 'she is not married; nay, she hath been and is yet very sick; albeit it is true that since none she hath mended marvellously.' The king readily apprehended what this amendment meant and said, 'In good sooth, 'twere pity so fair a creature should be yet taken from the world. We would fain go visit her.' Accordingly, a little after, he betook himself with Bernardo and two companions only to her chamber and going up to the bed where the damsel, somedele upraised,[460] awaited him with impatience, took her by the hand and said to her, 'What meaneth this, my mistress? You are young and should comfort other women; yet you suffer yourself to be sick. We would beseech you be pleased, for the love of us, to hearten yourself on such wise that you may speedily be whole again.' The damsel, feeling herself touched of his hands whom she loved over all else, albeit she was somewhat shamefast, felt yet such gladness in her heart as she were in Paradise and answered him, as best she might, saying, 'My lord, my having willed to subject my little strength unto very grievous burdens hath been the cause to me of this mine infirmity, whereof, thanks to your goodness, you shall soon see me quit.' The king alone understood the damsel's covert speech and held her momently of more account; nay, sundry whiles he inwardly cursed fortune, who had made her daughter unto such a man; then, after he had tarried with her awhile and comforted her yet more, he took his leave.

This humanity of the king was greatly commended and attributed for great honour to the apothecary and his daughter, which latter abode as well pleased as ever was woman of her lover, and sustained of better hope, in a few days recovered and became fairer than ever. When she was whole again, the king, having taken counsel with the queen of what return he should make her for so much love, mounting one day to horse with many of his barons, repaired to the apothecary's house and entering the garden, let call Master Bernardo and his daughter; then, the queen presently coming thither with many ladies and having received Lisa among them, they fell to making wonder-merry. After a while, the king and queen called Lisa to them and the former said to her, 'Noble damsel, the much love you have borne us hath gotten you a great honour from us, wherewith we would have you for the love of us be content; to wit, that, since you are apt for marriage, we would have you take him to husband whom we shall bestow on you, purposing, notwithstanding this, to call ourselves still your knight, without desiring aught from you of so much love but one sole kiss.' The damsel, grown all vermeil in the face for shamefastness, making the king's pleasure hers, replied in a low voice on this wise, 'My lord, I am well assured that, were it known that I had fallen enamoured of you, most folk would account me mad therefor, thinking belike that I had forgotten myself and knew not mine own condition nor yet yours; but God, who alone seeth the hearts of mortals, knoweth that, in that same hour whenas first you pleased me, I knew you for a king and myself for the daughter of Bernardo the apothecary and that it ill beseemed me to address the ardour of my soul unto so high a place. But, as you know far better than I, none here below falleth in love according to fitness of election, but according to appetite and inclination, against which law I once and again strove with all my might, till, availing no farther, I loved and love and shall ever love you. But, since first I felt myself taken with love of you, I determined still to make your will mine; wherefore, not only will I gladly obey you in this matter of taking a husband at your hands and holding him dear whom it shall please you to bestow on me, since that will be mine honour and estate, but, should you bid me abide in the fire, it were a delight to me, an I thought thereby to pleasure you. To have you, a king, to knight, you know how far it befitteth me, wherefore to that I make no farther answer; nor shall the kiss be vouchsafed you, which alone of my love you would have, without leave of my lady the queen. Natheless, of such graciousness as hath been yours towards me and that of our lady the queen here God render you for me both thanks and recompense, for I have not the wherewithal.' And with that she was silent.

Her answer much pleased the queen and she seemed to her as discreet as the king had reported her. Don Pedro then let call the girl's father and mother and finding that they were well pleased with that which he purposed to do, summoned a young man, by name Perdicone, who was of gentle birth, but poor, and giving certain rings into his hand, married him, nothing loath, to Lisa; which done, he then and there, over and above many and precious jewels bestowed by the queen and himself upon the damsel, gave him Ceffalu and Calatabellotta, two very rich and goodly fiefs, and said to him, 'These we give thee to the lady's dowry. That which we purpose to do for thyself, thou shalt see in time to come.' This said, he turned to the damsel and saying, 'Now will we take that fruit which we are to have of your love,' took her head in his hands and kissed her on the brow. Perdicone and Lisa's father and mother, well pleased, (as indeed was she herself,) held high festival and joyous nuptials; and according as many avouch, the king very faithfully kept his covenant with the damsel, for that, whilst she lived, he still styled himself her knight nor ever went about any deed of arms but he wore none other favour than that which was sent him of her. It is by doing, then, on this wise that subjects' hearts are gained, that others are incited to do well and that eternal renown is acquired; but this is a mark at which few or none nowadays bend the bow of their understanding, most princes being presently grown cruel and tyrannical."

THE EIGHTH STORY

SOPHRONIA, THINKING TO MARRY GISIPPUS, BECOMETH THE WIFE OF TITUS QUINTIUS FULVUS AND WITH HIM BETAKETH HERSELF TO ROME, WHITHER GISIPPUS COMETH IN POOR CASE AND CONCEIVING HIMSELF SLIGHTED OF TITUS, DECLARETH, SO HE MAY DIE, TO HAVE SLAIN A MAN. TITUS, RECOGNIZING HIM, TO SAVE HIM, AVOUCHETH HIMSELF TO HAVE DONE THE DEED, AND THE TRUE MURDERER, SEEING THIS, DISCOVERETH HIMSELF; WHEREUPON THEY ARE ALL THREE LIBERATED BY OCTAVIANUS AND TITUS, GIVING GISIPPUS HIS SISTER TO WIFE, HATH ALL HIS GOOD IN COMMON WITH HIM

PAMPINEA having left speaking and all having commended King Pedro, the Ghibelline lady more than the rest, Fiammetta, by the king's commandment, began thus, "Illustrious ladies, who is there knoweth not that kings, when they will, can do everything great and that it is, to boot, especially required of them that they be magnificent? Whoso, then, having the power, doth that which pertaineth unto him, doth well; but folk should not so much marvel thereat nor exalt him to such a height with supreme praise as it would behove them do with another, of whom, for lack of means, less were required. Wherefore, if you with such words extol the actions of kings and they seem to you fair, I doubt not anywise but those of our peers, whenas they are like unto or greater than those of kings, will please you yet more and be yet highlier commended of you, and I purpose accordingly to recount to you, in a story, the praiseworthy and magnanimous dealings of two citizens and friends with each other.

You must know, then, that at the time when Octavianus Cæsar (not yet styled Augustus) ruled the Roman empire in the office called Triumvirate, there was in Rome a gentleman called Publius Quintius Fulvus,[461] who, having a son of marvellous understanding, by name Titus Quintius Fulvus, sent him to Athens to study philosophy and commended him as most he might to a nobleman there called Chremes, his very old friend, by whom Titus was lodged in his own house, in company of a son of his called Gisippus, and set to study with the latter, under the governance of a philosopher named Aristippus. The two young men, coming to consort together, found each other's usances so conformable that there was born thereof a brotherhood between them and a friendship so great that it was never sundered by other accident than death, and neither of them knew weal nor peace save in so much as they were together. Entering upon their studies and being each alike endowed with the highest understanding, they ascended with equal step and marvellous commendation to the glorious altitudes of philosophy; and in this way of life they continued good three years, to the exceeding contentment of Chremes, who in a manner looked upon the one as no more his son than the other. At the end of this time it befell, even as it befalleth of all things, that Chremes, now an old man, departed this life, whereof the two young men suffered a like sorrow, as for a common father, nor could his friends and kinsfolk discern which of the twain was the more in need of consolation for that which had betided them.

It came to pass, after some months, that the friends and kinsfolk of Gisippus resorted to him and together with Titus exhorted him to take a wife, to which he consenting, they found him a young Athenian lady of marvellous beauty and very noble parentage, whose name was Sophronia and who was maybe fifteen years old. The term of the future nuptials drawing nigh, Gisippus one day besought Titus to go visit her with him, for that he had not yet seen her. Accordingly, they being come into her house and she seated between the twain, Titus proceeded to consider her with the utmost attention, as if to judge of the beauty of his friend's bride, and every part of her pleasing him beyond measure, what while he inwardly commended her charms to the utmost, he fell, without showing any sign thereof, as passionately enamoured of her as ever yet man of woman. After they had been with her awhile, they took their leave and returned home, where Titus, betaking himself alone into his chamber, fell a-thinking of the charming damsel and grew the more enkindled the more he enlarged upon her in thought; which, perceiving, he fell to saying in himself, after many ardent sighs,

'Alack, the wretchedness of thy life, Titus! Where and on what settest thou thy mind and thy love and thy hope? Knowest thou not that it behoveth thee, as well for the kindness received from Chremes and his family as for the entire friendship that is between thee and Gisippus, whose bride she is, to have yonder damsel in such respect as a sister? Whom, then, lovest thou? Whither lettest thou thyself be carried away by delusive love, whither by fallacious hope? Open the eyes of thine understanding and recollect thyself, wretch that thou art; give place to reason, curb thy carnal appetite, temper thine unhallowed desires and direct thy thoughts unto otherwhat; gainstand thy lust in this its beginning and conquer thyself, whilst it is yet time. This thou wouldst have is unseemly, nay, it is dishonourable; this thou art minded to ensue it behoveth thee, even wert thou assured (which thou art not) of obtaining it, to flee from, an thou have regard unto that which true friendship requireth and that which thou oughtest. What, then, wilt thou do, Titus? Thou wilt leave this unseemly love, an thou wouldst do that which behoveth.'

Then, remembering him of Sophronia and going over to the contrary, he denounced all that he had said, saying, 'The laws of love are of greater puissance than any others; they annul even the Divine laws, let alone those of friendship; how often aforetime hath father loved daughter, brother sister, stepmother stepson, things more monstrous than for one friend to love the other's wife, the which hath already a thousand times befallen! Moreover, I am young and youth is altogether subject to the laws of Love; wherefor that which pleaseth Him, needs must it please me. Things honourable pertain unto maturer folk; I can will nought save that which Love willeth. The beauty of yonder damsel deserveth to be loved of all, and if I love her, who am young, who can justly blame me therefor? I love her not because she is Gisippus's; nay, I love her for that I should love her, whosesoever she was. In this fortune sinneth that hath allotted her to Gisippus my friend, rather than to another; and if she must be loved, (as she must, and deservedly, for her beauty,) Gisippus, an he came to know it, should be better pleased that I should love her, I, than another.' Then, from that reasoning he reverted again to the contrary, making mock of himself, and wasted not only that day and the ensuing night in passing from this to that and back again, but many others, insomuch that, losing appetite and sleep therefor, he was constrained for weakness to take to his bed.

Gisippus, having beheld him several days full of melancholy thought and seeing him presently sick, was sore concerned and with every art and all solicitude studied to comfort him, never leaving him and questioning him often and instantly of the cause of his melancholy and his sickness. Titus, after having once and again given him idle tales, which Gisippus knew to be such, by way of answer, finding himself e'en constrained thereunto, with tears and sighs replied to him on this wise, 'Gisippus, had it pleased the Gods, death were far more a-gree to me than to live longer, considering that fortune hath brought me to a pass whereas it behoved me make proof of my virtue and that I have, to my exceeding shame, found this latter overcome; but certes I look thereof to have ere long the reward that befitteth me, to wit, death, and this will be more pleasing to me than to live in remembrance of my baseness, which latter, for that I cannot nor should hide aught from thee, I will, not without sore blushing, discover to thee.' Then, beginning from the beginning, he discovered to him the cause of his melancholy and the conflict of his thoughts and ultimately gave him to know which had gotten the victory and confessed himself perishing for love of Sophronia, declaring that, knowing how much this misbeseemed him, he had for penance thereof resolved himself to die, whereof he trusted speedily to make an end.

Gisippus, hearing this and seeing his tears, abode awhile irresolute, as one who, though more moderately, was himself taken with the charms of the fair damsel, but speedily bethought himself that his friend's life should be dearer to him than Sophronia. Accordingly, solicited to tears by those of his friend, he answered him, weeping, 'Titus, wert thou not in need as thou art of comfort, I should complain of thee to thyself, as of one who hath transgressed against our friendship in having so long kept thy most grievous passion hidden from me; since, albeit it appeared not to thee honourable, nevertheless dishonourable things should not, more than honourable, be hidden from a friend; for that a friend, like as he rejoiceth with his friend in honourable things, even so he studieth to do away the dishonourable from his friend's mind; but for the present I will refrain therefrom and come to that which I perceive to be of greater urgency. That thou lovest Sophronia, who is betrothed to me, I marvel not: nay, I should marvel, indeed, if it were not so, knowing her beauty and the nobility of thy mind, so much the more susceptible of passion as the thing that pleaseth hath the more excellence. And the more reason thou hast to love Sophronia, so much the more unjustly dost thou complain of fortune (albeit thou expressest this not in so many words) in that it hath awarded her to me, it seeming to thee that thy love for her had been honourable, were she other than mine; but tell me, if thou be as well advised as thou usest to be, to whom could fortune have awarded her, whereof thou shouldst have more cause to render it thanks, than of having awarded her to me? Whoso else had had her, how honourable soever thy love had been, had liefer loved her for himself[462] than for thee,[463] a thing which thou shouldst not fear[464] from me, an thou hold me a friend such as I am to thee, for that I mind me not, since we have been friends, to have ever had aught that was not as much thine as mine. Now, were the matter so far advanced that it might not be otherwise, I would do with her as I have done with my other possessions;[465] but it is yet at such a point that I can make her thine alone; and I will do so, for that I know not why my friendship should be dear to thee, if, in respect of a thing that may honourably be done, I knew not of a desire of mine to make thine. True it is that Sophronia is my promised bride and that I loved her much and looked with great joyance for my nuptials with her; but, since thou, being far more understanding than I, with more ardour desirest so dear a thing as she is, live assured that she shall enter my chamber, not as my wife, but as thine. Wherefore leave thought-taking, put away melancholy, call back thy lost health and comfort and allegresse and from this time forth expect with blitheness the reward of thy love, far worthier than was mine.'

When Titus heard Gisippus speak thus, the more the flattering hopes given him of the latter afforded him pleasure, so much the more did just reason inform him with shame, showing him that, the greater was Gisippus his liberality, the more unworthy it appeared of himself to use it; wherefore, without giving over weeping, he with difficulty replied to him thus, 'Gisippus, thy generous and true friendship very plainly showeth me that which it pertaineth unto mine to do. God forfend that her, whom He hath bestowed upon thee as upon the worthier, I should receive from thee for mine! Had He judged it fitting that she should be mine, nor thou nor others can believe that He would ever have bestowed her on thee. Use, therefore, joyfully, thine election and discreet counsel and His gifts, and leave me to languish in the tears, which, as to one undeserving of such a treasure, He hath prepared unto me and which I will either overcome, and that will be dear to thee, or they will overcome me and I shall be out of pain.' 'Titus,' rejoined Gisippus, 'an our friendship might accord me such license that I should enforce thee to ensue a desire of mine and if it may avail to induce thee to do so, it is in this case that I mean to use it to the utmost, and if thou yield not to my prayers with a good grace, I will, with such violence as it behoveth us use for the weal of our friends, procure that Sophronia shall be thine. I know how great is the might of love and that, not once, but many a time, it hath brought lovers to a miserable death; nay, unto this I see thee so near that thou canst neither turn back nor avail to master thy tears, but, proceeding thus, wouldst pine and die; whereupon I, without any doubt, should speedily follow after. If, then, I loved thee not for otherwhat, thy life is dear to me, so I myself may live. Sophronia, therefore, shall be thine, for that thou couldst not lightly find another woman who would so please thee, and as I shall easily turn my love unto another, I shall thus have contented both thyself and me. I should not, peradventure, be so free to do this, were wives as scarce and as uneath to find as friends; however, as I can very easily find me another wife, but not another friend, I had liefer (I will not say lose her, for that I shall not lose her, giving her to thee, but shall transfer her to another and a better self, but) transfer her than lose thee. Wherefore, if my prayers avail aught with thee, I beseech thee put away from thee this affliction and comforting at once thyself and me, address thee with good hope to take that joyance which thy fervent love desireth of the thing beloved.'

Although Titus was ashamed to consent to this, namely, that Sophronia should become his wife, and on this account held out yet awhile, nevertheless, love on the one hand drawing him and Gisippus his exhortations on the other urging him, he said, 'Look you, Gisippus, I know not which I can say I do most, my pleasure or thine, in doing that whereof thou prayest me and which thou tellest me is so pleasing to thee, and since thy generosity is such that it overcometh my just shame, I will e'en do it; but of this thou mayst be assured that I do it as one who knoweth himself to receive of thee, not only the beloved lady, but with her his life. The Gods grant, an it be possible, that I may yet be able to show thee, for thine honour and thy weal, how grateful to me is that which thou, more pitiful for me than I for myself, dost for me!' These things said, 'Titus,' quoth Gisippus, 'in this matter, an we would have it take effect, meseemeth this course is to be held. As thou knowest, Sophronia, after long treaty between my kinsfolk and hers, is become my affianced bride; wherefore, should I now go about to say that I will not have her to wife, a sore scandal would ensue thereof and I should anger both her kinsfolk and mine own. Of this, indeed, I should reck nothing, an I saw that she was thereby to become thine; but I misdoubt me that, an I renounce her at this point, her kinsfolk will straightway give her to another, who belike will not be thyself, and so wilt thou have lost that which I shall not have gained. Wherefore meseemeth well, an thou be content, that I follow on with that which I have begun and bring her home as mine and hold the nuptials, and thou mayst after, as we shall know how to contrive, privily lie with her as with thy wife. Then, in due place and season, we will make manifest the fact, which, if it please them not, will still be done and they must perforce be content, being unable to go back upon it.'

The device pleased Titus; wherefore Gisippus received the lady into his house, as his, (Titus being by this recovered and in good case,) and after holding high festival, the night being come, the ladies left the new-married wife in her husband's bed and went their ways. Now Titus his chamber adjoined that of Gisippus and one might go from the one room into the other; wherefore Gisippus, being in his chamber and having put out all the lights, betook himself stealthily to his friend and bade him go couch with his mistress. Titus, seeing this, was overcome with shame and would fain have repented and refused to go; but Gisippus, who with his whole heart, no less than in words, was minded to do his friend's pleasure, sent him thither, after long contention. Whenas he came into the bed, he took the damsel in his arms and asked her softly, as if in sport, if she chose to be his wife. She, thinking him to be Gisippus, answered, 'Yes'; whereupon he set a goodly and rich ring on her finger, saying, 'And

I choose to be thy husband.' Then, the marriage consummated, he took long and amorous pleasure of her, without her or others anywise perceiving that other than Gisippus lay with her.

The marriage of Sophronia and Titus being at this pass, Publius his father departed this life, wherefore it was written him that he should without delay return to Rome, to look to his affairs, and he accordingly took counsel with Gisippus to betake himself thither and carry Sophronia with him; which might not nor should aptly be done without discovering to her how the case stood. Accordingly, one day, calling her into the chamber, they thoroughly discovered to her the fact and thereof Titus certified her by many particulars of that which had passed between them twain. Sophronia, after eying the one and the other somewhat despitefully, fell a-weeping bitterly, complaining of Gisippus his deceit; then, rather than make any words of this in his house, she repaired to that of her father and there acquainted him and her mother with the cheat that had been put upon her and them by Gisippus, avouching herself to be the wife of Titus and not of Gisippus, as they believed. This was exceeding grievous to Sophronia's father, who made long and sore complaint thereof to her kinsfolk and those of Gisippus, and much and great was the talk and the clamour by reason thereof. Gisippus was held in despite both by his own kindred and those of Sophronia and every one declared him worthy not only of blame, but of severe chastisement; whilst he, on the contrary, avouched himself to have done an honourable thing and one for which thanks should be rendered him by Sophronia's kinsfolk, having married her to a better than himself.

Titus, on his part, heard and suffered everything with no little annoy and knowing it to be the usance of the Greeks to press on with clamours and menaces, till such times as they found who should answer them, and then to become not only humble, but abject, he bethought himself that their clamour was no longer to be brooked without reply and having a Roman spirit and an Athenian wit, he adroitly contrived to assemble Gisippus his kinsfolk and those of Sophronia in a temple, wherein entering, accompanied by Gisippus alone, he thus bespoke the expectant folk: 'It is the belief of many philosophers that the actions of mortals are determined and foreordained of the immortal Gods, wherefore some will have it that all that is or shall ever be done is of necessity, albeit there be others who attribute this necessity to that only which is already done. If these opinions be considered with any diligence, it will very manifestly be seen that to blame a thing which cannot be undone is to do no otherwhat than to seek to show oneself wiser than the Gods, who, we must e'en believe, dispose of and govern us and our affairs with unfailing wisdom and without any error; wherefore you may very easily see what fond and brutish overweening it is to presume to find fault with their operations and eke how many and what chains they merit who suffer themselves be so far carried away by hardihood as to do this. Of whom, to my thinking, you are all, if that be true which I understand you have said and still say for that Sophronia is become my wife, whereas you had given her to Gisippus, never considering that it was foreordained from all eternity that she should become not his, but mine, as by the issue is known at this present. But, for that to speak of the secret foreordinance and intention of the Gods appeareth unto many a hard thing and a grievous to apprehend, I am willing to suppose that they concern not themselves with aught of our affairs and to condescend to the counsels[466] of mankind, in speaking whereof, it will behove me to do two things, both very contrary to my usances, the one, somedele to commend myself, and the other, in some measure to blame or disparage others; but, for that I purpose, neither in the one nor in the other, to depart from the truth and that the present matter requireth it, I will e'en do it.

Your complainings, dictated more by rage than by reason, upbraid, revile and condemn Gisippus with continual murmurs or rather clamours, for that, of his counsel, he hath given me to wife her whom you of yours[467] had given him; whereas I hold that he is supremely to be commended therefor, and that for two reasons, the one, for that he hath done that which a friend should do, and the other, for that he hath in this wrought more discreetly than did you. That which the sacred laws of friendship will that one friend should do for the other, it is not my intention at this present to expound, being content to have recalled to you this much only thereof, to wit, that the bonds of friendship are far more stringent than those of blood or of kindred, seeing that the friends we have are such as we choose for ourselves and our kinsfolk such as fortune giveth us; wherefore, if Gisippus loved my life more than your goodwill, I being his friend, as I hold myself, none should marvel thereat. But to come to the second reason, whereanent it more instantly behoveth to show you that he hath been wiser than yourselves, since meseemeth you reck nothing of the foreordinance of the Gods and know yet less of the effects of friendship:—I say, then, that you of your judgment, of your counsel and of your deliberation, gave Sophronia to Gisippus, a young man and a philosopher; Gisippus of his gave her to a young man and a philosopher; your counsel gave her to an Athenian and that of Gisippus to a Roman; your counsel gave her to a youth of noble birth and his to one yet nobler; yours to a rich youth, his to a very rich; yours to a youth who not only loved her not, but scarce knew her, his to one who loved her over his every happiness and more than his very life. And to show you that this I say is true and that Gisippus his action is more commendable than yours, let us consider it, part by part. That I, like Gisippus, am a young man and a philosopher, my favour and my studies may declare, without more discourse thereof. One same age is his and mine and still with equal step have we proceeded studying. True, he is an Athenian and I am a Roman. If it be disputed of the glory of our native cities, I say that I am a citizen of a free city and he of a tributary one; I am of a city mistress of the whole world and he of a city obedient unto mine; I am of a city most illustrious in arms, in empery and in letters, whereas he can only commend his own for letters. Moreover, albeit you see me here on lowly wise enough a student, I am not born of the dregs of the Roman populace; my houses and the public places of Rome are full of antique images of my ancestors and the Roman annals will be found full of many a triumph led by the Quintii up to the Roman Capitol; nor is the glory of our name fallen for age into decay, nay, it presently flourisheth more splendidly than ever. I speak not, for shamefastness, of my riches, bearing in mind that honourable poverty hath ever been the ancient and most ample patrimony of the noble citizens of Rome; but, if this be condemned of the opinion of the vulgar and treasures commended, I am abundantly provided with these latter, not as one covetous, but as beloved of fortune.[468] I know very well that it was and should have been and should be dear unto you to have Gisippus here in Athens to kinsman; but I ought not for any reason to be less dear to you at Rome, considering that in me you would have there an excellent host and an useful and diligent and powerful patron, no less in public occasions than in matters of private need.

Who then, letting be wilfulness and considering with reason, will commend your counsels above those of my Gisippus? Certes, none. Sophronia, then, is well and duly married to Titus Quintius Fulvus, a noble, rich and long-descended citizen of Rome and a friend of Gisippus; wherefore whoso complaineth or maketh moan of this doth not that which he ought neither knoweth that which he doth. Some perchance will say that they complain not of Sophronia being the wife of Titus, but of the manner wherein she became his wife, to wit, in secret and by stealth, without friend or kinsman knowing aught thereof; but this is no marvel nor thing that betideth newly. I willingly leave be those who have aforetime taken husbands against their parents' will and those who have fled with their lovers and have been mistresses before they were wives and those who have discovered themselves to be married rather by pregnancy or child-bearing than with the tongue, yet hath necessity commended it to their kinsfolk; nothing of which hath happened in Sophronia's case; nay, she hath orderly, discreetly and honourably been given by Gisippus to Titus. Others will say that he gave her in marriage to whom it appertained not to do so; but these be all foolish and womanish complaints and proceed from lack of advisement. This is not the first time that fortune hath made use of various means and strange instruments to bring matters to foreordained issues. What have I to care if it be a cordwainer rather than a philosopher, that hath, according to his judgment, despatched an affair of mine, and whether in secret or openly, provided the issue be good? If the cordwainer be indiscreet, all I have to do is to look well that he have no more to do with my affairs and thank him for that which is done. If Gisippus hath married Sophronia well, it is a superfluous folly to go complaining of the manner and of him. If you have no confidence in his judgment, look he have no more of your daughters to marry and thank him for this one.

Nevertheless I would have you to know that I sought not, either by art or by fraud, to impose any stain upon the honour and illustriousness of your blood in the person of Sophronia, and that, albeit I took her secretly to wife, I came not as a ravisher to rob her of her maidenhead nor sought, after the manner of an enemy, whilst shunning your alliance, to have her otherwise than honourably; but, being ardently enkindled by her lovesome beauty and by her worth and knowing that, had I sought her with that ordinance which you will maybe say I should have used, I should not (she being much beloved of you) have had her, for fear lest I should carry her off to Rome, I used the occult means that may now be discovered to you and caused Gisippus, in my person, consent unto that which he himself was not disposed to do. Moreover, ardently as I loved her, I sought her embraces not as a lover, but as a husband, nor, as she herself can truly testify, did I draw near to her till I had first both with the due words and with the ring espoused her, asking her if she would have me for husband, to which she answered ay. If it appear to her that she hath been deceived, it is not I who am to blame therefor, but she, who asked me not who I was. This, then, is the great misdeed, the grievous crime, the sore default committed by Gisippus as a friend and by myself as a lover, to wit, that Sophronia hath secretly become the wife of Titus Quintius, and this it is for which you defame and menace and plot against him. What more could you do, had he bestowed her upon a churl, a losel or a slave? What chains, what prison, what gibbets had sufficed thereunto?

But let that be for the present; the time is come which I looked not for yet, to wit, my father is dead and it behoveth me return to Rome; wherefore, meaning to carry Sophronia with me, I have discovered to you that which I should otherwise belike have yet kept hidden from you and with which, an you be wise, you will cheerfully put up, for that, had I wished to cheat or outrage you, I might have left her to you, scorned and dishonored; but God forfend that such a baseness should ever avail to harbour in a Roman breast! She, then, namely Sophronia, by the consent of the Gods and the operation of the laws of mankind, no less than by the admirable contrivance of my Gisippus and mine own amorous astuteness, is become mine, and this it seemeth that you, holding yourselves belike wiser than the Gods and than the rest of mankind, brutishly condemn, showing your disapproval in two ways both exceedingly noyous to myself, first by detaining Sophronia, over whom you have no right, save in so far as it pleaseth me to allow it, and secondly, by entreating Gisippus, to whom you are justly beholden, as an enemy. How foolishly you do in both which things I purpose not at this present to make farther manifest to you, but will only counsel you, as a friend, to lay by your despites and altogether leaving your resentments and the rancours that you have conceived, to restore Sophronia to me, so I may joyfully depart your kinsman and live your friend; for of this, whether that which is done please you or please you not, you may be assured that, if you offer to do otherwise, I will take Gisippus from you and if I win to Rome, I will without fail, however ill you may take it, have her again who is justly mine and ever after showing myself your enemy, will cause you know by experience that whereof the despite of Roman souls is capable.'

Titus, having thus spoken, rose to his feet, with a countenance all disordered for anger, and taking Gisippus by the hand, went forth of the temple, shaking his head threateningly and showing that he recked little of as many as were there. The latter, in part reconciled by his reasonings to the alliance and desirous of his friendship and in part terrified by his last words, of one accord determined that it was better to have him for a kinsman, since Gisippus had not willed it, than to have lost the latter to kinsman and gotten the former for an enemy. Accordingly, going in quest of Titus, they told him that they were willing that Sophronia should be his and to have him for a dear kinsman and Gisippus for a dear friend; then, having mutually done each other such honours and courtesies as beseem between kinsmen and friends, they took their leaves and sent Sophronia back to him. She, like a wise woman, making a virtue of necessity, readily transferred to Titus the affection she bore Gisippus and repaired with him to Rome, where she was received with great honour.

Meanwhile, Gisippus abode in Athens, held in little esteem of well nigh all, and no great while after, through certain intestine troubles, was, with all those of his house, expelled from Athens, in poverty and misery, and condemned to perpetual exile. Finding himself in this case and being grown not only poor, but beggarly, he betook himself, as least ill he might, to Rome, to essay if Titus should remember him. There, learning that the latter was alive and high in favour with all the Romans and enquiring for his dwelling-place, he stationed himself before the door and there abode till such time as Titus came, to whom, by reason of the wretched plight wherein he was, he dared not say a word, but studied to cause himself be seen of him, so he might recognize him and let call him to himself; wherefore Titus passed on, [without noting him,] and Gisippus, conceiving that he had seen and shunned him and remembering him of that which himself had done for him aforetime, departed, despiteful and despairing. It being by this night and he fasting and penniless, he wandered on, unknowing whither and more desirous of death than of otherwhat, and presently happened upon a very desert part of the city, where seeing a great cavern, he addressed himself to abide the night there and presently, forspent with long weeping, he fell asleep on the naked earth and ill in case. To this cavern two, who had gone a-thieving together that night, came towards morning, with the booty they had gotten, and falling out over the division, one, who was the stronger, slew the other and went away. Gisippus had seen and heard this and himseemed he had found a way to the death so sore desired of him, without slaying himself; wherefore he abode without stirring, till such time as the Serjeants of the watch, who had by this gotten wind of the deed, came thither and laying furious hands of him, carried him off prisoner. Gisippus, being examined, confessed that he had murdered the man nor had since availed to depart the cavern; whereupon the prætor, who was called Marcus Varro, commanded that he should be put to death upon the cross, as the usance then was.

Now Titus was by chance come at that juncture to the prætorium and looking the wretched condemned man in the face and hearing why he had been doomed to die, suddenly knew him for Gisippus; whereupon, marvelling at his sorry fortune and how he came to be in Rome and desiring most ardently to succour him, but seeing no other means of saving him than to accuse himself and thus excuse him, he thrust forward in haste and cried out, saying, 'Marcus Varro, call back the poor man whom thou hast condemned, for that he is innocent. I have enough offended against the Gods with one crime, in slaying him whom thine officer found this morning dead, without willing presently to wrong them with the death of another innocent.' Varro marvelled and it irked him that all the prætorium should have heard him; but, being unable, for his own honour's sake, to forbear from doing that which the laws commanded, he caused bring back Gisippus and in the presence of Titus said to him, 'How camest thou to be so mad that, without suffering any torture, thou confessedst to that which thou didst not, it being a capital matter? Thou declaredst thyself to be he who slew the man yesternight, and now this man cometh and saith that it was not thou, but he that slew him.'

Gisippus looked and seeing that it was Titus, perceived full well that he did this to save him, as grateful for the service aforetime received from him; wherefore, weeping for pity, 'Varro,' quoth he, 'indeed it was I slew him and Titus his solicitude for my safety is now too late.' Titus on the other hand, said, 'Prætor, do as thou seest, this man is a stranger and was found without arms beside the murdered man, and thou mayst see that his wretchedness giveth him occasion to wish to die; wherefore do thou release him and punish me, who have deserved it.' Varro marvelled at the insistence of these two and beginning now to presume that neither of them might be guilty, was casting about for a means of acquitting them, when, behold, up came a youth called Publius Ambustus, a man of notorious ill life and known to all the Romans for an arrant rogue, who had actually done the murder and knowing neither of the twain to be guilty of that whereof each accused himself, such was the pity that overcame his heart for the innocence of the two friends that, moved by supreme compassion, he came before Varro and said, 'Prætor, my fates impel me to solve the grievous contention of these twain and I know not what God within me spurreth and importuneth me to discover to thee my sin. Know, then, that neither of these men is guilty of that whereof each accuseth himself. I am verily he who slew yonder man this morning towards daybreak and I saw this poor wretch asleep there, what while I was in act to divide the booty gotten with him whom I slew. There is no need for me to excuse Titus; his renown is everywhere manifest and every one knoweth him to be no man of such a condition. Release him, therefore, and take of me that forfeit which the laws impose on me.'

By this Octavianus had notice of the matter and causing all three be brought before him, desired to hear what cause had moved each of them to seek to be the condemned man. Accordingly, each related his own story, whereupon Octavianus released the two friends, for that they were innocent, and pardoned the other for the love of them. Thereupon Titus took his Gisippus and first reproaching him sore for lukewarmness[469] and diffidence, rejoiced in him with marvellous great joy and carried him to his house, where Sophronia with tears of compassion received him as a brother. Then, having awhile recruited him with rest and refreshment and reclothed him and restored him to such a habit as sorted with his worth and quality, he first shared all his treasures and estates in common with him and after gave him to wife a young sister of his, called Fulvia, saying, 'Gisippus, henceforth it resteth with thee whether thou wilt abide here with me or return with everything I have given thee into Achaia.' Gisippus, constrained on the one hand by his banishment from his native land and on the other by the love which he justly bore to the cherished friendship of Titus, consented to become a Roman and accordingly took up his abode in the city, where he with his Fulvia and Titus with his Sophronia lived long and happily, still abiding in one house and waxing more friends (an more they might be) every day.

A most sacred thing, then, is friendship and worthy not only of especial reverence, but to be commended with perpetual praise, as the most discreet mother of magnanimity and honour, the sister of gratitude and charity and the enemy of hatred and avarice, still, without waiting to be entreated, ready virtuously to do unto others that which it would have done to itself. Nowadays its divine effects are very rarely to be seen in any twain, by the fault and to the shame of the wretched cupidity of mankind, which, regarding only its own profit, hath relegated it to perpetual exile, beyond the extremest limits of the earth. What love, what riches, what kinship, what, except friendship, could have made Gisippus feel in his heart the ardour, the tears and the sighs of Titus with such efficacy as to cause him yield up to his friend his betrothed bride, fair and gentle and beloved of him? What laws, what menaces, what fears could have enforced the young arms of Gisippus to abstain, in solitary places and in dark, nay, in his very bed, from the embraces of the fair damsel, she mayhap bytimes inviting him, had friendship not done it? What honours, what rewards, what advancements, what, indeed, but friendship, could have made Gisippus reck not of losing his own kinsfolk and those of Sophronia nor of the unmannerly clamours of the populace nor of scoffs and insults, so that he might pleasure his friend? On the other hand, what, but friendship, could have prompted Titus, whenas he might fairly have feigned not to see, unhesitatingly to compass his own death, that he might deliver Gisippus from the cross to which he had of his own motion procured himself to be condemned? What else could have made Titus, without the least demur, so liberal in sharing his most ample patrimony with Gisippus, whom fortune had bereft of his own? What else could have made him so forward to vouchsafe his sister to his friend, albeit he saw him very poor and reduced to the extreme of misery? Let men, then, covet a multitude of comrades, troops of brethren and children galore and add, by dint of monies, to the number of their servitors, considering not that every one of these, who and whatsoever he may be, is more fearful of every least danger of his own than careful to do away the great[470] from father or brother or master, whereas we see a friend do altogether the contrary."

THE NINTH STORY

SALADIN, IN THE DISGUISE OF A MERCHANT, IS HONOURABLY ENTERTAINED BY MESSER TORELLO D'ISTRIA, WHO, PRESENTLY UNDERTAKING THE [THIRD] CRUSADE, APPOINTETH HIS WIFE A TERM FOR HER MARRYING AGAIN. HE IS TAKEN [BY THE SARACENS] AND COMETH, BY HIS SKILL IN TRAINING HAWKS, UNDER THE NOTICE OF THE SOLDAN, WHO KNOWETH HIM AGAIN AND DISCOVERING HIMSELF TO HIM, ENTREATETH HIM WITH THE UTMOST HONOUR. THEN, TORELLO FALLING SICK FOR LANGUISHMENT, HE IS BY MAGICAL ART TRANSPORTED IN ONE NIGHT [FROM ALEXANDRIA] TO PAVIA, WHERE, BEING RECOGNIZED BY HIS WIFE AT THE BRIDE-FEAST HELD FOR HER MARRYING AGAIN, HE RETURNETH WITH HER TO HIS OWN HOUSE

FILOMENA having made an end of her discourse and the magnificent gratitude of Titus having been of all alike commended, the king, reserving the last place unto Dioneo, proceeded to speak thus: "Assuredly, lovesome ladies, Filomena speaketh sooth in that which she saith of friendship and with reason complaineth, in concluding her discourse, of its being so little in favour with mankind. If we were here for the purpose of correcting the defaults of the age or even of reprehending them, I might ensue her words with a discourse at large upon the subject; but, for that we aim at otherwhat, it hath occurred to my mind to set forth to you, in a story belike somewhat overlong, but withal altogether pleasing, one of the magnificences of Saladin, to the end that, if, by reason of our defaults, the friendship of any one may not be throughly acquired, we may, at the least, be led, by the things which you shall hear in my story, to take delight in doing service, in the hope that, whenassoever it may be, reward will ensue to us thereof.

I must tell you, then, that, according to that which divers folk affirm, a general crusade was, in the days of the Emperor Frederick the First, undertaken by the Christians for the recovery of the Holy Land, whereof Saladin, a very noble and valiant prince, who was then Soldan of Babylon, having notice awhile beforehand, he bethought himself to seek in his own person to see the preparations of the Christian princes for the undertaking in question, so he might the better avail to provide himself. Accordingly, having ordered all his affairs in Egypt, he made a show of going a pilgrimage and set out in the disguise of a merchant, attended by two only of his chiefest and sagest officers and three serving-men. After he had visited many Christian countries, it chanced that, as they rode through Lombardy, thinking to pass beyond the mountains,[471] they encountered, about vespers, on the road from Milan to Pavia, a gentleman of the latter place, by name Messer Torello d'Istria, who was on his way, with his servants and dogs and falcons, to sojourn at a goodly country seat he had upon the Tesino, and no sooner set eyes on Saladin and his company than he knew them for gentlemen and strangers; wherefore, the Soldan enquiring of one of his servants how far they were yet distant from Pavia and if he might win thither in time to enter the city, he suffered not the man to reply, but himself answered, 'Gentlemen, you cannot reach Pavia in time to enter therein.' 'Then,' said Saladin, 'may it please you acquaint us (for that we are strangers) where we may best lodge the night.' Quoth Messer Torello, 'That will I willingly do. I had it presently in mind to dispatch one of my men here to the neighborhood of Pavia for somewhat: I will send him with you and he shall bring you to a place where you may lodge conveniently enough.' Then, turning to the discreetest of his men he [privily] enjoined him what he should do and sent him with them, whilst he himself, making for his country house, let order, as best he might, a goodly supper and set the tables in the garden; which done, he posted himself at the door to await his guests.

Meanwhile, the servant, devising with the gentlemen of one thing and another, led them about by certain by-roads and brought them, without their suspecting it, to his lord's residence, where, whenas Messer Torello saw them, he came to meet them afoot and said, smiling, 'Gentlemen, you are very welcome.' Saladin, who was very quick of apprehension, understood that the gentleman had misdoubted him they would not have accepted his invitation, had he bidden them whenas he fell in with them, and had, therefore, brought them by practice to his house, so they might not avail to refuse to pass the night with him, and accordingly, returning his greeting, he said, 'Sir, an one could complain of men of courtesy, we might complain of you, for that (letting be that you have somewhat hindered us from our road) you have, without our having merited your goodwill otherwise than by a mere salutation, constrained us to accept of such noble hospitality as is this of yours.' 'Gentlemen,' answered Messer Torello, who was a discreet and well-spoken man, 'it is but a sorry hospitality that you will receive from us, regard had to that which should behove unto you, an I may judge by that which I apprehend from your carriage and that of your companions; but in truth you could nowhere out of Pavia have found any decent place of entertainment; wherefore, let it not irk you to have gone somedele beside your way, to have a little less unease.' Meanwhile, his servants came round about the travellers and helping them to dismount, eased[472] their horses.

Messer Torello then brought the three stranger gentlemen to the chambers prepared for them, where he let unboot them and refresh them somewhat with very cool wines and entertained them in agreeable discourse till such time as they might sup. Saladin and his companions and servants all knew Latin, wherefore they understood very well and were understood, and it seemed to each of them that this gentleman was the most pleasant and well-mannered man they had ever seen, ay, and the best spoken. It appeared to Messer Torello, on the other hand, that they were men of magnificent fashions and much more of account than he had at first conceived, wherefore he was inwardly chagrined that he could not honour them that evening with companions and with a more considerable entertainment. But for this he bethought himself to make them amends on the morrow, and accordingly, having instructed one of his servants of that which he would have done, he despatched him to Pavia, which was very near at hand and where no gate was ever locked, to his lady, who was exceeding discreet and great-hearted. Then, carrying the gentlemen into the garden, he courteously asked them who they were, to which Saladin answered, 'We are merchants from Cyprus and are bound to Paris on our occasions.' 'Would to God,' cried Messer Torello, 'that this our country produced gentlemen of such a fashion as I see Cyprus doth merchants!' In these and other discourses they abode till it was time to sup, whereupon he left it to them to honour themselves at table,[473] and there, for an improvised supper, they were very well and orderly served; nor had they abidden long after the tables were removed, when Messer Torello, judging them to be weary, put them to sleep in very goodly beds and himself a little after in like manner betook himself to rest.

Meanwhile the servant sent to Pavia did his errand to the lady, who, with no womanly, but with a royal spirit, let call in haste a great number of the friends and servants of Messer Torello and made ready all that behoved unto a magnificent banquet. Moreover, she let bid by torchlight many of the noblest of the townfolk to the banquet and bringing out cloths and silks and furs, caused throughly order that which her husband had sent to bid her do. The day come, Saladin and his companions arose, whereupon Messer Torello took horse with them and sending for his falcons, carried them to a neighbouring ford and there showed them how the latter flew; then, Saladin enquiring for some one who should bring him to Pavia and to the best inn, his host said, 'I will be your guide, for that it behoveth me go thither.' The others, believing this, were content and set out in company with him for the city, which they reached about tierce and thinking to be on their way to the best inn, were carried by Messer Torello to his own house, where a good half-hundred of the most considerable citizens were already come to receive the stranger gentlemen and were straightway about their bridles and stirrups. Saladin and his companions, seeing this, understood but too well what was forward and said, 'Messer Torello, this is not what we asked of you; you have done enough for us this past night, ay, and far more than we are worth; wherefore you might now fitly suffer us fare on our way.' 'Gentlemen,' replied Messer Torello, 'for my yesternight's dealing with you I am more indebted to fortune than to you, which took you on the road at an hour when it behoved you come to my poor house; but of your this morning's visit I shall be beholden to yourselves, and with me all these gentlemen who are about you and to whom an it seem to you courteous to refuse to dine with them, you can do so, if you will.'

Saladin and his companions, overcome, dismounted and being joyfully received by the assembled company, were carried to chambers which had been most sumptuously arrayed for them, where having put off their travelling gear and somewhat refreshed themselves, they repaired to the saloon, where the banquet was splendidly prepared. Water having been given to the hands, they were seated at table with the goodliest and most orderly observance and magnificently served with many viands, insomuch that, were the emperor himself come thither, it had been impossible to do him more honour, and albeit Saladin and his companions were great lords and used to see very great things, natheless, they were mightily wondered at this and it seemed to them of the greatest, having regard to the quality of the gentleman, whom they knew to be only a citizen and not a lord. Dinner ended and the tables removed, they conversed awhile of divers things; then, at Messer Torello's instance, the heat being great, the gentlemen of Pavia all betook themselves to repose, whilst he himself, abiding alone with his three guests, carried them into a chamber and (that no precious thing of his should remain unseen of them) let call thither his noble lady. Accordingly, the latter, who was very fair and tall of her person, came in to them, arrayed in rich apparel and flanked by two little sons of hers, as they were two angels, and saluted them courteously. The strangers, seeing her, rose to their feet and receiving her with worship, caused her sit among them and made much of her two fair children. Therewithal she entered into pleasant discourse with them and presently, Messer Torello having gone out awhile, she asked them courteously whence they were and whither they went; to which they made answer even as they had done to her husband; whereupon quoth she, with a blithe air, 'Then see I that my womanly advisement will be useful; wherefore I pray you, of your especial favour, refuse me not neither disdain a slight present, which I shall cause bring you, but accept it, considering that women, of their little heart, give little things and regarding more the goodwill of the giver than the value of the gift.' Then, letting fetch them each two gowns, one lined with silk and the other with miniver, no wise citizens' clothes nor merchants, but fit for great lords to wear, and three doublets of sendal and linen breeches to match, she said, 'Take these; I have clad my lord in gowns of the like fashion, and the other things, for all they are little worth, may be acceptable to you, considering that you are far from your ladies and the length of the way you have travelled and that which is yet to travel and that merchants are proper men and nice of their persons.'

The Saracens marvelled and manifestly perceived that Messer Torello was minded to leave no particular of hospitality undone them; nay, seeing the magnificence of the unmerchantlike gowns, they misdoubted them they had been recognized of him. However, one of them made answer to the lady, saying, 'Madam, these are very great matters and such as should not lightly be accepted, an your prayers, to which it is impossible to say no, constrained us not thereto.' This done and Messer Torello being now returned, the lady, commending them to God, took leave of them and let furnish their servants with like things such as sorted with their condition. Messer Torello with many prayers prevailed upon them to abide with him all that day; wherefore, after they had slept awhile, they donned their gowns and rode with him somedele about the city; then, the supper-hour come, they supped magnificently with many worshipful companions and in due time betook themselves to rest. On the morrow they arose with day and found, in place of their tired hackneys, three stout and good palfreys, and on likewise fresh and strong horses for their servants, which when Saladin saw, he turned to his companions and said, 'I vow to God that never was there a more accomplished gentleman nor a more courteous and apprehensive than this one, and if the kings of the Christians are kings of such a fashion as this is a gentleman, the Soldan of Babylon can never hope to stand against a single one of them, not to speak of the many whom we see make ready to fall upon him.' Then, knowing that it were in vain to seek to refuse this new gift, they very courteously thanked him therefor and mounted to horse.

Messer Torello, with many companions, brought them a great way without the city, till, grievous as it was to Saladin to part from him, (so much was he by this grown enamoured of him,) natheless, need constraining him to press on, he presently besought him to turn back; whereupon, loath as he was to leave them, 'Gentlemen,' quoth he, 'since it pleaseth you, I will do it; but one thing I will e'en say to you; I know not who you are nor do I ask to know more thereof than it pleaseth you to tell me; but, be you who you may, you will never make me believe that you are merchants, and so I commend you to God.' Saladin, having by this taken leave of all Messer Torello's companions, replied to him, saying, 'Sir, we may yet chance to let you see somewhat of our merchandise, whereby we may confirm your belief;[474] meantime, God be with you.' Thereupon he departed with his followers, firmly resolved, if life should endure to him and the war he looked for undo him not, to do Messer Torello no less honour than that which he had done him, and much did he discourse with his companions of him and of his lady and all his affairs and fashions and dealings, mightily commending everything. Then, after he had, with no little fatigue, visited all the West, he took ship with his companions and returned to Alexandria, where, being now fully informed, he addressed himself to his defence. As for Messer Torello, he returned to Pavia and went long in thought who these might be, but never hit upon the truth, no, nor came near it.

The time being now come for the crusade and great preparations made everywhere, Messer Torello, notwithstanding the tears and entreaties of his wife, was altogether resolved to go thereon and having made his every provision and being about to take horse, he said to his lady, whom he loved over all, 'Wife, as thou seest, I go on this crusade, as well for the honour of my body as for the health of my soul. I commend to thee our affairs and our honour, and for that I am certain of the going, but of the returning, for a thousand chances that may betide, I have no assurance, I will have thee do me a favour, to wit, that whatever befall of me, an thou have not certain news of my life, thou shalt await me a year and a month and a day, ere thou marry again, beginning from this the day of my departure.' The lady, who wept sore, answered, 'Messer Torello, I know not how I shall endure the chagrin wherein you leave me by your departure; but, an my life prove stronger than my grief and aught befall you, you may live and die assured that I shall live and die the wife of Messer Torello and of his memory.' 'Wife,' rejoined Messer Torello, 'I am very certain that, inasmuch as in thee lieth, this that thou promisest me will come to pass; but thou art a young woman and fair and of high family and thy worth is great and everywhere known; wherefore I doubt not but many great and noble gentlemen will, should aught be misdoubted of me,[475] demand thee of thy brethren and kinsfolk; from whose importunities, how much soever thou mightest wish, thou wilt not be able to defend thyself and it will behove thee perforce comply with their wishes; and this is why I ask of thee this term and not a greater one.' Quoth the lady, 'I will do what I may of that which I have told you, and should it nevertheless behove me to do otherwise, I will assuredly obey you in this that you enjoin me; but I pray God that He bring nor you nor me to such an extremity in these days.' This said, she embraced him, weeping, and drawing a ring from her finger, gave it to him, saying, 'And it chance that I die ere I see you again, remember me when you look upon this ring.'

Torello took the ring and mounted to horse; then, bidding all his people adieu, he set out on his journey and came presently with his company to Genoa. There he embarked on board a galleon and coming in a little while to Acre, joined himself to the other army[476] of the Christians, wherein, well nigh out of hand, there began a sore sickness and mortality. During this, whether by Saladin's skill or of his good fortune, well nigh all the remnant of the Christians who had escaped alive were taken by him, without blow stricken, and divided among many cities and imprisoned. Messer Torello was one of those taken and was carried prisoner to Alexandria, where, being unknown and fearing to make himself known, he addressed himself, of necessity constrained, to the training of hawks, of which he was a great master, and by this he came under the notice of Saladin, who took him out of prison and entertained him for his falconer. Messer Torello, who was called by the Soldan by none other name than the Christian, recognized him not nor did Saladin recognize him; nay, all his thoughts were in Pavia and he had more than once essayed to flee, but without avail; wherefore, certain Genoese coming ambassadors to Saladin, to treat for the ransom of sundry of their townsmen, and being about to depart, he bethought himself to write to his lady, giving her to know that he was alive and would return to her as quickliest he might and bidding her await him. Accordingly, he wrote letters to this effect and instantly besought one of the ambassadors, whom he knew, to cause them come to the hands of the Abbot of San Pietro in Ciel d'Oro, who was his uncle.

Things being at this pass with him, it befell one day that, as Saladin was devising with him of his hawks, Messer Torello chanced to smile and made a motion with his mouth, which the former had much noted, what while he was in his house at Pavia. This brought the gentleman to his mind and looking steadfastly upon him, himseemed it was himself; wherefore, leaving the former discourse, 'Harkye, Christian, said he, 'What countryman art thou of the West?' 'My lord,' replied Torello, 'I am a Lombard of a city called Pavia, a poor man and of mean condition.' Saladin, hearing this, was in a manner certified of the truth of his suspicion and said joyfully in himself, 'God hath vouchsafed me an opportunity of showing this man how grateful his courtesy was to me.' Accordingly, without saying otherwhat, he let lay out all his apparel in a chamber and carrying him thither, said to him, 'Look, Christian, if there be any among these gowns that thou hast ever seen.' Torello looked and saw those which his lady had given Saladin; but, natheless, conceiving not that they could possibly be the same, he answered, 'My lord, I know none of them; albeit, in good sooth, these twain do favour certain gowns wherewithal I, together with three merchants who came to my house, was invested aforetime.' Thereupon Saladin, unable to contain himself farther, embraced him tenderly, saying, 'You are Messer Torello d'Istria and I am one of the three merchants to whom your lady gave these gowns; and now is the time come to certify you what manner merchandise mine is, even as I told you, at my parting from you, might chance to betide.' Messer Torello, hearing this, was at once rejoiced and ashamed; rejoiced to have had such a guest and ashamed for that himseemed he had entertained him but scurvily. Then said Saladin, 'Messer Torello, since God hath sent you hither to me, henceforth consider that not I, but you are master here.' Accordingly, after they had mightily rejoiced in each other, he clad him in royal apparel and carrying him into the presence of all his chief barons, commanded, after saying many things in praise of his worth, that he should of all who held his favour dear be honoured as himself, which was thenceforward done of all, but above all of the two gentlemen who had been Saladin's companions in his house.

The sudden height of glory to which Messer Torello thus found himself advanced put his Lombardy affairs somedele out of his mind, more by token that he had good reason to hope that his letters were by this come to his uncle's hands. Now there had died and been buried in the camp or rather in the host, of the Christians, the day they were taken by Saladin, a Provençal gentleman of little account, by name Messer Torello de Dignes, by reason whereof, Messer Torello d'Istria being renowned throughout the army for his magnificence, whosoever heard say, 'Messer Torello is dead,' believed it of Messer Torello d'Istria, not of him of Dignes. The hazard of the capture that ensued thereupon suffered not those who had been thus misled to be undeceived; wherefore many Italians returned with this news, amongst whom were some who scrupled not to avouch that they had seen him dead and had been at the burial. This, coming to be known of his wife and kinsfolk, was the cause of grievous and inexpressible sorrow, not only to them, but to all who had known him. It were longsome to set forth what and how great was the grief and sorrow and lamentation of his lady; but, after having bemoaned herself some months in continual affliction, coming to sorrow less and being sought in marriage with the chiefest men in Lombardy, she began to be presently importuned by her brothers and other her kinsfolk to marry again. After having again and again refused with many tears, needs must she at the last consent perforce to do her kinsfolk's will, on condition that she should abide, without going to a husband, so long as she had promised Messer Torello.

The lady's affairs at Pavia being at this pass and there lacking maybe eight days of the term appointed for her going to her new husband, it chanced that Messer Torello espied one day in Alexandria one whom he had seen embark with the Genoese ambassadors on board the galley that was to carry them back to Genoa, and calling him, asked him what manner voyage they had had and when they had reached Genoa; whereto the other replied, 'Sir, the galleon (as I heard in Crete, where I remained,) made an ill voyage; for that, as she drew near unto Sicily, there arose a furious northerly wind, which drove her on to the Barbary quicksands, nor was any one saved; and amongst the rest two brothers of mine perished there.' Messer Torello, giving credit to his words, which were indeed but too true, and remembering him that the term required by him of his wife ended a few days thence, concluded that nothing could be known at Pavia of his condition and held it for certain that the lady must have married again; wherefore he fell into such a chagrin that he lost [sleep and] appetite and taking to his bed, determined to die. When Saladin, who loved him above all, heard of this, he came to him and having, by dint of many and urgent prayers, learned the cause of his grief and his sickness, upbraided him sore for that he had not before told it to him and after besought him to be comforted, assuring him that, if he would but take heart, he would so contrive that he should be in Pavia at the appointed term and told him how. Messer Torello, putting faith in Saladin's words and having many a time heard say that this was possible and had indeed been often enough done, began to take comfort and pressed Saladin to despatch. The Soldan accordingly charged a nigromancer of his, of whose skill he had aforetime made proof, to cast about for a means whereby Messer Torello should be in one night transported upon a bed to Pavia, to which the magician replied that it should be done, but that, for the gentleman's own weal, he must put him to sleep.

This done, Saladin returned to Messer Torello and finding him altogether resolved to seek at any hazard to be in Pavia at the term appointed, if it were possible, and in default thereof, to die, bespoke him thus; 'Messer Torello, God knoweth that I neither will nor can anywise blame you if you tenderly love your lady and are fearful of her becoming another's, for that, of all the women I ever saw, she it is whose manners, whose fashions and whose demeanour, (leaving be her beauty, which is but a short-lived flower,) appear to me most worthy to be commended and held dear. It had been very grateful to me, since fortune hath sent you hither, that we should have passed together, as equal masters in the governance of this my realm, such time as you and I have to live, and if this was not to be vouchsafed me of God, it being fated that you should take it to heart to seek either to die or to find yourself in Pavia at the appointed term, I should above all have desired to know it in time, that I might have you transported to your house with such honour, such magnificence and in such company as your worth meriteth. However, since this hath not been vouchsafed and you desire to be presently there, I will e'en, as I may, despatch you thither after the fashion whereof I have bespoken you.' 'My lord,' replied Messer Torello, 'your acts, without your words, have given me sufficient proof of your favour, which I have never merited in such supreme degree, and of that which you say, though you had not said it, I shall live and die most assured; but, since I have taken this resolve, I pray you that that which you tell me you will do may be done speedily, for that to-morrow is the last day I am to be looked for.'

Saladin answered that this should without fail be accomplished and accordingly, on the morrow, meaning to send him away that same night, he let make, in a great hall of his palace, a very goodly and rich bed of mattresses, all, according to their usance, of velvet and cloth of gold and caused lay thereon a counterpoint curiously wrought in various figures with great pearls and jewels of great price (the which here in Italy was after esteemed an inestimable treasure) and two pillows such as sorted with a bed of that fashion. This done, he bade invest Messer Torello, who was presently well and strong again, in a gown of the Saracen fashion, the richest and goodliest thing that had ever been seen of any, and wind about his head, after their guise, one of his longest turban-cloths.[477] Then, it growing late, he betook himself with many of his barons to the chamber where Messer Torello was and seating himself, well nigh weeping, by his side, bespoke him thus; 'Messer Torello, the hour draweth near that is to sunder me from you, and since I may not bear you company nor cause you to be accompanied, by reason of the nature of the journey you have to make, which suffereth it not, needs must I take leave of you here in this chamber, to which end I am come hither. Wherefore, ere I commend you to God, I conjure you, by that love and that friendship that is between us, that you remember you of me and if it be possible, ere our times come to an end, that, whenas you have ordered your affairs in Lombardy, you come at the least once to see me, to the end that, what while I am cheered by your sight, I may then supply the default which needs must I presently commit by reason of your haste; and against that betide, let it not irk you to visit me with letters and require me of such things as shall please you; for that of a surety I will more gladly do them for you than for any man alive.'

As for Messer Torello, he could not contain his tears; wherefore, being hindered thereby, he answered, in a few words, that it was impossible his benefits and his nobility should ever escape his mind and that he would without fail do that which he enjoined him, whenas occasion should be afforded him; whereupon Saladin, having tenderly embraced him and kissed him, bade him with many tears God speed and departed the chamber. The other barons then all took leave of him and followed the Soldan into the hall where he had caused make ready the bed. Meanwhile, it waxing late and the nigromant awaiting and pressing for despatch, there came a physician to Messer Torello with a draught and making him believe that he gave it him to fortify him, caused him drink it; nor was it long ere he fell asleep and so, by Saladin's commandment, was carried into the hall and laid upon the bed aforesaid, whereon the Soldan placed a great and goodly crown of great price and inscribed it on such wise that it was after manifestly understood to be sent by him to Messer Torello's lady; after which he put on Torello's finger a ring, wherein was a carbuncle enchased, so resplendent that it seemed a lighted flambeau, the value whereof could scarce be reckoned, and girt him with a sword, whose garniture might not lightly be appraised. Moreover, he let hang a fermail on his breast, wherein were pearls whose like were never seen, together with other precious stones galore, and on his either side he caused set two great basins of gold, full of doubloons, and many strings of pearls and rings and girdles and other things, which it were tedious to recount, round about him. This done, he kissed him once more and bade the nigromant despatch, whereupon, in his presence, the bed was incontinent taken away, Messer Torello and all, and Saladin abode devising of him with his barons.

Meanwhile, Messer Torello had been set down, even as he had requested, in the church of San Pietro in Ciel d'Oro at Pavia, with all the jewels and ornaments aforesaid, and yet slept when, matins having sounded, the sacristan of the church entered, with a light in his hand, and chancing suddenly to espy the rich bed, not only marvelled, but, seized with a terrible fright, turned and fled. The abbot and the monks, seeing him flee, marvelled and questioned him of the cause, which he told them; whereupon quoth the abbot, 'Marry, thou art no child nor art thou new to the church that thou shouldst thus lightly take fright; let us go see who hath played the bugbear with thee.' Accordingly, kindling several lights, the abbot and all his monks entered the church and saw that wonder-rich and goodly bed and thereon the gentleman asleep; and what while, misdoubting and fearful, they gazed upon the noble jewels, without drawing anywise near to the bed, it befell that, the virtue of the draught being spent, Messer Torello awoke and heaved a great sigh, which when the monks saw and heard, they took to flight, abbot and all, affrighted and crying, 'Lord aid us!' Messer Torello opened his eyes and looking about him, plainly perceived himself to be whereas he had asked Saladin to have him carried, at which he was mightily content. Then, sitting up, he particularly examined that which he had about him, and for all he had before known of the magnificence of Saladin, it seemed to him now greater and he knew it more. Nevertheless, without moving farther, seeing the monks flee and divining why, he proceeded to call the abbot by name, praying him be not afraid, for that he was Torello his nephew. The abbot, hearing this, waxed yet more fearful, as holding him as dead many months before; but, after awhile, taking assurance by true arguments and hearing himself called, he made the sign of the cross and went up to him; whereupon quoth Messer Torello, 'How now, father mine, of what are you adread? Godamercy, I am alive and returned hither from beyond seas.'

The abbot, for all he had a great beard and was clad after the Saracen fashion, presently recognized him and altogether reassured, took him by the hand, saying, 'My son, thou art welcome back.' Then he continued, 'Thou must not marvel at our affright, for that there is not a man in these parts but firmly believeth thee to be dead, insomuch that I must tell thee that Madam Adalieta thy wife, overmastered by the prayers and threats of her kinsfolk and against her own will, is married again and is this morning to go to her new husband; ay, and the bride-feast and all that pertaineth unto the nuptial festivities is prepared.' Therewithal Messer Torello arose from off the rich bed and greeting the abbot and the monks with marvellous joyance, prayed them all to speak with none of that his return, against he should have despatched an occasion of his; after which, having caused lay up the costly jewels in safety, he recounted to his uncle all that had befallen him up to that moment. The abbot rejoiced in his happy fortunes and together with him, rendered thanks to God, after which Messer Torello asked him who was his lady's new husband. The abbot told him and Torello said, 'I have a mind, ere folk know of my return, to see what manner countenance is that of my wife in these nuptials; wherefore, albeit it is not the usance of men of your habit to go to entertainments of this kind, I would have you contrive, for the love of me, that we may go thither, you and I.' The abbot replied that he would well and accordingly, as soon as it was day, he sent to the new bridegroom, saying that he would fain be at his nuptials with a friend of his, whereto the gentleman answered that it liked him passing well.

Accordingly, eating-time come, Messer Torello, clad as he was, repaired with his uncle to the bridegroom's house, beheld with wonderment of all who saw him, but recognized of none; and the abbot told every one that he was a Saracen sent ambassador from the Soldan to the King of France. He was, therefore, seated at a table right overagainst his lady, whom he beheld with the utmost pleasure, and himseemed she was troubled in countenance at these new nuptials. She, in her turn, looked whiles upon him, but not of any cognizance that she had of him, for that his great beard and outlandish habit and the firm assurance she had that he was dead hindered her thereof. Presently, whenas it seemed to him time to essay if she remembered her of him, he took the ring she had given him at his parting and calling a lad who served before her, said to him, 'Say to the bride, on my part, that it is the usance in my country, whenas any stranger, such as I am here, eateth at the bride-feast of any new-married lady, like herself, that she, in token that she holdeth him welcome at her table, send him the cup, wherein she drinketh, full of wine, whereof after the stranger hath drunken what he will, the cup being covered again, the bride drinketh the rest.'

The page did his errand to the lady, who, like a well-bred and discreet woman as she was, believing him to be some great gentleman, commanded, to show him that she had his coming in gree, that a great gilded cup, which stood before her, should be washed and filled with wine and carried to the gentleman; and so it was done. Messer Torello, taking her ring in his mouth, contrived in drinking to drop it, unseen of any, into the cup, wherein having left but a little wine, he covered it again and despatched it to the lady. Madam Adalieta, taking the cup and uncovering it, that she might accomplish his usance, set it to her mouth and seeing the ring, considered it awhile, without saying aught; then, knowing it for that which she had given to Messer Torello at parting, she took it up and looking fixedly upon him whom she deemed a stranger, presently recognized him; whereupon, as she were waxen mad, she overthrew the table she had before her and cried out, saying, 'It is my lord, it is indeed Messer Torello!' Then, running to the place where he sat, she cast herself as far forward as she might, without taking thought to her clothes or to aught that was on the table, and clipped him close in her arms nor could, for word or deed of any there, be loosed from his neck till she was bidden of Messer Torello contain herself somewhat, for that time enough would yet be afforded her to embrace him. She accordingly having arisen and the nuptials being by this all troubled, albeit in part more joyous than ever for the recovery of such a gentleman, every one, at Messer Torello's request, abode quiet; whereupon he related to them all that had betided him from the day of his departure up to that moment, concluding that the gentleman, who, deeming him dead, had taken his lady to wife, must not hold it ill if he, being alive, took her again unto himself.

The bridegroom, though somewhat mortified, answered frankly and as a friend that it rested with himself to do what most pleased him of his own. Accordingly, the lady put off the ring and crown had of her new groom and donned the ring which she had taken from the cup and the crown sent her by the Soldan; then, issuing forth of the house where they were, they betook themselves, with all the nuptial train, to Messer Torello's house and there recomforted his disconsolate friends and kindred and all the townsfolk, who regarded his return as well nigh a miracle, with long and joyous festival. As for Messer Torello, after imparting of his precious jewels to him who had had the expense of the nuptials, as well as to the abbot and many others, and signifying his happy repatriation by more than one message to Saladin, whose friend and servant he still professed himself, he lived many years thereafterward with his noble lady and thenceforth, used more hospitality and courtesy than ever. Such then was the issue of the troubles of Messer Torello and his beloved lady and the recompense of their cheerful and ready hospitalities, the which many study to practise, who, albeit they have the wherewithal, do yet so ill contrive it that they make those on whom they bestow their courtesies buy them, ere they have done with them, for more than their worth; wherefore, if no reward ensue to them thereof, neither themselves nor others should marvel thereat."

THE TENTH STORY

THE MARQUESS OF SALUZZO, CONSTRAINED BY THE PRAYERS OF HIS VASSALS TO MARRY, BUT DETERMINED TO DO IT AFTER HIS OWN FASHION, TAKETH TO WIFE THE DAUGHTER OF A PEASANT AND HATH OF HER TWO CHILDREN, WHOM HE MAKETH BELIEVE TO HER TO PUT TO DEATH; AFTER WHICH, FEIGNING TO BE GROWN WEARY OF HER AND TO HAVE TAKEN ANOTHER WIFE, HE LETTETH BRING HIS OWN DAUGHTER HOME TO HIS HOUSE, AS SHE WERE HIS NEW BRIDE, AND TURNETH HIS WIFE AWAY IN HER SHIFT; BUT, FINDING HER PATIENT UNDER EVERYTHING, HE FETCHETH HER HOME

AGAIN, DEARER THAN EVER, AND SHOWING HER HER CHILDREN GROWN GREAT, HONOURETH AND LETTETH HONOUR HER AS MARCHIONESS

THE king's long story being ended and having, to all appearance, much pleased all, Dioneo said, laughing, "The good man,[478] who looked that night to abase the phantom's tail upright,[479] had not given a brace of farthings of all the praises that you bestow on Messer Torello." Then, knowing that it rested with him alone to tell, he proceeded: "Gentle ladies mine, it appeareth to me that this day hath been given up to Kings and Soldans and the like folk; wherefore, that I may not remove overfar from you, I purpose to relate to you of a marquess, not an act of magnificence, but a monstrous folly, which, albeit good ensued to him thereof in the end, I counsel not any to imitate, for it was a thousand pities that weal betided him thereof.

It is now a great while agone since the chief of the house among the Marquesses of Saluzzo was a youth called Gualtieri, who, having neither wife nor children, spent his time in nought but hunting and hawking nor had any thought of taking a wife nor of having children; wherein he deserved to be reputed very wise. The thing, however, not pleasing his vassals, they besought him many times to take a wife, so he might not abide without an heir nor they without a lord, and offered themselves to find him one of such a fashion and born of such parents that good hopes might be had of her and he be well content with her; whereto he answered, 'My friends, you constrain me unto that which I was altogether resolved never to do, considering how hard a thing it is to find a wife whose fashions sort well within one's own humour and how great an abundance there is of the contrary sort and how dour a life is his who happeneth upon a woman not well suited unto him. To say that you think, by the manners and fashions of the parents, to know the daughters, wherefrom you argue to give me a wife such as will please me, is a folly, since I know not whence you may avail to know their fathers nor yet the secrets of their mothers; and even did you know them, daughters are often unlike their parents. However, since it e'en pleaseth you to bind me in these chains, I am content to do your desire; but, that I may not have occasion to complain of other than myself, if it prove ill done, I mean to find a wife for myself, certifying you that, whomsoever I may take me, if she be not honoured of you as your lady and mistress, you shall prove, to your cost, how much it irketh me to have at your entreaty taken a wife against mine own will.'

The good honest men replied that they were content, so he would but bring himself to take a wife. Now the fashions of a poor girl, who was of a village near to his house, had long pleased Gualtieri, and himseeming she was fair enough, he judged that he might lead a very comfortable life with her; wherefore, without seeking farther, he determined to marry her and sending for her father, who was a very poor man, agreed with him to take her to wife. This done, he assembled all his friends of the country round and said to them, 'My friends, it hath pleased and pleaseth you that I should dispose me to take a wife and I have resigned myself thereto, more to complease you than of any desire I have for marriage. You know what you promised me, to wit, that you would be content with and honour as your lady and mistress her whom I should take, whosoever she might be; wherefore the time is come when I am to keep my promise to you and when I would have you keep yours to me. I have found a damsel after mine own heart and purpose within some few days hence to marry her and bring her home to my house; wherefore do you bethink yourselves how the bride-feast may be a goodly one and how you may receive her with honour, on such wise that I may avouch myself contented of your promise, even as you will have cause to be of mine.' The good folk all answered joyfully that this liked them well and that, be she who he would, they would hold her for lady and mistress and honour her as such in all things; after which they all addressed themselves to hold fair and high and glad festival and on like wise did Gualtieri, who let make ready very great and goodly nuptials and bade thereto many his friends and kinsfolk and great gentlemen and others of the neighbourhood. Moreover, he let cut and fashion store of rich and goodly apparel, after the measure of a damsel who seemed to him like of her person to the young woman he was purposed to marry, and provided also rings and girdles and a rich and goodly crown and all that behoveth unto a bride.

The day come that he had appointed for the nuptials, Gualtieri towards half tierce mounted to horse, he and all those who were come to do him honour, and having ordered everything needful. 'Gentlemen,' quoth he, 'it is time to go fetch the bride.' Then, setting out with all his company, he rode to the village and betaking himself to the house of the girl's father, found her returning in great haste with water from the spring, so she might after go with other women to see Gualtieri's bride come. When the marquess saw her, he called her by name, to wit, Griselda, and asked her where her father was; to which she answered bashfully, 'My lord, he is within the house.' Thereupon Gualtieri dismounted and bidding all await him, entered the poor house alone, where he found her father, whose name was Giannucolo, and said to him, 'I am come to marry Griselda, but first I would fain know of her somewhat in thy presence.' Accordingly, he asked her if, an he took her to wife, she would still study to please him, nor take umbrage at aught that he should do or say, and if she would be obedient, and many other like things, to all of which she answered ay; whereupon Gualtieri, taking her by the hand, led her forth and in the presence of all his company and of every one else, let strip her naked. Then, sending for the garments which he had let make, he caused forthright clothe and shoe her and would have her set the crown on her hair, all tumbled as it was; after which, all marvelling at this, he said, 'Gentlemen, this is she who I purpose shall be my wife, an she will have me to husband.' Then, turning to her, where she stood, all shamefast and confounded, he said to her, 'Griselda, wilt thou have me to thy husband?' To which she answered, 'Ay, my lord.' Quoth he, 'And I will have thee to my wife'; and espoused her in the presence of all. Then, mounting her on a palfrey, he carried her, honourably accompanied, to his mansion, where the nuptials were celebrated with the utmost splendour and rejoicing, no otherwise than as he had taken to wife the king's daughter of France.

The young wife seemed to have, together with her clothes, changed her mind and her manners. She was, as we have already said, goodly of person and countenance, and even as she was fair, on like wise she became so engaging, so pleasant and so well-mannered that she seemed rather to have been the child of some noble gentleman than the daughter of Giannucolo and a tender of sheep; whereof she made every one marvel who had known her aforetime. Moreover, she was so obedient to her husband and so diligent in his service that he accounted himself the happiest and best contented man in the world; and on like wise she bore herself with such graciousness and such loving kindness towards her husband's subjects that there was none of them but loved and honoured her with his whole heart, praying all for her welfare and prosperity and advancement; and whereas they were used to say that Gualtieri had done as one of little wit to take her to wife, they now with one accord declared that he was the sagest and best-advised man alive, for that none other than he might ever have availed to know her high worth, hidden as it was under poor clothes and a rustic habit. Brief, it was no great while ere she knew so to do that, not only in her husband's marquisate, but everywhere else, she made folk talk of her virtues and her well-doing and turned to the contrary whatsoever had been said against her husband on her account, whenas he married her.

She had not long abidden with Gualtieri ere she conceived with child and in due time bore a daughter, whereat he rejoiced greatly. But, a little after, a new[480] thought having entered his mind, to wit, to seek, by dint of long tribulation and things unendurable, to make trial of her patience, he first goaded her with words, feigning himself troubled and saying that his vassals were exceeding ill content with her, by reason of her mean extraction, especially since they saw that she bore children, and that they did nothing but murmur, being sore chagrined for the birth of her daughter. The lady, hearing this, replied, without anywise changing countenance or showing the least distemperature, 'My lord, do with me that which thou deemest will be most for thine honour and solace, for that I shall be content with all, knowing, as I do, that I am of less account than they[481] and that I was unworthy of this dignity to which thou hast advanced me of thy courtesy.' This reply was mighty agreeable to Gualtieri, for that he saw she was not uplifted into aught of pridefulness for any honour that himself or others had done her; but, a little after, having in general terms told her that his vassals could not brook this girl that had been born of her, he sent to her a serving-man of his, whom he had lessoned and who said to her with a very woeful countenance, 'Madam, an I would not die, needs must I do that which my lord commandeth me. He hath bidden me take this your daughter and....' And said no more. The lady, hearing this and seeing the servant's aspect and remembering her of her husband's words, concluded that he had enjoined him put the child to death; whereupon, without changing countenance, albeit she felt a sore anguish at heart, she straightway took her from the cradle and having kissed and blessed her, laid her in the servant's arms, saying, 'Take her and punctually do that which thy lord hath enjoined thee; but leave her not to be devoured of the beasts and the birds, except he command it thee.' The servant took the child and reported that which the lady had said to Gualtieri, who marvelled at her constancy and despatched him with the child to a kinswoman of his at Bologna, praying her to bring her up and rear her diligently, without ever saying whose daughter she was.

In course of time the lady again conceived and in due season bore a male child, to her husband's great joy; but, that which he had already done sufficing him not, he addressed himself to probe her to the quick with a yet sorer stroke and accordingly said to her one day with a troubled air, 'Wife, since thou hast borne this male child, I have nowise been able to live in peace with these my people, so sore do they murmur that a grandson of Giannucolo should become their lord after me; wherefore I misdoubt me, an I would not be driven forth of my domains, it will behove me do in this case that which I did otherwhen and ultimately put thee away and take another wife.' The lady gave ear to him with a patient mind nor answered otherwhat then, 'My lord, study to content thyself and to satisfy thy pleasure and have no thought of me, for that nothing is dear to me save in so much as I see it please thee.' Not many days after, Gualtieri sent for the son, even as he had sent for the daughter, and making a like show of having him put to death, despatched him to Bologna, there to be brought up, even as he had done with the girl; but the lady made no other countenance nor other words thereof than she had done of the girl; whereat Gualtieri marvelled sore and affirmed in himself that no other woman could have availed to do this that she did; and had he not seen her tender her children with the utmost fondness, what while it pleased him, he had believed that she did this because she recked no more of them; whereas in effect he knew that she did it of her discretion. His vassals, believing that he had caused put the children to death, blamed him sore, accounting him a barbarous man, and had the utmost compassion of his wife, who never answered otherwhat to the ladies who condoled with her for her children thus slain, than that that which pleased him thereof who had begotten them, pleased her also.

At last, several years being passed since the birth of the girl, Gualtieri, deeming it time to make the supreme trial of her endurance, declared, in the presence of his people, that he could no longer endure to have Griselda to wife and that he perceived that he had done ill and boyishly in taking her, wherefore he purposed, as far as in him lay, to make interest with the Pope to grant him a dispensation, so he might put her away and take another wife. For this he was roundly taken to task by many men of worth, but answered them nothing save that needs must it be so. The lady, hearing these things and herseeming she must look to return to her father's house and maybe tend sheep again as she had done aforetime, what while she saw another woman in possession of him to whom she willed all her weal, sorrowed sore in herself; but yet, even as she had borne the other affronts of fortune, so with a firm countenance she addressed herself to bear this also. Gualtieri no great while after let come to him from Rome counterfeit letters of dispensation and gave his vassals to believe that the Pope had thereby licensed him to take another wife and leave Griselda; then, sending for the latter, he said to her, in presence of many, 'Wife, by concession made me of the Pope, I am free to take another wife and put thee away, and accordingly, for that mine ancestors have been great gentlemen and lords of this country, whilst thine have still been husbandmen, I mean that thou be no more my wife, but that thou return to Giannucolo his house with the dowry which thou broughtest me, and I will after bring hither another wife, for that I have found one more sorted to myself.'

The lady, hearing this, contained her tears, contrary to the nature of woman, though not without great unease, and answered, 'My lord, I ever knew my mean estate to be nowise sortable with your nobility, and for that which I have been with you I have still confessed myself indebted to you and to God, nor have I ever made nor held it mine, as given to me, but have still accounted it but as a loan. It pleaseth you to require it again and it must and doth please me to restore it to you. Here is your ring wherewith you espoused me; take it. You bid me carry away with me that dowry which I brought hither, which to do you will need no paymaster and I neither purse nor packhorse, for I have not forgotten that you had me naked, and if you account it seemly that this my body, wherein I have carried children begotten of you, be seen of all, I will begone naked; but I pray you, in requital of my maidenhead, which I brought hither and bear not hence with me, that it please you I may carry away at the least one sole shift over and above my dowry.' Gualtieri, who had more mind to weep than to otherwhat, natheless kept a stern countenance and said, 'So be it; carry away a shift.' As many as stood around besought him to give her a gown, so that she who had been thirteen years and more his wife should not be seen go forth of his house on such mean and shameful wise as it was to depart in her shift; but their prayers all went for nothing; wherefore the lady, having commended them to God, went forth his house in her shift, barefoot and nothing on her head, and returned to her father, followed by the tears and lamentations of all who saw her. Giannucolo, who had never been able to believe it true that Gualtieri should entertain his daughter to wife and went in daily expectation of this event, had kept her the clothes which she had put off the morning that Gualtieri had married her and now brought them to her; whereupon she donned them and addressed herself, as she had been wont to do, to the little offices of her father's house, enduring the cruel onslaught of hostile fortune with a stout heart.

Gualtieri, having done this, gave out to his people that he had chosen a daughter of one of the Counts of Panago and letting make great preparations for the nuptials, sent for Griselda to come to him and said to her, 'I am about to bring home this lady, whom I have newly taken to wife, and mean, at this her first coming, to do her honour. Thou knowest I have no women about me who know how to array me the rooms nor to do a multitude of things that behove unto such a festival; wherefore do thou, who art better versed than any else in these household matters, order that which is to do here and let bid such ladies as it seemeth good to thee and receive them as thou wert mistress here; then, when the nuptials are ended, thou mayst begone back to thy house.' Albeit these words were all daggers to Griselda's heart, who had been unable to lay down the love she bore him as she had laid down her fair fortune, she replied, 'My lord, I am ready and willing.' Then, in her coarse homespun clothes, entering the house, whence she had a little before departed in her shift, she fell to sweeping and ordering the chambers and letting place hangings and cover-cloths about the saloons and make ready the viands, putting her hand to everything, as she were some paltry serving-wench of the house, nor ever gave over till she had arrayed and ordered everything as it behoved. Thereafter, having let invite all the ladies of the country on Gualtieri's part, she awaited the day of the festival, which being come, with a cheerful countenance and the spirit and bearing of a lady of high degree, for all she had mean clothes on her back, she received all the ladies who came thither.

Meanwhile, Gualtieri, who had caused the two children be diligently reared in Bologna by his kinswoman, (who was married to a gentleman of the Panago family,) the girl being now twelve years old and the fairest creature that ever was seen and the boy six, had sent to his kinsman[482] at Bologna, praying him be pleased to come to Saluzzo with his son and daughter and take order to bring with him a goodly and honourable company and bidding him tell every one that he was carrying him the young lady to his wife, without otherwise discovering to any aught of who she was. The gentleman did as the marquess prayed him and setting out, with the girl and boy and a goodly company of gentlefolk, after some days' journey, arrived, about dinner-time, at Saluzzo, where he found all the countryfolk and many others of the neighbourhood awaiting Gualtieri's new bride. The latter, being received by the ladies and come into the saloon where the tables were laid, Griselda came to meet her, clad as she was, and accosted her blithely, saying, 'Welcome and fair welcome to my lady.' Thereupon the ladies (who had urgently, but in vain, besought Gualtieri to suffer Griselda to abide in a chamber or lend her one of the gowns that had been hers, so that she might not go thus before his guests) were seated at table and it was proceeded to serve them. The girl was eyed by every one and all declared that Gualtieri had made a good exchange; and among the rest Griselda commended her amain, both her and her young brother.

Gualtieri perceiving that the strangeness of the case in no wise changed her and being assured that this proceeded not from lack of understanding, for that he knew her to be very quick of wit, himseemed he had now seen fully as much as he desired of his lady's patience and he judged it time to deliver her from the bitterness which he doubted not she kept hidden under her constant countenance; wherefore, calling her to himself, he said to her, smiling, in the presence of every one, 'How deemest thou of our bride?' 'My lord,' answered she, 'I deem exceeding well of her, and if, as I believe, she is as discreet as she is fair, I doubt not a whit but you will live the happiest gentleman in the world with her; but I beseech you, as most I may, that you inflict not on her those pangs which you inflicted whilere on her who was sometime yours; for methinketh she might scarce avail to endure them, both because she is younger and because she hath been delicately reared, whereas the other had been in continual fatigues from a little child.' Thereupon, Gualtieri, seeing she firmly believed that the young lady was to be his wife nor therefore spoke anywise less than well, seated her by his side and said to her, 'Griselda, it is now time that thou reap the fruits of thy long patience and that those who have reputed me cruel and unjust and brutish should know that this which I have done I wrought to an end aforeseen, willing to teach thee to be a wife and to show them how to take and use one and at the same time to beget myself perpetual quiet, what while I had to live with thee; the which, whenas I came to take a wife, I was sore afraid might not betide me, and therefore, to make proof thereof, I probed and afflicted thee after such kind as thou knowest. And meseeming, for that I have never perceived that either in word or in deed hast thou departed from my pleasure, that I have of thee that solace which I desired, I purpose presently to restore thee, at one stroke, that which I took from thee at many and to requite thee with a supreme delight the pangs I have inflicted on thee. Wherefore with a joyful heart take this whom thou deemest my bride and her brother for thy children and mine; for these be they whom thou and many others have long accounted me to have barbarously let put to death; and I am thy husband, who loveth thee over all else, believing I may vaunt me that there is none else who can be so content of his wife as can I.'

So saying, he embraced her and kissed her; then, rising up, he betook himself with Griselda, who wept for joy, whereas the daughter, hearing these things, sat all stupefied, and tenderly embracing her and her brother, undeceived her and many others who were there. Thereupon the ladies arose from table, overjoyed, and withdrew with Griselda into a chamber, where, with happier augury, pulling off her mean attire, they clad her anew in a magnificent dress of her own and brought her again to the saloon, as a gentlewoman, which indeed she appeared, even in rags. There she rejoiced in her children with wonder-great joy, and all being overjoyed at this happy issue, they redoubled in feasting and merrymaking and prolonged the festivities several days, accounting Gualtieri a very wise man, albeit they held the trials which he had made of his lady overharsh, nay, intolerable; but over all they held Griselda most sage. The Count of Panago returned, after some days, to Bologna, and Gualtieri, taking Giannucolo from his labour, placed him in such estate as befitted his father-in-law, so that he lived in honour and great solace and so ended his days; whilst he himself, having nobly married his daughter, lived long and happily with Griselda, honouring her as most might be. What more can here be said save that even in poor cottages there rain down divine spirits from heaven, like as in princely palaces there be those who were worthier to tend swine than to have lordship over men? Who but Griselda could, with a countenance, not only dry,[483] but cheerful, have endured the barbarous and unheard proofs made by Gualtieri? Which latter had not belike been ill requited, had he happened upon one who, when he turned her out of doors in her shift, had let jumble her furbelows of another to such purpose that a fine gown had come of it."

Dioneo's story being finished and the ladies having discoursed amain thereof, some inclining to one side and some to another, this blaming one thing and that commending it, the king, lifting his eyes to heaven and seeing that the sun was now low and the hour of vespers at hand, proceeded, without arising from session, to speak thus, "Charming ladies, as I doubt not you know, the understanding of mortals consisteth not only in having in memory things past and taking cognizance of things present; but in knowing, by means of the one and the other of these, to forecast things future is reputed by men of mark to consist the greatest wisdom. To-morrow, as you know, it will be fifteen days since we departed Florence, to take some diversion for the preservation of our health and of our lives, eschewing the woes and dolours and miseries which, since this pestilential season began, are continually to be seen about our city. This, to my judgment, we have well and honourably done; for that, an I have known to see aright, albeit merry stories and belike incentive to concupiscence have been told here and we have continually eaten and drunken well and danced and sung and made music, all things apt to incite weak minds to things less seemly, I have noted no act, no word, in fine nothing blameworthy, either on your part or on that of us men; nay, meseemeth I have seen and felt here a continual decency, an unbroken concord and a constant fraternal familiarity; the which, at once for your honour and service and for mine own, is, certes, most pleasing to me. Lest, however, for overlong usance aught should grow thereof that might issue in tediousness, and that none may avail to cavil at our overlong tarriance,—each of us, moreover, having had his or her share of the honour that yet resideth in myself,—I hold it meet, an it be your pleasure, that we now return whence we came; more by token that, if you consider aright, our company, already known to several others of the neighbourhood, may multiply after a fashion that will deprive us of our every commodity. Wherefore, if you approve my counsel, I will retain the crown conferred on me until our departure, which I purpose shall be to-morrow morning; but, should you determine otherwise, I have already in mind whom I shall invest withal for the ensuing day."

Much was the debate between the ladies and the young men; but ultimately they all took the king's counsel for useful and seemly and determined to do as he proposed; whereupon, calling the seneschal, he bespoke him of the manner which he should hold on the ensuing morning and after, having dismissed the company until supper-time, he rose to his feet. The ladies and the young men, following his example, gave themselves, this to one kind of diversion and that to another, no otherwise than of their wont; and supper-time come, they betook themselves to table with the utmost pleasure and after fell to singing and carolling and making music. Presently, Lauretta leading up a dance, the king bade Fiammetta sing a song, whereupon she very blithely proceeded to sing thus:

If love came but withouten jealousy,
I know no lady born
So blithe as I were, whosoe'er she be.
If gladsome youthfulness
In a fair lover might content a maid,
Virtue and worth discreet,
Valiance or gentilesse,
Wit and sweet speech and fashions all arrayed
In pleasantness complete,
Certes, I'm she for whose behoof these meet
In one; for, love-o'erborne,
All these in him who is my hope I see.

But for that I perceive
That other women are as wise as I,
I tremble for affright
And tending to believe
The worst, in others the desire espy
Of him who steals my spright;
Thus this that is my good and chief delight
Enforceth me, forlorn,
Sigh sore and live in dole and misery.

If I knew fealty such
In him my lord as I know merit there,
I were not jealous, I;
But here is seen so much
Lovers to tempt, how true they be soe'er,
I hold all false; whereby
I'm all disconsolate and fain would die,
Of each with doubting torn
Who eyes him, lest she bear him off from me.

Be, then, each lady prayed

By God that she in this be not intent
'Gainst me to do amiss;
For, sure, if any maid
Should or with words or becks or blandishment
My detriment in this
Seek or procure and if I know't, ywis,
Be all my charms forsworn
But I will make her rue it bitterly.

No sooner had Fiammetta made an end of her song than Dioneo, who was beside her, said, laughing, "Madam, you would do a great courtesy to let all the ladies know who he is, lest you be ousted of his possession through ignorance, since you would be so sore incensed thereat." After this divers other songs were sung and the night being now well nigh half spent, they all, by the king's commandment, betook themselves to repose. As the new day appeared, they arose and the seneschal having already despatched all their gear in advance, they returned, under the guidance of their discreet king, to Florence, where the three young men took leave of the seven ladies and leaving them in Santa Maria Novella, whence they had set out with them, went about their other pleasures, whilst the ladies, whenas it seemed to them time, returned to their houses.

HERE ENDETH THE TENTH AND LAST DAY
OF THE DECAMERON

The Decameron of Giovanni Boccaccio - Part II

Conclusion of the Author

MOST noble damsels, for whose solace I have addressed myself to so long a labour, I have now, methinketh, with the aid of the Divine favour, (vouchsafed me, as I deem, for your pious prayers and not for my proper merits,) throughly accomplished that which I engaged, at the beginning of this present work, to do; wherefore, returning thanks first to God and after to you, it behoveth to give rest to my pen and to my tired hand. Which ere I accord them, I purpose briefly to reply, as to objections tacitly broached, to certain small matters that may peradventure be alleged by some one of you or by others, since meseemeth very certain that these stories have no especial privilege more than other things; nay, I mind me to have shown, at the beginning of the fourth day, that they have none such. There are, peradventure, some of you who will say that I have used overmuch license in inditing these stories, as well as in making ladies whiles say and very often hearken to things not very seemly either to be said or heard of modest women. This I deny, for that there is nothing so unseemly as to be forbidden unto any one, so but he express it in seemly terms, as meseemeth indeed I have here very aptly done. But let us suppose that it is so (for that I mean not to plead with you, who would overcome me,) I say that many reasons very readily offer themselves in answer why I have done this. Firstly, if there be aught thereof[484] in any of them, the nature of the stories required it, the which, an they be considered with the rational eye of a person of understanding, it will be abundantly manifest that I could not have otherwise recounted, an I would not altogether disfeature them. And if perchance there be therein some tittle, some wordlet or two freer, maybe, than liketh your squeamish hypocritical prudes, who weigh words rather than deeds and study more to appear, than to be, good, I say that it should no more be forbidden me to write them than it is commonly forbidden unto men and women to say all day long hole and peg and mortar and pestle and sausage and polony and all manner like things; without reckoning that no less liberty should be accorded to my pen than is conceded to the brush of the limner, who, without any (or, at the least, any just) reprehension, maketh—let be St. Michael smite the serpent with sword or spear and St. George the dragon, whereas it pleaseth them—but Adam male and Eve female and affixeth to the cross, whiles with one nail and whiles with two, the feet of Him Himself who willed for the salvation of the human race to die upon the rood. Moreover, it is eath enough to see that these things are spoken, not in the church, of the affairs whereof it behoveth to speak with a mind and in terms alike of the chastest (albeit among its histories there are tales enough to be found of anothergates fashion than those written by me), nor yet in the schools of philosophy, where decency is no less required than otherwhere, nor among churchmen or philosophers anywhere, but amidst gardens, in a place of pleasance and diversion and among men and women, though young, yet of mature wit and not to be led astray by stories, at a time when it was not forbidden to the most virtuous to go, for their own preservation, with their breeches on their heads. Again, such as they are, these stories, like everything else, can both harm and profit, according to the disposition of the listener. Who knoweth not that wine, though, according to Cinciglione and Scolajo[485] and many others, an excellent thing for people in health,[486] is hurtful unto whoso hath the fever? Shall we say, then, because it harmeth the fevered, that it is naught? Who knoweth not that fire is most useful, nay, necessary to mortals? Shall we say, because it burneth houses and villages and cities, that it is naught? Arms on like wise assure the welfare of those who desire to live in peace and yet oftentimes slay men, not of any malice of their own, but of the perversity of those who use them wrongfully. Corrupt mind never understood word healthily, and even as seemly words profit not depraved minds, so those which are not altogether seemly avail not to contaminate the well-disposed, any more than mire can sully the rays of the sun or earthly foulness the beauties of the sky. What books, what words, what letters are holier, worthier, more venerable than those of the Divine Scriptures? Yet many there be, who, interpreting them perversely, have brought themselves and others to perdition. Everything in itself is good unto somewhat and ill used, may be in many things harmful; and so say I of my stories. If any be minded to draw therefrom ill counsel or ill practice, they will nowise forbid it him, if perchance they have it in them or be strained and twisted into having it; and who so will have profit and utility thereof, they will not deny it him, nor will they be ever styled or accounted other than useful and seemly, if they be read at those times and to those persons for which and for whom they have been recounted. Whoso hath to say paternosters or to make tarts and puddings for her spiritual director, let her leave them be; they will not run after any to make her read them; albeit your she-saints themselves now and again say and even do fine things.

There be some ladies also who will say that there are some stories here, which had been better away. Granted; but I could not nor should write aught save those actually related, wherefore those who told them should have told them goodly and I would have written them goodly. But, if folk will e'en pretend that I am both the inventor and writer thereof (which I am not), I say that I should not take shame to myself that they were not all alike goodly, for that there is no craftsman living (barring God) who doth everything alike well and completely; witness Charlemagne, who was the first maker of the Paladins, but knew not to make so many thereof that he might avail to form an army of them alone. In the multitude of things, needs must divers qualities thereof be found. No field was ever so well tilled but therein or nettles or thistles or somewhat of briers or other weeds might be found mingled with the better herbs. Besides, having to speak to simple lasses, such as you are for the most part, it had been folly to go seeking and wearying myself to find very choice and exquisite matters, and to use great pains to speak very measuredly. Algates, whoso goeth reading among these, let him leave those which offend and read those which divert. They all, not to lead any one into error, bear branded upon the forefront that which they hold hidden within their bosoms.

Again, I doubt not but there be those who will say that some of them are overlong; to whom I say again that whoso hath overwhat to do doth folly to read these stories, even though they were brief. And albeit a great while is passed from the time when I began to write to this present hour whenas I come to the end of my toils, it hath not therefor escaped my memory that I proffered this my travail to idle women and not to others, and unto whoso readeth to pass away the time, nothing can be overlong, so but it do that for which he useth it. Things brief are far better suited unto students, who study, not to pass away, but usefully to employ time, than to you ladies, who have on your hands all the time that you spend not in the pleasures of love; more by token that, as none of you goeth to Athens or Bologna or Paris to study, it behoveth to speak to you more at large than to those who have had their wits whetted by study. Again, I doubt not a jot but there be yet some of you who will say that the things aforesaid are full of quips and cranks and quodlibets and that it ill beseemeth a man of weight and gravity to have written thus. To these I am bound to render and do render thanks, for that, moved by a virtuous jealousy, they are so tender of my fame; but to their objection I reply on this wise; I confess to being a man of weight and to have been often weighed in my time, wherefore, speaking to those ladies who have not weighed me, I declare that I am not heavy; nay, I am so light that I abide like a nutgall in water, and considering that the preachments made of friars, to rebuke men of their sins, are nowadays for the most part seen full of quips and cranks and gibes, I conceived that these latter would not sit amiss in my stories written to ease women of melancholy. Algates, an they should laugh overmuch on that account, the Lamentations of Jeremiah, the Passion of our Saviour and the Complaint of Mary Magdalen will lightly avail to cure them thereof.

Again, who can doubt but there will to boot be found some to say that I have an ill tongue and a venomous, for that I have in sundry places written the truth anent the friars? To those who shall say thus it must be forgiven, since it is not credible that they are moved by other than just cause, for that the friars are a good sort of folk, who eschew unease for the love of God and who grind with a full head of water and tell no tales, and but that they all savour somewhat of the buck-goat, their commerce would be far more agreeable. Natheless, I confess that the things of this world have no stability and are still on the change, and so may it have befallen of my tongue, the which, not to trust to mine own judgment, (which I eschew as most I may in my affairs,) a she-neighbour of mine told me, not long since, was the best and sweetest in the world; and in good sooth, were this the case, there had been few of the foregoing stories to write. But, for that those who say thus speak despitefully, I will have that which hath been said suffice them for a reply; wherefore, leaving each of you henceforth to say and believe as seemeth good to her, it is time for me to make an end of words, humbly thanking Him who hath, after so long a labour, brought us with His help to the desired end. And you, charming ladies, abide you in peace with His favour, remembering you of me, if perchance it profit any of you aught to have read these stories.

HERE ENDETH THE BOOK CALLED DECAMERON AND SURNAMED PRINCE GALAHALT

FOOTNOTES

Page numbering refers to the original publication only.

[294] Lit. for their returning to consistory (del dovere a concistoro tornare).

[295] Messer Mazza, i.e. veretrum.

[296] Monte Nero, i.e. vas muliebre.

[297] i.e. who are yet a child, in modern parlance, "Thou whose lips are yet wet with thy mother's milk."

[298] i.e. women's.

[299] See ante, p. 43, Introduction to the last story of the First Day.

[300] Lit. Family wine (vin da famiglia), i.e. no wine for servants' or general drinking, but a choice vintage, to be reserved for special occasions.

[301] A silver coin of about the size and value of our silver penny, which, when gilded, would pass muster well enough for a gold florin, unless closely examined.

[302] Il palio, a race anciently run at Florence on St. John's Day, as that of the Barberi at Rome during the Carnival.

[303] Lit. knowing not whence himself came.

[304] Or, as we should say, "in his own coin."

[305] A commentator notes that the adjunction to the world of the Maremma (cf. Elijer Goff, "The Irish Question has for some centuries been enjoyed by the universe and other parts") produces a risible effect and gives the reader to understand that Scalza broaches the question only by way of a joke. The same may be said of the jesting inversion of the word philosophers (phisopholers, Fisofoli) in the next line.

[306] Baronci, the Florentine name for what we should call professional beggars, "mumpers, chanters and Abrahammen," called Bari and Barocci in other parts of Italy. This story has been a prodigious stumbling-block to former translators, not one of whom appears to have had the slightest idea of Boccaccio's meaning.

[307] i.e. of the comical fashion of the Cadgers.

[308] An abbreviation of Francesca.

[309] "Or her."

[310] Lit. to avoid or elude a scorn (fuggire uno scorno).

[311] Cipolla means onion.

[312] The term "well-wisher" (benivogliente), when understood in relation to a woman, is generally equivalent (at least with the older Italian writers) to "lover." See ante, passim.

[313] Diminutive of contempt of Arrigo, contracted from Arriguccio, i.e. mean little Arrigo.

[314] i.e. Whale.

[315] i.e. Dirt.

[316] i.e. Hog.

[317] A painter of Boccaccio's time, of whom little or nothing seems to be known.

[318] Perpendo lo coreggia. The exact meaning of this passage is not clear. The commentators make sundry random shots at it, but, as usual, only succeed in making confusion worse confounded. It may perhaps be rendered, "till his wind failed him."

[319] Said by the commentators to have been an abbey, where they made cheese-soup for all comers twice a week; hence "the caldron of Altopascio" became a proverb; but quære is not the name Altopascio (high feeding) a fancy one?

[320] It does not appear to which member of this great house Boccaccio here alludes, but the Châtillons were always rich and magnificent gentlemen, from Gaucher de Châtillon, who followed Philip Augustus to the third crusade, to the great Admiral de Coligny.

[321] Sic (star con altrui); but "being in the service of or dependent upon others" seems to be the probable meaning.

[322] Apparently the Neapolitan town of that name.

[323] The name of a famous tavern in Florence (Florio).

[324] Quære a place in Florence? One of the commentators, with characteristic carelessness, states that the places mentioned in the preachment of Fra Cipolla (an amusing specimen of the patter-sermon of the mendicant friar of the middle ages, that ecclesiastical Cheap Jack of his day) are all names of streets or places of Florence, a statement which, it is evident to the most cursory reader, is altogether inaccurate.

[325] Apparently the island of that name near Venice.

[326] i.e. Nonsense-land.

[327] i.e. Land of Tricks or Cozenage.

[328] i.e. Falsehood, Lie-land.

[329] i.e. paying their way with fine words, instead of coin.

[330] i.e. making sausages of them.

[331] Bachi, drones or maggots. Pastinaca means "parsnip" and is a meaningless addition of Fra Cipolla's fashion.

[332] A play of words upon the primary meaning (winged things) of the word pennate, hedge-bills.

[333] i.e. The Word [made] flesh. Get-thee-to-the-windows is only a patter tag.

[334] Or Slopes or Coasts (piaggie).

[335] ?

[336] Industria in the old sense of ingenuity, skilful procurement, etc.

[337] i.e. the tale-telling.

[338] Lit. the northern chariot (carro di tramontana); quære the Great Bear?

[339] Alluding to the subject fixed for the next day's discourse, as who should say, "Have you begun already to play tricks upon us men in very deed, ere you tell about them in words?"

[340] See p. 144, note 2.

[341] i.e. pene arrecto.

[342] i.e. a fattened capon well larded.

[343] i.e. eggs.

[344] So called from the figure of a lily stamped on the coin; cf. our rose-nobles.

[345] i.e. the discarded vanities aforesaid.

[346] i.e. the other ex votos.

[347] There is apparently some satirical allusion here, which I cannot undertake to explain.

[348] Syn. professor of the liberal arts (artista).

[349] i.e. inhabitants of Arezzo.

[350] Riporre, possibly a mistake for riportare, to fetch back.

[351] Lit. wished her all his weal.

[352] Boccaccio writes carelessly "for aught" (altro), which makes nonsense of the passage.

[353] Or, in modern parlance, "twopennny-halfpenny."

[354] Syn. encourager, helper, auxiliary (confortatore).

[355] This sudden change from the third to the second person, in speaking of Nicostratus, is a characteristic example of Boccaccio's constant abuse of the figure enallage in his dialogues.

[356] i.e. those eyes.

[357] i.e. the Siennese.

[358] i.e. from discovering to his friend his liking for the lady.

[359] Or, in modern parlance, logic-chopping (sillogizzando).

[360] i.e. with that whereof you bear the name, i.e. laurel (laurea).

[361] Or "on this subject" (in questo).

[362] Quære, "half-complines," i.e. half-past seven p.m. "Half-vespers" would be half-past four, which seems too early.

[363] Carolando, i.e. dancing in a round and singing the while, the original meaning of our word "carol."

[364] i.e. half-past seven a.m.

[365] Where the papal court then was. See p. 257, note.

[366] Or, as La Fontaine would say, "aussi bien faite pour armer un lit."

[367] Or apron.

[368] Se n'andò col ceteratojo; a proverbial expression of similar meaning to our "was whistled down the wind," i.e. was lightly dismissed without provision, like a cast-off hawk.

[369] A play of words upon the Italian equivalent of the French word Douay (Duagio, i.e. Twoay, Treagio, Quattragio) invented by the roguish priest to impose upon the simple goodwife.

[370] Or in modern parlance, "making her a connection by marriage of etc.," Boccaccio feigning priests to be members of the Holy Family, by virtue of their office.

[371] i.e. Good cheer.

[372] A play upon the double meaning of a denajo, which signifies also "for money."

[373] A kind of rissole made of eggs, sweet herbs and cheese.

[374] Vernaccia, a kind of rich white wine like Malmsey.

[375] i.e. not strait-cut.

[376] Sforzandosi, i.e. recovering his wind with an effort.

[377] i.e. love him, grant him her favours. See ante, passim.

[378] i.e. in the malaria district.

[379] i.e. great ugly Ciuta.

[380] Quarantanove, a proverbial expression for an indefinite number.

[381] i.e. how they might do this.

[382] i.e. in the old sense of "manager" (massajo).

[383] i.e. white wine, see p. 372, note.

[384] i.e. embarked on a bootless quest.

[385] A proverbial way of saying that he bore malice and was vindictive.

[386] Lit. out of hand (fuor di mano).

[387] Boccaccio here misquotes himself. See p. 389, where the lady says to her lover, "Whether seemeth to thee the greater, his wit or the love I bear him?" This is only one of the numberless instances of negligence and inconsistency which occur in the Decameron and which make it evident to the student that it must have passed into the hands of the public without the final revision and correction by the author, that limæ labor without which no book is complete and which is especially necessary in the case of such a work as the present, where Boccaccio figures as the virtual creator of Italian prose.

[388] Lit. face, aspect (viso).

[389] i.e. thy lover's.

[390] V'è donato, i.e. young lovers look to receive gifts of their mistresses, whilst those of more mature age bestow them.

[391] Lit. red as rabies (rabbia). Some commentators suppose that Boccaccio meant to write robbia, madder.

[392] i.e. resource (consiglio). See ante, passim.

[393] Boccaccio appears to have forgotten to mention that Rinieri had broken the rounds of the ladder, when he withdrew it (as stated, p. 394), apparently to place an additional obstacle in the way of the lady's escape.

[394] Quære, the street of that name?

[395] Danza trivigiana, lit. Trevisan dance, O.E. the shaking of the sheets.

[396] i.e. with the doctor's hood of miniver.

[397] The colour of the doctors' robes of that time.

[398] The commentators note here that on the church door of San Gallo was depicted an especially frightful Lucifer, with many mouths.

[399] Legnaja is said to be famous for big pumpkins.

[400] i.e. they think of and cherish us alone, holding us as dear as their very eyes.

[401] i.e. Fat-hog and Get-thee-to-supper, burlesque perversions of the names Ipocrasso (Hippocrates) and Avicenna.

[402] i.e. love her beyond anything in the world. For former instances of this idiomatic expression, see ante, passim.

[403] Syn. cauterized (calterita), a nonsensical word employed by Bruno for the purpose of mystifying the credulous physician.

[404] Syn. secretary, confidant (segretaro).

[405] A play of words upon mela (apple) and mellone (pumpkin). Mellone is strictly a water-melon; but I have rendered it "pumpkin," to preserve the English idiom, "pumpkinhead" being our equivalent for the Italian "melon," used in the sense of dullard, noodle.

[406] According to the commentators, "baptized on a Sunday" anciently signified a simpleton, because salt (which is constantly used by the Italian classical writers as a synonym for wit or sense) was not sold on Sundays.

[407] Syn. confusedly (frastagliatamente).

[408] La Contessa di Civillari, i.e. the public sewers. Civillari, according to the commentators, was the name of an alley in Florence, where all the ordure and filth of the neighbourhood was deposited and stored in trenches for manure.

[409] Nacchere, syn. a loud crack of wind.

[410] Syn. smelt (sentito).

[411] Laterina, i.e. Latrina.

[412] Lit. Broom-handle (Manico della Scopa).

[413] Lit. "do yourself a mischief, without doing us any good"; but the sequel shows that the contrary is meant, as in the text.

[414] i.e. what he is worth.

[415] Bucherame. The word "buckram" was anciently applied to the finest linen cloth, as is apparently the case here; see Ducange, voce Boquerannus, and Florio, voce Bucherame.

[416] i.e. in needlework.

[417] "It was the custom in those days to attach to the bedposts sundry small instruments in the form of birds, which, by means of certain mechanical devices, gave forth sounds modulated like the song of actual birds." —Fanfani.

[418] Syn. that which belongeth to us (ciò che ci è,) ci, as I have before noted, signifying both "here" and "us," dative and accusative.

[419] i.e. procure bills of exchange for.

[420] i.e. we must see what is to be done.

[421] i.e. having executed and exchanged the necessary legal documents for the proper carrying out of the transaction and completed the matter to their mutual satisfaction.

[422] The song sung by Pamfilo (under which name, as I have before pointed out, the author appears to represent himself) apparently alludes to Boccaccio's amours with the Princess Maria of Naples (Fiammetta), by whom his passion was returned in kind.

[423] According to the Ptolemaic system, the earth is encompassed by eight celestial zones or heavens; the first or highest, above which is the empyrean, (otherwise called the ninth heaven,) is that of the Moon, the second that of Mercury, the third that of Venus, the fourth that of the Sun, the fifth that of Mars, the sixth that of Jupiter, the seventh that of Saturn and the eighth or lowest that of the fixed stars and of the Earth.

[424] D'azzurrino in color cilestro. This is one of the many passages in which Boccaccio has imitated Dante (cf. Purgatorio, c. xxvi. II. 4-6, "... il sole.... Che già, raggiando, tutto l'occidente Mutava in bianco aspetto di cilestro,") and also one of the innumerable instances in which former translators (who all agree in making the advent of the light change the colour of the sky from azure to a darker colour, instead of, as Boccaccio intended, to watchet, i.e. a paler or greyish blue,) have misrendered the text, for sheer ignorance of the author's meaning.

[425] Scannadio signifies "Murder-God" and was no doubt a nickname bestowed upon the dead man, on account of his wicked and reprobate way of life.

[426] i.e. balls for a pellet bow, usually made out of clay. Bruno and Buffalmacco were punning upon the double meaning, land and earth (or clay), of the word terra.

[427] Scimmione (lit. ape), a contemptuous distortion of Simone.

[428] Chiarea. According to the commentators, the composition of this drink is unknown, but that of clary, a sort of hippocras or spiced wine clear-strained (whence the name), offers no difficulty to the student of old English literature.

[429] i.e. the doublet.

[430] i.e. do me a double injury.

[431] Syn. goodly design of foresight (buono avviso).

[432] Giovani di tromba marina. The sense seems as above; the commentators say that giovani di tromba marina is a name given to those youths who go trumpeting about everywhere the favours accorded them by women; but the tromba marina is a stringed (not a wind) instrument, a sort of primitive violoncello with one string.

[433] "Your teeth did dance like virginal jacks."—Ben Jonson.

[434] Adagiarono, i.e. unsaddled and stabled and fed them.

[435] i.e. hog.

[436] Lit. a backbiter (morditore)

[437] i.e. conjured him by God to make peace with him.

[438] i.e. from a serious or moral point of view.

[439] Apparently Laodicea (hod. Eskihissar) in Anatolia, from which a traveller, taking the direct land route, would necessarily pass Antioch (hod. Antakhia) on his way to Jerusalem.

[440] i.e. arrectus est penis ejus.

[441] See p. 372, note.

[442] i.e. fortune.

[443] Cattajo. This word is usually translated Cathay, i.e. China; but semble Boccaccio meant rather the Dalmatian province of Cattaro, which would better answer the description in the text, Nathan's

estate being described as adjoining a highway leading from the Ponant (or Western shores of the Mediterranean) to the Levant (or Eastern shores), e.g. the road from Cattaro on the Adriatic to Salonica on the Ægean. Cathay (China) seems, from the circumstances of the case, out of the question, as is also the Italian town called Cattaio, near Padua.

[444] i.e. to show the most extravagant hospitality.

[445] Or as we should say, "After much beating about the bush."

[446] i.e. jealousies.

[447] i.e. all sections of the given theme.

[448] Lit. accident (accidente).

[449] i.e. with news of her life.

[450] Dubbio, i.e. a doubtful case or question.

[451] i.e. who would have recognized her as Madam Catalina.

[452] Compassione, i.e. emotion.

[453] Lit. I leave you free of Niccoluccio (libera vi lascio di Niccoluccio).

[454] i.e. Ansaldo, Dianora and the nigromancer.

[455] i.e. the money promised him by way of recompense.

[456] i.e., nicety, minuteness (strettezza).

[457] A town on the Bay of Naples, near the ruins of Pompeii.

[458] Per amore amiate (Fr. aimiez par amour).

[459] In si forte punto, or, in modern parlance, at so critical or ill-starred a moment.

[460] Sollevata, syn. solaced, relieved or (3) agitated, troubled.

[461] Sic, Publio Quinzio Fulvo; but quære should it not rather be Publio Quinto Fulvio, i.e. Publius Quintus Fulvius, a form of the name which seems more in accordance with the genius of the Latin language?

[462] Or "his" (a sè).

[463] Or "thine" (a te).

[464] Lit. "hope" (sperare). See note, p. 5.

[465] i.e. I would have her in common with thee.

[466] Or "arguments" (consigli).

[467] i.e. of your counsel.

[468] i.e. my riches are not the result of covetous amassing, but of the favours of fortune.

[469] Sic (tiepidezza); but semble "timidity" or "distrustfulness" is meant.

[470] i.e. perils.

[471] i.e. to cross the Alps into France.

[472] Adagiarono; see p. 447, note.

[473] i.e. to place themselves according to their several ranks, which were unknown to Torello.

[474] Sic (la vostra credenza raffermeremo); but the meaning is, "whereby we may amend your unbelief and give you cause to credit our assertion that we are merchants."

[475] i.e. should any rumour get wind of death.

[476] Sic (all' altro esercito). The meaning of this does not appear, as no mention has yet been made of two Christian armies. Perhaps we should translate "the rest of the army," i.e. such part of the remnant of the Christian host as fled to Acre and shut themselves up there

after the disastrous day of Hittin (23 June, 1187). Acre fell on the 29th July, 1187.

[477] It may be well to remind the European reader that the turban consists of two parts, i.e. a skull-cap and a linen cloth, which is wound round it in various folds and shapes, to form the well-known Eastern head-dress.

[478] i.e. he who was to have married Madam Adalieta.

[479] See p. 325.

[480] Or "strange" (nuovo); see ante, passim.

[481] i.e. his vassals.

[482] i.e. the husband of his kinswoman aforesaid.

[483] i.e. unwetted with tears.

[484] i.e. of overmuch licence.

[485] Two noted wine-bidders of the time.

[486] Lit. living folk (viventi).

CPSIA information can be obtained
at www.ICGtesting.com
Printed in the USA
LVHW050907261020
669822LV00001B/39